PRISONERS AND WERELORDS

Drake turned to Drew and prodded a finger in the young Wolflord's chest. "You need to wake up, and fast," he said. "This—you and me shooting our mouths off—this is fun. This feels almost normal, like how folk talk to one another beyond the walls of the Furnace. Only we'll never get to experience that, will we? We're stuck here, and thinking about any other life is sheer folly. You're a gladiator, Drew, and gladiators fight and die. Don't ever forget that."

He was about to jab Drew in the chest again with his final comment when Drew caught his finger.

"There's something you've forgotten, Drake. We may be prisoners for now, at the mercy of Ignus and Kesslar, but we're Werelords. Think of the power each of us possesses, and what we could do if we worked together. There *is* a life for us beyond these walls. And I intend to return to it."

UNLEASH THE BEAST WITHIN!

RISE OF THE WOLF

RAGE OF LIONS

SHADOW OF THE HAWK

NEST OF SERPENTS

STORM OF SHARKS

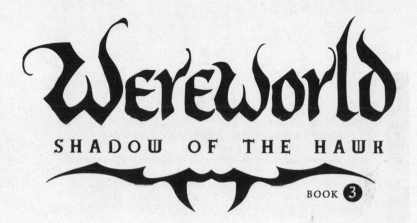

Wereworld

SHADOW OF THE HAWK

BOOK 3

CURTIS JOBLING

PUFFIN BOOKS
An Imprint of Penguin Group (USA) Inc.

PUFFIN BOOKS
An imprint of Penguin Young Readers Group
Published by the Penguin Group
Penguin Group (USA) Inc.
375 Hudson Street
New York, New York 10014, U.S.A.

USA / Canada / UK / Ireland / Australia / New Zealand / India / South Africa / China
Penguin Books Ltd, Registered Offices: 80 Strand, London WC2R 0RL, England

For more information about the Penguin Group visit www.penguin.com

First published in the United States of America by Viking,
an imprint of Penguin Young Readers Group, 2012
Published by Puffin Books, an imprint of Penguin Young Readers Group, 2013

THE LIBRARY OF CONGRESS HAS CATALOGED THE VIKING EDITION AS FOLLOWS:
Jobling, Curtis.
Shadow of the hawk / by Curtis Jobling.
p. cm. — (Wereworld ; bk. 2)
Summary: Enslaved by the Goatlord Kesslar, young werewolf Drew finds himself on the
volcanic isle of Scoria, forced to fight in the arena for the Lizardlords.
ISBN 978-0-670-78455-4 (hardcover)
[1. Werewolves—Fiction. 2. Adventure and adventurers—Fiction. 3. Fantasy.] I. Title.
PZ7.J5785 Sh 2012
[Fic]
2011046347

Puffin Books 978-0-14-242192-5

Printed in the United States of America
Book design by Jim Hoover

3 5 7 9 10 8 6 4

For Mum and Dad

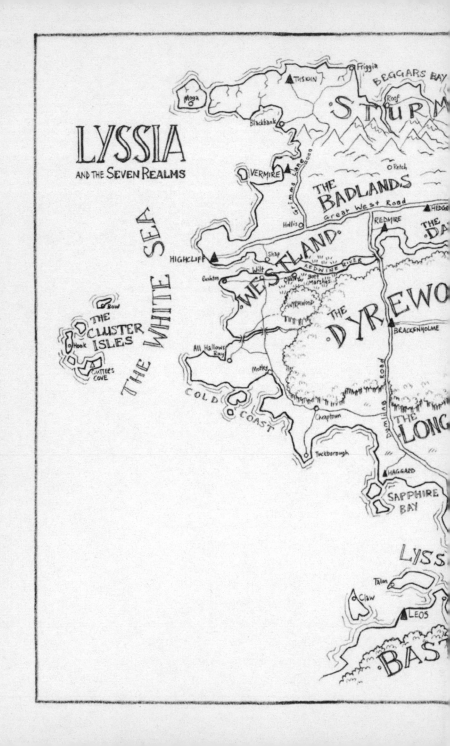

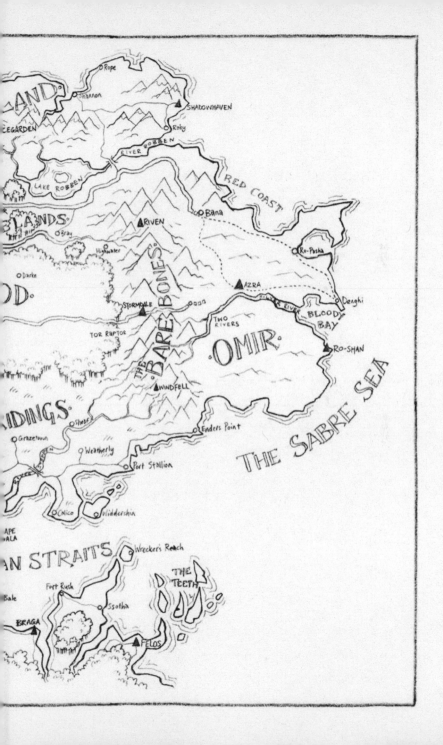

CONTENTS

PART I

SURVIVORS

I

SAVAGE SHORES

THE SHRIEKS OF strange beasts heralded his approach: a chorus of barks, booms, and bellows that echoed through the jungle. Creatures dotting the riverbanks ran for cover in the dense forest, dashing out of sight at the figure's frantic approach. His legs powered through the brackish water, feet struggling for purchase on the sandy riverbed as he put distance between himself and the beach behind him at the mouth of the shallow river. Spots of sunlight broke through the emerald canopy overhead, illuminating him briefly as he passed, leaving frothing waves in his wake.

Drew Ferran looked back all the while, eyes searching the landscape for those who followed. He had to keep moving, couldn't stop for one moment. If they found him it would be

3

back into the belly of the slave ship. The harsh cry of a nearby animal surprised him, causing him to stumble with a splash. Indistinct shapes darted from tree to tree on either side of him, leaping through branches, shadowing his every step. Not so far away he could hear the shouts of Count Kesslar's men tracking him. Drew pushed on; he much preferred taking his chances in the wild.

He'd left chaos behind on the beach. The *Banshee* had dropped anchor only to allow the quartermaster to take men ashore to gather provisions. Those crew members remaining had made the most of the break, swimming in the bay or relaxing on deck. When the ship's cook had brought Drew his meal—foul-smelling strips of rancid meat on a heavy steel dish—the guard had casually unlocked his cell door. Drew had acted fast. Within moments both cook and guard lay unconscious, the dish having proved a surprisingly adequate improvised weapon.

Emerging on a deck loaded with slavers, Drew hadn't stopped for good-byes. He'd instantly spied the nearby jungle-covered shore and had leaped overboard. The chill ocean had been a shock to his system, but Drew was made of hardy stuff; growing up, he and his brother, Trent, had frequently swum in the White Sea. These clear waters had nothing on the Cold Coast. When he'd surfaced he'd kept his head down, swimming hard, not looking back as he headed for the beach. His newly missing hand caused him grief and made it difficult to swim, but the promise of freedom more than made up for this hindrance, granting him unexpected energy.

Manacled by the Ratlord Vanmorten in the palace of High Stable and surrounded by a horde of approaching undead, Drew had been left with little choice. By biting his own hand from his wrist, he'd lived to fight another day, but the phantom pains in the stump were a constant reminder of his loss.

Scrambling up the golden sand he'd glanced back to see rowing boats making for the shore, men-at-arms shouting to one another as they made to recapture him. Farther along the beach he'd seen the quartermaster's team emerge from the trees, dropping their baskets of fruit and giving chase when they spotted Drew dashing toward the jungle's edge.

The river he was following had emerged into the sea from deep within the jungle. As the tropical forest on each bank looked impenetrable, Drew had opted to follow the river itself away from the beach. He scratched at his throat, cursing the collar Kesslar's slavers had secured around it. With the metal ring removed he would have been free to change, to embrace the Werewolf. He was amazed how quickly he'd come to rely upon his lycanthropic ability. A relatively short time ago he'd been a simple farm boy, content with his lot in life. With the discovery of his powers and the events that had followed, he'd initially resented his true identity—the last of the shape-shifting Wolflords. In time he'd learned to control the beast, call upon it in times of need, to save his friends and defeat his enemies.

5

Drew's feet caught against something hard on the river-bed, sending him tumbling forward, face disappearing beneath the turbulent water. Frantically, he spluttered back to the surface, struggling for air in a panic. Something large brushed against his side before hitting his legs hard. Drew was propelled through the air and then back beneath the water, unable to tell up from down. He opened his eyes, squinting against the storm of churning water and sand. A dark shape emerged, huge mouth opening wide to reveal rows of jagged teeth. Drew found his bearings at the last moment, kicking clear and dodging the jaws as they snapped shut.

Rising from the water, Drew gasped for breath, realizing with horror that he had been propelled into a lake. He caught a full view of the circling monster. Perhaps fifteen feet long, it bore no resemblance to anything he'd ever seen. Its skin was dark green with tough, gnarled ridges rising along the length of its body down to its great, swishing tail. Its head briefly surfaced and the beast's yellow eyes regarded him. Dozens of filthy teeth interlocked the length of its immense three-foot-long jaws, clasped together like miserly fingers. It seemed reptilian, like the rock lizards that inhabited the cliffs back home, but owed more in its terrifying appearance to the dragons from Drew's childhood storybooks.

The water erupted as the monster propelled itself at Drew, causing him to scramble backward. Teeth took hold of his leg, threatening to pull him under as the creature began to roll.

Drew disappeared beneath the foaming surface, his body spinning as the beast turned ferociously, trying to drown him. Drew felt his trousers tear, realizing with relief that the monster had only taken hold of the tattered material. With a kick he was free, propelling himself away from the chaos.

He hit the bank, scrambling against the muddy incline, struggling to find a purchase. The fingers on his remaining hand tore into the wet clay, the bank falling away around him. Exposed roots hung overhead, agonizingly out of reach. He leaped up, snatching at them before splashing pathetically back into the water. Drew staggered to his feet, working his way along the muddy slope, slipping and sliding as he searched vainly for an escape route. He caught a branch that was floating by and used it to try and hook the roots, pull them down within reach. Then the sound of surging water caused him to turn.

The monster's jaws had emerged from the water; the beast was launching itself at Drew. He turned the branch quickly, shoving it into the creature's open maw as it came in for the kill. The branch disappeared into its red fleshy gullet like a sword into its sheath. Instantly the monster broke away, thrashing and snapping its teeth, trying to dislodge the maddening branch. Drew didn't wait around. He kicked on, swimming once more as he headed for the lake mouth. Behind, he could hear crunching and splintering as the creature turned the branch into kindling. *Move, Drew, it'll be your bones next!*

Drew had no strength left, exhausted from fleeing his captors and then fighting the ferocious animal. He collapsed against a fallen tree that ran down from the jungle into the water, the monster racing up behind him. Drew tried to climb the trunk, crying out loud when a strip of bark came away in his hand.

But the killing blow never arrived. A rope net sailed through the air, weighted down along its edges by lead balls. The net descended over the creature, swiftly entangling the beast as it rolled. The more it struggled, the tighter the net bound. More ropes flew into the lagoon, lassoing the monster and holding it fast as the crew of the *Banshee* appeared along the banks of the lake.

The fallen tree trunk shuddered as something landed overhead. Drew turned, backing away while looking up its length and squinting. The unmistakable figure of the slaver Djogo stood silhouetted in a shaft of sunlight. The leather patch over his left eye covered the empty socket Drew had left him with back in Haggard. For the first time, Drew saw an unusual scar on Djogo's bare shoulder, a triangle within a circle. *Like a brand we'd give the animals back home on the farm.*

"Nearly got yourself killed, Wolf."

Drew looked back at the beast as the sailors subdued it, securing its limbs together, binding its jaws shut. "What kind of monster is it?"

"A crocodile. If you think that's monstrous you'll love the Furnace!"

The crack of Djogo's whip made everyone in the water jump, as the long lash of leather snared Drew around the throat. His hand went to the noose as he struggled to breathe. Djogo tugged at the whip, the cord tightening its hold around the captive therian's throat, causing his eyes to bulge from their sockets.

"Struggle all you like, boy," said the slaver, grinning as he yanked the lash tight, winding the whip in and hauling the choking Wolflord ever closer to him. "It's back to the *Banshee* for you!"

2

PRISONERS OF WAR

THE TWO CAPTAINS knelt on the *Maelstrom's* deck, each showing very different spirit. The older man kept his head bowed, although his eyes scanned the surrounding audience, weighing up the futile situation. In his twilight years, he should have been in some distant port, warming himself by a roaring fire instead of cowering on the pitching deck of a pirate ship. The fellow at his side kept his back straight, chest out, staring his enemies down, shouting and swearing all the while. Younger, cockier, and with far too much to say, it looked increasingly likely he'd get them both killed.

Count Vega paced back and forth in front of them, letting the younger captain exhaust himself with his torrent of abuse. Behind Vega stood Duke Manfred, the Werestag of Stormdale, watching impassively. Queen Amelie stood beside the duke, leaning on his arm for support as the ship lurched against the waves. Bethwyn, her lady-in-waiting and constant shadow, stood at her shoulder. The Werelords were ringed by a crowd of pirates who kept a respectful distance.

Baron Hector, the young Boarlord of Redmire, stood behind the two kneeling men, watching the pacing Sharklord. Hector and his fellow therianthropes had fled Highcliff in the wake of the attack by the Doglords of Omir and the Catlords of Bast. As founding members of the Wolf's Council, he, Vega, and Manfred had been instrumental in supporting Drew Ferran, the young Werewolf and rightful heir to the throne of Westland, as they defeated King Leopold, the Werelion. With the Lion trapped within Highcliff Keep, the Wolf's Council had held control of the city, laying siege to the overthrown king and waiting for his surrender. After the unexpected arrival of Leopold's allies, the group had narrowly escaped Highcliff with their lives. Their enemy had given chase, the remaining allies of the Wolf jumping on board the pirate ship, the *Maelstrom*, as the Wereshark captain tried to spirit them away from their foes.

The prisoners knew him. Vega's reputation as Pirate Prince of the Cluster Isles ensured he was known across the White Sea. When the small, ragtag fleet that had escaped Highcliff had been spotted off Vermire, three ships had come after them. Knowing that their companion vessels weren't built for battle,

11

Vega had sent them on ahead, with the plan to regroup at the Sturmish port of Roof. The *Maelstrom* had then turned about and engaged the enemy. She'd charged into their midst, breaking their formation, leading them back toward the coast, away from the fleeing civilian ships.

"When the Kraken gets a hold of you he'll drag you down to Sosha's bed, leave you there for the crabs. You'd save Ghul a lot of time by dropping on your sword," spat the younger captain, while his companion remained silent.

Vega sighed. "I would, dear boy, but I fear it wouldn't kill me."

He's not wrong, mused Hector. As a therianthrope the Sharklord was immune to most injuries, his accelerated healing repairing wounds that would be fatal for a mortal. There were exceptions to the rule, of course; silver and the physical attack of another werecreature could each lead directly to death, as could any very grave injury.

There's always magick, too, brother, hissed the Vincent-vile in Hector's ear. *Can't forget the magick now, can we?*

Hector shivered, shrugging the dark spirit away. It was unnerving to have the disembodied voice of one's dead brother following him around, especially as only Hector could hear him. The Boarlord had played his part in the death of his twin, and he paid the price each and every day. Hector rubbed the gloved palm of his left hand with the thumb of his right nervously, the leather squeaking as he circled the dark mark that stained the flesh beneath. The black spot had appeared the first time he had communed with the dead Wylderman shaman, back in the Wyrmwood. Talking with the dead was forbidden to all magisters, but desperate measures had been called for in order that he and Drew could save their friend Lady Gretchen from the wild men and their mistress, the Wereserpent. Each following occasion when he'd dabbled in communing, the dark spot had grown, the flesh corrupting with every dark act. Shivering, he clenched his gloved hands into fists and returned his gaze to the captured pirates.

"You think you're smart, Vega, but you're just lucky! It was rocks what ripped the belly out of the *Ace o' Clubs*, not any fancy move on the *Maelstrom*'s part!"

The captain was bitter that his ship had struck the submerged rocks, and understandably so. The following vessel had plowed into the back of it, the two keeling over as men dived away from the wreckage of twisted timber and lashing ropes. That had left one ship for the *Maelstrom* to engage: the bigger, slower *Leviathan*. Pitched against the deadliest crew and craftiest captain of all the Cluster Isles, the big boat hadn't stood a chance. Vega's ship had outmaneuvered it, dodging its catapults and sending flaming arrows, cannon fire, and heavy bolts into masts and deck. The battle was over and the white flag now fluttered from the mainmast—the *Leviathan*'s captain having had no choice but to surrender to the count.

"Luck didn't enter into it, Fisk," said the elderly Ransome, captain of the *Leviathan*. "It wasn't chance that you were led into those rocks. Your enemy knew the battlefield. If you'd held back as I commanded, the *Ace* might not have been reduced to driftwood. Stop whining; you were well beaten."

Vega smiled. "What can I say? I know these waters. Now if you're quite done, I'd like to hear about your masters."

Captain Fisk laughed haughtily, spitting at the Sharklord. "We won't tell you nothin', fish! The Kraken'll fillet you when he finds you!"

Hector shivered to think about what fate the Wolf's Council might face should they fall into the hands of the Squidlord Ghul, known throughout Lyssia by his nickname "the Kraken." Ghul's reputation was fearsome, built upon a lifetime of tyranny across the White Sea, showing little mercy to those poor souls he plundered. The Squidlord had been the eyes and ears of King Leopold, the Werelion, for many years, taking all that had once belonged to Count Vega in the process.

Vega nodded. "Yes, yes, so you keep saying. The Kraken this, Ghul that, blah blah, cut me up—all very tiresome! You forget that forty-faced fool used to work for me; I know the squid *all* too well."

"Then you know he don't take kindly to disappointment."

"Well he should prepare himself for a world of disappointment if he thinks his army of sprats will ever catch the *Maelstrom*. Last chance, Fisk: what are Ghul's plans? What does his fleet consist of? Tell me and I'll spare your life."

"I'd sooner embrace Sosha," snarled Fisk defiantly, throwing the sea goddess's name in the Sharklord's face once more.

Vega's cutlass flew from its scabbard, sliding gracefully into the man's heart and out again in a fluid motion. The assembled crowd gasped, none louder than Queen Amelie. The captain of the *Ace o' Clubs* collapsed to the deck, dying eyes wide with disbelief.

He's a cold-hearted monster, whispered Vincent to Hector. The young Boarlord nodded slowly as the Sharklord flicked the blood from his blade. His chief mate, Figgis, stepped over Fisk's body, giving it a couple of kicks as he rolled it along the deck and hauled it over the side. Vega turned to Captain Ransome, who stared back calmly.

"Been a while, Eric," said Vega.

"Indeed, lad. You're still painting the sea red, then?"

"Only when I have to, old friend."

"Spare the talk of friendship, Vega, if you're going to do me in like that idiot Fisk."

"He had it coming. Parlay will only protect a pirate for so long, Captain. This is war, after all."

"You're on the wrong side, Vega." Ransome sighed. "You saw what sailed north from Bast. I heard what the Catlords did to your sorry fleet. There's good money to be made working for the Cats. Perhaps it's not too late. Maybe Lord Onyx can find a place for you in his navy."

"I've burned my bridges there, Ransome. I've sided with the Wolf, if you couldn't already tell. I'm not sure the Catlords are as forgiving as you believe. A man is judged by the company he keeps, and I fear my choice of friends tells a terribly sorry tale." He waved a hand in the direction of Hector, Manfred, and Amelie.

Ransome nodded. "Shame. You're a good captain. It would have been nice to sail alongside you once again."

Vega crouched in front of the old pirate. His skin had taken on a gray hue, eyes darkening. Sharp white teeth glinted within the shadows of his face. "Ghul's plans, Ransome?"

The captain of the *Leviathan* shivered, a lifetime serving the Werelords of the Sea still no preparation for the sight of one on the change. "Half of Onyx's fleet has returned to Bast, the remainder is mooring up in Highcliff. It's unlikely they'll leave port until their cargo returns."

"Their cargo?" asked Hector.

"Bastian warriors—thousands of 'em. Seems the Cats are making Westland their own."

"So who patrols the White Sea?" said Vega.

"A handful of Bastian dreadnoughts are out there, but for the most part it's the pirates of the Cluster Isles. Ghul's sat on his backside for too long, growing fat on taxes he claimed in Leopold's name. Onyx has set him to work, now."

"Doing what?" asked Manfred.

"Hunting you."

Amelie gripped the Staglord's arm, face blanching.

"There were only three of you," said the Sharklord. "Where's the rest of your fleet, Ransome?"

16

"There's maybe twenty ships between Vermire and Blackbank, putting the word out that the *Maelstrom*'s a wanted vessel. There's a bounty, too; you'll have every privateer in Lyssia hunting you before long."

"He sees the *Maelstrom* as that much of a threat?" marveled Vega.

"He sees the Wolf's Council as the threat. As long as the councilors live he fears Lucas's kingship is in peril."

Hector's ears pricked up at mention of Werelion Prince Lucas. Having served his magister's apprenticeship under the Ratlord Vankaskan, the young Boarlord had spent a great deal of time in the prince's company. He had endured the young Werelion's violent temper throughout his teenage years and had finally been saved from the Catlord's cruelty when Drew had crashed headlong into their lives. A bully and a brat, Lucas had been spoiled by his father, and his planned marriage to the Werefox Lady Gretchen had been scuppered by the uprising of the Wolf's Council.

But what has happened to Leopold if his son now stands to inherit the throne? Hector thought, glancing at Queen Amelie, the Lion Prince's mother.

"Lucas?" said Amelie. "What of Leopold?"

"Dead, Your Majesty," said Ransome respectfully. He might have been a pirate, but he recognized royalty when he saw it. Manfred embraced her as she buckled at the news.

It sounds like the Werepanther has taken the Lion cub under his

17

wing, hissed the vile. *See how the old woman sobs! Her record for keeping husbands alive is decidedly poor!*

"How did he die?" whispered the queen.

"Duke Bergan killed him, they say, although the king slayed the Bearlord in the process."

Hector felt dizzy suddenly, the news of Bergan's demise hitting him like a hammer blow. He glanced at Manfred, who looked back pale faced. The Stag and the Bear had been like brothers. Such news so soon after the death of his younger brother, Earl Mikkel, would wound Manfred deeply.

"What was Ghul's last command?" asked Vega, pushing past the dreadful news.

"Follow the coast. Get word to the Isle of Moga, bring the Sturmish pirates on board. If the price is right Baron Bosa might aid us."

"He'll never join the fray," said Vega confidently. "He's a die-hard neutral; that'll never change."

Vega had told Hector about the Whalelord Bosa on the journey. Another old friend of his father's—the Sharklords were well known across the White Sea, it appeared—Bosa would deal with any party when there was money to be made. He'd retired from piracy long ago, although there were many villains who took their booty to the old Whale. Vega had intended to visit Bosa, but Hector now wondered whether avoiding Moga altogether might not be a better idea.

Ransome shook his head, smiling grimly. "Your old man

might have been friendly with Bosa once upon a time, Vega, but that's history. Onyx is confident Bosa will sign up: it's join him or sleep with Sosha. There are only friends and enemies in the Catlords' world."

Vega flexed his cutlass blade in his hands, sharing a look with Hector and Manfred. Ransome looked up, eyeing the sword worriedly.

"If you're going to run me through, get it done would you!"

Vega sheathed the blade, smiling at the *Leviathan's* captain. "Fisk was an arrogant thug. He had it coming. You, on the other hand, Ransome, have my respect. I doubt you take a great deal of pleasure in hunting the *Maelstrom* and a few boatloads of townsfolk. I give you the *Leviathan* back, your crew, and the survivors of the *Ace o' Clubs* and the *Wild Fiddler*. Your lives are your own. I don't expect you to follow us; not only are you overladen with bodies, you have to replace those burned sails before you can go anywhere."

Ransome looked astonished. "Thought you were going to do me in . . ."

"You thought wrong," said Vega. "I *do* suggest you reconsider your decision, however, and certainly think twice about rejoining the hunt. If we should encounter one another again under these circumstances, I'll take great pleasure in tearing your throat from your body and feeding your guts to the gulls."

Ransome nodded, struggling to his feet as Figgis cut his bonds. "You won't see me again," said the captain, but Vega was no longer listening, leading the Werelords away toward the rear of the ship.

Hector fell in behind, passing his own men, Ringlin and Ibal, once henchmen of his brother, as he followed. The two men of the Boarguard looked up, acknowledging him briefly with nods.

You seem to have straightened those two out, the Vincent-vile chimed in. *Do you trust them?*

"More than some," murmured Hector, his eyes on Vega ahead. Hector had once admired the count, the only fellow beside Drew who had ever stood up to Duke Bergan and the Wolf's Council. He'd looked out for Hector when all others had deserted him. Drew was gone and the Bearlord had turned his back on him. Vega had been there for him when Vincent had been slain, disposing of the body, tidying up loose ends, and remaining silent throughout.

But as time went on, the debt he owed the count became oppressive, weighing heavy on the young magister's shoulders. Vega had betrayed his "friends" before: the Sharklord had been the one to leave Highcliff undefended when King Leopold took the throne from the old king, Wergar the Wolf. Could Hector truly trust him? What was to stop Vega from selling Hector out and revealing his dirty secret, if the price was right? The idea of owing anyone anything, especially the Wereshark, was unbearable. He needed to pay the debt. He needed to be free of Vega.

The nobles gathered on the quarterdeck, away from the activity below. Ransome and his men were already being transferred back to the *Leviathan*, which remained lashed to the *Maelstrom* by boarding ropes. None of the ship's sails remained, the smoldering remnants hanging limply from the masts.

"It'll be days before they get her moving again," said Vega, looking down at the sea chart that was laid out over a raised hatch.

"You realize he'll send word straight to his masters?" said Manfred.

"By the time that old girl limps back into harbor, we'll be long gone."

"Is Bergan really dead?" whispered Hector suddenly. Manfred and Vega looked at him, their faces grim as they nodded.

"So it sounds, Brenn bless his soul," said Manfred.

Vega placed a hand on Hector's shoulder and gave him a squeeze. "Bergan would have wanted us to continue, Hector. We need to go on to Icegarden."

"Is that still the plan, then?" asked the Staglord.

"It has to be," said Hector. "We need to seek audience with Duke Henrik and find where his allegiance lies."

"Let's hope he's feeling hospitable," said Manfred. "There'll be plenty of folk looking for refuge in the Whitepeaks once the Catlords march through Westland. I'd imagine half of the

Dalelands are already on their way after the Omiri Dogs tore a path across Lyssia."

"Death everywhere," murmured Amelie, staring at the map, her eyes moist. "It's hopeless."

What think you, brother? Does she weep for Lyssia or her dead Lion?

Hector ignored the vile, reaching a black-gloved hand across to take hold of the queen's. She looked up at the young Boarlord.

"Your Majesty, we must stay together, stay strong. We need to show the people that they don't have to serve the Catlords—they have a choice. And Drew is out there, somewhere—he lives, I'm sure of it."

Amelie looked warily at Vega, who kept his eyes fixed on the chart. "Do you feel no remorse, Count?" she asked. "Captain Fisk was unarmed; you could have thrown him in irons. You didn't have to kill him."

"Please don't shed tears for Fisk, Your Majesty. He was a killer."

"As are you, Vega."

He looked up from the map, nodding. "As am I, Your Majesty. Only I'm a killer who is on *your* side. We are at war. Fisk's fate helped loosen Ransome's tongue, I'm sure you'll agree. Please don't lecture me on board my ship. The kings you married were hardly shy of bloodshed."

Amelie shuddered, releasing her hand from Hector's and turned to her lady-in-waiting. "Come, Bethwyn," she said. "Let us return to our cabin. We might be stuck on board this cursed ship, but we can still choose the company we keep."

Lady Bethwyn curtsied to the men and followed the angry Amelie as she departed. She flashed her big brown eyes at Hector as she passed, causing his heart to flutter.

That cow-eyed girl, Hector? And I thought you were toughening up. It seems you're still soft inside. Vincent chuckled.

"This 'cursed ship' is the reason we still live," muttered Vega. He looked across to Manfred, who was watching the queen depart.

"Do you want to go with her, Manfred? Make sure she gets to her quarters all right?"

The Staglord glowered back at Vega. Hector watched the two Werelords, the air crackling with tension. Manfred's brow darkened, bumps beginning to appear beneath the skin.

The antlers, gasped the vile. *Here they come!*

"Watch your tongue, Vega," said the duke slowly, trying to keep the beast in check. "I don't appreciate what you're insinuating."

"I insinuate nothing, Manfred. It's clear to me you care for her, that's all. As a friend, of course, nothing more," said the Sharklord.

Your ridiculous little council is tearing itself apart, said the vile.

Look at them, bickering over that old widow like schoolchildren. You're doomed, Hector. All of you: doomed.

"Shut up!" he shouted, his black-gloved fist striking the map. Manfred and Vega both looked at him in surprise. Vega smiled before returning his attention to the sea chart.

"Moga," he said at last, poking at the island on the map. Hector avoided Manfred's gaze. His cheeks were flushed with embarrassment, but also something else. He might have spoken out of turn, but they'd listened to him; he'd silenced them. *Am I indeed their equal?*

"Moga? Really?" asked the Lord of Stormdale gruffly.

"Onyx has yet to make the Whale his offer. If we get in early, who knows? Perhaps he'll be struck by a rare moment of conscience. Maybe he'll do the right thing."

"I would suggest we avoid Moga altogether," said Manfred. "Continue straight on to Sturmland. You're inviting danger by going ashore in such a dangerous port. The forces of the Werewalrus, Lady Slotha, are harbored there, are they not?"

Hector had heard all about Slotha, the Walrus of Tuskun. The tribal people of her remote region were known as the Ugri, fiercely loyal, owing more to the Wyldermen of the Dyrewood than the more civilized people of Sturmland. When Leopold had overthrown the old king, Wergar the Wolf, she had sided with the Lion, gaining governance over the northwestern tip of Lyssia in return for the muscle she added to the fight. In the following years she'd fortified her position in the frozen wastes, waging war on her neighbors in the Whitepeaks and striking fear into the hearts of sea traders. There was no love lost between the Walrus and the Wolf's Council.

"She has forces there, certainly, but Moga itself is still considered a free port. If anyone rules there, it's Bosa. Let me speak with him, see if I can win his aid before Onyx comes knocking."

"We should sail on," said Manfred. "Hector, your thoughts?"

"We're low on supplies, Your Grace. We should stock up on fresh water and food. The few provisions we had on board when we left Highcliff are virtually gone."

"Besides which," said Vega, "our five fellow ships that fled Highcliff are ahead of us, somewhere. Chances are good that someone in Moga will have sighted them. Bosa has answers. Trust me, Manfred; we need to pay him a visit."

The Staglord massaged his brow between thumb and forefinger, the argument lost. "I think we're making a mistake."

"We'll take a couple of boats ashore. Hector—can you oversee the securing of provisions? Manfred—you and I shall speak with Bosa. We keep our heads down, keep a low profile."

Look at him, hissed Vincent. *He's enjoying this. Skulking about, piracy—he's in his element. He's pulling the strings, Hector. He's in control now.*

Vega grinned at the Boarlord and winked slyly. "In and out. The Werewalrus Slotha won't even know we're there."

3

THE BLACK STAIRCASE

THE DRIVERS CRACKED their whips, urging the procession of wagons and horses onward and away from the curving cliff edge. The wagon wheels found their way into the ancient ruts worn into the dark rock road by centuries of traffic. To the people of the island the circling road was known as the Black Staircase, running all the way from the harbor below, through the city, around the mountainous island.

Drew pushed his face against the bamboo bars, looking down the cliff as the wagon he traveled in drove ever higher. There were six of them in the jail wagon, each equally miserable. No doubt Drew's fellow slaves had been picked up by Kesslar on his travels, and each bore the scars of the journey. Battered and beaten, the men were weary from the long time spent in the hold of the slave ship. The Goatlord Kesslar traveled at the front of the procession in a sumptuous caravan, his ill-gotten gains of blood, flesh, and bone following miserably behind.

The Black Staircase rose from the docks through the strange city, past bazaars and merchants' stalls, before winding through the town houses higher up. Far below in the harbor Drew spied the *Banshee*, bobbing lazily in the crystal-clear water, her cargo delivered.

At the highest point of the Black Staircase there was no sign of vegetation; the slopes of the mountain were covered with rocks and boulders as dark as jet. The road leveled out briefly as they reached the summit, turning in toward the mountain's center. Here the wagons passed through a tall, white gatehouse. Lightly armored guards stood to either side, inspecting the carts and their slaves as they trundled past. The people of the island reminded Drew of Djogo, Kesslar's captain, tall and rangy with dark, leathery skin. *Perhaps this is where the brute hails from?*

The wagons were moving downhill now into a bowl-shaped valley that marked the mountain's summit, a palace sitting at its center. An outer wall curved around the grand palace structure, echoing the concentric circles of the Black Staircase. Terra-cotta rooftops dipped in toward its center, the courtyard beyond not yet visible on the approach. Towers thrust up from the outer wall toward the clouds, their brickwork an ornate tapestry of black and white banded marble. The heat was oppres-sive; Drew felt it roll over him in waves. Occasional jets of steam broke through fissures in the ground on either side of the road, and hot gases belched violently from the earth. He held his hand to his mouth, gagging at a familiar scent in the air.

Drew's mind flew back to Hector's communing. He blanched as he remembered his dear friend's necromancy, speaking with the souls of the departed. The Boarlord had used a foul-smelling yellow powder, tracing out warding symbols and binding circles as part of the ritual. Despite the heat, Drew shivered. He remem-bered the undead playthings of Vankaskan in Cape Gala, and how they had cost him his hand. With a manacle fastened tight around his hand and a crowd of monsters hungry for his flesh, the choice between life and death had been a torturous one to make. When he closed his eyes, he could imagine the hand was still connected, could feel the flexing of ghostly fingertips. It was going to take some getting used to. Drew stared at his wrist, fully healed now, a scarred stump of flesh and bone. He sniffed at the air once again.

"Brimstone," he said, as much to himself as to anyone who might listen.

"That's right," said another slave, leaning against the bars on the opposite side of the wagon. "Sulfur. What else would you expect from a volcano?"

28

"Welcome to Scoria!"

If the heat outdoors was stifling, inside the palace it was unbearable. Guards had led the shackled slaves into the colossal building, past crowds of onlookers into a huge, circular hall. Stone tables ringed the room, littered with food from the previous night's feasting. Flies buzzed over discarded pieces of meat, adding to the grim atmosphere. Torches burned along the wall, while a large metal grille covered the center of the chamber, riveted to the polished basalt floor. A steady flow of steam emerged through the grating, turning the chamber into a sauna. A metal brazier, stacked with red-hot coals, stood beside the grille, long-handled brands buried deep within the glowing embers. Drew winced as he spied them, imagining what they might be used for.

The man who addressed the slaves rose from a tall, marble chair. He was wearing no more than a loincloth, gold jewelry, and a wide, slick smile. Three similarly garbed figures stood behind his throne, cloaked in shadow and steam. There wasn't a trace of hair on the speaker's body—the man didn't even have eyebrows, giving his face a permanently surprised look. His oiled skin glistened in the torchlight, reflecting different colors in the glow of the flames. Drew squinted, convinced his eyes were playing tricks on him. The man's flesh seemed to shimmer, first gray and then green, with a brief flash of blue before darkening once more.

Count Kesslar finally appeared from the rear of the group of slaves, accompanied by the Werehawk Shah, and made his way directly to the almost naked man. Djogo stood beside Drew, his one good eye fixed upon the young Wolflord. Kesslar and the bald, barely dressed man embraced, shaking hands heartily and laughing all the while.

"My dear Kesslar," said the man in the loincloth. "By the Wyrms, you've brought the enchanting Lady Shah with you, too! How is the Goat treating you, my lady?" He licked his lips, reaching a hand toward her. She backed away a step.

"Well enough," she said pointedly. "I trust you have kept *your* end of our bargain, Ignus?"

The bald man nodded, stroking his fingers over his smooth, oily chest. "Like family, Shah. Like family."

Drew didn't follow what they were discussing, but he paid attention nonetheless. He needed to return to Lyssia, to his friends and his people, so any information he could glean might hasten his escape. Shah was a strange one, staying close to Kesslar at all times. *Odd*, thought Drew, *considering the dark looks she always throws him*. He had his suspicions about her. The Werehawk had rescued him from certain death at the hands of the Catlords and carried him through the air, out of Cape Gala, bloodied and broken, only for him to wake up as Kesslar's prisoner. The notion made his head spin.

Ignus turned to Kesslar, pulling his eyes away from Shah. "I feared you weren't returning. I was ready to send your remaining stock into the arena to celebrate your demise!"

"I wouldn't make it that easy for you, Ignus," said the Goatlord. "I need every one of those souls in the Furnace, especially our brother therians. I've brought them a *true* champion to fight!"

"Really?" said Ignus, walking toward the crowd of slaves. "Bring them forward so I may better see."

The guards lowered their spears, jabbing at the slaves, forcing them to walk across the metal grille. Drew grimaced at the feel of hot iron against his feet, but he pushed the pain to the back of his mind. All those hours training to be a warrior under the watchful eye of Manfred back in Buck House were standing the young Wolflord in good stead.

He walked forward and stood before the man in the loincloth.

"So you're Kesslar's prize specimen, then?" said Ignus. Drew turned, looking back to the others who all struggled, stumbling, none daring to cross the hot metal floor. He stared back at Ignus, getting a good look at their oily host.

Ignus was maybe in his eighth decade. His neck looked deformed, strangely long, and he had a wide mouth with reed-thin lips that seemed to stretch almost back to his ears. His eyes were bulbous, pale, and honey colored with misshapen pupils.

Ignus peered down at Drew's arm. Djogo had clapped his stump in a smaller, tighter iron, just to ensure he couldn't slip his handless arm from the manacle.

31

"He has only one hand, Kesslar," Ignus said dismissively. "Damaged goods. You really expect me to buy this one from you? This boy probably can't even wipe his own rear; he's not fit for slavery, let alone my ludus. I take only the *best* in my gladiatorial school."

Drew's ears pricked up at mention of Ignus's ludus: *A gladiatorial school*? he wondered. *Is this connected to the Furnace that Kesslar and his cronies keep mentioning?*

"I'd be careful what you say, Ignus," said the Goatlord, stroking his short, forked beard. "There's more than one weapon a therian can use in battle, as well you know. This one bites!"

Ignus chortled. "Go on then, Kesslar. Tell me what beast you've brought to Scoria, and I'll tell you what he's worth."

"No, Ignus," said Kesslar, wandering over to one of the tables and picking up a rotten piece of meat. He batted the flies away and collapsed into a marble chair, tearing into the rancid hunk with splintered yellow teeth. "You guess what he is and I'll tell you what you're going to pay me."

Ignus glanced at his companions who hovered behind his throne. The three other men were also bald, bug-eyed, and smooth-skinned; no doubt, Drew thought, relatives of the ugly fellow. Ignus returned his gaze to Drew, looking him up and down, standing back to better judge him.

"From Lyssia?"

Kesslar nodded, devouring the meat.

"The north, I'd say. A Ramlord?"

Kesslar spat on the ground. The spittle hit the metal grille, sizzling where it landed.

"The next Ram I see I'll fleece and gut. I've had all I can stomach from my pathetic cousins."

"A Wereboar then?"

"Too lean," said Kesslar. "Look at his physique. He's built for the kill."

"Some kind of Doglord?"

"Bigger."

"A Bearlord!" exclaimed Ignus, clapping his hands together triumphantly. "Have you brought me a Bearlord?"

"You were closer with dog . . ."

Ignus turned slowly, looking at Drew with a fresh, inquisitive gaze. He stepped closer, their faces inches apart. Ignus's bulbous eyes narrowed and his thin lips peeled back, his foul breath washing over Drew.

"Wolf?"

Kesslar began a slow handclap from the marble chair.

Ignus spun around. "I don't believe you! The Wolves are dead. Wergar was the last, the Lion made sure of that!"

"He missed one of them in his eagerness to put them to the sword!"

"You're lying!"

"He's telling the truth," snapped Shah. "You could take the

silver collar off and see for yourself, if you're so confident."

Djogo reached into a pouch at his hip, withdrawing a short hammer and flat-headed chisel, used by the captain to remove his slaves' collars. He held them out to Ignus. The Lord of Scoria shook his head, sneering at the tall slaver.

"I see you're still making use of this beast," he said to Kesslar.

"Djogo? Of course. One of the finest deals we ever made."

"He's not bitten your hand yet as he did mine?"

"No, he's been dutiful to the last."

Ignus puffed his chest out, oiled skin rippling as he suddenly grew in size. Djogo, for all his height, took a faltering step back as Ignus towered over him. He was threatening to change, intimidating Djogo, keeping the beast in check. *Interesting*, thought Drew. *Another therianthrope—but what kind?*

"I should have fed you to the volcano when I had the chance," said Ignus. He dismissed the slaver with a shove, sending Djogo stumbling backward.

"If you break him, you pay for him," joked Kesslar. Shah kept her attention fixed on Drew, as Ignus rounded on him once more.

"Your master says you're a Werewolf?"

"He's not my master," said Drew, after a long pause.

Ignus laughed. "Very confident for one who is destined for the Furnace, aren't you?"

"If I knew what the Furnace was, I might tremble for you."

"You'll tremble soon enough," said Ignus. He looked Drew over again like a piece of meat, licking his lips. The swollen eyes blinked quickly. He called back to Kesslar.

"How much then?"

"Remember what you paid for Stamm? Double it!"

Ignus spluttered. "You're not serious?"

"Oh I am, Ignus. You wouldn't *believe* the lengths I've gone to, bringing this Werelord to Scoria. He's the most wanted therian in Lyssia, Bast, too, no doubt, now that the Catlords are after him. He's the last of the Gray Wolves— disputed heir to the throne of Westland!"

Kesslar rose and joined Ignus. He offered an open palm to the Lord of Scoria. Ignus moved to take it, snatching at thin air as Kesslar withdrew it for a moment. He stroked his short beard, nodding to himself and giving Drew a sly look.

"Twice Stamm's fee? No, I'm cheating myself." He held out his hand once more. "Make it *three* times, and we have a deal!"

Ignus took the Goatlord's palm and shook it firmly. "You'll cheat me out of house and home, Kesslar, if I'm not careful."

The slave trader grinned as one of Ignus's guards walked to the brazier of coals. Two more took hold of Drew by his shoulders, holding him in a tight grip as the guard stoked the embers.

"You'll need the silver one for the Wolf," said Ignus, as the man withdrew a metal poker from the coals. Drew recognized the glowing silver symbol on the end of the device, a triangle within a circle; the same as the one Djogo bore on his shoulder. His rage rose, the thought of these villains scarring his flesh— the last of the Gray Wolves and rightful king of Westland— almost bringing on the change. To shapeshift now, with a collar about his throat, would prove fatal. He struggled as the guard advanced. A punch to his stomach from one of the soldiers sent him wheezing to the metal-grilled floor as the men held him still and the brand seared his flesh.

Drew's scream could be heard far below in the harbor.

4

HOUSE OF THE WHITE WHALE

A BITTER WIND blew through Moga's cobbled streets, sending shutters rattling and townsfolk scurrying for shelter. The autumnal weather was shifting across Lyssia, winter drawing ever nearer, and the north was always the first to feel the change. Inns and taverns crowded the seafront, jostling for the affections of passing sailors and fishermen, offering food, drink, and company on this grim evening. The Torch of Moga, an ancient watchtower, stood proud on the town's natural stone jetty. Forty feet tall, the monolith rose from the promontory, centuries old steps carved around its perimeter leading to a timber platform. A solitary lookout stood atop, watching over the town and harbor.

The grandest tavern of all was the House of the White

Whale, its style owing more to a castle than a drinking establishment. Three stories high and taking up the space of four
regular inns, the roof was bordered with granite battlements,
complete with turrets on each of the four corners. While providing fine food and ale to the wealthy of Moga, the White
Whale was also famed for its gambling hall, where a man could
bet on and with anything his heart desired, from the toss of a
coin to the blood in his veins.

At the rear of the hall, beyond the gamblers and glut-
tons for punishment, a flight of steps rose to a mezzanine that
overlooked the tables and bars, protected by a gaggle of rough-
necks who looked more like pirates than guards. Here, on two
huge satin cushions, sat Count Vega and Duke Manfred before the imposing figure of Baron Bosa. The Whale of Moga
was busy decanting wine into three golden goblets. Manfred
struggled to keep his balance—and dignity—on the cush-
ion, while Vega sat cross-legged, looking annoyingly at ease.
Bosa took a drink in each hand, rings and jewels jangling,
and passed them across. Taking up the third, he raised it
into the air.

"A toast," he said, in a deep, fruity voice that belonged on
a stage. "To my dear old boating chum, Vega, and his delightful
friend, Manfred!"

Manfred looked surprised by the baron's flowery language,
but Vega didn't hold back.

"To the glorious health and long life of our most gracious host, the divine Bosa!"

This made the baron squeal with delight. He was the most unlikely looking pirate Lord Manfred had ever seen. Bosa was a giant, a whale in every aspect. His vast mass filled a chaise longue, his enormous belly resting on his thighs. His arms were lost within a black silk blouse that wouldn't have looked out of place on a dancing girl. Wobbling jowls linked up with a roll of double chins, his face a picture of jollity.

"It's been too long since we last shared a drink, dear Vega," said Bosa, sinking his goblet of claret. His men stood nearby, keeping a respectful distance, but watching the two guests' every move.

"Indeed it has. I've been busy, in case you hadn't noticed. There was the small matter of Leopold stealing my islands from me."

"Heard all about that, dear chap. Terrible business. Sounds like the Kraken's been riding roughshod over your archipelago with impunity!"

"He's a mollusc on the rear end of the Cluster Isles."

"Is that any way to speak of a fellow Werelord?"

"Fifteen years, Bosa," said Vega, sucking his teeth as he swilled the wine in his goblet. "That's an awful long time for bad blood to fester."

The Whalelord looked to Manfred and smiled. "I must

say it is a *tremendous* honor to have the Lord of Stormdale visit my little establishment. You're a long way from home, Duke Manfred. I can't imagine what drama has brought you all the way to Moga."

Manfred could feel the color rise in his cheeks and cleared his throat with a gruff cough. "I'm sure you know full well what's brought us here, Baron Bosa."

Vega raised a hand, making to apologize for his friend's straight talking, but the baron waved him away.

"They don't mince their words, these mountain men, do they, Vega?"

"I don't play these games very well either," added Manfred. "I'm not one for dancing around the issues."

"You don't love dance?" gasped Bosa dramatically, before leaning over toward them, his face suddenly more serious, the fat cheeks hardening and his jaw now set. The smell of roses washed over the Werelords like a wave.

Bosa's voice was quiet when he spoke again, the playfulness gone. "No more games, then. Tell me why you're here."

Vega shuffled forward, trying to diffuse the tension between the Whale and the Stag. "You'll be aware of the events in Highcliff. I'm sure word has reached every rock in the White Sea by now. The Catlords of Bast have marched to the Lion's aid; though Leopold is now dead, they're putting Lucas on the throne."

"But *why* did they come to Lyssia?" The Whalelord jabbed

his fat forefinger at the two Werelords. "Did you not turn on the king and take the throne as yours? Is this not lawful retaliation by the Cats?"

"Not so," said Manfred. "Leopold had imprisoned the last surviving son of Wergar, a boy named Drew Ferran. He was rescued from the Lion's murderous rampage when he was a babe-in-arms, and had grown up as a farmer's boy on the Cold Coast. The king was about to execute the lad on the eve of his son's marriage to Lady Gretchen. We ensured that didn't happen."

"Wergar really has an heir? So, the rumors are true?"

"Indeed," said Vega. "The rightful king of Westland. That's why Onyx came to Lyssia, to ensure a felinthrope of his choosing remains on the throne and controls the Seven Realms."

"Where is this son of Wergar now?"

Manfred and Vega looked at one another awkwardly.

"We don't know," said the Sharklord. "It's complicated."

"You've *misplaced* your king?" said Bosa, hiding a smirk.

"The boy is strong-willed," said Manfred. "He's his father's son, but with something else. He headed south recklessly, no army at his back, to save the life of a friend. He knows right from wrong, but has an empathy with others that's rare among the Werelords: he has the common touch."

The three therians were quiet for a moment, each staring out over the gambling hall as the music played.

"My dear, sweet Vega," said Bosa eventually. "If you and your allies came here seeking sanctuary, I'm afraid you came to

41

the wrong place. I won't stand in the way of these Bastians, and I'm certainly not looking to pick a fight with Ghul. It's been many a year since my rear sat in a ship; I'm not sure it would fit anymore!"

"We're not seeking your swords or support, old friend," said Vega. "I know what kind of hoard you sit on here, Bosa. You've the wealth of ten Werelords on this island, hidden Sosha knows where, the spoils of half a century's piracy in the Sturmish seas. You're sitting on a war chest."

"I make no apologies for my good fortune. It's been hard earned, Vega. I'm a trader, a gambler, an opportunist; make your point."

"The Beast of Bast will come knocking, Bosa. I merely ask you *not* to be drawn into this coming war on the side of the Catlords. I respect your decision not to fight alongside us, but please, don't assist those who'd see us dead."

Bosa rubbed his jowls, tweaking the flesh between thumb and finger.

"Agreed, my dear Vega; I give you my word. If Ghul and the Catlords *do* come ashore, they can expect a dazzling smile, sparkling wit, and a glass of the Redwine's finest, nothing more."

Vega and Manfred rose from their cushions, each offering hands to shake on the deal. Bosa staggered to his feet, batting the hands away and embracing the Werelords, one in each arm. Manfred could just about see the count's smiling face over the

Whalelord's shoulder; it appeared the Wereshark found great amusement in the Stag's embarrassment.

Below the mezzanine, toward the front of the gambling hall, Vega noticed a crowd was gathering, looking out of the huge bay windows that faced out on to the harbor street. He recognized a mob when he saw one, men and women jeering excitedly at a commotion outdoors. He pulled away from Bosa as all three Werelords turned to look.

"Moga might be my home, and a freeport aligned to no Realm, but there are other dangerous individuals on my isle. Did you bring anyone else ashore from the *Maelstrom*?" asked Bosa.

Manfred looked at Vega, answering for both of them.

"Hector."

"Back to the *Maelstrom!*"

A dozen of Vega's men ran along the harbor front, struggling to carry barrels and sacks between them, the wind in their faces and the battle at their backs. Hector remained in the middle of them, urging them back to the landing boats. Half the goods they'd picked up lay abandoned in the marketplace, dropped in their hasty flight. Behind the fleeing sailors the fight continued, swords clashing as the rear guard covered their retreat. Hector cursed his ill luck.

His mission should have been straightforward. While

Vega talked with Bosa, Hector was to requisition provisions for the *Maelstrom*. Vega's mate, Figgis, had accompanied him, guiding Hector to his regular supplier and leaving the Boarlord to strike the deal. It should have been uneventful; pay the man and take the goods back to the ship. Hector hadn't accounted for the distractions the port had on offer.

While he, Figgis, and the more reputable crew members had got on with their job, a few of the men had slipped into a tavern for a stolen drink. One drink had led to five, and by the time they were ready to return to the *Maelstrom* an altercation had taken place. Unfortunately for Hector, his men, Ringlin and Ibal, were at the heart of the disagreement. The argument had become a fist fight, and the fists had led to knives. Two men lay dead on the stoop of the Lucky Nine tavern, cut open by the Boarguard. Chaos had erupted.

Passing beneath the Torch of Moga, the sailors ignored the shouts of the guard in the watchtower, instead concentrating on getting what goods they'd saved onto their craft. The fight drew ever closer, Hector making his way toward the battle to hasten the men along.

What fools they were to trust the Baron of Redmire with such a daring mission, rasped the Vincent-vile. *Who'd have thought a shopping errand could result in such bloodshed?*

Ringlin and Ibal were in the thick of it, three of Vega's men shoulder to shoulder with them engaged with ten Moga men, two-deep along the stone jetty, jabbing and hacking with knives and cutlasses. More appeared, rushing toward the me-lee, reinforcing the enemy.

"Disengage!" shouted Hector, his voice lost in the com-motion. The goods were on the boats now; they had to beat a retreat and fast. There was no sign of Manfred and Vega, but they had to move—if they stayed they'd be cut down. He yelled again, but his orders fell on deaf ears. Ringlin and Ibal seemed to be enjoying the fight a little too much.

They're not listening, brother! Can you not command your own men?

Hector glanced down the jetty to where Figgis waited, beckoning him to get on the boat. The Boarlord turned back to the fight, slipping on the wet stone floor just as a cutlass ripped down across his torso. An opponent had broken the line, hav-ing felled one of Vega's pirates. The man had intended to slash the magister's belly open. Hector's hapless balance might just have saved his life, his jerkin torn open as he landed on his rear.

The attacker was instantly on top of him, striking Hector's forehead with the basket handle of his cutlass. The Boarlord saw stars, throwing his arms up and clawing at the man's eyes in desperation. The man screamed as Hector's fingers found their targets, raking his face. The sound of battle was all around him, the air thick with screams and curses. A stray boot con-nected with Hector's temple, sending fresh shockwaves racing through his skull. He brought a knee up, connecting with the enemy's nether regions, making him release his grip with a cry.

Run, brother! Run!

Hector rolled over, crawling on all fours through puddles, vision yet to return. He could just make out Figgis ahead, calling him frantically. Then an impact in the small of his back flattened him, the knees of his foe crushing his kidneys. The man grabbed a handful of his hair, yanking Hector's head back, throat taut, exposed. He'd have unleashed the vile on the man, but all control was lost. Since the death of Vincent by his hand, Hector had been haunted by his brother's tormented spirit. However, with Hector's knowledge of dark magistry growing, he'd learned to control the vile, acquiring an ability to project the shadowy specter forward like an attack dog. In the heat of battle, though, he now found his composure lost. Hector felt the touch of cold steel at his neck.

No sooner had the blade touched his throat than it was gone, along with the man from his back. He heard a shrill wail and a *snap*, very possibly from his attacker. Hector rolled over. Both Vega and Manfred were in the middle of the mob, transformed into beasts. While many of the enemy leaped clear of the changed therians, some of the braver, more foolish souls stayed for the fight.

The Werestag threw his fists into the men, dropping his antlers to catch and launch them aside. Bodies flew as he made short work of those who stood in his way. The Wereshark was more reckless, not caring how gravely he harmed his enemy. Limbs were torn free, fountains of blood erupting as Vega went into a frenzy. Within moments the pier was clear, the men from the *Maelstrom* regaining their composure, their foes defeated.

"Thanks for coming when you did, Captain—"

Vega, still transformed, backhanded the speaker across the face, sending him sliding along the wet stone pier.

"Shut your rattle, Carney," roared Vega. "If I didn't need you on the *Maelstrom*, I'd have left you here to be skinned alive! They'll be back shortly, and there'll be more of them. Get to the ship, we sail immediately!"

The men didn't move, staring at the transformed Sharklord fearfully.

"Are you deaf?" he screamed furiously, death-black eyes bulging, rows of razor-sharp teeth bared. "Move it!"

The men moved quickly, all but Ringlin and Ibal who had a self-satisfied swagger about them as they passed a prostrate Hector by. The short, fat one patted the other on the back as they returned their weapons to their belts. Vega lunged, catching each by the throat and lifting them high. The men kicked at thin air, hands raking at the Sharklord's muscular gray forearms. Manfred stepped forward to stop him, but the Pirate Prince wouldn't be halted.

"Back off, Manfred," said Vega, focusing on the two rogues. "This is your doing, isn't it? Pick a fight in Moga? They were Slotha's men. *Slotha's!* My boys are many things, but they're not suicidal!"

"They . . . dishonored us . . ." gasped Ringlin.

"You have no honor!" yelled Vega. "Why shouldn't I kill you both here and now?" He tightened his dark claws in their throats, a squeeze away from ending their lives.

"Because they're the Boarguard," said Hector, over the mournful wail of the wind. He was back on his feet again, and Vega looked at him with disbelief. "An attack on my men is an attack on Redmire. And on me."

Vega let go of them, the two men crumpling to the ground in a heap. Both scrambled over one another to get away, scurrying to the end of the long pier and joining the other men on the rowboats. Only the three Werelords remained on the stone promontory, in an uneasy standoff. They could hear Slotha's men calling for assistance, the beaten mob quickly growing into a fighting force.

"We need to return to the *Maelstrom*," said Manfred, taking Vega by the upper arm. The Sharklord shrugged him loose, looking overhead at the Torch of Moga. The lookout had already set light to the pyre on top, the fire burning hungrily and devouring the stacked timber. Bright flames and dark smoke belched into the stormy night sky.

"Your idiot Boarguard might just have drawn Lady Slotha on to our wake. If you ever reprimand me again ..." Vega choked on his words, furious with the young Baron of Redmire. He pointed at Hector. "Control your dogs, magister. Or I'll control them for you."

5

THE EIGHTH WONDER

THE SPEAR STRUCK Drew's temple. The skin split as his head recoiled and he crashed into the dust, ears ringing and head spinning. The weapon may have been blunt and fashioned from wood, but it was deadly enough. Drew scrambled clear as the spear stabbed into the ground where his head had been a second earlier. His attacker let the weapon glance off the floor and pirouetted, bringing it back down to Drew's new position on the baked earth of the ludus. Another roll from the young Wolf enabled him to evade the next lunge, this one destined for his bare belly. His enemy anticipated Drew's next tumble, jumping swiftly ahead of him to place a well-aimed kick at his jaw.

Just as Drew had hoped.

His hand was already coming up, snatching the foot from the air as it swung down. At the same moment he scissor-kicked his combatant's standing ankle, sweeping her legs from beneath her. She landed beside him, the wind knocked from her lungs. He reached for her, momentarily forgetting that he no longer had both hands, his left arm flailing at thin air. Cursing to himself, Drew rolled across, pinning her body while throwing his handless forearm over her throat. One of her arms was trapped beneath her, while the other was held in Drew's grasp. He needed to strike her one more time to the head. Currently, their contest stood at two strikes apiece, the next hit being the winner.

She struggled, writhing to break free, but he held her fast. She gnashed her teeth, trying to bite at his forearm, but he kept his flesh clear of her teeth. They were bright white, and sharp. Her eyes were amber, the black pupils narrowing into slits. He looked at the collar around her throat, silver like his own. *If she changes, she'll die.*

"Finish it!" shouted their gladiator master, a wiry, old fellow named Griffyn. He cracked his whip at the earth a foot from them. A cloud of dust exploded into their faces, and Drew chose the moment to release his opponent and roll away.

She was on her feet quickly, hissing at Drew while reaching for her wooden spear. Drew remained on his knees, panting heavily, looking up at the cruel sky. His skin was slick with sweat, the flesh sore from hours under the sun's burning glare.

"I won't fight her!" shouted Drew, glaring at Griffyn. The old man shook his head and readied another whiplash. The girl moved fast, leaping and landing behind Drew. He made no effort to evade her. They were both prisoners, both victims, being made to perform this foul game for the amusement of Kesslar and Ignus. He hoped his mercy might strike a chord with the girl.

He was mistaken.

"Then you'll die," she said, striking the wooden spear shaft hard across his head.

The clattering of plates and pots stirred Drew from his slumber, stabbing his skull like hot knives. He had the mother of all headaches, every noise hitting home as a hammer strikes an anvil. He'd been deposited on a trestle table in the mess, a corner of the ludus that doubled as both dining area and surgery. His presence hadn't prevented his fellow slaves and gladiators from taking their seats. They surrounded him, glowering as he tried to shuffle clear. A canopy of palm fronds overhead protected them from the worst of the midday heat, the training having halted while the gladiators ate and drank.

Drew swung his feet around from the end of the table and stood up gingerly, scanning the ludus. The other therians stood out against the rest of the slaves, together at a table of their own. While the humans wore their dull pig-iron collars, the therians wore silver chokers. Drew noticed that all gladiators and slaves bore the same mark upon their arms—the triangle within the circle—just as he'd seen upon Djogo. He looked at the scar upon his own left shoulder. His anger at Ignus and Kesslar for further disfiguring him remained undiminished. When he closed his eyes he could still feel the touch of the hot metal against his skin. The flesh was raised, the silver brand having done its damage well. *Djogo was a slave also, then? Or a gladiator?*

Shah stood nearby, in conversation with Griffyn. Both looked across when they saw him rise. Shah came over immediately, but the old man remained a distance away, watching keenly.

"Well, if it isn't the Eighth Wonder of the Furnace, a new Werelord the crowds can cheer for. You nearly got yourself killed out there this morning," she said.

"They were wooden weapons," said Drew, rubbing the back of his head. "What harm could they really do?"

"Don't be arrogant, Wolf. Taboo has other weapons, remember—her claws could have removed your throat if she'd so desired."

"Whatever therianthrope she is, she'd have risked death if she'd changed, and she didn't strike me as suicidal." He looked across the ludus to where the woman sat dining with the other therians. "Ungrateful. But not suicidal."

"You underestimate your opponent. Had you not considered she has more control of her therianthropy than you?"

Drew glowered at Shah. "I didn't expect my kindness to be thrown back in my face."

"Kindness will get you killed."

"Excuse me," said Drew stiffly. He didn't much like Shah and was in no mood to be patronized by one of Kesslar's cronies. He passed by a serving table where a couple of the slaves were dishing out the gruel. Drew snatched up a pot of the anemic-looking slop and made his way to the therian table. There were seven seated in all.

"Mind if I join you?" he asked, his voice unsteady.

Each figure was fearsome looking, and none seemed especially pleased to see him. A look passed between two on the end who appeared to be brothers, heavy-set men with broad shoulders and massive hairy arms. One of them opened the palm of his hand and gestured toward a seat opposite. Drew smiled and sat down beside another large man who left him little room on the end of the bench. He glowered briefly at Drew, his broad nose and lips curling with contempt before turning away.

"Don't mind Krieg," said one of the hairy brothers. "The Rhino can be a bad-tempered beast at the best of times."

"What's a Rhino?"

The brothers looked at each other in disbelief. Even the brute named Krieg allowed Drew a glance before shaking his head. Drew slunk low in his seat, embarrassed by his ignorance, scooping up the gruel with his fingers and shoveling it into his mouth hungrily.

"You're a Lyssian, then?" asked the other brother.

"They say he's a Wolf," said the first. "Is that right?"

Drew nodded, wondering where the conversation was headed.

"You're a long way from home," said number two. "Got a lot to learn, too."

"What do you mean?"

"Well, firstly, showing Taboo down there kindness is a surefire way of getting yourself killed."

The young woman with the amber eyes at the opposite end of the table shot them a glare. The two brothers laughed.

"She doesn't play nice with others, poor little princess!" said the second brother.

"Shut your mouth, Balk, or I'll shut it for you!" she shouted. Balk waved her away dismissively.

"Save your boasts for the Furnace, little girl," said Balk's brother. "My brother and I will teach you some manners in the dust."

Drew noticed that none of the others joined the conversation, each concentrating on their eating and ignoring the bickering.

"You're brave when you're with your brother, Arik," the girl said. "I'd watch your back; you can't always hide in his shadow."

Arik grinned aggressively at the girl, baring all his teeth.

"Secondly, sleep with one eye open, Wolf," continued Balk. "I haven't seen you in the Furnace yet, but I suspect you can fight. Makes sense that your rivals will try to dispose of you in the night rather than risk death by tooth and claw beneath the sun."

Drew looked at the others at the table, shivering to think that any one of them might happily murder him.

"And lastly," said Balk, whispering the final piece of advice. Drew leaned closer to hear the words. The big man's breath was rancid. "You'll find no friends here."

Without warning Balk smashed Drew's face down into the bowl of gruel. His head bounced up back into the waiting fist of Arik. This time he flew back, the brother's knuckles catching him across the jaw. Drew toppled off the bench, his body slumping into the baked earth as the brothers tossed their bowls onto him, laughing and clapping as they departed. Drew lay in a heap, shaken and angry.

"Here."

He looked up and saw the open hand of Krieg. Drew eyed it warily.

"Or stay down there like a dog. The choice is yours."

Drew snatched at the hand, the big fingers closing around

his palm. Krieg lifted him as if he were a child, plonking him back on to the bench.

"Thanks," said Drew sheepishly.

"Don't get used to helping hands, boy," grumbled the broad-nosed man. The Werelord opposite him chuckled. If Krieg was large, the other man was a giant—over seven feet tall, Drew guessed. He'd seen these two massive therians sparring in the ludus, hammering at one another with all their might.

"You should give the Apes a wide berth," said the giant. "They single out the weak. They're relentless once they get their teeth into you."

"You sound like you speak from experience."

"They've baited everyone here. They move on if you ignore them." He looked down the table to the girl at the end. "Taboo has yet to learn this lesson."

The young woman snarled. "They bite me, I bite back. They'll learn soon enough."

The giant shook his head sadly. "Seems felinthropes are incapable of turning the other cheek."

"Felinthrope?" said Drew, shuddering. "You're a Catlord?"

"What of it?" she asked sharply. "You've met my kind before?"

"I've had my run-ins."

A shaggy-haired fellow the other side of Krieg leaned around the Rhino.

"You might want to put your differences aside. Once you get into the Furnace, you may depend on one another."

Drew kept hearing mention of the Furnace. This was the arena where combat would take place, so named because of the battleground's location, Scoria's volcanic plateau.

"Depend on each other?" asked Drew. "I thought he wanted us to fight each other?"

"That happens occasionally, if Ignus and his guests are in a sadistic mood, but for the most part we therians are the main attraction," said the shaggy man. Even in human form, the fellow's shoulders were oversized and stacked with muscles, his mass of dark-brown hair framing his head like a matted thatch. His eyes were dark and heavy-lidded, his lips wide and downturned, giving his face a somber, thoughtful appearance. "The Lord of Scoria owns you, as he owns all of us. Our lives are over beyond the walls of the Furnace. We fight whatever they send out, be it human, beast, or monster."

"Monster?"

"You heard Stamm right," said Krieg.

Drew had heard the roars of whatever animals Ignus kept for the arena. They were housed within the circular walls of the Furnace, out of sight of Drew and the other gladiators.

"So we look out for one another?" said Drew, struggling to make sense of the situation. The Apes, as the giant had described them, were clearly a wicked pair, and he doubted they'd spare a moment's thought for Drew if he got into trouble in the Furnace. The girl, Taboo, seemed likewise unhinged, waiting to explode.

The giant sighed, long and hard. He was around Bergan's age, but time and the arena hadn't been kind to him. He was heavily scarred, his leathery skin dusty and gray. His dark eyes seemed sad, their lids downturned.

"You do what you must to survive. If you're looking for wise words, you've come to the wrong table. If you survive your first fight, take it from there. Live for each day, that's the only advice I have for you. Don't make plans for the future."

The giant rose, nodding to Krieg and Stamm before lumbering slowly away.

"The Behemoth speaks the truth," came a voice from the far end of the table. The last of the seven Werelord gladiators was a lean, languid youth around Drew's age, lying on his back on the bench. He drummed his fingers against his stomach, the sound like the rapping of a woodpecker's beak, the flesh hard as teak.

"The Behemoth? Is that his name?"

"It's the name we know him by. I'm Drake, by the way. Just so you know . . . when I have to kill you."

Drew chuckled, causing the others to look up. Even Drake leaned up from where he lay, twisting to stare as Drew's laughter grew in volume. The young Wolflord slapped his hand on to the table top.

"I get it," he said, wiping a tear from his eye and rising to his feet.

"You get what?" asked Stamm, confused.

"All of this. I'm the new arrival. Some of you, like the Ape brothers, will be the cruel ones who'll taunt me. Then there'll be the one who I can't get close to for fear of losing my throat— that'd be you, Taboo."

The woman remained seated, her face twisting angrily.

"Which brings us to the old timers: you, the Behemoth, and Stamm, right, Krieg? I guess you've been here the longest? That just leaves the sarcastic, smart-mouthed loose blade at the end there . . ."

Drake was already up off the bench and leaping across the table at Drew. Stamm and Krieg wrestled him back, while Taboo squealed excitedly at the conflict. Drew stood still, defiantly. He could feel the bile in his throat, thought he might vomit at any moment. His heart pounded, willing him to change, to embrace the Wolf. He couldn't show them how scared he was, couldn't let them see that they'd got to him.

"I see only one *smart mouth* here, Wolf!" spat Drake. "Who do you think you are? Where's your respect for your betters?"

"I was prepared to give my fellow Werelords all the respect they deserved. You each threw that back at me. It's good to know that therians are the same the world over; arrogance isn't unique to Lyssia!"

"You jumped up little turd!" grunted Stamm, letting go of Drake to reach over the table himself now. Stamm's huge mane of matted hair shook as the therian snatched at Drew, the young Wolf just dodging clear of a great, dirty hand. Taboo punched the table with delight. Krieg found himself holding back both of his fellow gladiators now.

"Don't you see?" said Drew, his confidence now shifting to a heartfelt plea. "You're *letting* Ignus treat you like animals. It doesn't have to be this way!"

"Spare your breath, child," said Krieg wearily. "Many have uttered similar words and all are now turned to dust."

"Just so *you* know," said Drew, staring at the therianthropes, "I don't intend to remain here, let alone die in this sun-baked pit in the middle of the ocean. I'll be leaving Scoria as soon as I find a way. It's up to you whether you'll join me or not. I lost a hand in Lyssia, was beaten, tortured, and terrorized by my enemies. I need to return there, to help my people and settle some scores. You may be broken at the moment, but if you remember what it was that once made you great Werelords, come find me. I could do with some tooth and claw at my side."

With that, Drew turned and walked away, leaving the therians staring at one another, lost for words.

On the outside Drew might have been the rightful king of Westland and the best hope for a free Lyssia, but on the inside he was still a farmer's son from the Cold Coast. *I just faced down a gang of Werelord warriors*, he thought. *They could kill me as quick as blinking*. It took every piece of will and nerve on the shepherd boy's part not to stumble as he went.

6

BLAZETOWN

HIS MOUTH WAS thick with the taste of smoke. Hacking up a glob of dark spittle, he smeared it on the dirty material of his red cloak. He shuddered, thinking about the homes they had burned, the villages they had sacked, all in the name of the cause; all in the hope of finding the Wolf.

Trent Ferran looked at the burning farms around him. The sound of families sobbing mixed with the crackling of their blazing homesteads. He recognized the people, not so dissimilar from those he'd grown up around back on the Cold Coast; simple folk, for the most part, who busied themselves with tending their flocks and fields. But these people of the Longridings had aligned themselves with the enemy, siding with the Wolf and his allies. He would shed no tears for those who stood against the Lion.

Nearby, a large group of townsfolk gathered in a huddle, a dozen Bastian warriors surrounding them. They looked pitiful, faces smeared with soot and tears, holding one another fearfully. Grazetown was one of the Longridings' largest settlements, a glorified village compared to other towns in Lyssia. They had no defensive walls, and the small militia had resisted as best they could, but they were vastly inexperienced compared to the Bastians and Redcloaks, and the fight had been brief and bloody. The surviving militia had been shackled. Trent didn't know what the plans were for them, but he hoped their families would be spared. He'd spilled enough blood for one night.

Trent looked at the Wolfshead blade in his hands, the sword stained dark from battle; his father's sword, found in the bloody ruins of Cape Gala, left behind by his traitorous brother, Drew. He wondered how many men Mack Ferran had killed with it in battle, fighting for the old Wolf Wergar many years ago. He thought back to the night he and his father had found his mother, freshly murdered by Drew after he'd transformed into the beast. Trent and Mack had had no other choice than to join the Lionguard to seek revenge. The old man had spent his life trying to dissuade Trent from a military life. But with his wife so brutally taken from him, he'd had no qualms in letting Trent sign up alongside him. While Mack was fast-tracked into the Royal Guard of Highcliff, Trent found himself a new recruit for the Lionguard, his skill at horsemanship ensuring a position as an outrider for the army.

When Highcliff was taken by Drew and his allies, Mack had been killed in the initial skirmishes, apparently at the hands of the young Wolf's friends. Trent shivered to think about Drew. They'd been as close as any brothers could be. He hadn't known what kind of monster Drew really was. When the change came and the beast took over, Trent had been helpless to stop him, as Drew betrayed his family and destroyed his world. Drew had taken both his mother and father from him. How many others would the Wolf murder? Trent had to stop him. He was no longer afraid of death. The cause was just, the Wolf his mortal enemy.

Sliding the Wolfshead blade into its sheath, he strode past the soldiers and their prisoners. Some nodded respectfully. He'd proven himself to his brother warriors now; there was no doubting his allegiance, his loyalty. Some had questioned whether he'd be able to stand up and be counted when the fight was on them; after all, he *was* the Wolf's brother. Those concerns had been quashed since their forces had left Cape Gala and begun their search of the Longridings; he was every bit the equal of his comrades.

An elderly woman broke from the huddle and rushed toward him, cradling a crying baby. She snatched at his cloak, bony knuckles clinging to the deep red material.

"Please," she implored. "Winter approaches and you leave us with nothing!"

The child wailed in her embrace. The mop of curly blond

hair was filthy, the face a mask of misery. The baby's cries cut Trent to the bone. Here was one of the few innocents of Grazetown. Trent tore the woman's hand loose.

"I'm sorry," he said regretfully, pushing the woman away. "I can't help you."

With that Trent strode away, the child's screams haunting him as he departed. He walked between the torched homes toward the tall wooden building at the town's heart. This was the seat of power for Grazetown. The doors were wide open, soldiers carrying provisions and whatever else they could find from within—crates of food, barrels of wine, golden candlesticks, precious tapestries. He entered the building.

The Lord's hall had been stripped of all valuables. Bodies of slain militiamen lay about, including a few soldiers wearing the garb of the Horseguard of the Longridings. Trent stepped over the bodies as he made his way toward the soldiers gathered in front of the Lord's Table. Two figures knelt before them.

Lord Gallen and Lady Jenna, the masters of Grazetown, were broken figures. Gallen's long gray hair had been shorn off, a sign of disrespect to the Horselords. His wife sobbed quietly at his side. To the rear of the table the remaining family members stood, helpless at the hands of the Lionguard. Sorin stood directly behind the Lord and Lady, a grin as wide as the Lyssian Straits filling his broken-nosed face. The Redcloak captain remained at loggerheads with Trent, having still not forgiven the young outrider for snatching Mack Ferran's Wolfshead blade from him back in Cape Gala. Sorin made no attempt to disguise his contempt for Trent, taunting him for being the Wolf's brother whenever the opportunity arose. He nodded at Trent, throwing him a filthy wink. Trent disliked the man, but he was an accomplished soldier.

"I ask you again: where's the Wolf?" said Frost.

The albino Catlord paced in front of the kneeling Horselords, every movement smooth, almost lazy. He carried his staff in his hands. Gallen lifted his gaze to Frost.

"I've told you already, we don't know his whereabouts. Since your people sacked Cape Gala, my wife and I have been on the road, heading home. We were not party to the violence that took place there."

"Come now, my lord," said Frost. "This isn't a difficult question, yet you insist on telling mistruths. You were seen fleeing the city with your fellow Horselords, those who had revolted against Lord Vankaskan."

"He was no lord to us!" spat Jenna tearfully, instantly catching a look of warning from her husband.

"Now we're getting somewhere. I know he was an unpopular choice as Protector of the city in my family's absence, but he was your lord nonetheless. I do not seek a confession here; we know all we need to know from the noble Viscount Colt. He has very honorably told us *exactly* who participated in the revolt."

Jenna sneered. "That old nag is a traitor to the Longridings!"

"Yet he sits on the throne in Cape Gala now—imagine that!" The albino stopped pacing, swinging his staff behind his back and hooking it between his crooked elbows.

"Where—is—the—Wolf?" he said slowly.

Gallen sighed. "We don't know. Brenn be my witness, we don't know."

"You must know! You and your cohorts freed him!"

"Drew was gone when we arrived in the courtroom. All that remained were the dead and unliving, thanks to your friend the Ratlord!"

Trent trembled at the memory of the risen dead they'd encountered in Cape Gala, the handiwork of the Ratlord Vankaskan. The dark magister hadn't been content with killing his enemies in High Stable, instead raising them from death to torment them anew. Sorin withdrew his sword, the sound of the metal against scabbard causing the husband and wife to look warily over their shoulders. The sword shone, silver runes catching the light of the fires that burned beyond the hall's windows. Trent watched Sorin. He'd seen him question people every day since they'd left Cape Gala. It always ended the same way.

Gallen's eyes widened.

"I swear to you, we don't know where he went!"

"Wait," said Trent, interrupting the interrogation. "Perhaps he doesn't know the whereabouts of the Wolf. But there were others present who might."

"Go on," said Frost, gesturing to Trent to continue. Trent stepped forward.

"The Wolf had friends in Cape Gala, did he not? Lady Gretchen of Hedgemoor—the Werefox was close to him, wasn't she? She was with you when you left your city. Where did she head to?"

Jenna nodded at Trent, tears flowing as she looked at him imploringly.

"Wife, please—" began Gallen, but she spoke over him.

"If I tell you, how do I know you won't kill me? You have slaughtered so many of our people!"

"You have my word we shan't harm you, my lady," promised Trent, his face grim. "Please, answer the question and this torment shall be finished."

"Calico," she stammered. "She heads to the coast."

Trent straightened, turning to Frost. "If she heads to Calico, then the Wolf will follow."

"You're sure of this, Ferran?"

"He chased her all the way to Cape Gala. If he lives, he'll find her, I guarantee it."

"Good," said Frost, spinning his staff. "Find the Fox, find the Wolf."

He banged the base of his staff on the floor, the metal-shod end striking the stone flags. An eight-inch spike projected from the top, the silver blade appearing in a flash. Frost turned the staff and lunged, the blade sinking deep into Gallen's heart.

Frost held it there as the Horselord spluttered, his wife and family screaming in horror. The Lord of Grazetown slid from the end of the silver spear, collapsing on to the cold floor. Frost flicked off the blood before striking the base once more and the blade disappeared from whence it came. He turned, putting an arm around Trent and walked away, as Lady Jenna wailed mournfully over the body of her dead husband.

"You promised you'd spare us!" she screamed as they left.

"He said we'd spare *you*, my lady," called Frost as he stalked out of the room, the young outrider at his side. "Be grateful we're men of our word!"

Trent looked back at the Horselord's family grieving around their slain father.

"Well played, Ferran." The albino chuckled. "You're a shrewd young man. Come with me; that sword of yours is missing something."

PART II

RED SAND, DEAD SEA

I

A BEAST AT ONE'S BACK

FOR A MOMENT he didn't recognize his own reflection. His face was tanned, beaten by the elements, while his black hair hung over his eyes, cloaking them in shadow. The water rippled as he ran his fingertips across the surface, the image fracturing with their passing, soon gone from sight.

Clasping the barrel's edge with his one hand, Drew dipped his face forward, submerging his whole head beneath the water. Although it was dusk, the water was warm after standing all day beneath the hot Scorian sun. He shook his head from side to side, the water cleansing the blood, dust, and filth from his face.

When his head came up he was momentarily blinded, dragging his mutilated left arm across his eyes, blinking the water away. Slowly, he was adjusting to life without the hand, relying on his right for every little task. The phantom sensa-tions would probably never leave him, but he could learn to tolerate them in time. As his vision returned he realized he was no longer alone. The roofless bathhouse was deserted; the human and therian gladiators had disappeared to the ludus to eat. Having spent the day surrounded by others, fighting and sparring, Drew had taken a moment for himself, disappearing into the baths of the gladiator school to reflect in solitude on his predicament. He should have known better. Privacy was a luxury he no longer enjoyed, and a lone soul separated from the pack would always be a target for predators.

Arik and Balk had appeared at the far end of the open chamber, casting long shadows in Drew's direction as they watched him, waiting for him to move. Drew could feel the adrenaline coursing through his exhausted body, preparing him for the coming fight. He wasn't ready for this. His body was battered and bruised from hours of punishing drills and contests. He eyeballed each of the brothers, baring his teeth, putting on a show of strength. But it was bravado.

The Apes had both sparred with him over the course of the day, and he'd bested each of them under the watchful eye of Griffyn, the old gladiator master. Drew had put his victories down to good luck and survival instinct. He was approaching each fight as if it were his last, each opponent in the ludus an obstacle to overcome if he was ever to see Lyssia again. Beating the Wereapes in single combat was one thing; defeating them both at once, however, was a feat that no gladiator had ever accomplished. The two brutes grinned, their huge white teeth shining within their ugly faces as they stepped forward.

Then they halted.

Their smiles transformed into sneers. Arik spat on the floor and Balk stalked away. The remaining Wereape growled, the sound deep and bassy, bouncing off the bathhouse walls and making Drew's guts quake. Then the warrior turned and lumbered after his brother. Drew remained motionless, suddenly realizing that he'd been holding his breath. Slowly he exhaled, his lips trembling as the air escaped in a steady, relieved stream. His extremities shook, his body still prepared for a fight that wasn't going to happen. *What had made them stop?*

"I can't always have your back, Wolf."

Drew turned at the voice, surprised to see Drake standing a few feet behind him.

"I didn't see you there."

Drake pointed after the departed Wereapes. "They did."

He walked past Drew toward the water barrel, grasping the wooden frame before plunging his head beneath the water's surface. For the first time, Drew got a good look at him. Drake was perhaps a year older than he, and by the look of his body he'd spent a great deal of time in the Furnace. As toned and muscular as he was, his torso was hatchmarked with old injuries, a grisly map of scars. Drew thought about his own awful injuries—the severed hand, the whipmarks on his back from

Highcliff, his brand from the Furnace—and felt an empathy for another person that until that moment had been missing since he left Lyssia.

With alarm, he realized that Drake's head had been submerged for a dreadfully long time. Was Drake trying to take his own life? Drew lurched forward, grabbing the other therian by the shoulder and yanking him back out of the barrel. The two tumbled into the dirt, Drake beating Drew away with an expression of deep irritation on his face.

"What are you doing?"

"You'd been under for ages," said Drew. "I thought . . ."

"You thought what? I'd drowned?"

Drake got to his feet, shaking himself off, his torso and head soaking. He ran his hands through his hair, slicking it away from his face.

"You've got a lot to learn about the therians of Bast, Wolf." Drake chuckled. "I'm a Werecrocodile. Water is the least of my worries."

Drew gasped. "I fought one of those croc-creatures. They're like *dragons*!"

Drake laughed. "I suppose so. My father always told me we were descended from the dragons. Perhaps he was on to something."

Drake held his hand out to Drew, snatching his arm and helping him to his feet.

"I'm not the only Reptilelord—there are a few of us," he

said wearily, glancing toward the open archway that led from the baths back into the ludus.

"You're different when you're away from the others," said Drew, warming to the other therian.

"I have a reputation to keep up, Wolf. I'm a killer. It'd do me no good if they all thought I was stepping into everyone else's fight. They'd think I was going soft."

"So what was this? A rare moment of compassion?"

Drake looked hard at Drew. "You and I aren't so different."

"You feel that, too?" said Drew. "It's been so long since I've had a proper conversation with someone, I'd almost forgotten what it felt like. This was the last place I expected to find friendship."

Drake arched a thin eyebrow at Drew's words. "Friendship? You're getting ahead of yourself, Wolf. I see myself in you, back when I first arrived on Scoria."

"When was that?"

"Nine years ago."

"Nine years?" exclaimed Drew, unable to hide his astonishment. He tried to imagine what he was doing nine years ago. He was probably playing with the lambs on the farm, or hanging off his mother's apron strings. Drake had been in the ludus all that time, a child, just like Drew?

"I know," replied Drake, thinking for a moment. "I've spent half my life in this hellhole. I can hardly remember my life before the Furnace."

Drew expected to see a change in Drake's mood, but it didn't happen. The Crocodile simply leaned back against the stone wall of the baths and stared up into the darkening sky.

"What was your story, before all this?" Drake asked.

Now it was Drew's turn to smile. "How long do you have?"

He gave Drake a brief summary of his life, from growing up on the farm to the discovery of his lycanthropy and all that had followed.

"The last of the Gray Wolves of Lyssia, eh?" said Drake, sucking his teeth. "You know, your old man was like a bogeyman to the people of Bast. He was 'the enemy across the water,' the monster who was going to sail south and attack our lands. Little did we know the real foe was closer to home."

"Closer to home?"

"The Catlords," muttered Drake. "They're the reason I'm here. They conquered my people, took our land for their own, and stole hundreds of children, like me. I often wonder what became of my family, whether the Cats spared my mother's life or killed her as they did my father."

"Have you been fighting since then?"

"By the Wyrm's teeth, no! After I was brought to Scoria, I was put to work as a slave in Ignus's palace. When I began to change from child into youth they tired of me quickly—I was a liability. The last thing they needed was a Werecrocodile on the cusp of the change wandering around the palace. They sent me down here, under Griffyn's tutelage. I started in the ludus the same time as Taboo."

"He seems strict."

"Griffyn? I suppose he is. The old man's doing you a favor. If he cracks his whip or shoves you back into the sand to spar one more time, just remember: he's helping you stay alive. If he shows you no mercy, that's because you can expect none in the Furnace. Believe me, if anyone knows how to survive the arena, it's him."

"Griffyn? Why?"

"He was a gladiator once himself, possibly the greatest to ever fight in the Furnace. Five years or so he fought for Ignus and his brothers. He was the crowd's favorite, a true champion. If ever a gladiator earned his freedom, it was him."

"He doesn't look free to me."

Drake shrugged. "He's as free as you can ever expect to be when you're owned by Ignus. He no longer wakes each morning wondering whether the day will be his last. You and I don't have that luxury."

Drew thought about the old man, finding it hard to imagine how he had ever been a gladiator, let alone a champion.

"How is it that Taboo is here—a prisoner, a gladiator—if she's a Felinthrope?"

"That's a question you need to ask Taboo. She'll tear my throat out if I go blabbing about her past."

"You know her well, then?"

"Well enough, Wolf. She's the closest thing to a friend I'll ever have."

"That's sweet."

Drake cackled. "Don't talk soft, Wolf. I'll still have to kill her if we come face to face in the Furnace."

Drew shivered at the Crocodile's cold words. "How can you say that so matter-of-factly?"

Drake turned to Drew and prodded a finger in the young Wolflord's chest. "You need to wake up, and fast," he said. "This—you and me shooting our mouths off—this is fun. This feels almost normal, like how folk talk to one another beyond the walls of the Furnace. Only we'll never get to experience that, will we? We're stuck here, and thinking about any other life is sheer folly. You're a gladiator, Drew, and gladiators fight and die. Don't ever forget that."

He was about to jab Drew in the chest again with his final comment when Drew caught his finger.

"There's something you've forgotten, Drake. We may be prisoners for now, at the mercy of Ignus and Kesslar, but we're Werelords. Think of the power each of us possesses, and what we could do if we worked together. There *is* a life for us beyond these walls. And I intend to return to it."

Drew turned toward the ludus. "Thanks for stepping in with the Ape brothers," he added over his shoulder as he made for the archway from the bathhouse. "But if you're worried about losing face in front of the other gladiators, next time feel free to leave me to fight my own battles."

The Werecrocodile watched the Wolf go. "You're on your own, Wolf!" he shouted after him, chuckling hollowly as Drew disappeared.

2

DEADLY WATERS

THE *MAELSTROM* REMAINED tantalizingly out of reach of the two chasing ships' cannons, her eight white sails faintly visible in the dim light of dusk. The pursuers had been dogging the pirate ship for days now, hot on her heels since she'd fled Moga in a mist of blood. The ships represented the twin enemies of the *Maelstrom* on the high seas: the *Rainbow Serpent* of Lady Slotha and the *Quiet Death* from the Cluster Isles. Slotha had not sat idle since hearing of the bloodshed in Moga, sending the *Rainbow Serpent* out immediately. The *Quiet Death* had joined the chase not long afterward, the lead ship in the Weresquid Ghul's fearsome fleet.

While the captain of the *Rainbow Serpent* wasn't known to the crew of the *Maelstrom*, they knew the *Quiet Death*'s commander all too well. Captain Klay was another of the Sealords, a therian of the ocean like Vega and Ghul. A pirate first and a Werelord second, the Barracuda was a butcher of men and a maker of widows. Sticking close to the *Rainbow Serpent*, Lord Klay was determined to be the Werelord to capture the elusive Count Vega and, better still, put the Shark to the sword.

Klay stood at the prow of the *Quiet Death*, as she sailed slightly ahead and to starboard of the *Rainbow Serpent*, willing his vessel to greater speeds, but his ship remained at a distance from the *Maelstrom*. Vega's ship was the fastest for sure, but the *Quiet Death* was a close second. If Klay could capture the count's ship, he might even end up with the two fastest pirate ships in the known seas. Imagine that! And here was the *Quiet Death*, keeping apace with the Shark. He grinned to himself. Klay had been waiting for his chance to come up against Vega. The man was a braggart and a showman, grown soft over the years on a fading reputation. His time was over. Vega didn't have the nerve to cut it as a pirate anymore, better suited to flouncing around in the courts of Lyssia. *Leave the piracy to the true Sealords, Vega.*

An explosion of fire along the port side of the *Rainbow Serpent* caused Klay's head to whip around. The Sealord ran to the *Quiet Death*'s starboard to better see the destruction, the other ship only forty feet from his own. Two more eruptions along the *Rainbow Serpent*'s flank sent fire racing across her frame, snaking through the cannon hatches below deck. The screams from the men within mixed with the roar of the hungry flames. In moments the ship was careering wildly out of control as the deckhands rushed to put out fires, abandoning their posts—the Tuskun ship was lurching toward the *Quiet Death.*

"Hard to port!" screamed Klay as his own crew rushed to their posts, their pursuit of the *Maelstrom* halted by the devastation that had struck their companion vessel. Fire now covered the decks of the *Rainbow Serpent,* her crew desperately trying to tame the inferno. The *Quiet Death* was able to turn aside just in time as the other lunged across her bow, wails and flames trailing in her wake. A loud *boom* within the middle of the ship sent timbers splintering into the night sky as something exploded in the *Rainbow Serpent's* belly. Klay's crew watched in horror as burning men leaped from the other warship into the sea.

Fire and yelling on board the *Quiet Death* now caused fresh chaos as Klay's men rushed about in a panic. The Sealord saw his mizzenmast aflame, the orange fire licking up the sails and devouring them hungrily. How could this be happening? He snatched hold of his first mate by the throat, shaking him like a doll.

"What's going on?"

"The fire, Captain!" cried the man. "The fire and the monster!"

Monster? Klay tossed him aside into the path of more fleeing men. They looked over their shoulders, clearly fearful of whatever awaited them there.

"Get back, you dogs!" Klay yelled, his face morphing as he began to channel the Barracuda. He whipped out his saber as his eyes grew luminescent, teeth sharpening into long white needles. His skin took on a pale silver pallor, his mouth splitting the flesh as the jaw receded toward his ears.

"Screaming like women—I'm the only monster here! I see you running to the foredecks and I'll cut you in two myself! Get that mast down, and quench those fires!"

To emphasize the point he took a swipe at the air in front of them, the saber scything inches from the men's throats. They fell back as one, terrified into returning to the flames, the first mate leading the way. Buckets were hurried along lines as the crew of the *Quiet Death* was forced to clamber up the burning rigging. Flaming sails fell to the deck as the men struggled to kill the fire. Captain Klay nodded contentedly, pleased that his men were now shaping up.

He was about to return to the rest of his crew when the wet *thunk* of something hitting the deck made him halt. Klay glanced down, thinking a bucket had fallen from a sailor's grasp. The sight of a decapitated head staring back at him did not instantly register.

He looked up as a severed arm spun through the air, narrowly missing his face. Through the smoke and shadows he could see shapes moving frantically, men running, swords slashing, as a melee broke out beneath the flaming mast. He shifted his saber in his grip before stalking through the choking gray clouds. An arc of blood sprayed him as he emerged into the fight. His first mate's carotid artery had been opened up like a bottle of the Redwine's finest. As the body tumbled onto a pile of equally lifeless corpses, Klay squinted through the smoke, trying to spot the killer. He opened his mouth wide, teeth glistening, an armory of shining daggers. He tried to call his men to him, rally them to his aid, but no sound came forth. With surprise and horror he felt a wet sensation washing down his chest and soaking his shirt. He reached a faltering hand up to his throat, finding a gaping hole where it used to be.

The Werefish Klay, commander of the Kraken Ghul's fleet, tumbled onto the corpses of his shipmates. As his life slipped away he stared up at the monstrous silhouette that towered over him; broad gray head, dead black eyes, and razor-sharp teeth that went on forever. *So fast: never saw him coming.* The Wereshark, Count Vega, tossed the lump of torn throat and severed vocal cords on to the Barracuda's body. The last thing Klay heard was the captain of the *Maelstrom*'s voice, dark as the night.

"How's that for your *Quiet Death*, Klay?"

Hector watched the burning ships from the rear deck, the crew of the *Maelstrom* cheering all around him. The ship's rocking left him feeling constantly ill; a life at sea didn't suit the young magister's weak constitution. Hector had found it impossible to keep a meal down since boarding the *Maelstrom* and couldn't wait until they hit land once more. Lady Bethwyn stood at his side, shivering despite her thick cloak. He wanted to put a comforting arm around her but found his limbs unwilling.

What are you afraid of? She won't bite!

Hector snarled at the taunts of the Vincent-vile, and Bethwyn heard the noise that escaped his lips. He smiled awkwardly, embarrassment never far away. A commotion on the main deck caused a crowd to gather. Bethwyn turned and followed the men as they rushed to their returning captain. Vega was soaking, his white shirt clinging to his torso as he shook the excess water from his body. Duke Manfred passed the Sharklord his cloak.

"That was some piece of work, Vega," said the Staglord, impressed.

"I did what had to be done. That's put their lead ships off our tail for the time being. We might be able to put some distance between ourselves and the remaining pack."

"Klay's dead, then?" asked Hector as he approached.

Vega looked up, tousling his long, dark locks dry with the cloak.

"Very much so," said the Shark, his characteristic smile not present. "Klay's reputation was built upon hitting hard and showing no mercy. He got what he deserved."

Vega's plan had been as cunning as one might have expected from the Pirate Prince of the Cluster Isles. As twilight fell they'd lowered a small boat overboard, loaded up with flasks of Spyr Oil and a hooded lantern. The Shark had then clambered in and rowed silently back toward the pursuing ships, ensuring he ended up between the two.

Once in position he'd lit the flasks and launched them at the *Rainbow Serpent*, saving the last to throw at the *Quiet Death*. Diving from the boats he'd clambered onto the pirate ship while the crew were distracted by the fires. Transformed into his therian form, he'd added to the madness, slaughtering the enemy and dispatching their captain, the terrible Lord Klay.

Vega clapped his hands, attracting the crew's attention. "Enough lollygagging, lads! We need to make the most of Sosha's blessings. Ghul and Slotha aren't far behind. These are uncharted waters and we mean to reach Roof—let's not get complacent!"

The crew immediately dispersed back to their posts, leaving the Werelords to return to the aft deck. Queen Amelie stared at the burning ships in the west.

"Will there be survivors?"

"I should think so," said Vega. "I'm not a *monster*, Your Majesty. But their fate isn't our concern."

"That's cold," said the queen.

"That's war." Vega sighed. "With respect, Your Majesty, it's the business we're in."

"Don't patronize me, Vega. You forget my people are from this part of the world. The White Wolves of Sturmland are a tough breed."

"So tough they were chased out of Shadowhaven when the Lionguard arrived."

Amelie slapped the Sharklord hard across the face.

"Do not mock me! The White Wolves were lucky to escape Shadowhaven with their lives. If I hadn't agreed to wed Leopold, he'd have slaughtered all my people. Who knows where my brethren are now? My people are *lost*, Vega!"

See how poisonous the Sharklord is to your precious Council? I can't imagine the Wolf would be pleased to hear how the Shark speaks to his mother!

"Show some respect to the queen, Vega," said Hector, the words out before he'd even considered them. He wished he could take them back, but it was too late.

Very good, brother!

Vega looked up, his left eyebrow threatening to lift off his head. Even Manfred was surprised to hear Hector speak to the Sharklord in such a manner. Vega bowed to Hector, smiling through a split lip he'd sustained in the melee.

"My apologies," said the sea marshal. "I meant no offense."

"This quarreling does us no good," said Manfred. "We need to remain unified. If we're at one another's throats, then we're doomed. With my brother and Bergan gone and Drew still lost, we only have each other."

"I'm sorry, Count Vega. I spoke out of turn," said the queen. "I worry about all lives in these terrible times, even those of our enemy."

"That's understandable, Your Majesty," said Vega, his voice now respectful. "The beast sometimes gets the better of me."

"The hour's late, gentlemen. We shall retire for the evening and see you at first light."

The three male Werelords all bowed as the queen and Bethwyn departed. Hector watched Bethwyn go, the girl glancing back just once before disappearing belowdecks. His heart briefly skipped a beat.

"Speaking to her wouldn't hurt," said Vega, causing Hector to start. The sea marshal didn't look up, unfurling his sketchy maps and inspecting them hopefully by lantern light. Hector's anger flared at Vega's remark, but he remained tight-lipped.

"I'd have thought we'd have encountered one of our own ships by now," said Manfred, casting his thumb across the waters ahead of them on the parchment. "They're out here somewhere, Brenn help them."

"If they're lost then they're at Sosha's mercy," said Vega. "Hopefully they'll all make it to Roof and we can regroup there."

Hector looked away, back toward the door that led to the cabins.

Yes, go and speak with her, Hector. She won't be able to resist you: you're the Baron of Redmire now, remember?

Hector shivered, stepping away from the two therians as they looked back to the faded sea charts. He made his way down the staircase back to the main deck, stepping aside as sailors rushed about. The sails clapped as the wind caught them, speeding them away from the burning ships.

He spied Ringlin and Ibal, skulking in the shadows before the poop deck. Since the fight in Moga, Hector had been forced to show control over the duo, ordering them to work alongside Vega's men.

They nodded briefly as he passed them by, but didn't speak.

They don't trust you anymore, brother, and who can blame them? Letting Vega take a whip to them? Flogging them in front of his crew? You're lucky they haven't slit your throat in your sleep!

"They had to be punished," said Hector under his breath. He strode to the side of the ship, gloved hands clutching the rail. He could feel his evening meal rising in his throat, the sickness returning.

Yes, but by you, surely? Not by the Shark!

"Don't worry about me, Vincent. I know what I'm doing."

The vile's gurgling laughter made Hector's skin crawl. He felt its cold breath rasp against his ear, while bile raced toward his mouth.

"I'll be fine," he whispered to himself, but his words felt hollow.

3

BLOOD IN THE DUST

"YOU'RE UP, WOLF!"

Drew remained seated, ignoring Griffyn's words. The din was deafening, dust falling from the ceiling into his holding pen. A grilled door barred his entrance into the Furnace, beyond which he could hear the bloodthirsty crowd's cheers. Drew had just witnessed the Wereapes, Balk and Arik, tear through ten gladiators. The brothers now stood in the center of the arena, caked in blood and gore, roaring triumphantly at the ghoulish spectators.

"I shall not fight innocent men."

"Then you'll die."

Drew looked around. The old gladiator master stood behind bars at his back, there to ensure the Wolf entered the arena. He held Drew's collar in his hand, having removed the silver choker once he'd been locked into the cell. Two of Ignus's warriors stood either side of Griffyn, each carrying polearms. The foot-long blades on their ends shone brilliantly, the silver reflecting flashes of sunlight into Drew's face. He winced, raising his wrist stump to his eyes.

"Pick up your weapons, boy," said Griffyn, insistent now. The guards began to lower their weapons toward the grilled door. "Kesslar didn't bring you all this way to be run through in this stinking pen."

"Then he's in for a disappointment."

"Banish all thought of these men being innocent," said Griffyn. "They're killers, Wolf. Gladiators. They live to fight and die."

The Apes had now departed and the bodies of their opponents had been removed. Drew heard the grating of metal cogs as the door mechanism ground into action. The metal bars rose, hard clay falling from the spiked ends that had been buried in the baked earth. Drew choked as the hot dust blew into the cell, catching in his throat.

Griffyn reached through the bars for one of the weapons lying on the floor that had been given to the Werewolf. Drew snatched the old man's forearm, holding him fast. The two glared at one another.

"If you want to live, Wolf, pick up the weapons," he said quietly.

"Why do you care if I live or die?"

Griffyn smiled. "You remind me of someone I used to know."

A guard grabbed hold of Griffyn's shoulder, trying to pull the gladiator master back.

"Pick them up and *fight!*" said Griffyn.

With that, the warriors pulled Griffyn clear and readied their polearms to strike. Drew could hear the crowd chanting and booing now, growing restless with the delay. He examined his weapons.

The two blades were old and pitted, each caked with dried blood and rust. The first was a trident dagger with a basket handle, no doubt formerly the property of some other single-armed gladiator. Drew pulled it over his stump, using the pommel of the other weapon, a shortsword, to bang it home. The fit was tight.

Rising, Drew took a couple of deep breaths before looking back at Griffyn. The old gladiator nodded to Drew, pointing toward the exit. Saying a silent prayer to Brenn, he turned and stepped out into the Furnace.

The first thing that hit Drew was the unbearable heat. The sun glared down, while the ground felt like a bed of hot coals. The sulfurous smell was overwhelming, pockets of the noxious gas leaking from the cracked arena floor. The sand was stained crimson and brown from the day's earlier battles, the blood drying swiftly in the soaring temperature. He was walking into the heart of hell, with no turning back.

The mob filled the seating all around, a mixture of the wealthy and poor of Scoria, all united in their blood-lust. They bayed at Drew as he walked into the center of the Furnace, screaming obscenities and howling wildly. One side of the terrace was taken up by guests from the palace of Lord Ignus, the viewing deck jutting out from the black and white marble walls. Great sails of colorful cloth kept the heat from Ignus's guests while they lounged and feasted, enjoying their sport.

On the opposite side of the arena, Drew saw a trio of figures entering the Furnace. The heat haze caused them to shimmer into focus as they approached. One carried a net and trident, a broad helmet covering his face. Another carried a spear and shield, a pot helm hiding his head from view. The last carried a pair of shortswords, spinning them in his hands as he advanced.

"Behold!" cried Ignus from his viewing deck. He wore a long white robe, open to his midriff, baring his smooth, oiled chest. His three brothers stood leaning on the balcony, similarly undressed, ugly and misshapen. Beside Ignus, Drew spied Kesslar, Shah, and Djogo.

"I give you Drew of the Dyrewood, the last Gray Wolf of Lyssia!"

The mob found new volumes, roaring their approval and chanting for blood.

"He faces Haxur of the Teeth; Obliss of Ro-Shann; and our very own Galtus, the Swords of Scoria!"

The crowd chanted the gladiators' names, each having their favorites. The one named Galtus—whom Drew had to assume carried the two swords—seemed to be popular, clearly one of Scoria's champions. They each raised their weapons to the crowd, soaking up their adulation. *They're* enjoying *this madness!*

The gladiators split formation, fanning out as they circled Drew. Each was clearly a seasoned slayer of men—better armed and armored than the ten the Apes had slaughtered—and they moved with deadly grace. Nevertheless, Drew had no intention of killing anyone. His fight was with Ignus and Kesslar.

"I don't want to fight you . . ." began Drew, but the one with the trident moved quickly. The net flew through the air landing over Drew, the lead balls clattering about his waist as he became entangled.

"Too bad!" yelled Obliss, leaping forward to drive his pronged spear home. Drew twisted clear as the weapon ripped through the air where his stomach had been a second previously. He dived into a roll, arms pinned by the netting as he powered himself toward the spot Obliss had vacated, just as Haxur's spear struck the earth where he'd stood.

"See how he runs with his tail between his legs!" Haxur laughed.

Drew scrambled to his knees, sawing at the net with sword

and parrying dagger, desperate to free himself. The crowd laughed and jeered, disappointed to see how quickly this great Wolf from the Northern continent had fallen. The gladiators laughed, clapping Galtus on the back as he stepped forward.

"You're a long way from home, Lyssian cur," said the Scorian champion. Drew scrambled back, toppling and kicking into the dirt as he retreated. Galtus relentlessly closed in.

"Change for me, dog, and I'll have your pelt as a cloak!"

Galtus kicked Drew, sending him rolling across the hot clay. The last thing he wanted was to let the Wolf loose, but it looked increasingly like he was going to have to. Drew's short-sword arm suddenly came free from the netting, allowing him to bring it up as Galtus bore down. He parried the first sword away, but the second scored a wound across his bicep, causing the shortsword to fly from his grasp. The crowd booed, throwing stones and bits of rubbish into the Furnace.

Galtus held his swords out to either side, turning on the spot as he looked around the arena.

"This is the best Lyssia has to offer?" he bellowed. "Let me kill him, Lord Ignus! Let me end this embarrassment before he ridicules the Furnace any further!"

Ignus stood on the platform, the subject of much of the crowd's booing. They had come to see battle, see blood. He glared across the terrace at Kesslar, then marched over to him, his face red with fury. His brothers joined him, circling the Goatlord.

"You make a mockery of my arena!" spat the outraged Lord of Scoria. "You sell me this worthless hound for a king's ransom and have the gall to watch as I'm humiliated!"

The Scorians continued to curse and bay. Fights broke out as the mob turned on one another in anger. From where Drew lay, surrounded by killers, he could see the confrontation on the balcony, Kesslar shifting back as Ignus and his brothers began to transform. Shah and Djogo took a step away from the enraged Werelords.

Ignus's neck elongated, his jaws widening and cracking. His thin lips ripped even farther back, the flesh tearing as he opened his mouth wide. His gray oily skin rippled, shifting quickly to a sickly green, while his bulbous eyes almost popped from their sockets. He brought his hands up, now transformed into scaly claws, readying a fist to strike the Goatlord. Kesslar stood his ground, horns breaking free as the therians put on a show of their own. Even the gladiators looked up, their attention pulled away from Drew.

"You steal from me, Kesslar, and I would seek recompense!" yelled the Lizardlord of Scoria, his black tongue flicking over serrated teeth.

"You bought the Wolf fair and square," brayed Kesslar, stamping a hoof angrily. "It's not my fault if he won't fight for you!"

"I'll take what you owe me, Kesslar!" roared Ignus. "In blood if I have to!"

With that, the Scorian swung around with lightning speed and grabbed Djogo by his throat. In one savage motion he hurled him off the viewing deck.

"No!" shouted Shah as Kesslar's captain landed twenty feet below on the red clay floor of the Furnace. Before she could move, the three other Werelizards took hold of her, wrestling her into submission.

"Now we'll see a show!" Ignus laughed as his warriors joined his brothers, forming a ring around Kesslar and Shah.

"He can't *do* this!" cried Shah. The Goatlord made no effort to intervene.

Djogo struggled to rise as the Lizard bellowed: "Scoria shall have blood!"

From where he lay on the floor of the Furnace, entangled in the net, Drew watched the desperate Djogo struggling to rise. *How quickly loyalty can shift*, he thought. The slaver hobbled gingerly to his feet, scrabbling for a weapon as Obliss and Haxur advanced. *They'll kill him*, Drew mused, for a moment seized by inaction. Here was the man who had tormented him in Haggard and aboard the *Banshee*. Djogo was a monster—why should Drew care if the trio of gladiators ran the killer through? Finding only his whip, Djogo looked up to the balcony.

"Throw me a blade, I beg you!"

Ignus picked up a blunt knife from his banquet table and tossed it below, the tiny sliver of metal plinking on the hard clay. The crowd roared with laughter as Djogo ignored the insult and cracked his whip overhead, trying to ward off the gladiators.

"Been a while since you fought in the Furnace, Djogo," sneered Obliss, avoiding the lash.

"I bet you thought you were done with the arena once the old Goat bought you!" Haxur laughed as he moved to flank the slaver. Djogo got one more whiplash away before they lunged in and brought him down, spear and trident slashing and stabbings sending him to the dirt.

The lanky ex-gladiator was brought to his knees to a chorus of roars from the crowd. Galtus raised his swords in the air as his companions held Djogo down. The spectators suddenly went wild. Too late, Galtus realized the mob was agitated not by the imminent slaughter of the slaver, but by what was happening directly behind him. He turned quickly, but not quick enough. A powerful lupine leg kicked out, connecting with Galtus's knee and breaking it at the joint. The leg buckled back at an impossible angle, sending the gladiator tumbling in a fit of wailing agony.

The transformation had taken place swiftly, Drew's body now more than accustomed to the change. He rose with the net still wrapped about his dark torso, snarling at the man and roaring in his face. Spittle hit Galtus as he slashed out with his blades, the swords tearing through net and fur as they cut into the Werewolf's flesh. The net fell away like a tattered cloak as Drew shook it loose, ignoring the fresh wounds. A mighty fist caught the man in the jaw, sending him skidding along the dirt, a cloud of dust erupting in his wake.

The two other gladiators stared at the scene, shocked at the sudden and violent metamorphosis and the dramatic reversal of fortune for their fellow gladiator. Djogo winced, his body checkered with cuts as the gladiators disengaged from their fight with him to face the Wolf. They moved to flank Drew, Haxur banging his spear against his shield, calling for the Wolf to attack while Obliss readied to lunge. Drew feinted to attack Haxur, stepping forward on his left before leaping back toward Obliss. The man was already committed, throwing his weight behind his trident. Knowing what the gladiator's move would be allowed Drew to leap above the blow, high into the air as his opponent passed beneath.

Obliss looked up as the shadow descended, the Werewolf landing on him from on high. His companion having taken Drew's attack, Haxur tried to skewer the beast on his spear, a blow that would surely find its home in the therian. Instead he halted mid-thrust, the crack of Djogo's whip signaling the attack. The whip coiled around Haxur's throat, catching fast. Djogo rose in the dust, pulling hard, the throttled man spinning toward him, spear flying from his grasp. Pirouetting across the Furnace floor, Haxur whirled inexorably toward Djogo to be caught in the slaver's arms.

Haxur's eyes widened as he looked down at his chest, the blunt banquet knife piercing deep through his breastplate and into his heart. Djogo let the body fall to the floor as Drew rose from the unconscious form of Obliss.

The crowd were silent for a brief, dreadful moment, before bursting into rapturous applause. Drew stood opposite Djogo, still changed, chest heaving, as he weighed the slaver up. Djogo teetered, torso bloody, ready to collapse at any moment. He fell forward as Drew lunged, changing as he moved. Back in human form, Drew caught the slaver as they landed, the beast receding as the guards of Ignus emerged from the pens, advancing toward the combatants.

"Thank you," panted the one-eyed warrior through bloodied teeth.

"Don't thank me yet, Djogo," said the young therian as the guards surrounded them. "The enemy of my enemy is still my enemy."

4

THE BOLD THUNDER

THE CREW OF the *Maelstrom* had never seen anything like it. The fog that surrounded the ship was the thickest they'd ever encountered, a great bank of sea mist that swallowed everything in its path. The crew stood around every rail, squinting into the gloom. Men muttered prayers, some chanting, others whispering, the atmosphere sinister. A dread sense of foreboding filled the soul of everyone. Nobody, human or therian, was immune.

It had come on fast. The ship's lookout boy, Casper, spied it easily enough, pointing it out to Count Vega and allowing the *Maelstrom* to change course and avoid it. But somehow the fog had still intercepted them. Few ships sailed through the Sturmish Sea, its grim reputation making it a body of water to avoid whenever possible. The sails were lowered as they cut their speed, at the mercy of the mysterious fog. With Figgis holding the wheel, Vega, Duke Manfred, and Baron Hector all stood on the foredeck, looking out into the mist.

"Ship ahead!" cried out a crewman as a black shape appeared out of nowhere. Figgis turned the wheel hard, bringing the *Maelstrom* about to avoid a collision. Manfred and Hector backed away as Vega stood firm on the prow, feet apart and legs locked as the other vessel drew ever closer. The *Maelstrom* ran beside it, the distance between the ships a matter of mere feet. To their relief, the other ship wasn't in flight, simply drifting on the currents.

The ship's name painted down the side proclaimed her to be *Bold Thunder*. She was one of theirs, another escapee from Highcliff that had carried civilians when they'd fled. This was the first ship from their tiny fleet the *Maelstrom* had encountered.

"Grapples and ropes!" cried out Vega as he paced along the deck, Manfred and Hector close at his heel. Lines were hastily thrown, securing the *Bold Thunder* to the *Maelstrom* and bringing her alongside.

"Captain Crowley!" called out Vega, hailing the other ship's skipper. He waited for an answer, but none came—the ship appeared deserted. The sea marshal turned to look at his puzzled companions.

"Perhaps they're all sleeping in their cabins," said Vega

with a grim smile, unsheathing his cutlass. "After me, lads—and stay on your toes!"

With that, Vega placed his blade between his teeth before taking hold of a mooring rope and beginning to drag himself across. Hector looked at Manfred worriedly.

"I think he means us to follow, Hector," said the Staglord, taking hold of the rope and clambering after the count.

Hector watched him go, his insides knotting, hands sweating inside the leather gloves.

Well? Aren't you going to follow, brother? Afraid of what you'll find?

The young magister ignored the vile's taunts, stepping up onto the rails and taking a grip on the rope. It bounced in his grasp as Manfred disappeared into the fog ahead. Hector threw his legs around it, letting his body swing until he was suspended beneath it, gripping with his arms and legs. The waves lapped ten feet below him between the two ships, clapping against the hulls in anticipation of his falling.

Hector glanced back before setting off, spying Queen Amelie and Bethwyn at the edge of the rail. He'd summoned enough courage to speak to Bethwyn in the last few days—only small talk, light banter that didn't lead anywhere—but it was a start. His life felt empty without his friends: Drew, Gretchen, and Whitley were lost to him, possibly forever. A blossoming friendship with Bethwyn might fill that void.

"Be careful," whispered Bethwyn, her eyes never leaving him.

His heart beat faster now, the weight of expectation having doubled suddenly with this unexpected audience. He just needed to get across without making a fool of himself. He began to move.

At the middle point between the ships, the rope sagged, swinging wildly. Hector closed his eyes, inching his hands forward one over the other, dragging his knees onward while gripping on for dear life. He could swear he felt the waves slapping his back, could imagine the horrors lurking in the depths waiting to take a bite. Nearing the *Bold Thunder* he found his grip slipping. Panic rising, he feared he might fall at any moment.

A firm hand took hold of his jerkin, hefting him up through the air, away from the rope, and down on to the deck of the *Bold Thunder* in one motion. His legs wobbled as he steadied himself. Vega patted him down.

"Are you all right, Hector?" asked the count.

"I'm fine, thank you, Vega," he replied, trying to sound confident while his trembling voice betrayed him. He looked around as more men from the *Maelstrom* joined them.

The *Bold Thunder* was a ghost ship.

There was no sign of anyone on deck, the wheel unmanned and the sails flapping idly in the faint breeze. The men fanned out, calling to one another, remaining in earshot when the fog threatened to hide them from their shipmates. Hector unsheathed his dagger, holding it warily before him. The Lord of

Stormdale pulled a lantern from its housing on the main mast, and taking out his flint and steel he set about lighting it.

"Have you seen anything like this before, Vega?" asked the Staglord as he worked on his tinderbox.

"Very rarely; sometimes piracy can be the cause of an abandoned ship, but more often than not the pirates take the ship." He smiled at his fellow therians. "I've done it myself!"

Hector walked toward the cabin hatch that led belowdecks. He flexed his left hand, the black skin of his palm rippling beneath the glove as he held it toward the handle. A hand on his shoulder caused him to jump.

"You want me to go first?"

It was Vega again; ever present, shadowing his every move.

And you thought I was bad? said the vile in his ear.

Hector turned to the captain as assuredly as he could. "You're welcome to accompany me, Vega."

The sea marshal looked impressed, gesturing to the door. "After you, dear baron."

Hector grasped the handle and opened the door. The dark below was impenetrable. Hector shivered, his courage deserting him. He was about to turn and suggest Vega lead when the lighted lantern was offered by Manfred.

"Here, Hector. Looks like you'll need light down there."

Hector smiled, gratefully taking the lantern before proceeding down into the belly of the *Bold Thunder*. He heard the footsteps of the following Werelords, relieved he had them at his back. The stairs led down into a cramped corridor that ran to the officers' cabins at the rear, and forward to a cargo hold.

"The *Bold Thunder*'s a merchant ship," said Vega, ducking as he entered the corridor behind Hector. "Crowley's been a regular trader along the Cold Coast since I was a boy. He'd never leave his ship, not under any circumstances. This is his home, his life."

He slapped the wall as if to emphasize the point, as Hector entered the cargo hold. Crates and barrels were lashed down against the walls, provisions that had been stowed in the hold before the violence had broken out in Highcliff. Crowley had taken as many civilians onto the *Bold Thunder* as possible, crowding them belowdecks as the ship had set sail. Empty bedrolls littered the floor, with not a single body occupying them.

"Where *is* everybody?" gasped Hector.

"It's like a tomb down here," said Manfred.

"A tomb without any bodies," added Vega quietly.

Manfred pulled his cloak tight around his chin. "I don't like this one bit."

Hector inspected the lashed-down goods, checking what Crowley had been shipping. Manfred followed, reading the words aloud that marked each crate and barrel.

"Grain, vegetables, wine; there's enough here to feed the *Maelstrom* for a couple of weeks. Why would they leave it behind?"

"Crowley wouldn't," said Vega, rubbing his jaw thoughtfully. He headed toward the cabins. Manfred and Hector hurried along behind him.

The captain's quarters were well furnished. A leather-backed chair swiveled lazily behind his huge desk; ledgers, sea charts, and maps remained unfurled on the table, open inkpots holding them in place. Vega skirted the desk and went over to the bunk. Rummaging beneath it he found a chest. He pulled out a knife and jammed it into the lock. With a crack the box opened, revealing gold, silver, and personal artifacts; all of Crowley's worldly possessions. Vega stared up at his companions.

The three men returned above deck, where the *Maelstrom*'s away party had gathered. Vega addressed the group.

"There are goods below that we need aboard the *Maelstrom*. Whatever happened to the crew and civilians of the *Bold Thunder*, we can't neglect the fact that we left Moga in a hurry, without anywhere near the provisions we required."

Vega couldn't help but glance Hector's way at the mention of the disastrous encounter in Moga. Hector simmered silently.

Any opportunity to stick the knife in . . . and twist . . .

Hector looked at the gaudy dagger he always carried with him—the dagger that had ended Vincent's life. Thin wisps of black smoke materialized before his eyes as the vile's thin hand appeared to claw at its hilt.

Vega continued, aware that his men were uneasy aboard the abandoned vessel. "I know none of you wants to be on this ship any longer than need be, so be quick about it. Peavney, you're in charge."

One of the *Maelstrom*'s mates stepped forward as the three Werelords paced back toward the mooring ropes that held the two vessels together. Hector spied Ringlin and Ibal among them, lurking at the rear of the bunch. Both men nodded to their lord.

Seems they've found their respect again, whispered the vile. *But for how long, brother?*

Hector skidded on the deck, his legs threatening to fly from beneath him, his dagger flashing wildly as he steadied himself.

The duke and the count caught him, "Careful, Hector." Vega grinned. "You could have someone's eye out."

The vile hissed in Hector's ear. *Every barbed word the Shark says hides a meaning just for you, brother!*

"I know what I'm doing, thank you, Vega."

Vega didn't respond to the riposte, instead crouching and inspecting the deck. He traced his hand across the timber planks where Hector had slid, his fingers slick with brackish slime. He flicked it, the gelatinous liquid spattering on to the deck a few feet away.

"What is it?" asked Manfred, frowning.

"I have no idea," said Vega, the mischief in his voice re-placed by concern. "I have absolutely no idea."

5

RECRIMINATION AND RECUPERATION

THE LIZARD LOUNGED in his stone chair, alone, staring at the open balcony that overlooked the Furnace. The last of his guests from yesterday were finally gone, having remained during the night to share in the debauched entertainment. His brothers had retired to their own quarters in the palace, nursing their heads and stomachs after their excesses.

The rap of a spear on the door, followed by it swinging open, brought the Lizardlord's attention back to the rear of the hall.

"Count Kesslar and Lady Shah, my lord," the guard announced.

"Send them in."

The guard stepped into the chamber, followed by the Goatlord and the raven-haired lady, and three more warriors fell in behind them. They came to a halt before the metal grate. The guards stood to the side of the pair, not retreating from the chamber. Kesslar eyed them, stroking his gray beard between bony knuckles.

"You took your time," snapped Ignus, reaching down beside his throne to pick up a terra-cotta bowl. He scooped up a handful of yellow oil out of it, slapped it onto his chest, and began to massage it into his skin. Shah wrinkled her nose at the sight.

"I didn't realize we were to come rushing like your lackeys, Ignus. We are still guests, are we not?"

"For the time being," said the Lizardlord, the threat evident in his voice. "I plan another contest in two days' time and don't want the same debacle we witnessed yesterday. What guarantees do you give that this Wolf will cause no further chaos?"

"None, Ignus. He's troublesome, but it's not my place to break him to your will. That's *your* job. I simply supply the raw meat."

Ignus threw the bowl at Kesslar, the pot shattering against his shoulder and sending the hot oil over his face. The Goatlord cried out, wiping the amber liquid from his eyes.

"Do not dare to enter *my* home and tell me how *I* should

run my affairs, Goatlord! You made a mockery of my arena with your incompetence! I'll make a gladiator out of the Wolf, mark my words, but our business isn't finished. You still owe me for the shame you brought to the Furnace."

"I owe you nothing," said Kesslar.

The guards shifted at his words, spears twitching menacingly. A jet of sulfurous steam erupted from the grate, as if the volcano was adding its voice to the proceedings. Ignus pointed a clawed finger at the slave trader, his face contorting as his rage rose.

"Say that one more time, Kesslar, and you'll pay with more than blood, flesh, and bone!"

The Goatlord sulked, smearing the last of the oil's residue from his face on to his sleeve. Shah remained silent, watching the guards warily.

"Good," said the Lizard, reclining on his throne once more. "I think you know what I ask of you."

"Consider it done," muttered Kesslar.

"Speak up!"

"He's yours once more!" shouted the Goat. "Do with him as you please!"

Shah suddenly understood and became animated. "You can't do this, he's a free man!"

"Be quiet, Shah," snapped Kesslar. "Have you not yet learned? None who are in my service are truly free. What part of being a slaver do you not yet grasp?"

112

"But he's your friend! This is unfair!"

"This is business," said the Goat, glaring at Ignus.

"That's the spirit, Kesslar," said the Lizardlord. "And I'd mind your tongue if I were you, Shah. You forget that I hold your father still. His wings may be clipped but I can do an awful lot more if I so please!"

Shah looked between them, unable to decide which she despised more.

"If you're done with me, I would like to retire to my room," she said, her voice raw with anger.

Ignus nodded and waved a hand dismissively. Kesslar snatched at Shah's arm as she turned to depart.

"Do not do anything foolish, woman. I'd hate to lose you, too."

Shah tugged herself free, tearing her sleeve. She took a staggering step away from Kesslar before storming from the foul hall.

Drew stared into his bowl, his stomach knotting as the grains shifted. He deftly picked out the tiny grubs from the two-day-old rice, flicking them away before proceeding to eat. His insides rumbled, hunger ensuring his search for unwanted visitors in the meal was short-lived. If there were any more of the creatures in the gloopy mush, they'd be dead soon enough once they hit his belly.

He kept his head down, not wanting to attract further attention. It had been a chaotic time since his appearance in the Furnace. Many of the human gladiators had given him a wide berth, wary of what he was capable of after defeating three of their best. Galtus and Obliss glowered at him from across the ludus, still mourning the death of Haxur and blaming the young Werewolf for his part in the gladiator's demise. Galtus's right leg was strapped in a splint, and the man never took his eyes off Drew.

The therians had been less evasive, Arik and Balk wasting no time in continuing their taunts. Drew gave them nothing, taking their insults. The remaining Werelords had kept a respectful distance, although he'd sparred in the ludus with Krieg the Rhino and Stamm the Buffalo. He'd trained alongside them for hours that afternoon, trading blows, parrying, and wrestling, but not a word had passed between them. Presently the pair sat down at Drew's table.

"You fought well in the Furnace the other day," said Stamm from beneath his shaggy mane. For once, the Buffalo's somber face seemed a touch less miserable. His sad eyes twinkled as he looked at Drew with newfound respect from beneath his thick fringe.

"When you finally fought, that is." Krieg laughed. "I thought they were going to finish you in the pen before you got out of the gate!"

Drew wondered whether this was the precursor to more insults like the cruel games of the Ape brothers. Neither therian showed signs of aggression. Indeed, Stamm was now smiling, his thick, matted hair shaking as he rocked in his seat, his laughter low and rumbling.

"I didn't know how that would play out," Drew muttered. "I won't take a life without just reason."

"I could have told you the crimes those three committed in the outside world before you were led into your pen, Wolf," said Krieg. "That may have made your decision to fight that bit easier."

"What do you mean?"

"All three were murderers. They were bought by Ignus to perform. None will leave alive."

"Seems Ignus might have done something right there," said Drew.

"Ignus serves himself when buying the lives of these killers," said Stamm. "His reasons are entirely selfish. He wants the very *best* killers to walk on to the red clay and do battle."

Drew looked over his shoulder, spying the human gladiators still watching him.

"They knew Djogo. Did the slaver fight here in the past?"

"He used to be one of them, a gladiator, and a fine one for a human," said the Wererhino, snorting as he threw his rice down his throat. "Kesslar struck a deal with Ignus, buying the man and making him his own. Djogo's worked his way into a position of power for the Goat by all accounts. He's the exception to the rule."

"He's a ruthless killer," said Drew. He hadn't seen the slaver since the fight in the Furnace. He wondered what had become of him.

"The young Wolf catches on fast." Stamm chuckled, scooping the remainder of the rice out of his own bowl. The Buffalo shoved it into his wide mouth, slurping the last grains from his thick, dirty fingertips.

Drew shook his head. "Why did Ignus throw him into the arena?"

Krieg leaned across the table, keeping his voice low. "Ignus and his brothers own *everything* on Scoria. Anyone who comes here is a guest of the Lizards so long as they remain in favor. It appears Kesslar displeased Ignus when his star gladiator failed to live up to expectations. That would be you, of course."

Stamm added his voice. "In Ignus's eyes, the Goatlord deceived him. He took Djogo as payment for Kesslar's bad business. You cost the Lizard a great deal of gold, Wolf."

Just then the Behemoth came over, sitting down at the opposite end of the table from them. Drew felt the bench bow as he took his seat.

"Won't you join us?" asked Drew, making the most of the thaw in relations between the therians.

The Behemoth turned slowly as he was about to take his first mouthful of food. The man's eyes were spaced farther apart than one might expect on a human, and his skin had a hard, hide-like quality, as if whatever beast he was remained hidden just below the surface. Without speaking, the Behemoth rose. Any fears Drew had that he'd offended the giant disappeared, as he paced farther down the long table to join them, the ground trembling beneath his footsteps.

"Thank you," said the Behemoth as he sat. "Am I joining you to dine, or for something else?"

Stamm and Krieg looked at one another, unsure what to make of the Behemoth's question. Drew wasted no time.

"What else could you be joining us for?"

"The grand speech you made the other day—I dismissed it as sunstroke initially. But now I see you're a man of conviction. You really intend to escape the Furnace, don't you?"

"I do."

Stamm waved his hand dismissively. "You waste your words; talk of escape is futile."

"How is it futile?" said Drew urgently. "I was told the Werelords were noble; look what you've been reduced to!"

"Be quiet, boy," said Krieg, big lips curling back to reveal teeth like blocks of granite. The therians may all have been wearing silver collars, but each was more than capable of killing Drew in human form if they put their mind to it. Nevertheless, Drew would not back down.

"You've become used to fighting alone, looking after your own skin in the Furnace. But imagine what we could do if we were to *combine* our strength and make a stand! Do you not want to see your homelands again?"

"Our homelands are enslaved, just as we are, Wolf," said Stamm. The laughter that had earlier been evident had disappeared, the Werebuffalo's thick mane casting shadows over his face once again, sad eyes drooping as he stared at the floor. "Do you think Lyssia is the first of the Catlords' conquests?"

"The boy does not speak for me," said Krieg, shaking his head.

"If we escape the arena, we can work together, Krieg. We can unite against our common enemy. You risk your life every time you enter the Furnace. Why not risk it for something noble for once?"

Krieg snatched angrily at Drew, but the young Werewolf was too quick for the Rhino, dodging out of reach. The debate was descending into a fight.

"Leave the Wolf alone, Krieg," said the Behemoth. Krieg growled and snorted, bringing his fist back but keeping his glare on the young man.

"He's right," the giant continued quietly. "Each of us has been dragged to this purgatory. We all have scores to settle with Ignus and his friends, like Kesslar and the Catlords."

"And where would your grand plan start?" asked Stamm, his voice a whisper.

The Behemoth sighed. "Thinking was never my strength. My strength . . . would be my strength."

Drew looked around the ludus at the other gladiators. Galtus and Obliss couldn't be trusted, but there had to be other humans present who wanted to escape. He saw Taboo eating at another table with Drake. His eyes suddenly recognized a familiar face being led out of the small surgery tent at the rear of the ludus by master Griffyn.

"Excuse me," said Drew, rising immediately and making his way between the tables, ignoring the jeers of Galtus and Obliss on one side and the Apes on the other.

Griffyn was in deep conversation with his man, heads close together as they spoke quietly. Drew slowed his pace. The two appeared to know each other very well. The aged gladiator had his arm around the other's shoulder in a fashion more familiar than Drew might have expected. *Almost paternal*, thought Drew. He thought back to the rare occasions as a boy when Mack Ferran would put a consoling arm around him when he was hurt. He stepped before the two men, who looked up with a mixture of surprise and shock. Griffyn seemed flustered.

"Can I help you, boy?" asked the wiry old man, his hands scratching at the silver collar that encircled his ragged throat. *So Griffyn's a therian*, thought Drew. *Yet Ignus ensures the collar remains around his neck. It seems freedom in Scoria still comes with conditions attached.* The man beside him wore a newly forged collar of iron.

"You might be able to," said Drew, before turning to the Furnace's latest recruit. The man stared back at Drew with one good eye, the other missing from a recent fight. "But it's Djogo I really wanted to talk to."

6

Song of the Sirens

SHE SWAM IN a lake, crystal-clear waters breaking with each stroke of her arms. The shore was comfortingly close by; the silence deafening yet beautiful. She was alone, the only soul in the world, content with her solitude. Rolling over, she made a series of backstrokes, her hands cutting through the heavenly water and propelling her gently backward. She looked up at the sun, its warm rays invigorating and caressing her from above. She let her arms trail as she kicked her feet, turning once more on to her chest, allowing a giggle to escape her lips. She dipped her head beneath the water and opened her eyes.

The darkness consumed her. If the surface world was the beautiful day, the terrible night lurked in the depths. Black shapes moved in the deep, snaking their way up, up through the black water, up toward her. Slits of light broke the shadows, opening into round globes of light.

Eyes: terrible pale eyes with pinprick pupils. She struggled to return to the surface, hitting a sheet of glassy ice above. Beyond, she could see the sunlight, tantalizingly out of reach. She hammered the ice with the balls of her fists, her lungs bursting, trying to find an escape route. She looked down once more into the darkness, as the first of the phantoms took a grip on her legs, its claws cutting deep into her flesh, and a scream burst from her mouth in a cloud of bubbles.

Bethwyn's eyes flicked open, the nightmare replaced by the cabin's darkness. She looked to the bunk opposite, the sleeping form of Queen Amelie faintly visible in the gloom. She reached a hand beneath the covers to feel her legs, the sensation of the monster's claws still evident on her skin. Finding no wounds, she relaxed once more, her head collapsing onto her pillow.

Sleeping on board the *Maelstrom* was proving difficult for the young Wildcat. She had grown up on an island in the middle of a lake, and her father, Baron Mervin, the Lord of Robben, had regularly taken her boating. They were good times, happy times. But life on board the pirate ship was quite different from a lazy day on the lake.

She'd felt no split loyalties when Leopold had been overthrown. Although she shared the felinthrope heritage of the Catlords, their similarities ended there. The Wildcats were creatures of the north, native to Lyssia; they had as little in common with the Cats of Bast as with the Dogs of Omir.

Mervin had wasted no time in swearing allegiance to Lord Drew, returning home to Lake Robben after the uprising, leaving his daughter behind to care for his queen.

With only Amelie and the staff of Buck House for company, Bethwyn had found herself looking forward to the visits of Baron Hector. He'd been a frequent visitor to the Staglord mansion in Highcliff, often on official business with Drew. She sensed he'd wanted to make a formal introduction to her, but the shy Boarlord had never seized the moment back in the city. Even now, on board Count Vega's ship, he struggled to find something to talk about with her.

She made a silent promise to make more effort with the magister, starting in the morning. There was something there—it just needed coaxing out. Bethwyn's heartbeat began to slow again, as sleep promised to return.

Then she heard it.

Initially she dismissed it as the sound of the waves lapping against the *Maelstrom*, sloshing against the thick timber hull. Yet the noise was constant, a gurgling sound shifting from high to low, as water might disappear down a drain. There was something musical about the sound, an undulating rhythm that built gradually, as if in a chorus. Soon the noise was all around her, crawling through the cabin and creeping through the shadows.

Bethwyn swung her legs out of the bunk and dropped to the floor. She reached for the lamp that swung from the ceiling, unhooking it and turning up the burner. The light chased the darkness away as the queen stirred in her cot.

"What is it?" she whispered. "What's the matter, Bethwyn?"

"Don't you hear it, Your Majesty?"

Amelie lay still, a hand shielding the light from her face, listening intently. Her eyes widened as the gurgling sound registered. The queen pushed the covers away and climbed out of her bed, joining Bethwyn barefoot on the floorboards. She took her robe, wrapping it about herself, while her lady-in-waiting picked up her own cloak.

"That song," said the queen. "Where's it coming from?"

The girl opened the cabin door a crack, expecting to see crew members rushing by to investigate the strange sounds. The corridor was empty.

Bethwyn turned to the queen. "Please, Your Majesty, remain here while I investigate."

Amelie shook her head. "If you think I'm going to allow you to go up there alone, you're sorely mistaken, my girl. I'm coming with you."

The women walked along the corridor, the ship's constant creaking adding to the sinister chorus that filled the air. Bethwyn leaned against the wall as she advanced, one hand trailing along the varnished wood as she drew closer to the steps that led to the main deck. Taking hold of the rail in her free hand she rose up the staircase toward the open air. The hatch door was swinging on its hinges, left open to the night.

The men of the *Maelstrom* were gathered on the deck, standing like statues in the fog. They swayed with the motion of the ship, shifting like a field of barley. The sound was louder now, clearly coming from the sea, surrounding the ship.

"What's the matter with them?" asked the queen.

Each man stood as if under a spell, mesmerized by the gurgling drone as it came high and low through the cold night air. Bethwyn spied Hector and Manfred among them, the Boarlord and old Stag still wearing their nightshirts. She moved through the crew toward the magister, maneuvering in front of him.

Hector's face was slack, his mouth parted slightly, eyes staring through her like she wasn't there. She waved her hand across his field of vision, but he didn't even blink, as if hypnotized. Bethwyn took his hand in hers, giving it a squeeze—nothing. She raised his wrist up and gripped harder, digging her nails in—no reaction. She glanced down at the palm, usually hidden by a glove, and was shocked to see a dark mark that filled it like an ink stain.

"Bethwyn!" called Amelie fearfully.

Bethwyn looked for the queen, unable to see her through the bewitched crew and the unnatural fog. She kept hold of Hector's hand and began to lead him, his steps clumsy and staggering, as if sleepwalking.

"Your Majesty?"

"Bethwyn!" A scream now.

She moved fast, dragging Hector behind her like a stumbling corpse, bumping into the crew, none showing any reaction. Bethwyn burst from their midst, the magister coming to an immediate halt beside her. Queen Amelie was retreating from the railing on the port side of the *Maelstrom*. The gurgling chorus had grown louder still, rising from the depths and rolling over the decks. Bethwyn moved in front of her queen, raising the lantern to provide illumination.

A scaly green hand clung to the rails, webbing spanning the gaps between each clawed finger. Another hand lurched up beside it, this time the forearm reaching over to grasp an upright post. A dark shape followed, its head looming from the mist as its torso came over the side. Scales covered the creature's entire body, its squat skull sunk low between the shoulder blades, merging with its chest. Two enormous eyes the size of saucers blinked at the lantern light, as the beast's mouth hung open, the terrible song guttering from its throat through a maw of needle-sharp teeth. Seaweed hung from the creature like an emerald shawl, clinging to its skin as it landed with a wet *thump* on the deck.

Bethwyn and Amelie screamed and clung to each other as the monster crawled toward them. Below its waist they could see the beast had a fish's body that snaked along the deck, flapping movements propelling it forward as its clawed hands dug into the decking. A long spiked dorsal fin ran along its spine to an enormous tail, the fin rattling as it advanced. Bethwyn spied pendulous breasts hanging from its chest.

"Get back!" she screamed, swinging the lantern, causing the beast to back up, its song lifting into a gurgling screech. The chorus grew from every side of the ship as Bethwyn and Amelie looked about. With rising dread the women saw more of the shapes emerging over the side. Still the crew remained motionless, oblivious to the nightmare that unfolded around them.

"What are they?" came a shout above. Bethwyn glanced up, spying the shape of the lookout boy, Casper, straddling the spar overhead. Like the women, he seemed immune to the ghastly song of the creatures.

"Stay where you are, child!" warned Amelie.

The women moved closer to the sailors, bumping into them as the creature nearest closed in. Another joined it, this one slightly different in shape and color, its skin a mottled red. She could hear them crawling over the decks, surrounding the crew.

"There must be nearly twenty of them, my lady!" gasped Casper, his voice tearful. "They're going for the lads!"

One of the sailors suddenly went down, caught in the grip of one of the sea creatures. He was quickly followed by another and in seconds, six of the men had been thinned from the crowd. None cried out. All the while the creatures sang as they tossed the sailors over the side.

The swinging hatch door slammed open suddenly as Count Vega emerged on deck. He wore his leather breeches and nothing else, having been rudely woken by the commotion and not a moment too soon. Cutlass in hand he leaped forward toward the nearest creature, which reared up on its tail. He lunged in, catching the creature across the belly, the cutlass splitting the flesh. The monster's arms shot out, grabbing the sea captain by his shoulders and pulling him toward its jaws. Vega began to transform instantly, chest and shoulders rippling and causing the beast to lose its grasp. He brought his head down, mid-change, butting it in the face, its teeth scraping furrows across his brow as its mouth crumpled. The two tumbled to the deck, Vega having badly underestimated the strength of the beast.

"Captain!" Bethwyn cried, moving to help the Wereshark, whose changed head now emerged from the violent struggle.

"Get back!" he yelled, his monstrous mouth flying down to bite at the creature's throat. Black blood fountained, spraying the count and the deck around him as the beast clawed wildly at the Shark's face.

More creatures appeared, avoiding the two women, skirting around them as they went for the men instead. Bethwyn stepped forward as the one they'd first encountered hissed, clawing at the motionless Hector beside her.

"No you don't!" she shouted, smashing the lantern over the creature's head. The Spyr Oil within erupted, sending flames over the beast and back across Hector. Monster and magister shrieked at the fire, Hector waking instantly. He swiftly patted down the flames, trying to comprehend what was happening.

"What in Brenn's name is that?" he gasped as the burning sea creature thrashed about, its face aflame.

Bethwyn noticed that the guttural singing had ceased, the creatures now distracted by their fight with the Wereshark and her fire.

"The lantern!" called Amelie. "They're afraid of the flames!"

Bethwyn snatched up the broken lantern from the floor, sloshing the remaining oil at another beast. It roared and recoiled as the oil burst into flame, scuttling away in terror. Still it was not enough. The men continued to fall and the creatures departed with their prizes. But now the crew were being woken up by the noise and heat of the battle. They were confused and terrified but instead of being dragged over the side, limp and lifeless, they screamed, kicking and clawing at the creatures as they tried to wrestle them overboard.

Bethwyn and Amelie moved swiftly through the men now, waking them up, the song's spell broken. The creatures were among them, bringing the men down quickly. They screeched as they attacked, huge eyes closing each time they clamped their jaws around the pirates.

"Into them, lads!" bellowed Vega as the crew of the *Maelstrom* rallied, aiding him in the fight. They picked up cudgels, knives, axes—whatever was to hand—weighing in to battle against the monstrous creatures. Duke Manfred charged into the fray, his head lowered, transformed, antlers tossing the beasts from the decks, tearing them in two in the process.

Feet thundered across the deck around Bethwyn as the crew of the *Maelstrom* fought back. A clawed hand grabbed hold of her leg, in exactly the same place where she was seized in her nightmare. She shrieked as she fell, the creature crawling up her legs and hips, over her stomach toward her face. Bethwyn raised a hand, claws springing from her fingertips as she slashed down at the monster, tearing strips from its wide face. The huge milky eyes didn't even blink, its cavernous mouth yawning open as it came to bite her. Putrid, salty breath rolled over her in a tide. She tried to scream but nothing came out, gripped as she was by fear and the beast from the deep.

Suddenly the creature halted as if on a choke chain, huge eyes bulging. Bethwyn held it away from her, still gnashing its teeth, but instead of her it bit at the air, snatching and claw-ing at an invisible foe. Its hands went to its throat, Bethwyn watched as it struggled for breath. Then, with a harsh *crack* its head spun around, slime and seaweed spraying the young Wildcat as its corpse collapsed on top of her.

All around her limbs were snapped and severed as gradu-ally Vega's men pushed the foul creatures back, forcing them off the gore-slicked deck. Through the crowd of fighting men and monsters, Bethwyn saw Hector. *Had he saved her?* The ma-gister's left arm was raised, the black-stained palm open to-ward her, fingers splayed, a look of deadly concentration on his face. He was ten yards away from her. *How in the world could he have stopped the beast?*

129

7

HUNTER'S MOON

THE LUDUS WAS quiet, the hour late, and the palace of Ignus asleep. Inside the labyrinth of chambers that riddled the volcano's cone, the Lizardlord's gladiators slumbered in bunks and bedrolls within the hot, carved rock. Locked away from the outside world, they were alone with one another, brother warriors who might die at each other's hand in the morning, for tomorrow Lord Ignus would bless Scoria with the blood of his finest gladiators.

One solitary figure stood in the paddock, clad in only a loincloth, his skin scarred from battle, staring at the full moon overhead. Drew took in the heavens, the moon huge and bloody in a dark sky. It reminded him of his childhood on the Cold Coast. Mack Ferran would take his boys hunting on nights like this during the autumn equinox; the "Hunter's Moon" it was known as in Lyssia. He couldn't think of his father without thinking of the others he'd lost. He said a silent prayer to the old man, willing him to look after his mother in the afterlife. Mack Ferran had saved his life, just when it had appeared that Leopold might execute him, losing his own in the process. The little solace he took from his father's passing was that the man had absolved him of any guilt he might have felt over his mother's death. He thought of his brother, Trent, hoping he was far away from whatever war and misery the Catlords had brought upon his homeland. Most of all, he wished he could see him again.

He grimaced as he eyeballed the moon. There'd been a time when the moon had been something for Drew to fear, the beginning stages of a sickness that had transformed him into the Werewolf, setting him upon his epic path. He'd resented his destiny once, but that seemed long ago. He was the last of the Wolves of Westland, and a survivor. Now the full moon wasn't to be feared; it was his friend.

But the Hunter's Moon had its own meaning for the Scorians. When the moon was full and blood red, their volcano demanded a sacrifice. Tomorrow the fire mountain would be served a feast.

Standing with a silver collar around his throat, standing before a full moon and resisting the change, was the ultimate test of will for Drew. The Werewolf was dying to rip free. Drew was pushing his body to its limits, toughening it up for what lay ahead. His muscles flexed as he curled his hand into a fist, the stump on his other arm trembling. He could feel the moon's rays across his flesh, their touch electric. A bank of clouds passed, casting shadows over the paddock and releasing the moon's grip on Drew momentarily.

"A dangerous game you play, Wolf."

Drew hadn't heard Djogo approach, turning suddenly to find the slaver a few yards away. Drew panted, the strain proving great, his skin slick with sweat on the humid red night.

"Do you always creep around?" he rasped to the slaver.

Djogo didn't answer, walking closer to stand beside Drew and look up at the sky.

"Have you considered my offer?" asked Drew, dragging his forearm across his wet brow.

"I have indeed, and I still say you're a lunatic, Wolf."

"That's not an answer. Yes or no, Djogo; I'm not looking for your opinion of my sanity."

"Your plan is madness."

"To a broken man, perhaps, but not to a man who has hope in his heart. Which are you, Djogo?"

The slaver sneered at Drew. "Watch what you say. We're equals now, and wearing that silver collar means you've no beast to call upon."

"You're right. We *are* equals. How does it feel to be an owned man?"

"It's nothing new. I was a slave and gladiator before, until Kesslar freed me from the Furnace. The Goatlord let me rise."

"And now he's let you fall. He's discarded you. If he'd respected you he wouldn't have handed you over to Ignus!"

"He'll barter with Ignus to have me released."

"You believe that? How long have you worked for the Goat? You know what Kesslar's capable of. Can you really afford to wait?"

"There's too much to lose . . ."

"You've nothing to lose!" cried Drew, reaching out to grab the man's arm.

"I've everything to lose," spat Djogo, shoving Drew away angrily. "There are more ways to wound a man than with a sword."

Drew shook his head. "I don't understand."

Djogo turned his back on Drew. "He can hurt those I care about."

Drew considered the man's words. "You fought here for many years, Djogo. You know the Furnace and the palace better than anybody. The old master—Griffyn—I've seen you with him. You care about him, don't you?"

Djogo said nothing.

"I don't know what your relationship is. I don't *care*, truth be told. You and I have been enemies since we first met. I don't see how the pair of us being gladiators now makes us brothers. Tomorrow I fight back, and I hope those who share my desire to be free of Scoria will stand up and be counted."

Djogo paced back to the sleeping chambers silently. Drew watched him go, wondering if he'd angered the man further. He looked up. The sky was clear again, the moon casting her spell over the young Werewolf once more. He snarled through clenched teeth as he basked in her cold white light.

8

A World Away

THE GROUND WAS hard and uneven beneath his bedroll, promising an uncomfortable night's sleep, but Trent Ferran didn't care. He stared at the Hunter's Moon overhead. Not so long ago they'd run through fields and meadows, stalking deer under the bright night sky: Trent, his father, and his brother, Drew. He sucked his teeth, thinking of the young man who had ruined his life. He sighed, closing his eyes and willing the memories from his mind.

This had been the first day for weeks that he and his men had seen no combat. While his companions seemed indifferent, it was a relief for Trent. He'd joined the Lionguard for one reason: revenge. He hadn't signed up to burn people out of their farms and turn wives into widows. Of the hundred or so fighters he traveled with, the majority were Bastians. They were emotionless, carrying out their officer's instructions to the letter and never breaking rank. The Lionguard were sadly less disciplined than their southern counterparts, recklessly meting out their own justice in Prince Lucas's name.

It was only a matter of time before Lucas was made king: the Pantherlords from Bast, Onyx, and Opal would ensure that. While Onyx marched across Lyssia, Opal was in Highcliff watching over the prince's education while he awaited confirmation of his ascension. Trent had met Onyx briefly in the Horselords' plundered court of High Stable. The Beast of Bast cut a monstrous figure, a giant among men. It chilled Trent's heart to imagine how fearsome the transformed Werepanther might look in battle. King Leopold had been slain in the fight for Highcliff, and Queen Amelie had been kidnapped by Duke Manfred and Count Vega, two Werelords whose names now topped the kingdom's most-wanted list alongside Drew's. Lucas was now without a father or a mother. With Lyssia in such a state of flux, the vacuum was waiting to be filled. As Trent's fellow Redcloaks often said, the sooner Lucas was crowned the better.

"Asleep so soon?"

Trent opened his eyes. The Catlord Frost was standing over him. He sat up, instantly alert.

"Resting my eyes is all, sire."

"Did your blade get blessed as I said?"

"With silver, sire." Trent made to stand up.

Frost waved his hand, dropping on to his haunches beside the youth.

"Drop the titles, Trent. Frost will suffice. I like you, and see no need for you to jump to attention whenever I'm close by. You're not like the other Lyssians. You're honest and true, like the best Bast has to offer."

Trent felt his heart swell at Frost's words, recognition for his efforts warming his spirit. He felt honored that the Catlord could be so informal in his company. He began to relax a little.

"Any word from Westland?" asked Trent.

"Onyx makes huge strides. The Great West Road is ours already, and whatever resistance the Wolf's army had provided is all but broken. Our main force marches east, through the Dalelands. I don't expect them to find much of a fight there. The real battle lies ahead with the Barebones and the Dyrewood. This war will be over once we crush the Stags and the Bears."

Frost smiled as he stared at the moon, pink eyes glowing with an unearthly light.

"Does it have an effect on you, as it does the Wolf?" Trent asked.

"The moon? It affects all therians in different ways. The more passive Werelords find calm and clarity under her light. For the more aggressive, it stirs the blood, fires passion and power." He clapped his hands. "I could fight an army of Lyssian turncoats presently without breaking sweat." He laughed. "As for the Wolves? Different beasts altogether. They're more connected to the lunar cycles than any of us. I'm too young to have ever faced Wergar, but those who fought him said he was at his most ferocious while the moon was full."

"Is Drew really the last one left?"

"The last of the Gray Wolves, most certainly. But your queen, Amelie, she's a White Wolf of the north. They were always fewer in number, so I'm told, but fled their home of Shadowhaven when Leopold came to power. There may be some left, vagabonds. But I'd be surprised if any other White Wolves still survive, to be honest. The queen and Drew may be the last of the true Werewolves."

"We'll find him, Frost. I promise."

The albino put an arm around the youth. "I'm sure we will. If anyone can sniff the beast out it's you. It sickens me to think of what he did to those who raised him as their own. The Wolves of Westland are a vile breed—a blight on your land. They need to be extinguished. Utterly."

Trent nodded. "He won't stray far from Lady Gretchen," he promised Frost. "He stole her from Prince Lucas once, and no doubt he'll try it again. We just need to find her, quickly."

"That's the spirit, Trent," said Frost, clapping his back. "And when we do, hiding in Calico no doubt, I want you by my side. Then your blade can truly be blessed, with the Wolf's blood."

Trent's smile was bittersweet. "That's the greatest gift I could receive."

Frost held his open palm out, head bowed and voice low. "You have my word, Trent. Lead us to him and the Wolf is yours."

Trent took Frost's hand and shook it heartily.

"Now rest, my friend. We've another march tomorrow. The Longridings are riddled with the Wolf's allies. The Werefox may be heading to Calico, but who knows where she might be hiding along the road as she makes her way there. We can leave no stone unturned."

Trent nodded as the Catlord rose gracefully before stalking away through the tall grass toward his tent.

"So you think you're his favorite now?"

The voice was Sorin's, from his bedroll nearby.

"I wouldn't say that," muttered Trent, relaxing onto his mat. He pulled his blanket back up, staring up at the moon once again.

"Don't get me wrong, Ferran, you're a good soldier. But a Werelord calling you his friend? That's laughable, you have to admit!"

Trent tried to block Sorin's words from his head, but he went on.

"He's plumping you up, making you feel more than you are. You're a grunt, Ferran, like the rest of us. Don't think just because his lordship says you can call him 'Frost' he means anything he says."

Sorin rustled through the grass toward him, his voice low.

"He doesn't trust you," he said jealously. "At the end of the day you're the Wolf's brother. When push comes to shove, Frost worries you'll betray him, betray all of us."

Trent closed his eyes, but Sorin's words were poisonous. He heard Sorin crawl closer, his voice inches away when he next spoke.

"I think he's right."

Trent was out of his bedroll and on top of Sorin in an instant, hunting knife at the other's throat. Sorin chuckled, his eyes wide as he looked down. Trent followed his gaze to where Sorin held his own knife to Trent's belly, ready to be driven home.

"You've got me wrong," spat Trent angrily. "I want the Wolf dead."

"So you say," snarled the broken-nosed captain of the Lionguard.

"Nobody has more reason to see Drew Ferran dead than I!"

Sorin pushed him off, the knife fight over before it had begun.

"It might be argued . . . *Ferran*," said Sorin, slinking back toward his bedroll, "that nobody would have more reason than you to see him live."

Trent collapsed back on to his mat, shaking his head. *Sorin knows nothing. Drew's a monster. Monsters need to be killed.* What did Sorin know about him? Trent tried to push his captain's malignant words away, but they just kept coming back at him.

9

BITTER BLOWS

"SIRENS?"

Duke Manfred was incredulous. He stood beside the two Wereladies in the captain's quarters.

"Some call them that," said Vega from behind his desk. "Others call them the Fishwives. Either way I thought they were creatures of myth before last night."

"They were vile." Queen Amelie shuddered, her arm around Lady Bethwyn. It was dawn, but the previous night's encounter was still all too fresh in their minds.

Hector winced at Amelie's mention of the word "vile."

If she only knew the true meaning of the word now, eh, brother?

Hector spoke over Vincent's whispered words. "They were like no therians I've seen before."

"Some therians turn their back on their human form, fully embracing the beast," said Vega. "Legend has it the Sirens did that very thing; the once noble wives of the Fishlords swam to the seabed, accepting their bestial nature totally. Is it really so unlikely, Hector? Didn't you face and defeat the Wereserpent, Vala, in the Wyrmwood not so long ago?"

Hector nodded, his thoughts returning to the encounter with the giant Snake. He'd had Drew at his side then, his tower of strength. It seemed a distant memory.

"How was it that some were affected by their song while others weren't?" asked the magister.

"I can't explain it," said Vega, "although I have a theory. The Sirens of nautical mythology can enchant only males, not females. Alluring beauties, so tales tell. If these beasts are in any way connected to those of legend, that would explain why Queen Amelie and Lady Bethwyn were unaffected by their dreadful chorus."

"But their song had no effect on you, Count," said Amelie.

"Hazarding a guess, perhaps it's because I, like them, am a beast of the sea. Maybe the Sealords are immune to their enchantments?"

"And the boy, Casper?" added Manfred, pointing out the only other member of the crew who had not been captivated by the Siren song.

Vega shrugged. "He's still a child, not yet grown. Maybe that's why he was spared their spell."

"The Sturmish Sea is a dreadful place," muttered Manfred. "The sooner we reach land the better. Where are we, Vega?"

The count looked at the map on his desk, shaking his head.

"Hard to say. These are waters I've never ventured through. My charts are old and that cursed fog has thrown out our navigation. I reckon we're somewhere north of Tuskun, but I'd wager nothing!"

"Manfred's right," said Amelie. "We need to find the mainland soon. Who knows what else lurks in this awful sea?"

"Your guess is as good as mine." Vega sighed, scratching his head and running his hand through his long dark locks. He stretched in his chair, exhausted from the night's activities, as was everyone.

"The *Maelstrom* is eighteen souls light after last night. I can't decide what's best for her when we reach Roof. Do I crew up and head back out to sea? Or disembark and continue on with you, to Icegarden?"

"That's for you to decide," said Manfred, not about to be drawn on Vega's tormented morals.

"Thank you, Your Grace. Ever helpful with your counsel," said the Sealord sarcastically.

"Your Majesty," said Bethwyn, turning to the queen, a tired smile across her face, "if you could excuse me, may I head above decks?"

"You look exhausted, my dear," said Amelie.

"Here," said Hector, seizing the moment to step forward and offer his arm. "Let me escort you."

Amelie smiled at the Boarlord approvingly, while Bethwyn blushed at the show of courtesy.

"Really, Baron Hector, I'm quite all right," replied the girl. "Please don't mistake me for a damsel in distress. I merely need to take some air."

"Sounds like a fine idea," said Hector. "If you'd allow me to join you?"

"Persistent fellow, isn't he?" said Vega with a grin.

See how he can't resist making a joke at your expense, brother? hissed the Vincent-vile.

Hector ignored his brother's voice and held a gloved hand out to Bethwyn. The young woman looked at it tentatively before taking it.

"Your Majesty," she said to Amelie, managing a clumsy curtsy before allowing herself to be led away by Hector.

The two made their way to the main deck.

She's putty in your hands, the vile persisted.

Hector shivered, trying to shake the spirit loose.

"Are you cold?" Bethwyn asked.

"A little, my lady," he said awkwardly, hating his tormenting brother with every step.

They emerged on deck into bright daylight, the cold morning air bracing. The remaining crew were busy, rushing about their business with even greater industry than before. Figgis stood steady at the wheel, keeping the *Maelstrom*'s course steady. Casper stood beside him, watching Hector with suspicious eyes.

Even that wretched urchin distrusts you, brother.

Hector walked Bethwyn over to the rail and out of the way of the busy crew, many of whom were still scrubbing the gore and slime from the decks. The corpses of the Sirens had been tossed overboard once the battle was over, Vega waiting until they'd put some distance between themselves and the scene before burying his slain crew at sea.

"Your hand," said Bethwyn, holding the railing. "Is it wounded?"

"Pardon?" asked Hector, alarmed by the question.

"Your left hand: I saw it last night. You've a burn in your palm, a big one. What happened?"

"Oh, that," said Hector, flustered. "I burned it on a lamp. I know; I'm a fool."

"It should be looked at."

"Don't worry, really," said Hector. "I'm a magister after all. It's nothing I can't take care of."

She nodded, seeming to accept his answer. She looked pale, exhaustion and terror having chased the warmth from her face. The crew had begun to sing a shanty, sailors chiming in as they worked to the tune's rhythm. Hector spied Ringlin and Ibal near the ship's aft, apart from their fellows, shying away from work again.

"I'd have thought we'd heard enough singing after last night," said Bethwyn.

"They're a tough breed, aren't they? They buried their brothers only hours ago and they're finding their voices again."

Hector rapped his gloved fingers along the rail's edge to the beat of the shanty, trying to look relaxed while his insides were in turmoil.

"You were very brave," he finally said. "If you and the queen hadn't acted so swiftly, who knows what might have become of us. Thank you, Bethwyn."

"It's I who should thank you, Hector. You stopped the Siren that would have killed me, didn't you? How did you *do* that?"

Hector smiled nervously.

"I don't follow."

"I saw you: you strangled it! You broke its neck, yet you were a great distance away. How could that be?"

She's on to us, Hector. She saw your little parlor trick, sending me out to do your dirty work. Tell her about me, brother. Tell her about your shadow hand . . .

"I wasn't so far away, my lady. Perhaps it seemed farther from where you lay?"

"I could've sworn you were many yards from my struggle," she said, raising a hand to rub her brow.

"I can't remember the night's events clearly myself. In the chaos of battle it's hard to see straight, let alone recall what happened."

He plucked up the courage to place his hand over hers on the rail. He gave it a reassuring squeeze.

"You're safe now, my lady. That's all that matters."

Vega, Manfred, and Amelie emerged from the cabins nearby, the captain heading to the wheel while the duke and queen promenaded along the deck.

If this is courtship, brother, I was getting it wrong *all these years.* The vile laughed.

"You've been the queen's lady-in-waiting for some years now," said Hector, his hand still on top of Bethwyn's. "Do you not long for your own life, away from service?"

"I'm the queen's confidante," replied the young Wildcat. "I was appointed her companion, and that's more important than ever now."

"How long must you remain with her?"

She turned, puzzled, her big brown eyes narrowing. He kept his hand over hers, Bethwyn having not yet pulled away.

"For as long as she needs me. In Highcliff my responsibilities were manifold: music, languages, writing letters for the queen. Out here, however, I do whatever she asks."

Hector nodded.

"You're most noble, Bethwyn. You do your father and Robben proud."

"I do my duty, Hector."

Don't make a fool out of yourself, piggy. What could she ever see in you? A sickly bookworm with a penchant for dark magistry . . .

Hector cleared his throat, taking a big lungful of sea air. His heart felt like it might leap from his chest as he squeezed her hand once more.

"I would speak with Baron Mervin once this war is over, my lady."

"Regarding what?"

"Regarding your hand, Lady Bethwyn."

She didn't react immediately, but when his words registered, a shocked look flew across her face as she whipped her hand away. Hector raised his black-gloved palms by way of apology.

"My lady, I'm sorry if my words cause offense!"

You clumsy oaf! Do you really think this is how one asks a Werelady for her hand in marriage? Stick to your books and scrolls, fool!

"You caught me unawares, my lord," she gasped, bringing her hands to her bosom and clenching them together. She backed away, the color having returned to her cheeks in a crimson blush. Her big brown eyes looked anywhere but at Hector. He took a step forward as she retreated.

"My lady—" he began, but he was interrupted by her flustered response.

"I must return to the queen. Thank you, again, for your kindness last night, and just now. Walking up. Thank you. The fresh air . . ."

With that she was hurrying after the queen, leaving

Hector alone by the rail. He turned, grinding his fists into the timber banister, shaking his head.

That went well, I thought!

"Curse you, Vincent! Cease your incessant chatter!"

Too late, brother: I'm already cursed!

Hector opened his left hand, the black leather creaking as he splayed his fingers. His head was splitting, an ache cutting into his temple. He could feel anger rising, threatening to erupt in glorious fury: anger at their predicament, at Vega, at Bethwyn, and at his own hapless attempts to charm her.

Hector clenched his hand tight, his eyes alone seeing the black smoke curling around it, the vile in his grasp, choked in his fist.

"Hold your tongue, vile. You forget the control I have over you. The Siren last night was a reminder. You're mine, Vincent, to do my bidding, as and when I please!"

Hector waited for a smart-mouthed response from the vile, but nothing came. He kept his fist closed, thumping it on to the rail as he closed his eyes, letting his head slump miserably into his chest.

Count Vega looked down from the poop deck, watching the Boarlord of Redmire rage. He winced as Hector snarled and spat, holding a heated discussion with himself. Vega worried about the magister, after all he'd been through—continued to go through. He knew Hector had a good heart, and prayed the young man stayed out of the shadows.

The cabin boy, Casper, handed the sea marshal his goblet. Vega smiled as he took it, washing the day's first brandy down his throat. He'd purloined a bottle from the *Bold Thunder* for himself, while handing the rest over to Cook. He'd make sure the lads had a drink this day. They'd earned it after last night's horrors.

"Captain," said the boy, still at the count's side.

"What is it, lad?" asked Vega, giving the cabin boy his full attention.

"Last night, those Mermaids—I saw what happened."

Vega put a hand on the boy's head, ruffling his hair.

"Saw what, lad?"

Casper looked across the deck. Vega followed his gaze as it settled upon the irate Boarlord.

"I saw what he did to that monster."

Vega's cheery mood vanished in an instant. He crouched down beside the boy, turning him to face him. Casper looked shocked, and more than a little frightened. When Vega spoke again, his voice was a whisper.

"What did you see, Casper?"

"Wasn't natural, the way he killed it. His hand, Captain: that black hand. It was dark magick, I swear to Sosha. The magister scares me."

"Then stay close to me, my boy," said the Wereshark. The boy smiled nervously at Vega, the captain, his hero, his everything. The count brushed Casper's mop of dark hair out of his eyes.

"Stay close to me."

PART III

THE FIRES OF THE FURNACE

I

BATTLE OF THE BEASTS

THE CROWD HAD enjoyed their fill of blood. Fifty gladiators had entered the Furnace and only twenty-five had walked away. Every appetite had been catered to. Horseback warriors had jousted, boxers had dueled with bare fists, bowmen had peppered opponents with arrows, while spearmen had launched their javelins. Swords, scimitars, axes, and tridents had clashed across the volcanic earth, limbs and heads severed and hoisted as trophies. The Bestiari, specialists in fighting animals, had come up against lions, bears, jackals, and wolves. The cruelest contests involved two recently condemned criminals pitted against each other: one armed but blindfolded, the other unarmed but clear-sighted. The blindfold ultimately proved too great a handicap. Now the Scorians quieted as Lord Ignus appeared upon his balcony.

"People of Scoria, I give you the rarest gift. I show the fire mountain the greatest generosity—my therian warriors from across the known world. You all saw the Blood Moon last night, signaling the need for sacrifice. Those gladiators who have fallen thus far today have gone some way to quench the mountain's thirst, but she hungers for yet more. We must honor Scoria with the mightiest offerings in order to appease her fire. My Eight Wonders enter the Furnace. The contest is over when only five remain standing."

He cast his hands over the arena below, oily skin glistening in the midday sun.

"Behold: the Battle of the Beasts!"

Eight iron gates were cranked open around the Furnace, each one sending clouds of dust billowing into the arena. From out of the pens the therian gladiators strode forward. Ignus clapped his hands, turning to his fellow nobles and Lizardlords who had gathered as honored guests. He'd just witnessed his most recent acquisition from Kesslar provide the fight of his life. Djogo had triumphed against the trident-wielding Obliss of Ro-Shann. Of the Goatlord there had been no sign. Ignus suspected Kesslar was still smarting from the humiliation he'd dealt him.

Drew squinted through the dust clouds as he looked

around the Furnace. He'd seen Djogo moments earlier when the gladiator had returned to the gates, the two sharing a look as they'd passed. Drew walked forward as the sand settled, taking in the combatants. The Behemoth had entered from a gate directly opposite. To his side the Wereapes, Arik and Balk, had appeared, immediately moving together into a pair. Between Drew and the brothers stood Taboo, limbering up as she prepared for the fight. To the other side of Drew stood the Rhino, Krieg, flanked by the lean figure of Drake. The Werecrocodile looked the most relaxed of all, turning to look toward the chanting crowd. Last of all, between Drake and the Behemoth, Stamm could be seen, the Buffalo shaking the dust from his shaggy mane. Drew wondered who—if any—would follow his lead.

None of the other Werelords carried weapons. In a cruel twist devised by Ignus, they were to use tooth, claw, and their therian strength alone to best their opponents. Only Drew's trident dagger remained on his stumped wrist. Drew hoped to avoid the Behemoth in the coming fight. The giant had been responsive to the idea of breaking out, but that was yesterday. Here, in the heat of the arena, it might count for naught. There had to be a fight, and that fight would separate those who were with Drew and those who were against him. Arik and Balk were certain enemies, while questions remained over Drake and Taboo.

Then the battle began.

It happened so fast, triggered by the two brothers. As if reacting to Drew's thoughts, the Apelords wasted no time, rushing Taboo as their opening gambit. As they charged they changed, forearms exploding with muscles while their backs expanded, silver bristles bursting from their skin. Within seconds the brothers flanked the young woman, their mouths open to reveal huge, deadly canines.

Taboo was ready. She kicked up the dust, sending a cloud into the air to provide cover. By the time Arik brought his huge hand down at her, the girl had gone. She shot a lithe leg through the dusty air, her clawed foot striking and piercing the Ape's shoulder, sending him tumbling away. When Balk's fist flew through the air where he'd imagined she stood, Taboo rolled out of the dust, transformed, her body shimmering with dark black stripes across orange skin. The Weretiger snarled, unfazed by the brutes.

Drew turned just in time to see the bowed head of Krieg charging him. The Rhino was transformed, head down and shoulders thick with hide armor. Dodging the great horn, Drew caught the brunt of the attack from the Rhino's shoulder. The collision was colossal, the pain immense. Drew was catapulted into the air and back toward his gate and landed in the dirt. As he flew he tried to breathe, the air having been crushed from his lungs.

Drew rolled, choking and gasping as he saw Krieg skid, changing his angle of attack. The head was his primary weapon and the ground thundered as he sped back toward Drew.

"Krieg!" he yelled, his breath returned. "What are you doing? We can fight *together*!"

"It can't work, boy!" Krieg snorted as he charged. "Better let me finish you, end this quickly. Three of us have to die, and I won't be one of them!"

Drew hadn't wanted to fight Krieg. He had believed he'd be an ally, but he'd got it wrong. Drew let the Wolf in, and the transformation was rapid. He leaped up from the floor on powerful, lupine legs, his clawed feet digging into the dirt for extra purchase. The specially built trident dagger sat snugly on his left arm, while his clawed right hand was open. His yellow eyes blazed with purpose as he peeled back his lips to reveal deadly teeth. He let out a deafening roar to alert Krieg.

The crowd screamed deliriously as Drew changed, but he ignored their cheers, his attention focused on the Rhino. The armor plating over Krieg's head, shoulders, and back afforded him a confidence in battle that few therians would know.

Drew's trident dagger bounced off the main horn, sending his arm ringing with shock. He dropped to one side as the brute raced to the center of the Furnace, allowing his clawed hand to rake the Rhino's flank. Drew felt the claws struggle for any purchase, scraping harmlessly over Krieg's armored skin.

The Rhino was far bigger than the Wolf, but what Drew lacked in size he made up for in agility. He readied himself for Krieg's next attack using the same defense as before, raising the dagger again. At the last moment, with Krieg almost on top of him, Drew leaped in the air, spinning and coming down to land on the Rhino's shoulders. Krieg snorted, swinging his head, legs still pumping, momentum carrying him forward. Drew held on tight, his arms around the Rhino's throat as Krieg charged on.

Krieg looked up suddenly as the arena wall appeared before him. He felt Drew's feet dig into the armor of his back as he sprang away to safety, the Rhino struggling vainly to slow down. He crashed into the wall with a sickening crunch, rocks and rubble coming loose and showering him as he collapsed to the Furnace floor in a heap.

Drew landed gracefully, looking around the arena at the other battles that raged. Taboo had been joined by Stamm, evening up the fight against the Apes. The Crocodile, Drake, was darting around the Behemoth, who now stood transformed. Drew was amazed by the sight.

He'd heard about mammoths as a child, giant beasts from Bast, dismissing them as being as mythical as dragons. The animals the other therians were brethren to—crocodile, rhino, ape, and buffalo—he could comprehend. But the Weremammoth was beyond all his experience. He was monstrously impressive—twice Drew's height, with legs like battering rams, the Behemoth dominated everything around him. Enormous fists smashed down, narrowly missing his opponent. Huge ears flapped from the side of his boulder-sized head, while curling ivory tusks jutted from his mouth. A snaking trunk swung through the air, smacking Drake across his long, toothy snout and sending the Werecrocodile flying.

The Apes were brutal. Their silver backs rippled with muscles as their powerful arms lashed out at their enemies. While Stamm was holding his own with Arik, Taboo was faring less well with Balk, tiring under the relentless blows of the Wereape, as his fists connected with alarming frequency.

Having assessed the field, Drew chose his opponent.

With a couple of bounds he bowled into Balk, hitting him square in the back and the two of them went down.

"Dog!" snarled the Ape. "The Cat can wait! Let's see the color of your blood!"

Drew didn't answer, squirming out of reach of the Ape's mighty arms. He'd made a mistake, choosing to wrestle the monster. Balk bit into his shoulder. Drew roared, snapping his own jaws down the side of the Ape's face. A black ear came away with a wet rip. Wailing, Balk disengaged, lifting a hand to the wound.

"I see yours is red," spat the Werewolf, poised for the next attack. Then suddenly an arm slid over his throat from behind, muscles flexing as Arik snatched hold. *I thought he was fighting Stamm!* Drew's head thundered as the blood struggled to find a way through his restricted arteries.

Balk was about to join the attack when his jaw cracked, a flying kick from Taboo sending his head recoiling. Teeth flew as the Tiger landed, panting hard. The Ape went for her, drawn away from his brother's fight with the Wolf.

Drew was seeing lights—fading fast. With a desperate burst he yanked his left arm free of Arik's other fist, burying the trident dagger in the Ape's forearm. The beast roared, releasing its grip, the dagger tearing a lump of flesh with it. The enraged Ape smashed his other arm down on to Drew's back, flattening him. He rolled over in time to see both Arik's arms raised, fists curled and about to strike.

Then without warning, the horns of the Buffalo, Stamm, crashed into Arik's back, the two Werelords going down beside the stunned Drew. He saw the damage the Apes had done to Stamm, one of his arms broken and limp at his side, his torso ripped and torn. Balk now returned to the fracas, while some distance away, Drew saw Taboo lying wounded and still.

Seizing Stamm's curling horns, Balk hauled the Buffalo's head up, holding the neck exposed. From beneath, Arik opened his jaws wide as his teeth connected with Stamm's throat. Drew caught a despairing look in Stamm's eyes as his neck was torn open.

Drew pounced, his heart full of rage. He had known Stamm from only their few exchanges in the ludus, but the Buffalo's valiant assistance had struck deep. Balk tried to bat Drew away, but the Wolf wouldn't be halted. He took three, four more punches as he dragged the Ape off Stamm, the butchered

Buffalo landing on Arik beneath him. The fifth punch came and Drew opened his mouth, closing his jaws around Balk's fist. Bones, knuckles, and tendons crunched as he ground his muzzle closed.

Balk screamed, trying to prize the Wolf's jaws apart with his other hand, but Drew's teeth snapped together, taking four fat fingers off with two quick bites. The bloodied Ape fell, kicking at the Wolf, but Drew was too swift, his clawed hand snatching hold of Balk's jaw. The monster grasped at him with broken, bloody hands, but Drew's grip was solid. He raised his powerful leg and brought his foot down hard on Balk's chest. A sickening crunch sounded above the noise of combat in the Furnace, and the Wereape lay dead in the dust.

Drew turned to see Arik struggle from beneath the slain Buffalo, letting loose a despairing wail at the sight of his brother's demise. The Ape bounded high, blotting out the sun as he came down toward Drew.

The Werewolf readied himself for the impact, but the expected blow didn't come from above, but from the side—Drew was thrown clear of Arik's attack. Krieg had replaced him, taking the Ape's barrage. The two went down, Arik landing directly on top of Krieg with a wet *crack*, throwing a cloud of red dust into the air. The combat between the Ape and Rhino was over instantly. As the cloud settled, Drew could see Krieg's huge horn, standing proud from the silverback of the Wereape.

Krieg pushed him back, the dead Arik sliding off his horn into the bloody dust.

"Thank you," Drew whispered, embracing Krieg. Taboo stood nearby, battered but not beaten. The bloodthirsty crowd were wild with excitement. Ignoring the mob of onlookers, the three therians walked across the Furnace toward the two who still fought.

The Behemoth and Drake still battled, trading blows, but not dealing any true damage to each other. This combat took place beneath the viewing balcony of the palace, but all eyes had been fixed upon Drew's battle.

"Enough!" yelled Ignus. "We have our victors!"

Drake and the Behemoth parted as Drew joined them, Krieg and Taboo following.

"The fire mountain has been appeased!" cried Ignus as the audience cheered. "We are blessed for another year. The glorious death of these noble Werelords has sated Scoria's hunger!"

The Lizardlord was so busy performing to the crowd that he paid little attention to the five therians who stood below. Drew stepped in front of the Behemoth and nodded to him.

"You're sure?" asked the Weremammoth.

Drew smiled, grimly. The Behemoth bent his head, allowing Drew to clamber on to his tusks, crouching low.

"Today the Furnace has witnessed the greatest contest Scoria has ever seen!" continued Ignus, arms open and enjoying his oratory. "The fire mountain has had her fill of blood, both human *and* therian!"

The Weremammoth swung his head, tossing Drew skyward. The lycanthrope, springing from his haunches to gain extra speed, flew through the air toward the balcony.

"Not quite!" he shouted, landing on the balcony with deadly grace to a chorus of frantic screams. "Your fire mountain is still thirsty!"

2

THE UPPER CLAW

THE GUESTS ON the balcony fled as the Werewolf of Westland rose to his full height. Instantly the palace guards rushed him, sending him leaping clear onto the stone banquet table. Plates and goblets scattered beneath his clawed feet, clattering across the floor as the rich and powerful of Scoria screamed. The guards fanned out, trying to anticipate the Wolf's next move, but Drew was on the prowl, making his way closer to Lord Ignus, who was already changing.

The Lizardlord shook off his robe, his long neck ballooning as it stretched and twisted, mouth gaping open. His skin turned a mottled green, and hooked, black claws burst from his fingers as a reptilian tail snaked out behind him. Panic increased as Drake landed on the balcony to join the fray, and then Taboo followed her brother therians into the palace.

Below, the Furnace gates broke open. Scoria's human gladiators surged through, carrying poles, ladders, anything that might help them clamber out of the arena. Deep within the walls of the coliseum, fighting had broken out as others chose different escape routes. The cage doors that had kept them imprisoned had been mysteriously unlocked, allowing them to surge over any astonished soldiers who dared stand in their way. The wild beasts were freed from their pens, running riot through the corridors that encircled the arena. Soldiers, civilians—all fell beneath their teeth and claws. The breakout had caught the Scorians by surprise.

Drake and Taboo darted between the guards' spears, striking home with ease, filling the air with a fine red spray. The guards, so used to bullying manacled slaves around, struggled to hold the therian warriors back. With the guards preoccupied, that left Drew facing just the Lizardlord.

"Where's Kesslar?" snarled Drew as Ignus stood transformed, bathed in the sulfurous steam that billowed through the floor grate. His eyes bulged, thin rubbery lips peeling back to reveal jagged teeth.

"Kesslar isn't your concern, Wolf! You'll put your collar back on if you know what's good for you!"

Ignus's three siblings emerged through the yellow mist behind him, Lizards like their brother. None looked lean or fit like Drew and his companions. The Lizards of Scoria had grown used to a life of gluttonous luxury, feeding their addictions with whatever took their fancy. One was a tall, skinny wretch, while his fat brother loped beside him. The third one was top heavy with stunted legs, and then there was Ignus, their glorious leader, too used to letting others fight his battles.

The Lizardmen rushed Drew, all four attacking in clumsy unison. *These weren't the odds I'd hoped for*, thought Drew, bounding over their heads as they dived across the stone table. He landed with a *clang* on the grille, just behind the slowest of them. He lashed out his leg, clawed feet tearing the top-heavy one's hamstring in two and putting him out of action.

Down to three.

The fattest Lizard leaped back over the table, directly on top of Drew, but the Werewolf was ready for him, catching him on his clawed feet. His knees compressed up to his chin as the monstrous mouth snapped inches from his face and scaly hands clawed at Drew's throat. The grille vent groaned and buckled beneath the impact of their combined weight. Drew snarled and kicked back. The fat Lizardlord's eyes widened as he was propelled through the air, disappearing over the balcony's edge.

Two down. Two to go.

Drew jumped away from the grille, landing before the stone throne. Ignus and his last sibling separated, the lanky one snatching a silver spear from a fallen guard.

"It's been a while since I slew another therian," the Lizard rasped, Ignus grinning at his side.

"I'd like to say the same," said Drew.

The Lizard lunged, but Drew parried the spear away with the trident dagger. The reptile came a second time, and Drew knocked him the other way. Snarling, the Lizard put his weight behind the spear, stabbing high at Drew's chest. The Wolf caught hold of the spear in the crux of the trident dagger, its progress halting. His foe looked shocked as Drew bit down on the wooden pole, snapping the gleaming blade off. Before he could react, Drew buried the spearhead in the Lizard's chest, the hapless therian still clutching the broken spear shaft as black blood gushed from his bosom.

And then there was one.

Ignus screamed to his men for assistance, but they were occupied by the therian gladiators. Silver weapons or not, none was a seasoned warrior like Taboo and Drake. The pile of Scorian corpses grew.

Drew was about to offer Ignus a chance to surrender, to end the bloodshed, but he was spared the speech. Ignus ducked low, flicking his tail out and around, whipping Drew's legs from beneath him. The Wolf toppled backward, crashing on to the throne. Before he could rise, Ignus had leaped, straddling him, pinning Drew to the chair.

The Wolf struggled to escape the Lizard's hold, but the hooked claws were buried in his arms, fixing him in place. He snapped his jaws at Ignus's reptilian face, the Lizard's eyes blinking as a wicked grin spread across his reed-thin lips. The

Lord of Scoria's bony forehead came down like a hammer blow, cracking Drew's muzzle and leaving the Werewolf stunned. He was aware of the Lizard's mouth gaping open, its jaws separating, but he was helpless to stop it.

Darkness enveloped him, the world hot, wet, and terrible. With sick dread he realized his head was in the Lizardlord's gullet. He tried to shake it loose, open his jaws to bite the monster from the inside, but the Lizard's constrictive mouth was too powerful, too tight. He could smell Ignus's stomach acids, noxious and overwhelming, heavy with the stench of bacteria and infection. The monster meant to suffocate him, and was close to succeeding.

Drew's feet scrabbled at the base of the chair, struggling for purchase on the polished stone floor. His clawed toes found a crack in the flags. Digging in with all his might, he pushed back, straightening his legs. Slowly, the stone throne rocked. With each push the chair shifted looser off its back legs. He felt the Lizard's tongue flickering over his closed jaws inside its throat. A final shove sent the throne back hard, crashing into the wall behind before lurching forward, sending Wolf and Lizard flying from the seat.

They landed on the grilled floor, the iron grate buckling again. Drew's arms were now free and he jabbed with the trident dagger and clawed with his hand as he pounded Ignus's leathery torso. The Lizard choked and gagged, coughing the strangulated Werewolf's head from its ballooned throat. Drew shook the reptilian Werelord's saliva from his eyes, glancing up in time to see the stone throne rocking back toward them, sheering from its plinth.

The Wolf rolled clear on to the polished stone floor as the throne crashed down on to Ignus. It landed with a bone-crunching *clang*, metal screeching as the grate tore free from its housing. Lizard, throne, and twisted grille all disappeared into the sulfurous hole, the screaming of iron against rock mixing with the wails of Ignus as the Lord of Scoria plummeted to his doom.

Black smoke rolled through the palace of the Lizardlords and fires raged deep within the ludus, the house of the gladiators burning out of control. The corridors that encircled the Furnace were a scene of carnage and the sounds of combat still rang from the vaulted walls. An enormous lion lay on a pile of bodies, chewing on a corpse as if relaxing with its kill in the wild. Screams echoed through the thoroughfare as the coliseum burned.

Drew and his companions emerged into the sunlight. The air was parched and dry, unlike the humid, chemical atmosphere in the throne room, and Drew could feel his sweat already drying. He looked at Taboo and Drake at his side, his fellow therians shifting back to their human forms. All three bore many wounds, but most were superficial.

They headed away from the smoking palace, the curved black and white walls cracking as the fires raged at their backs. Huge portions of the terra-cotta roof broke away, crumbling into the arena, as Ignus's coliseum threatened to collapse in on itself. The survivors of the battle, a crowd of gladiators and slaves, had gathered by the gatehouse at the top of the Black Staircase.

"Friends, we feared the Furnace had taken you!"

Krieg smiled as he greeted them. Beside him stood the Behemoth and a hundred or so fighters.

"That's the first time I've seen you smile," said Drew, shaking the Rhinolord's hand. The greeting was warm and earnest. Drew looked up at the Behemoth, nodding respectfully.

"Thank you. We couldn't have done that without you."

"We couldn't have done that without many people," said the Behemoth, standing to one side as three other figures emerged from the crowd.

Shah walked with her arm around Griffyn, the wizened trainer weary as he leaned on her. Drew could see the family resemblance now, the same shaped nose and sharp cheekbones.

"Your grandfather?"

"Father," corrected Shah.

Drew was shocked. He'd have put sixty years between the old man and his daughter. He could only imagine how hard the trainer's life must have been beneath the boot of Ignus.

"You risked a great deal unlocking the gates in the house

of gladiators, Shah. If Ignus or Kesslar had discovered your complicity, you'd have been killed."

"Strange how the actions of one can inspire others, Drew of the Dyrewood," she said, smiling as she glanced up at the other man beside her. The one-eyed warrior looked down at Drew.

"Come, Wolf," said Djogo. "We need to get you back to Lyssia."

3

THE WHITE ISLE

IT MIGHT HAVE been missed had it not been for the keen eyesight of the cabin boy, Casper, perched atop the *Maelstrom*'s crow's nest. Count Vega extended his spyglass to better see the island—a barren stack of chalk-white rocks that erupted from the gray waters. It looked unremarkable, a pile of bleached bones floating on the Sturmish Sea, the flesh picked bare from a long-dead leviathan.

"It's land all right," said Vega, "but I've seen more life hanging from a gallows."

"Can we not alight there, even if only briefly?" asked Baron Hector.

Vega stared at the Boarlord as if he'd grown another head. "For what possible reason?"

"This life at sea is all too familiar to you and your crew, Vega. You forget that myself, Manfred, and the ladies are *land-lubbers*, as your crew so eloquently put it." Hector smiled. "Solid ground beneath our feet would make a welcome interruption to our journey."

Vega rubbed his chin and looked at Manfred. "You feel this way, too?"

The Duke tipped his head to one side. "To be honest I'd rather we kept going until we hit the mainland. The longer we're in these foul waters, the less safe I feel. Hanging around out here, we're giving Ghul and Slotha every opportunity to capture us."

Hector turned to the Staglord, opening his gloved hands in a show of reasoning.

"Vega *did* say we needed to plot a new route, calculate where we are. Where better than a spot of dry land? Don't worry about our enemies. Anyone who follows us through that green fog will struggle to emerge on this side anywhere near us. Besides, think of Queen Amelie and Lady Bethwyn. Wouldn't this provide a pleasant, albeit brief, distraction from their journey?"

The Duke looked over his shoulder as if the queen might suddenly appear. He rubbed a hand over his stubbled jaw.

"Hector may have a point there."

"Exactly," said Hector, smiling as he clapped his hands

together. "Then it's agreed. We stop to take some air. Really, what harm can it do?"

There was a knock at Hector's cabin door. He hurriedly threw the blanket over the satchel on his bunk.

"Enter."

The door swung open and the tall figure of Ringlin stepped in, ducking beneath the low door frame.

"Close it behind you," said Hector, waiting for his man to shut the door before pulling his blanket back once again. The Boarguard rogue looked over the magister's shoulder, watching Hector as he packed his bag. Hector's ungloved hands rolled bottles and jars over the rough mattress, glass containers clinking as they collided, his fingers hurriedly sorting what was needed. There was also the narrow mahogany box containing the silver arrow that Bergan had entrusted to him in Highcliff. Hector's hands hovered over the black candlestick, fingers brushing the dark wax before stowing it in the satchel.

"You're packing a lot of gear there if you're only going to stretch your legs, my lord," observed Ringlin slyly.

"If I were visiting the island for a constitutional, I'd hardly need you accompanying me, Ringlin."

The tall man smiled.

"Is Ibal also ready?"

"He is, my lord. He's on deck now, making sure he gets us a spot together on the same landing boat."

"Good," said Hector, fastening the clasps on his bag and throwing it over his shoulder. He was about to pass Ringlin when the tall man placed a hand on his chest, stopping him. Hector's face instantly darkened.

"Your hands, my lord," reminded the Boarguard. Hector glanced back to the bunk, spying the black leather gloves by the pillow.

Hector smiled nervously, snatching them up and pulling them on. Ringlin watched as his master tugged the glove over the left hand, the black scar now almost filling the palm.

"On the island," said Hector, taking hold of the door handle, "you and Ibal are to stay close to me. You'll be my eyes and ears if need be."

"I don't follow."

"You will," said the magister, opening the door.

Two longboats rowed away from the *Maelstrom* in the twilight, the ship anchored a safe distance from the White Isle. Vega was on the first, accompanying Manfred, Amelie, and Bethwyn, as six of his men rowed them ever nearer the rocky outcrop. Behind came Hector's boat, Ringlin and Ibal helping with the rowing.

Very clever, brother, whispered Vincent's vile. *You've got them all dancing to your tune. You're getting good at this.*

Hector sat at the rear, his knees drawn up, satchel on his lap, arms crossed over it. The men were too busy rowing to hear or notice him muttering to himself.

"Hardly. There was some truth to my suggestion. Stretching one's legs on solid ground is a good idea."

But stretching one's legs on this *solid ground, brother? Why did you not tell them of the voice? Do you fear they'll think you mad?*

Hector had heard the voice for the last two nights, calling him across the water, teasing him as to the White Isle's whereabouts. Hector winced, thinking about the sensation. Voice wasn't the correct word, as no true words were recognizable within the call. More it was a series of images lancing through his mind, feelings and flashes of knowledge tantalizingly out of reach. The strange language was archaic, but somehow Hector recognized it. In his heart he knew the call held the answers to a world of questions, answers that he'd find in no ancient tomes or scrolls. It was connected to the communing, he was sure, the telepathy similar to his bond with Vincent's vile. But there was a great power behind this; the call promised something. Hector needed to discover what.

"Is it mad to search for the answers to one's questions?"

Perhaps if it means putting those you care for in peril, brother. But what do I know? I'm just a wicked spirit sent here to torment you. It's not my place to suffer from a guilty conscience. I'll leave that to you. . . .

The launches drew closer. The rocks thrust skyward at jagged angles, reaching up like bony fingers. The island was perhaps half a mile long and maybe a hundred feet tall at its highest point, a pyramid of splintered stone, bereft of plant life. As the boats searched for a mooring point, the sailors took special care to avoid the rocks beneath the surface, faintly visible through the waves. If the *Maelstrom* had drawn nearer, such hidden dangers could have ripped a hole in her hull.

As if to prove this point, the call came up from the lead boat as the shell of a wrecked ship was spied. The vessel was on her side, broken masts clinging onto the rocks, a jagged wound in her belly suffering the constant pounding of the waves. Beyond the wreck, the crew could see a rocky stretch of beach, perhaps a few hundred feet long and the perfect place to get ashore.

Hector felt the call again, an alien tongue rich in old magick, luring him closer. He looked at the crewmen, checking their reactions, convinced they too heard the summons. But the sailors rowed on, oblivious, the message inaudible to all but the magister. As the lead boat hit the shore, Vega leaped off the prow, his booted feet landing on the shingle beach. At this precise moment Hector felt a stabbing pain behind his eyes, as if a blade had been slipped into his skull. He wavered at the rear of the boat, one hand grasping the seat while the other snatched at his temple.

Images flashed: *skin against rock; blood on stone; a black eye opening suddenly. A recognizable word:* welcome.

Hector opened his eyes, snorting for breath. His throat burned as if scorched by acid. Ringlin glanced up, catching sight of his master's shocked expression.

"You all right, my lord?"

You're not all right, are you, brother? I heard it, too. It's expecting you.

The second boat hit the beach, the sailors jumping out and dragging it onto the pebbles alongside the first. Amelie and Bethwyn were already ashore, their winter cloaks wrapped tightly around them. Vega stood beside Manfred, looking up and down the length of beach.

"Everybody stay close," said the captain. "No wandering off. Keep a shipmate at your side at all times. Last thing we need is to lose anyone on this white rock."

Casper appeared between the count and the duke, a wooden case on his back. The captain removed it and laid it flat on the beach, opening it up.

"What's this then, Vega?" asked Manfred, watching the sea marshal at work.

"Our best bet at working out where in Sosha's big blue we are," said Vega, removing a sextant from the box and placing it gently to one side. The navigational artifacts were all utterly fascinating to Manfred, who reached a tentative hand toward one. Vega smacked at the hand, shooing the duke away.

"An astrolabe, Your Grace," said Vega. "You know how to use one?"

"Um . . ." muttered Manfred sheepishly as Amelie watched, smiling.

"Might be best if you leave it to someone who does, eh, Manfred?" The Sharklord grinned.

Manfred managed a chuckle despite the admonishment.

"This is actually the best time of day for me to take a sighting," said Vega. "It may be only twilight, but the sun's still up and the first stars are in the sky. I should be able to pinpoint our whereabouts. Seems Hector was paying attention after all when he recommended we stop here."

"Talking of our Boarlord," said Manfred, looking about. "Where's he got to?"

Hector paced along the shore, Ringlin and Ibal at his side, the landing party left behind around the bluff. The pebbles disappeared now, replaced by sheets of seaweed-slicked rock that sloped off beneath the surface of the waves. Hector slipped occasionally but wouldn't be slowed.

"Take care, my lord," said Ringlin as he caught a stumbling Ibal. "It's treacherous here; you need to watch your footing."

Oh, bless him, hissed Vincent. *See how he cares? He doesn't want you breaking your neck. Not while they still need paying, anyway!*

Hector didn't answer either soul, instead keeping up his pace. He could feel the pull, close now, promising answers.

Images flashed again: *the dark, a black curtain, a mouth, a kiss.*

Hector could feel his heart quicken as he slipped over the rocky ledge, dropping into a rock pool up to his knees. He clambered up again, and his gloved hands scrabbled over the white stone as he rounded the next outcrop, revealing another smaller cove beyond. The beach was empty and gloomy, broken in its center by a tall, thin crevice in the rock. The black crack snaked twenty feet up the stunted chalk cliff, the high-tide water washing in through its entrance and rushing out once again. Hector dropped from the ledge into the water and waded the remaining distance, the Boarguard joining him.

Hector stood ankle deep in the water as the sea surged into the cave. Perhaps a foot across, the gap was just wide enough to allow single file entrance. As the tide sluiced back between his feet, he could have sworn he heard the word again: *welcome.*

He turned to his henchmen. Ibal held his sickle in his hand, turning the blade nervously in his grasp while glancing at Ringlin. The tall man simply stared at the thin cave entrance, his serrated long knife still sheathed.

"You're going in there, aren't you?"

Hector nodded.

"And you won't follow, unless you hear me scream. Understand?"

Ringlin and Ibal nodded, the short man letting loose a nervous giggle before throwing a fat hand over his mouth.

"Brenn be with you," muttered the tall man.

Don't count on it, brother, whispered Vincent as Hector squeezed through the gap. *Brenn deserted you long, long ago.*

4

NEW OATHS

SCORIA WAS A changed island. It had once known law and order, albeit the bloodthirsty variety of the Lizardlords. But now chaos reigned. The mansions of the Black Staircase had been sacked, stripped of all their worth, the merchants and nobles who lived there long gone. When the Werewolf and his allies had leaped on to Lord Ignus's balcony, the island's wealthiest had fled the coliseum with their guards and entourages in tow, grabbed what they could carry, and raced to the harbor, sailing on the first ships they found. All else was left to those who remained: the slaves, prisoners, and gladiators.

With the Lizardlords gone, it had been left to Drew and the surviving therians to assume control; there were few on Scoria who would argue with their word.

Those freed slaves who could work as sailors were guaranteed passage, crewing up on the remaining ships as, one by one, they set sail from Scoria. Those with trades or families also secured transport, with the remainder forced to stay on the island.

By now, only one ship remained in the harbor, anchored beyond the cove. She was all too familiar to Drew: the *Banshee*, the commandeered slave vessel that had belonged to Count Kesslar and would now take the young Wolflord home to Lyssia. Drew stood on the harbor walls, staring at the black ship, her decks alive with activity. The boat had been his prison as the Goatlord transported him to Scoria. Now she was going to return him to his homeland.

"She's ugly," came a voice from behind. Drew turned and found Djogo stood there, smiling grimly. "Though I'm one to talk."

Drew might have laughed if Djogo's words weren't so barbed. He looked at the eye patch.

"The eye, Djogo . . ." said Drew, trying to find the words to apologize for the wound he'd inflicted back in Haggard.

Djogo snorted, ignoring the young therian as he stared at the *Banshee*.

"Still no sign of Kesslar," he said. "His face is known throughout Scoria—if he remained he'd have been spotted by now. I think we can assume he was behind the theft."

While Drew and his companions had led their revolt

against the Lizardlords, Ignus's private chambers had been burgled, the true wealth of Scoria stolen from his personal vault. The rarest jewels and gems that the Lizard had stashed away down the years, ill-gotten gains from a lifetime trading in the misfortune of others, had been kept secure in a long-box under constant watch. The four warriors who guarded the hoard were found slain, gored from throat to navel or run clean through. Drew had no doubt whatsoever that the horns of the Goat were responsible. The treasure of Scoria was gone, and so was the count.

"Why didn't he take the *Banshee*?" asked Drew.

"Dragging that loot down the Black Staircase would have slowed his escape. By the time he hit the harbor he'd have been with the other rich pigs, struggling to get away. With the *Banshee* anchored so far from the shore, he must have jumped on to another ship."

Drew shook his head. "The Goat has so much to answer for. How many innocent souls fought and died in the Furnace so he could make a coin?"

Djogo nodded slowly. "He'd have happily harmed those closest to me. There can be no forgiveness."

"Who would he have harmed?" said Drew, although he already knew the answer: the Hawklady.

"Kesslar has never tolerated any divided loyalties within his ranks. My—friendship—with Lady Shah would have enraged him if he'd ever known how deep my feelings ran for her. Once he allowed Ignus to throw me into the Furnace, she was on her own, her safety hanging in the balance. Even her own father couldn't protect her from Kesslar because he was left languishing in the ludus. I would have my revenge on the Goatlord."

"With respect, Djogo—finding Kesslar's like searching for a needle in a haystack. Don't devote your life to hunting Kesslar down. Find a new future, with Shah."

Djogo grimaced. "She's a Werelady. What future would she want with a human?"

"It's clear she cares for you. You've a chance at a new beginning now."

"She needs to choose a therian as her mate. It is her duty as a Werehawk, is it not?"

"I'm not the best person to speak to about duty—I've run away from it at every opportunity. Only now do I see what I must do. I need to return to Lyssia."

"And I'll be at your side," said Djogo, staring at the black ship. Drew glanced sharply at the tall warrior. *Did I hear him correctly?*

"You'd accompany me?"

Djogo turned, his face deadly serious, one good eye trained on the Wolf.

"I worked for Kesslar for many years, first as his slave, then as his soldier. I've done many things in the Goat's name that I'm not proud of, terrible things that should've seen me put to the sword. The balance needs redressing. By serving you, Drew of the Dyrewood, I can set that in motion."

Drew was speechless. Here stood Djogo, Kesslar's own killing machine, offering his services. Did Drew *want* to have such a man associated with him—*serving* him? Could he stand shoulder to shoulder with the murderer who'd been his mortal enemy? Could Drew *trust* Djogo?

"I absolve you of any debt you feel you owe me, Djogo. You should go where you wish."

Djogo smiled, the expression hitting Drew like a slap to the face. He'd grown too used to seeing the tall warrior sneering.

"I'm not alone in wanting to aid you, Wolflord; there are others who'd benefit from hearing your words."

The Werelords had gathered aboard the *Banshee*, Djogo the only human present. The former slaver stood beside Drew, trying not to look across at where Shah stood with her father, Baron Griffyn. Taboo and Drake stood on either side of a large port-hole that looked out toward Scoria, while the Behemoth towered behind Krieg.

Drew faced the assembly. "Are you certain this is what you want to do with your freedom?"

Krieg spoke up. "We have our freedom thanks to you. If it weren't for your courage, we'd still be in the coliseum fighting for our miserable lives, or worse, dead. We'll stand by you, Drew.

We're all therian brothers—and sisters—of the Furnace."

"You didn't treat me like a brother when I arrived," said Drew.

"Do you think we were met with open arms when we first came to Scoria, Wolf?" Drake laughed. "You got the measure of the Ape brothers pretty quickly—they'd have killed you in your sleep if you'd trusted them."

"If you'd looked for friendship," said Krieg, "you'd be dead now. You're tough, Drew, as tough as any of us."

"This is my fight, though," said Drew. "Lyssia isn't your homeland."

A huge hand landed gently on Drew's shoulder and the Behemoth's deep voice made Drew's bones rattle. "Our homelands are enslaved. Do you not think our people would have sailed to Scoria to free us if they could? We share the same foe. The Catlords must be stopped."

"I don't understand," said Drew to Taboo. "Why would Onyx and the Catlords allow one of their own to fight in the Furnace? They're your family, aren't they?"

The Tiger looked up, baring her teeth. They all looked away, except Drew, who held her gaze.

"I have no family."

Drew hastily moved the subject away from Taboo's story.

"If you join me, you join my mission," Drew told the group. "Rescue Lyssia from these vicious Cats and restore power to the Lyssians—therians and humans alike. You've all tasted the bitterness of slavery; you know how it feels to live in servitude to another. We must unite with the people, start treating them as our equals. It's time for us, the Werelords, to serve the people." He held out his hand.

The therians looked at one another, Krieg nodding to each in turn as they bowed their heads in agreement.

Each of the therians stepped forward, placing their hands on the Wolf's single hand.

"What happens now?" said Drew, unsure of what they'd agreed to.

"You sail to Lyssia, and we go with you," said Krieg. "We fight at your side, Drew. Fight or die. The Furnace is behind us, but the battle goes on."

Drew smiled and nodded, looking at each of them in turn.

"You have my word, brothers and sisters. When Lyssia is won, we shall return to Bast and your homelands. We'll free your people from the reign of the Catlords."

5

THE HOST

WITH DAYLIGHT FADING behind him, Hector felt he'd stepped into the dead of night. A little illumination was provided by phosphorescent lichen that pockmarked the cave walls, covering the pale rock beyond the tide mark's reach. He'd expected to find sea creatures scuttling away in the shallow rock pools, but like the rest of the island the cave was devoid of life, barring the strange lichen. At its widest the cave was ten feet across, the fissure broadening like an opening eye, before closing once more at its rearmost point.

Where's your host? teased Vincent. *All alone again . . .*

Hector shook his head, dismissing the vile's words as his hands played over the chamber's walls. He leaned close, squinting, tracing the white stone with his gloved fingertips. The pale light revealed strange markings, symbols scrawled into the chalk that resonated with Hector.

"Language," muttered Hector to himself. He tilted his head, trying to translate the archaic shapes. To the magister, the markings read vertically, from floor to ceiling—or the other way around—and the more he stared, the more they struck a chord with the images that had flashed through his mind's eye.

He sensed Vincent's vile was still listening, and half expected it to chime in, but the phantom remained unusually silent, as if it knew Hector was approaching the truth. The higher Hector looked up the cavern walls, the more markings he discovered.

"A scripture, perhaps. Or a diary. But who wrote it?"

Still no responses were forthcoming from the vile. With the greatest mass of symbols being higher up, Hector tottered on tiptoe in the shallow pools, craning his neck to better examine the ceiling. The hanging stalactites were jagged and broken, severed in places where whoever marked the walls had smashed them from the roof in order to reach bare wall. Hector marveled at the many markings, the symbols crossing over one another, runes illegible, as if the author had gone mad over a tremendous period of time.

One long black stalactite hung in the ceiling's center, directly above Hector's head, the rock black and gnarly as opposed to smooth and white.

"Different from the others . . ." When Hector whispered to himself again, Vincent finally responded.

You don't know the half of it, brother.

Two long, skeletal arms separated from the dark mass like a threadbare fan, foot-long fingers splaying out as a pair of hands yawned open. Hector gasped, quickly realizing the figure was suspended upside down, the arms connecting with the shoulders at the base of the body mass. A bulbous head slowly swung down from where it had been tucked away close to the chest. Hector looked straight into the creature's face, nose to nose, trembling chin to pale white forehead.

The face was smooth and hairless, the skin almost translucent. Blue veins were faintly visible, like wisps of pale smoke frozen within marble flesh. It had no nose to speak of, just two angry-looking red holes puncturing the middle of its face. A pair of dark slits widened, revealing cloudy black eyes that stared soullessly at the magister. Then its mouth creaked slowly open. Long teeth, splintered like a graveyard fence, emerged from behind blood-red lips, the creature's fetid breath catching Hector fully in the face. The stench of death was unmistakable, causing the Boarlord to gag, but he couldn't pull his eyes away from those of the creature.

"Welcome."

Casper sat on the shingle beach, skimming pebbles into the water. He looked up the shore toward his captain and the Staglord, the two therians having finished consulting the captain's navigation equipment. The duke held a sea chart over the wooden case, the Sharklord scribbling on the map feverishly with an inked quill. Casper looked the other way down the beach, spying the queen and her lady.

Casper had taken quite a shine to Bethwyn. The noblewoman had been happy to talk with the cabin boy, answering his many questions about the fascinating continent of Lyssia. Casper was used to the sea—the mainland was a world he couldn't wait to explore once the *Maelstrom* reached Roof.

The sun had dropped below the horizon, the sky turning a deep indigo as night came on fast. Casper was ready to return to the ship now, regretting not bringing his cloak. Winter seemed especially bitter on the Sturmish Sea. He'd hoped to catch sight of an iceberg so far north, but when Figgis had mentioned how an ice floe could tear open the greatest warship, that had killed his interest swiftly. He reached down and grabbed at a thin white pebble, but it was rooted in the beach, resisting his attempts to pull it free. Another identical stone popped up beside it, and then another. They looked like razor shells at first glance, four of them side by side. It was only when a fifth emerged and closed tight around his hand that he realized they weren't pebbles at all.

They were fingers.

Casper's scream was heard on the *Maelstrom*.

The creature's mouth hung open, its voice as clear in Hector's head as that of his dead brother, although the vile was silent. The pale white head was connected to ragged shoulder blades by the scrawniest length of neck, giving the impression that the skull might tear loose with the slightest provocation. The black eyes remained fixed on Hector as a dark tongue emerged from between the teeth, flickering over the Boarlord's face like a serpent's kiss. Hector swayed, staring at his suspended host, moving left to right, wanting to pull away but locked into its gaze.

"Why have you sought me out?"

"I . . . I . . ." stammered Hector nervously, fear snatching the words from his throat. "I heard your call."

Again the tongue flickered, but still Hector couldn't step away. He had no trouble understanding the words now, in such close proximity. The telepathy that had drawn him to the island was now abandoned. The language was new and unnatural to Hector, yet somehow he was able to follow and respond.

"But you are not one of my kin. What are you?"

"I'm a Boarlord."

"Boarlord."

There was silence as the creature considered this. Hector

glanced at the rest of the body. The beast's head seemed to glow compared to the rest of its form, skeletal with black skin drawn tight across the bones. The torso was an emaciated bag of bones, while the creature's feet remained clamped to the ceiling.

"How is it you know the tongue of my kin? I have called them for many moons and they fail to come. Now you hear my call?"

"I can't explain," said Hector, his eyes on the creature's black pupils once more. They held him like a rabbit in a snare. Hector waved his hands toward the walls.

"This language—I recognize it, though I've never studied it. And I *know* languages. Where are you from?"

"My home is the isle."

"This island?"

"I dwell here, but this is not my home. Our isle is bigger. Much bigger. Another white isle."

"How did you come here? You mention others, but you seem alone. Are you lost? Separated from your people?"

"People."

His host made a sound, somewhere between a growl and a laugh. Hector shivered as if someone had walked over his tomb. He sensed that, fragile though the creature seemed, it was more powerful than anything he'd ever encountered, and that included the Wereserpent, Vala. This beast was born from old magicks, while somehow still being connected to theriankind like the Boarlord.

"Perhaps I can help you get home?"

"In return for what?"

"I don't know. What do you offer?"

"You have an understanding, Boarlord, that is rare beyond my kin. A magister, are you not? You are not the first of your order who has visited me seeking answers. You know some dark magick, Boarlord, but you only scratch the surface. Tell me: what do you know of the Children of the Blue Flame?"

Hector had to think for a moment. He was about to shrug and shake his head, about to say that he knew nothing, when his left hand spasmed involuntarily. He raised it before his face, black leather creaking as the palm and fingers clenched.

Images flashed: *the shaman of the Wyrmwood; the risen corpse of Captain Brutus in the Pits; pale blue eyes that flashed in the night.*

"The undead," whispered Hector.

The creature made the noise again.

"You are no stranger to the Children of the Blue Flame. You do not fear them?"

Hector puffed his chest out, confident he had the answers to the creature's riddles. He pulled the glove off his hand, showing the beast the black mark.

"Fear them? I command them!"

The creature's tongue snaked out, perhaps a foot in length, stroking the palm of Hector's hand. He shuddered at the touch but kept his arm up, elbow locked. He couldn't let the host see his fear.

"You do not understand them, Blackhand. You do not see how they can help you."

"What is there to understand? How can they help me?"

Again, the growling laughter from the creature.

"For one who hungers for knowledge, your appetite is easily sated."

"Tell me what I'm missing, then. Show me what you know!"

"Good," said the host. *"We have our bargain."*

"We do?" asked Hector. He was unsure where this was heading. Beyond the cave, Hector could hear screaming.

"We have a bargain, Blackhand. I show you what may come to pass, what can be yours."

"In return for what?"

"An embrace, magister."

The creature's mouth opened wider now, the splintered teeth trembling with anticipation. Again, a scream outside. Shouting from the beach. Hector had no time to waste.

"We have a deal," he said. The host's long, skeletal arms swept down toward him, enormous fingers reaching about Hector's skull. Its touch was as cold as death itself.

"Get back on the boats!"

Vega dashed along the shore, grabbing his men and tossing them toward the sea and away from the beach. He was partly transformed, his skin darkening as his hands and teeth sharpened with every step. In the eerie twilight moans rose from the beach as the bleached and buried dead hauled themselves from the shingle. Rocks and pebbles tumbled away from hands and heads emerging from the ground, grasping hungrily at the living.

Casper held tight onto Vega's torso like a limpet. He'd been the first to encounter the corpses, but not the last. Amelie and Bethwyn had been dragged to the ground, decayed hands tugging at them. Manfred had dashed to their aid as Vega hauled the boy out of danger, but more of the *Maelstrom*'s men were falling foul of the creatures.

One of the cursed souls had risen fully, taking hold of one of Vega's less agile crewmen. Its skin was parchment thin and clung to every bone on the dead man's body, drained of all fluid. Tattered breeches hinted at the dead man's life; perhaps it had once been a sailor from the wrecked ship. Twin blue fires danced in its eyes as it brought its mouth to the screaming sailor's throat, burying its teeth in warm flesh.

"Move!" screamed Vega as more of the dead emerged from their pebbly graves. Those who got too close took a blow from his clawed fingers, but Vega had no intention of tarrying. They had to get off this devil's rock, and quick.

He waded through the water toward the boats, where the last of his men struggled to clamber aboard.

"Did anyone see Hector?"

"Went around the shore with his men, captain," replied a sailor, pointing. "Beyond that outcrop."

Vega was waist high in the water now and passed Casper to Manfred.

He looked at the beach, counting around twenty of the shambling dead sailors, a clutch of them gathering around the body of his fallen shipmate and tearing hungrily into him. Their moans echoed across the island.

"Keep away from the shore, but try and get around that outcrop. I'll go ahead, see if I can find them."

Vega dived below the surface and swam, skirting the jagged rocks around the White Isle's coastline before heading back toward the beach. As he emerged from the waves he could see Hector's henchmen standing on guard before a tall, thin cave entrance. Both looked startled to see the transformed Sharklord, each of them glancing warily around their small stretch of beach.

"Why all the screaming?" asked Ringlin nervously. "It's enough to wake the dead!"

Ibal's giggles were cut short when Vega threw him a dark and serious look.

"Where's Hector?"

"The master said he wasn't to be interrupted," said Ringlin cockily, sneering at Vega defiantly. "Them's our orders."

"Out of my way," said Vega, making to push past them.

Both men raised their hands to bar his progress, but neither was a match for an angry Sharklord. He punched each in the stomach, grabbed them by their necks, and hurled them back into the water just as the first rowboat emerged into the cove.

"I don't have time for your idiotic loyalty!" he snarled. "Get on the boats. *Now!*"

As if on cue, the first of the risen dead crawled around the outcrop, blue eyes glowing in the dark. Ringlin and Ibal needed no further prompting, running to the boat as Vega disappeared into the cave.

Beyond, in the dark, Vega could hear movements. It was the sound of glass clinking against glass. Gradually the fissure opened into a tall, bell-shaped chamber. The seawater sloshed around his ankles. Vega shook his head, trying to comprehend what he witnessed.

Hector hung in the air, held tight in the long black arms of some creature that was suspended from the cavern's ceiling. The beast was upside down. Its thin fingers with bony knuckles reminded Vega of the spindly legs of a spider crab. He could see the bald white dome of its skull against Hector's neck, its face buried in his throat, the Boarlord's head lolling to one side. The glassy clinking sound came from the magister's satchel, which still hung around his shoulder, banging against his hip as his legs and feet trembled in the air above the rushing tide.

Vega raised up his hands to grab at Hector's shoulder.

Instantly the beast raised its head, still upside-down, revealing its hideous visage with a hiss. Its waxy skin was stretched over its smooth skull, enlarged black eyes narrowing at the Sharklord's interruption. The lower portion of its head was dedicated to a maw of sharp, splintered teeth that ran red with the Boarlord's blood. Vega recoiled, the wound bubbling at Hector's neck.

"Hector!" cried the Sharklord, as the creature screeched something unintelligible.

"No, Vega," said Hector, his voice weak, body trembling spasmodically in the monster's embrace.

What? He wants *this?* Vega shook his head, his mind collapsing at the notion that the young magister might have *willingly* let the creature attack him. The captain of the *Maelstrom* had seen men take leave of their minds enough times to know when they needed saving from themselves. He whipped out his cutlass, plunging it swiftly into the monster's chest.

The beast thrashed, screeching as it dropped the Boarlord. Hector landed in the swirling water below with a splash. Vega snatched at him with his free hand as he lunged in once more with his cutlass.

"No!" shouted the Boarlord, but the Wereshark took no notice, standing over the stricken magister as the creature lashed out with its long arms. A thin sheet of black flesh began to appear beneath the beast's arms and between its fingers, a dark elastic membrane that connected joint to joint. Its head snapped toward Vega, blood pooling in the two sword wounds in its torso. Its movements were frantic as its body continued its change. Vega wasn't about to wait and see any further transformation—if it was anything like a therian, then his cutlass would have caused it no harm at all. He brought his open hand back and swung.

The white, skeletal head ripped free from the creature's shoulders with the impact of the Wereshark's blow. The skull went flying across the cave and shattered against the scarred chalk wall. The decapitated body shook uncontrollably as Vega picked up Hector, the young man's eyes wild with madness as he stared over the Pirate Prince's shoulder.

"No," the magister whispered as Vega carried him from the host's cave, out into the cold night.

PART IV

THE KISS OF SILVER

I

THE HAWKLORD'S TALE

IF THE SURVIVORS of Scoria had hoped for a peaceful crossing to Lyssia, they were sorely disappointed. The farther the *Banshee* sailed north, the more restless the Saber Sea became. It was a credit to the crew that they handled the conditions without complaint, content to be out from under the cruel hoof of Count Kesslar. Djogo had assumed captaincy of the vessel, a position he'd held under the Goatlord, and this time the sailors were cooperative and his whip remained in his belt.

Slaves were no longer the cargo of the *Banshee*. Instead, her hold and decks were packed with warriors—former gladiators who had sworn allegiance to the Wolflord. They came from all across the world, each with his own story of enslavement and sorrow to tell. But now their spirits were high, and their loyalty to Drew seemed absolute. His small army numbered over a hundred, each man promising his blade to the cause. Not a moment of the journey was spent idle, with the soldiers training throughout, ensuring that they remained combat ready and fighting fit. Drills and exercises were overseen by the Werelords, with Baron Griffyn pulling the strings. When he wasn't training the Wolf's army, the Hawklord was deep in conversation with Drew.

"Was my father a good man?"

Griffyn sat on one side of the enormous window that spanned the rear of the *Banshee*, with Drew at the opposite end of the sill. The spacious quarters had once been home to Kesslar, but the Goat's belongings had been stripped from the cabin and now lay on the seabed in Scoria's harbor. Practical furniture, such as the captain's desk, chairs, table, and bunks had remained in place, now providing a home to Drew's Werelord companions, the seven therians sharing the cabin and making it their own. It was crowded, but still infinitely better than the labyrinth of the Furnace. While the others slept, the old Hawk and the young Wolf sat quietly, talking in whispered tones.

"I'd love to tell you a string of beautiful lies, Drew, truly I would. Wergar was a hard man. He'd never back out of a fight or argument; he was stubborn, hotheaded, and as tough as Sturmish steel. There was never a more fearsome sight than the Werewolf charging into battle, howling and roaring, scything Moonbrand through the bloody air. You couldn't imagine a more beautiful sword than your father's white blade. Wergar had friends and enemies and nothing in between."

Griffyn took a sip from the tankard he held in his gnarled hand. "I was honored to be considered his friend."

"The more I hear, the more he sounds like a brute."

"He was a man of conviction, Drew, and he was the king."

"King of Westland though, not the Barebones."

"It mattered little back then, just as now; whosoever ruled in Highcliff ruled over all the Seven Realms. Consider Westland as the head of a great beast, and the remaining realms the body. It's long been acknowledged that there's only one king in Lyssia, and that's the one who sits on the throne in Highcliff. The Wolves ruled for two hundred years, Drew; nobody ever contested their place until the Lion arrived."

Drew chewed his thumb as he stared out of the window, watching the churning waves as they flashed moonlight in the *Banshee*'s wake.

"So you knew Bergan, Manfred, and Mikkel then? Were they your friends, too?"

Griffyn smiled. "They were once."

"What changed?"

"Allegiances." The old Hawk sighed. "I'm sure you know all about Bergan's quandary when Leopold took power. He and the Staglords all played their parts in persuading Wergar to surrender his crown. They didn't know the Lion would go back on his word, but each of them deserted Wergar, and I hope each feels the pain of that betrayal to this day."

"You've got them wrong, Griffyn. They're good men; they were my Wolf's Council, my advisers after we took Highcliff. It's cruel to hope they still suffer for something that happened so long ago."

Griffyn looked surprised. "I apologize, Lord Drew. I didn't mean to offend, but my opinion stands. I've earned it."

"How?"

Griffyn rose stiffly, unfastening his jerkin. "I was a loyal Kingsman, right until the last, to the moment Leopold chopped off your father's head. And I continued to remain loyal afterward."

Drew flinched at mention of Wergar's execution. He'd never known the man, but they were still joined by the bond of blood. The old Hawklord shook off his jerkin, popping the buttons of his shirt. Drew shifted uncomfortably.

"The Hawklords would—and did—die for your father, Drew. We were his staunchest allies and one of the fiercest weapons Wergar had in his arsenal. 'Death from above' our enemies would scream when we soared into battle."

Griffyn's face was wistful as he shrugged off the shirt. "The other Werelords bowed and swore fealty to whoever sat on the throne. Not so the Hawklords, even after the Wolf and his pack were slain. We remained loyal to the dead king. This enraged the Lion, so much so that he made an example of me."

Griffyn turned, the moonlight that streamed through the window illuminating his back. Two enormous scars ran from his shoulders down to the base of his spine, great discolored swathes of pale, colorless skin. There was nothing neat or orderly about the old wounds, the torn flesh undulating in and out, jagged and angry, where his skin had been hacked away many years ago.

"Leopold took my wings. They held me down in the Court of Highcliff, the stench of your murdered and burned family still thick in the air, while the Bear and Stags watched. All the Werelords were there: Horses, Rams, Boars, the lot of them. The Lion took a silver blade to my beautiful wings. He carved them off."

Drew was nauseated. He turned away, unable to look at the Hawklord's awful scars. The image was there in his mind: Leopold holding Griffyn down while he sawed the Werehawk's wings from his back. When he looked back, Griffyn was already rebuttoning his shirt.

"So, as you can imagine, I find it difficult to forgive after all these years."

"I'm sorry, my Lord, I didn't . . ."

"You weren't to know," said Griffyn, dismissing Drew. "Bergan and Manfred are good men who were put in an awful situation. They escaped the Lion's wrath with their bodies intact but their pride battered. I might not have suffered this fate if I hadn't been so stubborn."

Griffyn grimaced as he continued. "Leopold's Lionguard dragged me back to Windfell, accompanied by the lickspittle Skeer—one of my Hawklord brothers—parading me before my people as a warning to all; if any Hawk should show their wings again, they were signing their own death warrant. Skeer was the only Hawk who sided with the Lion, happily swearing allegiance long before Wergar's murder. I was forced to deliver the message on behalf of Leopold. While the Lionguard displayed my severed wings to the Hawklords I recounted Leopold's decree, outlawing my people's falconthropy."

"Falconthropy?"

"The therianthropy of the Hawklords, Drew. You have your lycanthropes, felinthropes, caninthropes, and the like. The Hawks are the falconthropes."

"Leopold outlawed your transformation?"

"That's right," said Griffyn, sitting down again on the windowsill. "In addition, for their treasonous behavior, the Hawklords were forbidden to return to the Barebones. We were banished, chased from our homeland, to be executed should we return. Leopold's army put Windfell under Skeer's command, and I was kept in court as a plaything for the new baron, a reminder to our people of what insubordination led to."

"Where are the Hawklords now?"

"Dead. Gone. Forgotten. I honestly don't know. Leopold and Skeer destroyed my people. Windfell was emptied of Hawklords overnight, never to return. We were powerful and great in number, manning towers and keeps along the spine of the Barebones, acting as commanders and scouts in every army of the Seven Realms. But Leopold put us to the sword."

"But Scoria? How did you get from Windfell to the Furnace?"

"That's where our mutual acquaintance Kesslar comes in," said the Hawk, smacking his bony hand against the window frame.

"Kesslar and Skeer were friends from long, long ago. Opportunists, liars, thieves—they had so much in common. Kesslar was a frequent visitor to Windfell, the only place he was welcome, having taken advantage of his brother therians' kindness in the other courts of the Seven Realms. The Goat took a shine not just to me, but my daughter."

Griffyn paused, glancing toward where Shah slept in her bunk.

"How old was she?"

"Twelve, just a child. Kesslar made Skeer an offer and the old Falcon couldn't say no. Deal done, the Goat had me shipped over to Scoria to fight in the Furnace, while he kept Shah as his own."

Drew tried to imagine what kind of life that must have been for the young Shah. She'd been in a dark mood since he'd

212

met her, and even with their freedom secured, a shadow still hung over Shah's head.

"She must have been terrified."

"I don't doubt it for a moment, but we Hawklords are made of strong stuff. After four years in the Furnace, I'd earned the respect of my masters and freedom from the arena. I'd earned gold for my achievements, as well as lodging of my own away from the slaves and gladiators. While I moved into the ludus to train the Lizards' gladiators, my daughter was by then working for Kesslar, the eyes and wings that got him into places nobody else could reach."

"How did she and Djogo come to know each other?"

"She saw him fight in the Furnace," said the Hawklord. "He was the greatest human gladiator I ever trained. When Kesslar bought him from Ignus, he and Shah began to spend time together, aboard this ship while Kesslar traveled, picking up slaves. A fondness grew, surrounded by the misery the Goatlord thrived upon."

"She seems troubled," whispered Drew, staring at her dark form in the recesses of the cabin.

"If she could get her talons into Kesslar, she'd tear his throat out."

"Because of what he did to you?"

"No." The Hawk sighed. "Because of what happened to her child."

"Child?" gasped Drew.

"Hush, lad," said Griffyn, his voice low. He edged closer along the window seat toward Drew.

"She and Djogo have a child?"

"No, Drew, this was long before Djogo. My daughter met a fellow while she traveled with Kesslar, a charming, dangerous man who thought a little too much of himself—certainly not a marriageable prospect. She was a teenage girl and thought she was in love. Perhaps they were; we'll never know. Anyway, a child came from this union, unbeknown to Kesslar. The father was gone before my daughter even knew she was expecting. We hid the pregnancy from the Goat, Shah remaining in Scoria for the final months while Kesslar was away.

"The baby was born days before the Goat returned with the *Banshee* full of fresh slaves. Shah had no time at all with the child. I had it—him—taken away, using what coin I'd saved to have the baby taken to his father. If Kesslar had found my daughter with a child, Brenn knows what he'd have done with them. Punish her? Sell the child? I only hope the baby was delivered to the father. To this day I worry about what became of him. That child is my only regret."

Drew put a hand on the old Hawk's crooked shoulder. "You did what you had to, protecting your daughter and grandchild."

"If I had that time again, I'd have killed Kesslar before surrendering one of my own. My only regret," he repeated.

Drew wanted to comfort the old Hawklord but was unable to find the words.

"We all have regrets," he said eventually, thinking back to Whitley and Gretchen, how he'd never had the chance to say good-bye to them. He wondered where Hector was, what had become of his dear friend, whether he'd ever see him again.

Griffyn smiled, the grin creasing his weather-beaten face.

"You're too young for regrets, Drew. You've got time on your side. You can make changes and right your wrongs. Better still, right *others'* wrongs. And as long as I live and breathe I shall be by your side to help you do just that."

2

THE GAME

DIGGING HIS FEET into the loose earth, Trent scrambled the remaining distance up the hillside. He'd left the campsite behind him, his comrades' calls still echoing at his back as they searched for the escaped prisoners. They'd had forty captured men of the Longridings and Romari, all manacled and chained, and three of them had escaped. They had originally been caught in the grasslands, drawing ever nearer to Calico where Lady Gretchen no doubt hid.

For one prisoner to go missing was extraordinary; for three to have escaped sounded like there might have been a traitor in the camp. Not one to let the tracks go cold, Trent was immediately up and away once the shout went out.

The footprints disappeared up the bluff to the east of the

camp. Looking up, Trent could see a swaying rank of grass silhouetted against the moonlight, marking the highest point of the snaking ridge. He hauled himself to the summit, snatching at tufts of grass to stop himself from tumbling back. Breathing hard, he staggered to his feet and looked down. A huge meadow of unspoiled long grass disappeared into the darkness. The bluff was rocky on this side, a steep, treacherous bank of rough stones and loose earth filling the slope to the north and south. Trent watched his step as the rocks skittered underfoot, the scree plummeting sixty feet to the grasslands below.

He glanced along the ridge to see two figures to the north, a hundred feet or so feet away. By the clear night sky he recognized Sorin as one of them. The other was having his manacles removed, before being handed a shortsword by Sorin. With a hearty shove the prisoner was then sent tumbling down the embankment, a cloud of earth and stones erupting in his wake as he rolled and spun down into the grass.

"Wait!" called Trent, scrambling along the ridge, but by the time he'd caught up with Sorin the prisoner had disappeared from view below.

"What in Brenn's name are you doing? Are you behind this, Sorin? There's *three* of them that have escaped!"

"That's right, farmboy," said Sorin, winking at Trent. Three pairs of unlocked manacles lay at his feet. "Was me what freed them, wasn't it."

Trent struck the broken-nosed captain in the face, his

knuckles cracking as the two of them went down.

"Get off me, you fool!" shouted Sorin, hammering the side of Trent's head with his fists as the younger man tried to pin him down.

"Traitor!" yelled Trent, finding fresh strength as he grappled with his senior officer. He couldn't hear the captain's voice; his mind and struggle was focused on Sorin the traitor. Traitor, just like Drew.

Sorin's fist caught Trent across the jaw, sending the young outrider over the ridge and down the rocky embankment. He bounced and twirled, losing all sense of up and down, his body a whirling mass of limbs. His head struck hard rock—once, twice—his temple splitting before he shuddered to a halt in the grass at the base of the scree.

Trent tried to focus his eyes, stars spinning overhead. He lifted a hand, feeling the torn flesh over his eye, his fingertips coming away crimson.

"You'd call *me* a traitor, Ferran?" Sorin laughed from above, staggering back to his feet. "I was obeying orders. Lord Pinkeye told me to have three picked out and sent down here. For the game."

"The game?" called up Trent, dabbing at his streaming brow.

"Our lordship needs to hunt, Ferran. That's why I brought them away from the camp. He can lose control when his blood's up."

Trent rolled on to his belly and began to crawl up the

embankment, the loose earth falling down on top of him. He struggled frantically, trying to find purchase in the scree, but it was impossible. A scream from the long grass behind made him stop and turn, his eyes wide and fearful.

"You gave them swords?" he shouted to Sorin.

"Pinkeye likes his prey to have a little fight in 'em, doesn't he?" called down the captain, crouching over the incline. "I hope you brought your pa's Wolfshead blade with you, Ferran. Best of luck, eh?"

With that, Sorin turned and disappeared from view.

"Sorin!" Trent cried in vain. "Sorin!"

Trent looked up and down the ridge base, desperate to find a way of climbing out. He was blind to a means of escape; the tall grass to his right was as high as his head and constantly swaying. Reluctantly, he unsheathed the Wolfshead blade and started to follow the stony bank northward. He glanced up as he went, constantly searching for a route out.

Sorin had played the situation perfectly. He'd let Trent leap to his own conclusions, and before he knew it, he was lying at the bottom of an impossible slope waiting for the Catlord to tear him to pieces. The captain was a sly fellow.

"Brenn, help me . . ."

A gurgling cry came from the long grass nearby. Trent recognized the wet sound in the voice; blood, pooling at the back of the man's throat. He shook his head and moved onward. *Not your concern, Trent.*

"The beast," a voice sobbed. "Dear Brenn, the beast . . ."

Trent ground his teeth, ignoring the man's pleas. He had to look after his own skin, thanks to Sorin. The sobbing man's cries tugged at him as he walked past, like hooks beneath his skin. *Keep going, Trent. Don't stop now. You can't stop. The man's a traitor. His death rattle's on its way. He got what was coming.*

But with each step, the begging cries of the man snagged hold of Trent's conscience. He couldn't leave *anything* to die—that much Mack Ferran had taught him on the Cold Coast.

He cursed angrily, wiping the blood from his temple along his sleeve as he turned and set off into the long grass. Away from the ridge he strode, cutting the grass back with his long-sword, staggering hesitantly toward the cries of a scared and dying man.

Thirty or so paces from the slope, Trent found him, lying on a flattened bed of grass. The tall, feathery fronds lay bent and broken about him, his limbs spread-eagled as if he'd prepared a nest for the night. The man still held the shortsword that Sorin had given him, his right hand feebly raising it as Trent appeared. The man's head remained still against the floor, although his eyes stayed fixed on the Ferran boy as his lips trembled.

The man's mouth was awash with blood, pink spittle foaming between his teeth, his belly torn wide open. Trent gagged, the food from his evening meal racing up his throat. He turned away, trying to hold it down but only partly succeeding.

"Please . . ." begged the man, finding his words again. "Kill . . . me . . ."

Trent turned back, his face a mask of pity and horror. He raised the Wolfshead blade and faltered, unable to put the poor man out of his misery. Before he could act decisively, the grasses split to his right as a white shape sprang from the darkness, the moonlight catching the beast's shining fur as it flew. Trent just had time to parry the monster away, before the sword flew from his grasp and the two tumbled into the bloody grass.

The Catlord's white head was huge, the width of Trent's torso. The jaws snapped at his face, teeth the size of daggers. Claws held Trent's shoulders, pinning him to the ground and preventing his escape. He raised his left forearm toward the monster, catching the Cat's bite with it before it tore at his skull. The teeth clamped down hard, cutting into the steel-armored bracer and threatening to snap his arm in two. Trent screamed as the Cat's pink eyes shone, demonic in the moonlight; Frost was possessed by the change, by the hunt, by the kill. The bracer bowed, the metal sleeve groaning, about to break. Trent jabbed at the Catlord's eyes with his free hand, hooking his thumb in and striking home.

With a roar, Frost released his grip on the Redcloak, leaping off the boy and bounding back into the grasses. The shouting of soldiers echoed down from the ridge, as Bastians and Lionguard investigated the commotion. Trent rolled over on to the body of the dying man, but the beast was gone. The light had gone from the prisoner's eyes, life's last breath steaming from his still lips.

Trent scrambled about on the bloody ground, fingers searching for his dropped blade. A low growl emanated from the shadows; the beast was still close by. Did Frost know that it was Trent he was facing? *Surely he recognizes me?* Trent's hand brushed cold steel, fingers racing along its length until they found the handle. Snatching it up he tracked back through the grass, toward the voices on the ridge.

He stumbled from the tall grass, collapsing against the pebbled hillside. Above he heard Bastians and Lyssians alike, shouting for him to climb up, to keep moving. He resheathed the Wolfshead blade and began his ascent again, hands and feet clawing at the bank, every handful of loose earth sending him sliding back again. The growling sound drew closer as his comrades shouted their support, looking on with morbid fascination as the beast closed in.

"Keep moving, Ferran!"

"It's coming, man!"

"Climb for your life!"

Trent wanted to scream, but that was wasted energy. He was fighting for survival now—the changed Catlord behind him was out of his mind with bloodlust. Trent was just one more human delivered by Sorin, a mouse for the cat to play with until it stopped twitching.

Trent's hand caught a flat rock overhead, a few feet below a larger boulder that protruded from the scree bank. He didn't have time to check its suitability. His muscles strained and burned as he trusted his body weight to the flat ledge. It remained in place, deeply embedded, allowing him to finally make progress.

"It's on you, Ferran!"

"I can see it in the grass!"

Trent threw his right hand forward toward the larger boulder, his fingers scrabbling for purchase as he launched himself toward the higher point. The men cheered overhead, willing him on. This would put him clear of the grasses, give him the chance to find a route out while Frost regained his senses.

The boulder ripped free as it took Trent's weight, the bank collapsing as he fell in a shower of dirt, rock, and pebbles back to the base of the ridge. Trent spluttered, the dust cloud blinding and choking him as he struggled to rise from the debris. The grasses parted in front of him as a figure emerged.

Trent had expected a clawed paw to strike out, tear his throat, his stomach, put an end to his fight. Instead, a smooth, human hand was extended before him, as the lithe outline of Frost stood over him, naked in the moonlight. The albino Catlord flexed his fingers, beckoning Trent to take his offered palm. He rubbed his other hand against his injured eye, squinting and blinking as he focused on the terrified outrider.

"Got me good there, Trent," said the felinthrope, smiling through bloodied teeth. He nodded at his hand. The Redcloak hesitantly took it as Frost hauled him to his feet.

"A word of warning: never get in the way of a Catlord when he's hunting game. Come, let's return to camp. I owe you a hundred apologies."

3

THE BLOODY BAY

AT A GLANCE he looked like any other sailor on ship's watch in Denghi. A fringe of black hair poked out from the rim of his kash, the headdress popular with the men of the desert. A white scarf was wrapped around his face in the Omiri style, gray eyes peering out from the narrow slit, watching all who passed along the wharf. His bare torso was weather-beaten and tanned; three-quarter length white leggings covered his legs, leaving his bare feet exposed to the elements. His right hand rested on his hip, a shortsword lodged within the sash, while his left was missing, a basket-handled trident dagger sitting on the stump in its place. He stood between the rails at the head of the *Banshee*'s gangway, apparently relaxed. There were few captains in Denghi who could boast the rightful king of Westland as their watchman.

The port was crowded with a variety of ships, greater in number than any Drew had seen before. All Hallows Bay, Highcliff, and Cape Gala had been busy, bustling harbors, but there was a manic energy to Denghi. Griffyn had explained to Drew that this port on the Bloody Bay was the only truly neutral city in Omir. Ro-Pasha to the north was under the control of Lord Canan's Doglords, while Ro-Shann to the south was home to Lady Hayfa, the Hyena. Both Canan and Hayfa were enemies of the true ruler of Omir, King Faisal of Azra, but each respected the neutrality of Denghi. It was the only place in Omir where one could find agents of all three factions rubbing shoulders with one another.

The choice of where they should land had been limited. As predicted, they'd passed patrolling Bastian warships while they slunk across the Saber Sea. As the *Banshee* was known to the Bastians as a slaver, she was allowed on her way with little interference. Djogo and Shah had welcomed the captain of one such vessel aboard while the Werelords and small army of gladiators hid in the hold. They'd made their excuses for Kesslar's absence, telling the Bastians that the Goat was sleeping off a barrel of wine belowdecks. The captain had warned Djogo to steer clear of the southern waters, due to the military activity in the Lyssian Straits. The *Banshee* had no other option than to head for Denghi.

The former slave vessel was moored at the end of the port's longest pier, a five-hundred-foot-stretch of wharf that reached out into the Bloody Bay. Every inch of the pier was crowded with merchants, fishermen, sailors, and ne'er-do-wells, haggling with one another over goods. The air was alive with sounds and smells: music from cantinas clashing with shouting traders, monkeys chattering, dogs barking, spices burning, meats cooking. Apart from one Bastian warship, anchored a little farther around the bay, there was no sign of the military within the harbor. Lyssia may have been at war, but there seemed to be little conflict in Denghi.

Three figures approached the gangplank from the pier. Djogo came first, his face open, identity unhidden. He was known in Omir, with a fearsome reputation hard-earned. Denghi had been a regular stop-off for Kesslar down the years for buying and selling slaves. Behind came Griffyn and Krieg, their faces obscured by kashes. The trio traversed the gangway, Drew nodding as they passed. He followed them as they disappeared below, another sailor replacing him at the top of the planked walkway.

The Werelords gathered around the desk in the captain's cabin, Djogo standing by the door. A crude map of Lyssia was carved into the tabletop, which the Goat had used to plot his raids around the continent. The allies of the Wolf now used it to plan their next move.

Griffyn cast his hand across the map wearily.

"Lyssia is turbulent, more so than ever before," said the Hawklord, pinching his sharp nose between thumb and forefinger.

"Turbulent?" asked Drew. "Beyond that Bastian frigate, there's no sign of war in Denghi."

"The battle rages beneath calm waters," said Krieg. "It would appear the seaport has dodged much of Omir's fighting, but that could change at any moment."

"You said Denghi was neutral."

"So it is. But news is that Lord Canan is allied with the Catlords," said the Rhino.

"Cats and Dogs, unified?" The Behemoth chuckled, the noise like a grinding millstone.

"I know," agreed Griffyn. "Unlikely unions have sprung up across Lyssia. There is talk that Lady Hayfa has also agreed terms with Canan. Her forces are already mobilizing, ensuring that Faisal is surrounded to the north and south by powerful enemies allied against him. They mean to attack Azra."

"Are they powerful enough to succeed?" asked Drake.

"If the Catlords lend their claws, this Desert King will die," said Taboo, sneering out of the porthole toward the Bastian warship.

"Grim days indeed for the Jackal," said Drake.

"And the rest of Lyssia?" said Drew, keen to hear news of the west.

"Broken," said Djogo. "Highcliff has fallen to the Catlords, your Wolf's Council chased from Westland. Lucas sits on the throne in place of his dead father."

"Leopold, dead?" said Drew, clearly shocked.

"It's said that Duke Bergan killed him," said the old Hawklord.

Good old Bergan. I knew he wouldn't let us down if he got the chance.

Drew noticed Griffyn was avoiding eye contact. "What is it?"

"The duke is dead, too, Drew; killed in his battle with Leopold."

Drew stared at Griffyn's bowed head, the old man's words not sinking in straight away.

"The whereabouts of your mother and others—Duke Manfred and Baron Hector—aren't known, though Earl Mikkel was slain by the Doglords. The remains of your Wolf's Council are being bruited about as Lyssia's 'most wanted'; there's a price on their heads—and your own."

Drew hardly heard Griffyn. Mikkel and his dear friend and mentor, Bergan, dead. He'd always felt certain he would see the Bearlord again, didn't imagine that he would never get to make amends to the giant, bearded duke for fleeing Highcliff in secret.

Krieg tugged at the kash around Drew's face.

"It's more important than ever we keep your identity secret, my friend," said the Rhino, before placing a consoling hand on the Wolf's shoulder. "If Onyx offers riches in return for your head, you'll have fewer friends than ever."

"Hector and Whitley," said Drew, his attention still on the Hawklord. "And Gretchen. Any news?"

"As I said, Hector fled Highcliff when Onyx took the city. I couldn't tell you if he's alive. Lady Gretchen and Lady Whitley disappeared from Cape Gala after you were taken by Kesslar. Their whereabouts are unknown, but many of the Horselords fled Cape Gala to Calico on the coast, so your friends may have joined them. Duke Brand, the Bull, reigns there, his fortress city one of the few that makes a stand against the Bastians. A fleet of the Catlord's warships gathers off the coast, blockading the Lyssian Straits."

"Have the other realms not come to Westland's aid? What of Sturmland? The Barebones?"

Krieg raised his voice now as Griffyn shook his head. "The Lords of Sturmland have taken no side, while the Barebones are split—the Stags of Stormdale and Highwater stand in favor of the Wolf, while the Crows of Riven supposedly remain neutral."

"Supposedly?"

"Their contempt for the other Werelords of the Barebones is famous—they want the realm for themselves. I find it hard to believe they aren't involved in some way with the attacks on Highwater."

"Highwater's been attacked?" asked Drew.

"The Staglord cities are without their lords, one brother dead, the other missing," replied Griffyn, pointing a bony finger at the mountain range on the map. "Even now Onyx moves his pieces into play, his army having taken the Dalelands and now laying siege to Highwater."

"But surely Highwater is full of civilians?"

"Not so. Word reached the remaining Stags that a combined army of Bastians and Omiri approached. The innocents have evacuated south to the safety of Stormdale. Brenn willing, the civilians will be spared this conflict and the battle will play out in Highwater. The men of the Barebones are a tough bunch, and Highwater is well protected: they'll be prepared for a long siege."

"Is there *nobody* who can aid them?"

"The Stags have no allies. The Bear is gone from Brackenholme, and Windfell to the south remains deserted." Griffyn sighed. "My homeland is no more than a ghost town, while the Lion's lackey, Skeer, rules the roost."

Shah, at her father's side, now spoke up. "Not for long. Skeer's time is running out. When we return to Windfell, we'll turn the traitorous old bird out of the nest and make it our own again."

"Brave words, Hawk," said Krieg. "But what hope do you and your father have of defeating whatever force awaits you in Windfell? Where are your fellow Hawklords in your time of need?"

Griffyn looked up from the table, his eyes settling upon Drew again, who stared straight back, shocked at the old warrior's tide of bad news.

"Where are the Hawklords, Baron?" asked Drew, his voice quiet as he struggled with his grief.

"Scattered," replied Griffyn. "Many took on lives as normal, mortal men—like you, Drew, before you discovered your lycanthropy. Can you imagine? Forbidden to embrace the beast? Having your gift denied you? My people were broken just as Windfell was. They're lost."

"Is there no way of reaching them?"

Griffyn wavered, his eyes narrowing. The Hawklord sat down, looking back to the map. His finger traced a line up the Silver River from Denghi, past Azra, to the Barebones, coming to a halt. The Werelords were silent as they watched him, waiting for Griffyn to speak. He closed his eyes and spoke.

"There is a place most sacred to my people, the great mountain of Tor Raptor, ancient tomb of the Hawklords of Windfell. Only the just and rightful lord may safely enter the Screaming Peak."

"Screaming Peak?" Drew asked.

"It's a cavern within Tor Raptor's summit. When the stones are lifted, Tor Raptor screams to her children."

"Screams?" Krieg was fascinated, as were the others.

"It's the one way in which the true Lord of Windfell may call the Hawklords home. The only way."

232

"Sounds like a legend to me, old timer." Drake sighed. "We need more than wailing mountains to best our foes."

The Hawklord opened his eyes, settling them upon Drew. The young Wolf nodded.

"We need an army."

4

BACK FROM THE DEAD

"COME IN," CALLED Count Vega, as a series of knocks on the door took his attention away from his desk. A heavily cloaked Duke Manfred entered the cabin, stamping his feet and clapping his hands, tiny snowflakes shaking loose from his shoulders.

"Is it chilly outside, Your Grace?"

"It's as cold as Ragnor's chin!" grunted the duke miserably.

"Interesting you mention old Henrik's father. We're close to the coast of Sturmland again by my reckoning, maybe a day or two out of Friggia. That business with the Sirens and then the White Isle almost did for us—thank Sosha that I was able to get my bearings."

The two Werelords were silent for a moment, memories of their brief visit to the lonely island all too vivid. Vega reached into a cabinet and pulled out a bottle and glass, pushing them across the table toward Manfred.

"There really was no need for you to take a watch, you know. The last thing I need is a frozen Stag tumbling on to the deck, shattering into a thousand pieces. Would scare the lives out of my men."

"It's the least I can do, mucking in with your crew," said the old Duke, unstoppering the bottle and pouring himself a glass with shivering hands. He threw it down his throat swiftly, barking a spluttering cough at the drink.

"Friggia, you say?" muttered the duke. "Do you plan to stop there?"

"I'd hoped we could make it straight to Roof. Perhaps we still can. Stopping in Friggia would be dangerous. It's one of Slotha's ports; we want to bypass it if possible. There's no way Onyx's forces could have reached this far north yet. We should get to Icegarden through the back door, so to speak."

"How's Amelie?"

Vega smiled, a rakish grin breaking his handsome features. The captain of the *Maelstrom* had watched the tender friendship between Manfred and the queen blossom into something else. Neither of the therians would admit to such feelings—they'd deny it instantly—but there was no fooling the Sharklord.

"I invited her into my company, but she still needs rest. It appears the encounters on the White Isle have left their scars upon her."

Manfred nodded, staring back into the open stove, the flames warming his hands and soul.

"And Hector?" said the Staglord. "Any news?"

Vega ran a hand through his long black hair, wincing at the thought of the young magister. "He still sleeps."

"Sleep is a good thing. I thought he was dead."

"He might have killed us all."

"How can you say that, Vega? The poor lad was attacked by that creature, wasn't he?"

The count scratched at his scalp. "He was and he wasn't."

"Don't start with the cryptic talk, Vega!"

"Yes, the creature attacked him, could easily have killed him. But I think he deliberately allowed the beast to assault him."

"How so?" The duke sounded shocked.

"We landed on the White Isle on Hector's insistence. I suspect he wanted us to go there, knew what awaited us, and put all our lives in danger."

"How could he have possibly known what was on the is-land? That's preposterous, Vega!"

"I don't know. This communing he's confessed to carry-ing out, this necromancy—who knows what he's tapped into? You can't tell me Hector isn't a changed man. He *knew* there was something on that island. His actions led to one of my men getting killed. It has something to do with dark magistry, I'm sure of it. I don't have the answers, Manfred, but I believe Hector does."

The duke scratched at the gray stubble on his jaw, saddened to hear Vega's accusations, but he didn't defend the Boarlord. It was plain for all to see that the sickly Hector bore little resemblance to the happy young boy he'd first met ten years ago in the court of Redmire.

"Does Lady Bethwyn still attend him?"

"She has a soft spot for our magister," said Vega, staring at the cabin door, his thoughts distant. "She is another therian of the Dalelands after all. She seems a lovely girl, very trusting. I hope Hector doesn't betray that trust."

"What on earth do you mean?"

The count shook his head wearily and then smiled at the duke. "I'm thinking aloud, that's all. He's a complex character, our Baron of Redmire, Manfred."

"You worry too much," said Manfred, unfastening his cloak at last as his body warmed up. "He's not as misguided as you suggest, my friend. Just a little misunderstood."

Vega nodded but said nothing, his mind lingering on the memory of two bickering brothers on the staircase of Bevan's tower, arguing over their father's throne for a final, fatal time.

Bethwyn clenched the cloth in her fist, her knuckles turning white as she squeezed the excess water from it. Beyond the porthole, sleet raced past, blurring streaks of white against the pitch-black night. Bethwyn moved her hand over Hector's head, gently mopping his brow with the damp cloth, the warm scented water settling across his clammy skin. For seven days and nights she'd kept vigil over the Boarlord, Queen Amelie relieving her of her other responsibilities in order to care for the magister. She wondered if his terrible fever would ever break.

By the time the rowboats had returned to the *Maelstrom* from the White Isle, many had assumed the baron was bound for a watery grave, few giving him any chance of survival. His throat was torn and his blood loss great, the wound refusing to heal as a normal injury would for a therian. Using what medicinal knowledge she and others had, Bethwyn had patched Hector up, cleaning, staunching, and dressing the bite as best she could. She'd changed the bandage frequently over the following days, but the festering smell never went away. The Boarguard, Ringlin and Ibal, always lurked nearby, making Bethwyn uncomfortable. The tall one didn't have a nice word to say about anyone, and the looks the fat giggling one gave her made her skin crawl. All the while the Boarlord had clung to the sliver of life, refusing to give up his fight.

Bethwyn brushed the matted hair from Hector's brow. He'd lost a lot of weight since she'd first met him in Highcliff, his puppy fat all gone as his skin clung tightly to his cheek-bones. His skin had a deathly pallor to it, almost yellow beneath the lantern light. She shivered, throwing another piece of wood on to the stove. She closed the grille door with the poker before facing the sickly Boarlord once more.

Hector's left arm had found its way out of the covers. She picked it up at the wrist and elbow and was about to tuck it back below the blanket when she paused. She turned it over in her hands, revealing the palm. The black mark she'd seen when they'd encountered the Sirens had grown, the entire palm now blackened and the skin darkening between each finger. This wasn't the first time she'd examined the hand while Hector slept. While the rest of his body burned with a fever, the corrupted palm remained cold to the touch. *As cold as death itself*, thought Bethwyn.

Suddenly the hand snatched at her wrist, causing her to cry out in shock. It clasped hard, the chill flesh tight on her skin, fingers holding her in their grasp. Hector's eyes were open, watching her, his head motionless on the pillow.

"Gretchen."

His voice was a whisper, cracked lips trembling as he tried to smile. Bethwyn should have been happy to see his eyes and hear his voice, but she couldn't get over the shock of his grip. *He's mistaken me for another.* She tugged back, trying to free her wrist.

"I dreamed it was you. So caring and kind," he said slowly and quietly.

"Please, Hector; it's me, Bethwyn," she said, but he wouldn't relinquish his hold.

"I was in such a dark place, Gretchen, so cold and alone. And you were the warmth I could cling to. It was your light that brought me back from the darkness. It was your love."

"Hector, you're hurting me," she cried, as the magister's hand tightened its grip. *Can he not hear me?* It was as if he were unaware of his hand's action while her words simply didn't register.

"I knew you wouldn't abandon me to the dark," he said, eyes closing as tears rolled down his face. "I knew you'd save me from the nightmare, Gretchen . . ."

Bethwyn was crying out now, trying to prize his fingers away, but the more she struggled the tighter he held on. His words were rambling, making no sense, as if he were sleep talking. *Is he even conscious? Does he* know *he's hurting me?*

"I would speak with your father when the time comes, Gretchen. I would seek your hand my love, for we should be together. We *belong* together."

Bethwyn shrieked, frantically trying to shake him loose, as the door burst open. Vega was between the two of them immediately, trying to bat Hector's hand away. When he realized the Boar wouldn't relinquish his grip, he took his own fingers

240

to Hector's, pulling them back hard. The Sharklord was surprised by the magister's strength, the hold like a trap. Finally
the fingers opened enough to allow the girl to pull her arm
free, the flesh of her wrist livid with red welts.

"What are you *thinking*?" shouted Vega, shaking Hector by
the shoulders in his cot.

"What?" muttered Hector, his eyes blinking as if waking
from a dream. "I didn't . . ."

"You were *hurting* her!" said the count as Manfred and
Amelie appeared in the doorway. Bethwyn rushed into the
queen's arms.

"Bethwyn?" gasped Hector, deeply confused.

Manfred stood to one side, escorting Amelie and Bethwyn
from the room. He passed Ringlin and Ibal entering as he left,
the Staglord unable to resist glowering at the Boarguard. The
men watched the three leave before joining Vega in their sickly
master's cabin.

"I didn't know," whispered Hector. "I was dreaming . . ."

"Dreaming or not, Hector, that girl has tended to you for
the last seven days."

Vega leaned over the bed and brought his face close to
Hector's. "Tell me, Hector: did you *know* what was waiting for
us on that island? What kind of monster was that in the cavern? One of my men died on that beach, devoured by the dead,
while you explored that cave."

"I don't know . . . what you're talking . . ." stammered Hector, but the captain of the *Maelstrom* continued.

"I thought you and I had an understanding, Hector. I was there in Bevan's Tower, remember? I helped you with that mess. I thought it was an accident . . ."

"It *was* an accident, Vega!" cried Hector, fully awake now, his face contorting with resentment.

"That may be," said the Sharklord. "But our visit to the White Isle was no accident. Your encounter with that monster didn't look like a struggle to me, Hector. It looked like . . . like an *embrace* . . ."

Vega stood up, straightening his collar.

"I'm disappointed, Hector. I've looked out for you, shown you nothing but compassion and friendship, and this is how you repay me. Well, I'm watching you. You know more than you're telling us, only I'm not as foolish as the others. I know your secrets, just remember that."

Count Vega turned, barging between the Boarguard and slamming the cabin door shut as he left. Ringlin and Ibal watched him leave, then looked back to the Lord of Redmire as he lay in his sickbed. Hector's face darkened as he lifted his blackened hand to his throat. He took hold of the bandages, yanking them loose, the stained dressing crunching as he pulled it from his wound. The scar was scabbed over, slowly on the mend. He rubbed his black hand across his neck and heaved himself upright, swaying woozily on the bed. He looked at the two men, his face full of thunder, eyes bright with fury and revenge. The stare spoke volumes to the Boarguard. Ibal giggled and Ringlin nodded.

Hector's whisper hissed from his broken lips. "Vega must die."

5

OVERWHELMING ODDS

OPENING INTO THE ocean at Bloody Bay, the Silver River had earned its name on two counts. Firstly, as the main tributary from the Barebones to the Saber Sea, it was the swiftest and most profitable trade route for moving precious metals out of the mountains. It was said that whoever controlled the Silver River controlled Omir, the stewardship of the waterway being a constant bone of contention between the Werelords of the Desert Realm.

As Drew stood on the poop deck of the *Banshee* and looked east toward the sunrise, he marveled at the other cause for the river's name. With the sun's first rays breaking over the horizon, the mighty river threw its light back to the heavens. Drew squinted, raising his hand to shield his eyes from the metallic glare of the water.

"It's something else, isn't it?"

He blinked as his eyes slowly refocused on Lady Shah at his side.

"A jewel in the desert's crown," agreed Drew, turning from the blinding vision.

The crew made the most of the fair weather and unfurled the sails, grateful for the wind that spirited them westward up the river. Djogo stood at the wheel on the deck below, the former slaver enjoying his newfound freedom, even managing to share a rare joke with Drake, who lounged nearby. The sun's rays were warm on Drew's back, a welcome change from the freezing night. They might have been in the land of sand, but the night reminded him of the Cold Coast. Winter had arrived across Lyssia, even flirting with Omir. The snow-capped mountains of the Barebones straddled the horizon, their ultimate destination.

"When did you last visit the mountains?"

"Fifteen years ago," replied Shah, pausing to think about the long absence. "I was but a girl, handed over to Kesslar by Skeer, along with my father."

"And you've encountered no other Hawklords in your travels since then?"

"None. I hear mention of them occasionally, reported

sightings, but their spirits were broken when my father's wings were taken. We were a shamed species to King Leopold, lower than humans in his eyes."

"Do you really think your father can call them home? This Screaming Peak—it sounds like something from a storybook."

"He was taken there as a child by his father, its secrets passed on to him. I just hope we can find it."

The *Banshee* wasn't a huge ship, but she looked out of place on the Silver River. Her big black prow cut a great wake through the water, sending the smaller fishing vessels, barges, and skiffs toward the shores. The waterway was wide and deep, navigable to big ships such as the *Banshee* to where the river split at Two Rivers. This wild port town at the foot of the Barebones, where mountain met desert, was where the Werelords now headed. From Two Rivers they would disembark and hike on toward Tor Raptor. Drew's eyes settled on the former slaver who commanded the ship's wheel on the deck below, his thoughts returning to the private talks the two had shared.

"Djogo seems to be very fond of you," said Drew.

"What's he told you?"

"He says you're friends—that's all you can ever be, he a human, you a therian."

Shah shivered and smiled. "I've loved before, Drew, and it didn't end well ..." Her voice trailed off as she stared upriver to where a number of craft jostled against one another.

"What is it?" said Drake as he walked up to the poop deck to join them.

"A massacre," said Shah, still looking ahead, her face impassive. "An ambush."

"You can see *that*?" asked Drew, suddenly anxious. They had to retain their anonymity and stay out of the fray—the last thing the group needed was a fight, especially someone else's. He strained his eyes, seeing only blurs aboard the boats ahead, plus the occasional glint of steel.

"You have your nose, Wolf. I have my sight."

"Who's fighting?" asked Drake.

"Hard to tell, but the skiff in the middle is under attack from two others. They're badly outnumbered."

She arched an eyebrow. "A Doglord of some kind leads the assault."

"Really?" said Drew, mention of a therian so similar to his own kind piquing his interest. His instinct told him they should step in. The men of the *Banshee* had noticed the commotion as well, stopping their work to watch.

Shah saw that Drew was agitated. She placed a hand on his shoulder. "You cannot join every fight."

"It feels wrong," he growled as they watched the skirmish. He was about to say more when her fingers dug into his skin. He winced, noticing her nails had transformed into talons.

"What's the matter?" Drew gasped.

"A child's in danger!"

Before Drew could respond, Drake had taken a running jump, launching himself from the deck of the *Banshee*.

"Drake!" cried Shah, but the Crocodile was already gone, swimming speedily toward the fracas. The pair could see his long dark shape powering through the water in the direction of the three boats, transforming as he swam.

"He'll get himself killed!" fretted Shah.

"How many are there?" asked Drew.

"Too many."

Shah arched her back, gray wings emerging with a flourish. Her head was changing, features growing sharper, her nose and mouth blending together into an amber beak as a frill of charcoal feathers emerged through her black hair. A large avian eye stared down at Drew as he stood in the Hawklady's shadow.

She prepared to take flight, taking to the air from the *Banshee*'s wooden deck. Drew needed no invitation, catching hold of her legs as she took off. The Werehawk looked down, surprised at the presence of a passenger.

"You've carried me once before!" he shouted, as if to persuade her not to drop him. Shah shook him loose, his one hand not strong enough to keep hold, only to snatch him up again in her powerful talons. They quickly put the *Banshee* behind them as they closed in on the battle. Drake was there already, wading into the midst of the combatants, turning the air red around him. As they neared, Drew felt the change coming, the

Wolf's aspects gradually shifting through his body. By the time Shah was flying over the ambushed skiff, she was launching a changed Werewolf into a gang of shocked swordsmen.

Drew's claws flew, the lycanthrope spinning as he scattered the mob of attacking warriors along the deck. His foot crunched into a torso, ribs crumpling as the man was catapulted overboard. Drew's hand battered another, sending him colliding into his companion's blade, the two toppling in a bloody mess. A scimitar sailed down, one fighter finding a way past the claws toward the Werewolf's throat. Drew's trident dagger flashed, deflecting the blade off the basket hilt.

Drew took in the scene. The skiff's oarsmen lay dead, some floating facedown in the river, butchered in the attack. Two sleeker boats were moored alongside the skiff, grapples having hauled it in so the warriors could board. The dozen or so invaders wore crimson kashes, the splash of red reminding Drew of the Lionguard. He looked to the prow. A girl no more than ten years old cowered there, two warriors in white valiantly standing between her and the enemy, their dead comrades littering the deck.

Drake tried to cut his way through the red-kashed warriors toward the girl, but the attackers were ready for him, throwing their blades up as he tore into them. Drew was drawn to the towering dog-headed warrior in the middle of the skiff. He held an enormous spear in one hand, barking orders as he faced the therians.

"You've nothing to fear!" cried the Doglord to his soldiers. "Silver or not, they'll still bleed from your blades!"

The warriors attacked, spurred on by their master. Scimitars rained down on Drew and Shah. The Hawklady leaped off the boat to hover over the water, lashing out with her talons. Drew ducked and weaved, returning his own volley of claw, tooth, and dagger at the warriors. He glanced up to see the two brave defenders at the front of the skiff tumble lifelessly to their knees, the attackers' numerous scimitars too much for them. With mighty wing beats Shah rushed to the prow, landing over the girl and snatching up a pair of swords.

"Leave the girl alone!"

The red-kashed warriors hesitated for a moment, facing the transformed Werehawk armed with twin blades. The Doglord urged them forward, Shah's swords finding the first few who got too close, before the caninthrope turned to face the Werecrocodile. Bodies, oars, scimitars, and benches made the battleground uneven for all the combatants. The *Banshee* remained too far away, leaving the three therians alone in their fight against the men in red kashes. The Doglord's giant spear lanced through the air toward Drake, but the Crocodile stumbled clear and into the enemy mob. He went down beneath them as the Doglord turned his attention on Drew.

The spear splintered the deck where the Wolf had stood a moment earlier. Drew hurdled the weapon and leaped, kicking the Dog's jaw. The beast's head snapped back, the blow sending him crashing into his men. They pushed him forward once more, allowing him to take another stab at Drew. The Werehound was fast, and deadly with his spear, the blade finding Drew as he tried to dodge clear. The foot-long silver dagger tore deep into Drew's shoulder, tearing the flesh and glancing off bone. The Wolf howled in agony, dizzy with nausea from the deadly blade.

"You must be the Werewolf everyone's so keen to meet. Let's see what they make of you when I'm wearing your skin as a cloak!" the Doglord taunted.

The spear jabbed forward again, but Drew threw his head out of the way just in time, the blade missing his face by a hair's breadth. He took hold of the spear shaft as it passed, hooking it under his arm and throwing his weight behind it as he swung it hard to one side. The Doglord kept hold of the other end, unable to stop himself from being propelled into his own men. Three of them tumbled overboard and the Hound narrowly avoided joining them. But before Drew could press home his advantage the remaining red-kashed warriors leaped on him.

Drew lashed out blindly, but scimitar cuts crisscrossed his back as his attackers slashed at him, and blood pumped relentlessly from his shoulder wound. He was overwhelmed, knocking one red-kashed fighter off only to see two more take his place. The longer he remained on the deck, the more chance the fight would end badly. More sword blows were finding their mark now, the Doglord's warriors proving fearless and blindly obedient under his command.

But just as it began to look hopeless, the men in red started to fall away, their blows becoming less frequent as their numbers were thinned. Drew looked up to see hands, limbs, fingers, and flesh flying as Drake tore a path through the warriors toward him. The Doglord brought his spear around, striking out at the Werecrocodile, but Drake was too fast, his reptilian tail whipped out from behind. Two men went overboard, legs broken, before the tail struck the Doglord, sending him bouncing on to the deck, spear clattering down on top of him.

Two more soldiers stood over Drew, one aiming an executioner's blow to his neck. Drew knew all too well that no therian healing could replace a missing head. Drake was on them instantly, his reptilian body blocking the blows as he put himself in harm's way. The red warriors were strong but no match for a transformed therian gladiator. The executioner suddenly found he was missing a hand, Drake spitting it back at him as he toppled. The last man let loose a wail as the Crocodile's jaws closed around his neck and snapped closed. He let the body collapse to the deck before turning to his friend.

"Quick, Drew," gasped Drake, extending his clawed hand. "On your feet!"

One moment the Werecrocodile stood over Drew, the epitome of the heroic warrior, lit by the rising sun. The next, a foot-long silver spearhead burst from Drake's puffing chest. The Crocodile's face froze in agony. Drake's eyes rolled down to look at the bloody blade that protruded from his sternum. As Drew watched in horror the spearhead was savagely twisted before the Doglord whipped it free from behind with a roar of triumph.

Drew didn't wait for Drake's body to land.

The Wolf dived across the skiff to where the Doglord lay against the gunwales in a pile of broken oars, past the spear, hitting the monster with a ferocious impact. The hull splintered open, sending the wrestling therians into the Silver River, struggling for dominance as they sank. Drew's teeth found the Dog's muzzle and nose, biting down hard.

The Dog reached up, trying desperately to prize the jaws open, but it was hopeless. The struggling slowed, Drew's own head and chest thundering as he felt his last breaths escape his body. He released his hold and kicked back toward the surface, but not before he caught sight of the Doglord, choked and drowned on blood and water, sinking toward the bottom of the cold river.

Drew resurfaced as the *Banshee* neared, the two enemy boats having disengaged from the skiff now, beating a hasty retreat to the southern bank. Drew threw his arm over the skiff's broken side, taking a great lungful of air, his body already returning to human form. He clambered aboard, spying Shah with the girl in her arms, struggling to stand upright on the gore-slicked deck. Her face was ashen as she stared aft.

Drake lay on a bed of dead warriors, clawed hands over the hole in his chest. He, too, was returning to his human form while he clung to life, his lips smacking clumsily as he tried to smile at Drew. The young Wolflord crawled to him, placing his hand over the fatal wound.

"Never doubt it, Wolf . . ." whispered the dying therian as his eyes began to close. "I had your back . . ."

A tear rolled down Drew's cheek as he held Drake in his arms, the young Werecrocodile drifting off to sleep for the final time.

6

STRAIGHT AND TRUE

THE CANDLELIGHT CAST long shadows over the captain's desk as Count Vega dipped his quill pen into the inkpot. The nib swept across the open page, the Sharklord's handwriting as flamboyant as one would expect from the Pirate Prince. He'd kept a journal since his first commission as a captain, thirty of the leather-bound volumes filling the bookcase in his cabin. He was aware that the crew, many of whom were illiterate, considered the habit eccentric, but it was one of the few things that kept Vega feeling civilized during his travels.

The hour was late and the night quiet. With most aboard the *Maelstrom* asleep bar the skeleton crew, it was the perfect time to write uninterrupted. The ship, of course, was more crowded than usual; Vega had to wonder if he'd ever truly have

255

it back for himself. Although it was pleasant to spend time in the company of other Werelords, especially Manfred, his guests were beginning to overstay their welcomes. *Typical dirtwalkers*, his mother would have said. He'd get them to Roof all right, but he wasn't sure where his own path led. Perhaps he'd leave the *Maelstrom* with Figgis as he went inland with the queen and the duke—he couldn't abandon the Wolf's Council now.

Vega wondered if anyone truly considered him a changed character. He'd been described as "the count without a court," shamed for betraying Wergar to help Leopold rise to power. There was more to the story than that, of course. Bergan and Manfred had recovered well enough after bowing before Leopold, although Vega suspected the parts they'd played in the Wolf's downfall had kept them awake at night. He hoped so, anyway—he'd be cursed if he was the only Werelord who carried a guilty conscience wherever he went.

Vega's respect for Drew was a new feeling for the Sharklord. He'd sworn an oath of loyalty to the boy's father years ago, and Leopold since, but he'd taken those vows lightly. Young and impetuous, he'd been more concerned with gold, swashbuckling his way across the White Sea. Now, older and wiser, the count took his promise to the young Wolf seriously—to aid Wergar's son as they set about righting past wrongs and making Lyssia a safe place for all. With Bergan and Mikkel gone and Drew's whereabouts unknown, he held on to the hope that the Wolf's

Council still stood for something. He prayed to Sosha that the boy lived.

The ink burst from the nib suddenly, sending a small black puddle over his script. He cursed, blotting at it with a piece of paper. The stain slowly drying, Vega stared at the inkblot, and his thoughts drifted toward the last member of the Wolf's Council, the Baron of Redmire. Vega had seen Hector's palm while poor Bethwyn had nursed him. The girl had tried to keep the scarred hand hidden, possibly due to some misguided sense of loyalty, but the sea marshal had spied it all the same: a black mark. Hector's flesh was corrupted by something—but what?

Vega wasn't sure when it had happened, but things had gone very wrong for the Boarlord. The young man had been losing control long before the dreadful encounter on the White Isle. Had he started to unravel after the death of his brother? It had been an accident, of course. At least, Vega had *assumed* that was the case. He shook his head. No, Vincent was wicked; he'd have killed Hector that night if fate hadn't intervened. Perhaps Hector's ill luck had begun when he'd first communed with the dead Wylderman shaman in the Wyrmwood.

Hector's decline had really spiraled after Drew's departure. When they were all living in Highcliff, Vega had enjoyed the company of both young men, as had the entire Wolf's Council. It had been good to watch the boys' friendship blossom, each benefiting from the other's best traits. Drew had become more worldly wise with the Boarlord's help, whereas time with the Wolf had allowed Hector to become more confident, more vocal. Hector had changed further without Drew, but it was all for the worse.

The rapping of a loose rope against his cabin window pulled Vega away from his dark thoughts. He swiveled in his seat, staring back at the small panels of glass that filled the rear wall of the captain's quarters. The rope flashed faintly into view as it whipped down and struck the window. Vega grimaced: some fool hadn't tied the thing off. He hated seeing such lazy attention to detail on the *Maelstrom*, and if he did nothing about it now, it'd be sure to keep him awake all night. Replacing the quill in the inkpot, Vega rose from his desk, taking his black cape and fastening it around his throat. He checked the carriage clock that was fixed to his desk, which told him it was the second hour after midnight. Leaving the cabin he made his way above deck, heading aft.

Arriving aloft, Vega caught sight of a couple of crew members working on the foredeck. Only one sailor paid attention to the captain's arrival, the chief mate Figgis, who acknowledged him with a brief nod. The count glanced up the main mast, spying Casper on his way down from the midnight watch. Vega was proud of how seriously the lad took his duties as a cabin boy and lookout. He'd been up there for three hours, earning himself a warm bunk on his return. Marching up the steps to the poop deck, Vega passed the wheel, lashed down for the night, stepping through the darkness toward the stern.

Vega stopped at the railing. He'd expected the offending rope to be attached to a working part of the ship. Instead it was a relatively short length tied to the rail, serving no purpose. He looked over the side, spying the tattered end banging against his cabin windows as the water churned white below. *Who'd fasten a length of rope to the aft of the ship?* What good did it do other than annoy the count and bring him aloft? Vega looked at how the rope was tied; it wasn't a nautical knot, which meant it wasn't one of his crew. The Sharklord suddenly felt a sick, cold feeling in his stomach. He turned.

Hector stood behind him, flanked by two other figures in the shadows. His men kept an eye toward the prow of the *Maelstrom*, on the lookout for passersby, while the Boarlord's eyes were fixed on the count.

"What is this, Hector?" asked Vega, trying to keep his voice calm while his guts were in knots. *Why did he feel so anxious? How could Hector put him so on edge?*

"I needed to see you, Vega."

"Why the rope trick? You could have come and knocked for me. Don't you know, by now? My door's always open to friends, Hector."

Vega glanced past the trio, trying to spy anyone beyond them, but could see no one. They were alone.

"I needed you up here. On deck."

Hector's voice was rough from disuse. He'd not ventured

on to the deck since he'd awoken from his weeklong coma. Clearly, the Boarlord had chosen the time of this meeting carefully.

"Well," said Vega, opening his arms. "You have my attention. What do you want?"

Vega smiled, but it was a mask. The poop deck seemed charged with energy, the Sharklord's ears threatening to pop as if a great pressure was in the air.

"You kept pushing, Vega."

"What?"

"You kept poking, belittling me."

"What are you talking about, Hector?"

"You treat me like a child, a foolish boy who can't do anything right. Is that how you see me?"

Hector took a couple of steps forward. If he'd been in awe of Vega previously, he wasn't showing it. Hector didn't seem the least bit nervous about challenging the Wereshark.

"Hold on," said Vega, wanting to raise his voice but sensing that, if he did, something very bad might happen. The Sharklord's hunches rarely steered him wrong. "I don't know what you're talking about, but you're mistaken. I've stood by your side, my young friend, through every cursed thing that's happened."

"Don't patronize me, *friend*," spat Hector. "As for being at my side, perhaps *you're* the cursed one. Perhaps it's *you* who brings misery and death to all you touch."

260

Vega saw the young Boarlord's hands curled into fists at his side. His men were no calmer, each of them agitated as they shadowed him. Vega could see where this was heading.

"Hector," he said calmly. "Before you do anything stupid, just think—"

"*Silence!*" hissed Hector, throwing his ungloved hand up, palm open toward the captain of the *Maelstrom*.

Vega couldn't get another word out. His throat felt restricted, closed tight as if held by some invisible force. He clawed at his neck, fingers scratching the skin, trying to sever whatever constricted him but finding nothing. The sensation was sickening, an invisible noose around his throat, tightening as he struggled. He wanted to shout, to scream, but Hector had silenced him utterly. He took a step forward, grabbing Hector by the shoulders. He tried to mouth the word *please*, but all that came forth was spittle.

Vega's eyes widened as he felt something cold and sharp in his gut. He felt it cut through his flesh, burying itself among his internal organs as the blood flowed out around it. Hector's face contorted with both horror and sadness, eyes red with tears.

"Getting rid of Vincent," whispered Hector. "Did you think you could keep me in your debt forever? You're just like the others, Vega. Worse: you're a two-faced serpent. You belong on the seabed with the other bottom-dwellers."

Hector stepped back, as Vega, still spluttering, looked

down. In his hands the Boarlord held an arrow, its beautifully crafted silver head slick with blood. Where had Hector got it from? *It doesn't matter now*, thought Vega, his fingers fumbling over his stomach as his white shirt turned crimson.

Ringlin and Ibal stepped forward, the fat one giggling quietly as he handed a burlap sack with an attached rope to the tall one. Ringlin lifted the rope over Vega's head, a noose that fitted snugly around the count's neck. He pulled it tight before releasing it. Vega instantly staggered at the weight of the sack, recognizing the unmistakable clang of the heavy balls of shot from the *Maelstrom*'s cannons.

Hector snapped his left hand shut, black hand vanishing out of sight, as Vega struggled to breathe with the sack around his throat. He wanted to beg Hector, ask him to stop the madness, apologize for whatever wrongs the lad imagined the count had done him. But he didn't get the chance.

Hector nodded to his henchmen, who stepped forward and grabbed Count Vega, fearsome captain of the *Maelstrom*, Pirate Prince of the Cluster Isles and terror of the White Sea. They gave him a hearty shove, sending him flying back over the aft rail of the ship.

Hector turned away before Vega had even gone over the side. To his shock and horror he saw the cabin boy, Casper, barge past him out of nowhere and sprint between Ringlin and Ibal as they deposited the Sharklord into the cold Sturmish Sea.

Ibal was quick with his sickle, grabbing the boy by his mop of hair and whipping the curved blade to his throat.

"No!" gasped Hector, his old self returning briefly.

Kill the boy! snarled the Vincent-vile gleefully, fresh from throttling the Sharklord. *He's seen too much!*

Before Hector could issue any command, the lad bit down hard on the fat man's hand and stamped on his foot. Ibal relinquished his grip instantly and Casper didn't hesitate, leaping overboard after his captain.

Hector rushed to the rail and looked over, astonished by the boy's suicidal act of blind loyalty. All he saw was the white water disappearing behind the *Maelstrom*, the great ship leaving her dying captain to the ocean as a lonely length of rope whipped behind her in the black night.

7

THE JEWEL OF OMIR

IF HIGHCLIFF'S DEFENSES had once impressed Drew, the walls of Azra put them firmly in the shade. The shining city walls rose fifty feet high, encircling Omir's capital like a steel crown. Sandblasted by fierce winds, the mighty walls were polished like glass, breathtaking to the eye and intimidating to the enemy. The battlements were manned by gold-helmeted warriors, looking down at the people who crowded around the River Gate. Drew couldn't help but stare as he and his companions approached, jaw slack with awe behind his kash.

The *Banshee* remained moored in Kaza, a small port a mile south of Azra and used by the great city for access to the river. The Silver Road that ran between the two was marked by many small shops, inns, and trade posts, effectively forming a ramshackle town of its own. Those who couldn't gain access to Azra had settled on the Silver Road, waiting for their chance to enter, and many had put down roots, now calling the road their home.

Merchants from the river traveled up the road to queue and seek entrance into King Faisal's city. But there were others present: families with children, fearful-looking people who sought refuge in Azra. Drew was shocked by the number of slaves they also encountered, shackled to one another by chain and collar. Some ferried goods up and down the Silver Road, while others carried their masters and mistresses in silk-covered chairs over the heads of the crowd. It was in the middle of this throng where Drew found himself, jostled by slave and trader as he and his companions pushed toward the gate.

"Bringing the girl to the Jackal's door was a mistake. We should have handed her over to the port authorities," growled Djogo.

"I'd sooner leave her with Kesslar," said Drew, thinking back to the unruly dockers they'd encountered in Kaza. The girl was in a state of shock after the fight on the river that morning, too traumatized to speak. The Werelords had taken the slain body of Drake to the shore, breaking the journey to bury the brave Werecrocodile. They had worked alongside one another, digging deep into the hot sand as they prepared the grave. Krieg had said a few words for their fallen brother while the rest watched in silent respect. None would forget the sacrifice Drake had made in saving the lives of both Drew and the child. The young Wolflord and his companions had decided to take the girl to the city, delivering her safely to the gate guards. They would know what to do with her.

Walking beside Drew, Lady Shah carried the girl in her arms. The girl had warmed to Shah, and the Hawklady had taken her under her wing. In addition to the slain soldiers who'd accompanied the girl, Djogo had found the body of an older, noble-looking gentleman, a silver javelin piercing his chest. Judging by the choice of weapon, Drew assumed he'd been a known Werelord, the girl perhaps a relative. Either way, Azra was the safest place for her.

"Are random attacks common on the Silver River?" Drew asked Djogo as Shah pushed on ahead through the crowd, the exhausted girl sleeping in her arms.

"Yes, but they're usually river pirates, not Doglords and Omiri warriors. That was a coordinated attack; seems the dead Werelord back there had enemies."

Four warriors from the *Banshee* followed them, pulling a covered cart along behind. The body of the slain nobleman lay beneath the tarpaulin.

"Are there not safer ways to travel than the river?"

The tall warrior shrugged.

"In the Desert Realm? It's a balancing act. The smaller your group, the more chance you have of traveling unnoticed, but if you're attacked, you're in trouble. The larger your number, the more noticeable you are to your enemies, but the likelier you are to get there in one piece. The Omiri are a secretive people—they've turned subterfuge into a fine art. Misdirection and smokescreens have won numerous wars in the desert."

Djogo clapped the boards of the wagon behind them. "If war is on Omir's doorstep, then the realm's therians will be returning to their respective homes, quickly and quietly. Our friend here wasn't as well versed in subterfuge as his brethren."

"Perhaps he was betrayed?"

"Not our problem now. Let's drop the child and corpse off and be on our way."

"I can't believe how many slaves I'm seeing. I hadn't ex-pected to see this outside of Scoria."

"I'll say one thing for the Jackals," whispered Djogo. "They treat their slaves better than the Lizards do. But that wouldn't take much, would it?"

"Sounds like you don't want to be here."

"You don't know the half of it, Wolf," said the warrior as they neared the gate, pulling his kash across his face.

A dozen soldiers stood at the gate, checking the papers of anyone who sought admittance into Azra. Wearing golden hel-mets that rose to sharp points, some carried scimitars at their hips. Others carried the long spears that the Omiri favored. At nine feet long they were somewhere between a pike and javelin. The guards wore yolk-yellow capes around their shoulders. All in all, they looked both regal and lethal.

Suddenly, the crowd shuffling up toward the gate seemed to get thicker, and Drew found himself separated by the pushing throng, which drove a wedge between him and his companions.

"Djogo," called Drew, trying to catch the tall warrior's attention, but he and the other crew members pulling the cart had fallen behind. Looking forward, Drew saw Shah had reached the guards and was trying to reason with a man who appeared to be an officer. The girl shifted in the Hawklady's grasp, beginning to wake with the din of the crowd.

Drew found himself shoved to the front of the shouting and bickering traders, face-to-face with some more of the guards. One of them said something unintelligible to Drew.

"I'm sorry," he said. "I don't understand."

The guard's officer overheard Drew's remark, and left Shah momentarily, stepping closer to speak with the young Westlander.

"You're not Omiri?" he asked, his voice thickly accented but understandable.

"No." Drew smiled awkwardly.

"I tried to explain . . ." called Shah, but the man ignored her.

"Only Omiri enter Azra!" said the man harshly.

"I don't seek entrance!" said Drew, aware that he was shouting and struggling to be heard. Both the officer and Drew caught sight of a scuffle taking place, beyond where Djogo and the men from the *Banshee* stood with the handcart. An altercation between merchants had descended into a fistfight. The officer looked back at Drew.

"Then what do you seek?"

"If you'd let me finish . . ." yelled Shah, but the officer's attention returned to the brawl. Many in the crowd were jeering as the merchants fought, the guards standing back while the men exhausted themselves. A fat slaver watched from his silk-covered sedan chair, clapping with glee. The fight was spreading as one of the merchants knocked into a woman carrying a tall basket of fruit. The basket tumbled, clattering into Djogo and the *Banshee*'s men, sending an avalanche of lemons over them. More fists flew as the woman's companions joined the melee.

"Who is this man?" said the captain to Shah as he poked Drew's chest.

At that moment, the crowd barged into the fat slaver's litter and sent it over, crashing into the handcart. A wheel sheared off, clattering over onto the wailing slaver's body, while the Werelord's corpse toppled from the broken cart on to the road. Several women in the crowd screamed, spurring the guards to push forward through the panicking mob. Soldiers and civilians instantly recognized the slain therian. Acting quickly, half the guards tried to hold the crowd back while others moved toward the men from the *Banshee*.

At that moment, Djogo's kash fell loose as he was jostled by the crowd.

"Djogo!"

The guards' cries of recognition were not happy ones. *They know him*, realized Drew. *Curse the man and his business with Kesslar!*

The soldiers immediately lowered their long spears and unsheathed their scimitars. In response, the tall, one-eyed warrior whipped out his own weapons. The crowd parted as the fistfight suddenly escalated into sword fight. Not prepared to leave their man outnumbered, the warriors from the *Banshee* withdrew their daggers and shortswords.

"Wait!" cried Shah, making a grab at the officer. With the fight spiraling out of control, the captain mistook Shah's hand as an assault. He swung his arm back, scimitar pommel crashing into Shah's forehead, sending woman and girl to the ground, instantly lost in the crowd.

"Don't harm them!" shouted Drew, pushing past the guards to get to them.

To his horror Drew found the commander now turning on him, taking hold and twisting Drew's forearm in his grasp. He stumbled onto one knee, surprised at the other's strength. The officer forced Drew's hand up his back, the young man bellowing as he threatened to collapse. He couldn't get into a fight, yet he couldn't allow his companions to be harmed.

"You don't understand! We just want to leave the girl with you!"

He tried to plead, but the soldier wouldn't listen. Feet stamped around him as another turbaned warrior came forward, striking Drew over his head with the flat of his blade. Drew's head rang as he collapsed on to the sand-covered flags and the officer jumped on him. Through the legs of the crowd, he could see Shah, trampled by the wild mob.

Drew had no choice.

The first notion the captain had that he was no longer wrestling with a human was when the arm he held twisted violently, throwing him one hundred and eighty degrees through the air. He landed with a crunch, his view of the world on its head as the beast rose to its full height, towering over him. The crowd screamed as the Werewolf roared.

Drew's eyes scanned the crowd around the overturned cart as they backed away. Djogo and the gladiators were being overpowered by superior numbers, and the guards had already removed Shah from the chaos. Of the child, there was no sign. Drew felt sick, having brought the girl to the gates of Azra only for her to be lost.

Reinforcements flooded out of the gate as the Omiri circled him, scimitars and spears raised. They'd clearly fought Werelords before, and were treating Drew with a healthy dose of respect. He snapped his jaws, lashing out with the trident dagger while he frantically tried to decide what to do. Overhead, bowmen lined the walls, taking aim at the Wolf.

Fools, he thought. *Can't they see we were bringing an innocent to them?* But all the guards saw was a target to take down. He needed to get back to the *Banshee,* regroup with the others, and find a way of rescuing their companions. He couldn't be drawn into a fight here. These men were innocent—foolish, but innocent. He couldn't take their lives.

Dropping into a crouch he sprang backward, high, narrowly avoiding the guards' long spears before landing behind them. A dozen arrows rained down from the walls, half of them finding their target. The Werewolf crashed to the floor, the wind taken from his sails. The arrows weren't silver, but they hurt. Drew cried with agony as he scrambled to his feet, body still aching from the river battle wounds.

Drew stumbled down the Silver Road toward the port of Kaza, onlookers screaming and moving clear as he lurched along. The long spears flew, most hitting the paved road or bouncing off Drew's thick, furred skin, but a couple punched their way home, breaking flesh and jarring bone. He howled, going down again.

Booted Omiri feet surrounded him now as, dizzied, he tried to keep moving, willing his body on.

"Wolf!"

The shout came from the captain of the guard behind. The Werewolf looked back, guards parting to reveal the captured men of the *Banshee*. The captain forced Djogo to his knees, the prisoner's hands tied behind his back. Raising his scimitar high, the blade hovered in the air above the ex-slaver's neck, ready to fly.

PART V

DANGEROUS GAMES

I

WITNESS

LOOKING BACK NERVOUSLY, the young woman checked she wasn't being followed as she hurried along the lurching corridor. Clutching the bottle of water, Bethwyn walked past the queen's cabin and continued on, deeper into the belly of the *Maelstrom*. With a final glance to ensure she was alone, the girl from Robben opened the door to the dark cargo hold and slipped inside.

Closing the door firmly, Bethwyn weaved between the lashed-down crates and barrels, gingerly making her way toward the prow. The hold's contents were severely depleted, many weeks at sea having exhausted the *Maelstrom*'s provisions, leaving the pirates surviving on short rations and in desperate need of making land. Upon hearing the queen was thirsty, the ship's cook, a gaunt fellow named Holman, had handed over the bottle to the lady-in-waiting, telling her to make it last; fresh water was a luxury, more precious than food.

As Bethwyn neared the prow, she felt guilty for taking the bottle from Holman. He was a kind man who had always ensured she got a little extra when serving up the crew's meager portions of food. But she'd needed the bottle, an excuse to go belowdecks and disappear for a while, attending her mistress. There were prying eyes aloft that might question her absence without any plausible reason. She finally arrived at the thick curved wall that marked the head of the hold and the prow of the *Maelstrom*. The others waited, gathered around a hooded lantern that gave out a tiny amount of light.

"Nobody followed you?" asked Amelie, moving up along the crate where she sat to make room. Bethwyn collapsed beside her, shaking her head.

"He doesn't suspect you?" asked Duke Manfred.

"He asked where I was going. If he follows that up, Master Holman will tell him the same thing—I'm with the queen, not to be disturbed." Bethwyn raised the bottle as if to emphasize the ruse.

"Good," said Manfred, rubbing his knuckles against his temple. "What we discuss must never reach Hector's ears."

"Murderous traitor," said Figgis, eyes narrowing in his leathery old face.

"Steady on," said Manfred. "We don't know for sure he's a killer."

"You call me a liar? I saw it with my own eyes!"

"What on earth would young Hector gain from killing Vega? The count was his friend. I question what you saw. I have to. I owe that to Hector."

The first mate spat at mention of the magister's name.

"Gentlemen," said Amelie, raising her hand gently.

Figgis bowed to his queen before nodding to Manfred. The duke returned the gesture, to Bethwyn's relief. She'd watched the old pirate trying to hold his nerve over the course of the day. He'd reported what he'd seen directly to Amelie late last night, hot on the heels of the captain disappearing. A search of the boat had followed, whereupon the crew discovered that Casper was gone, too. Everyone aboard the *Maelstrom* was suspicious, none more so than Figgis, who'd stared daggers at Hector and his men all day long. It was only now, the following night, that the four had the opportunity to discuss the events in detail.

"It's as I said last night," said Figgis, his wiry arms sagging as he recounted what he'd seen. "I was doing my rounds when the captain come aloft, disappeared up to the poop deck, and never came back. The boy followed him up there, too. Then the three of them—Hector and his men—came down. Asked them where the captain was, I did. They said they'd never seen him.

When I got up there they was nowhere to be seen, neither the captain nor the boy."

Bethwyn was surprised to see tears rolling down Figgis's cheeks. The old man was as hard as they came, a long life of piracy behind him and many years by Vega's side. As first mate he'd taken command of the *Maelstrom*, but the responsibility didn't sit easy on his gnarled shoulders.

"Why didn't you challenge Hector at the time?" said Amelie.

"Question the Boarlord, Your Majesty?" Figgis shook his head. "I didn't know right away what had gone on. I went up there to find the captain gone, a bloodstain on the deck. By the time I returned your Lord of Redmire had scarpered to his cabin, along with his men."

Manfred shook his head wearily.

"It makes no sense. *Why* would Hector harm one of us, especially one who's looked out for him these recent months?"

"May well be that the captain looked out for him," said Figgis. "But look at what happened in Moga. Then we had the White Isle—that was his doing, too, so the captain said. That traitor let us land there when he knew it was cursed. He's a bad one, that boy."

"How can you say that? Hector's given everything in the service of the Wolf's Council, Figgis."

Manfred can't help himself, thought Bethwyn. *He has to defend*

Hector. He knows there's good in him, and can't believe there's any bad.

The Staglord continued. "Couldn't it be that Vega slipped? Struck his head? Fell overboard?"

Figgis laughed. "This is a Wereshark you're talking about, my lord. The captain knew every inch of the *Maelstrom* blindfolded. I never saw him slip on this deck in all the years I've been with him. And even if he fell overboard, he's a shark. He'd have swum back to the ship, wouldn't he?"

"Unless he was injured," said Amelie.

"Exactly, Your Majesty," said the first mate. "And regardless of whether the captain fell overboard or not, there's Casper going missing, too. Two going overboard and not a trace of either?"

"I have to agree with Duke Manfred here," Amelie put in. "Captain Figgis, I believe you saw what you say, I truly do. But the notion that this dear young man could have done something so out of character? It's simply too much."

Figgis looked like he might scream, his face shifting from bloodless white through angry red and then furious purple.

"I believe Figgis."

Manfred and Amelie turned to look at Bethwyn, the girl's big brown eyes wide with fright, but chin set with determination.

"You believe him?" asked Manfred incredulously. "But Hector's your friend!"

"I cannot let friendship stand in the way of the truth, Your Grace."

"What makes you think this is true, my dear?" said Amelie, placing her palms over the trembling lady-in-waiting's hands. "Is this on account of what happened when he woke from his long slumber? Surely you realized that was his fever talking?"

"That was upsetting, Your Majesty, but there were other things. His hand . . ."

"What about it?" said Manfred.

"Something . . . something *bad* has got into it. His hand is blackened, Your Grace. It's so cold to the touch, too. It reminds me of dead skin, all the life leached from it. I saw it well enough when I tended him."

"A diseased hand doesn't make for a diseased mind," said Amelie, but the girl from Robben continued.

"When the Sirens attacked the ship, Hector killed one that would have slain me, only from a great distance away. His left hand, the black palm—he had it open, as if controlling something. I know Hector's a magister, and I know he uses magicks and cantrips to heal, but this was something else."

Manfred sighed. "The communing."

Amelie looked at the Staglord with horror. "Hector has *communed*? When?"

"The first occasion was in the Wyrmwood, when he, Drew, and Gretchen encountered Vala."

"The *first* occasion?" gasped the queen. "This has happened more than once?"

"Yes, regrettably. We thought we'd steered him off that course, but perhaps he has continued to commune in secret."

The four were silent. Bethwyn tried to stifle her tears, holding them back with all her will. She felt as though she'd betrayed Hector, but he was a changed boy from the bumbling Boarlord who'd made his bashful appearances at Buck House. She feared for him.

"So," said Amelie quietly. "What do we do with him?"

"I've been on ships where the likes of him would've been thrown overboard like bait," spat Figgis. "So long as he's aboard the *Maelstrom* he's cursing us all. Who knows what he might do next?"

Amelie and Bethwyn shivered at the thought of the pirate's justice, but neither spoke up.

"No, we won't execute him," said the Staglord. "He'd need a trial before his peers and besides, we still have no evidence. If he *did* send Vega and the boy overboard, how did he do it? And how did he make sure the count never came back?"

"He can't stay on board," said Figgis, his voice calm. "The men already whisper. They won't hold back forever."

Manfred rose, stretching. "We need to return to our quarters, show our faces aloft before our absence alerts Hector."

The others stood, Manfred helping Amelie to her feet.

Figgis picked the lantern up, peering through the dark hold and checking the path ahead.

"Lead the way, Captain Figgis," said Manfred, placing a hand on the old man's shoulder.

"I wish you wouldn't call me that," muttered the old pirate. "There's only one captain of the *Maelstrom*, the best man I ever sailed with, and he's in Sosha's arms now."

The old pirate stopped, his free hand scratching at the thin white hair at the back of his head. He turned back to the therians, his eyes catching the lantern light and glowing like embers.

"There's one more thing I'd wanted to tell you, my lord and lady, but feared not on account of an oath."

"An oath?"

"Aye, my lord. To Captain Vega. Only thing is, he's dead now, ain't he? So, where does that leave my oath?"

Manfred glanced to Amelie and Bethwyn, but the women had no answer.

"If there's something you need to tell us, Figgis, go ahead man."

"The captain . . . he *did* something for your baron. He got rid of something for him."

"What's that supposed to mean?" said Manfred.

"We thought it was an accident, y'see? Captain didn't think it was done on purpose, but the more I think about it, the more I think Hector *meant* to kill him."

"Kill who?" said Amelie.

"Lord Vincent," said Figgis. "Hector killed his brother."

Amelie gasped.

"Why would Vega help Hector cover this up?" asked Manfred, shaking with shock.

"Like I say, the captain believed it was an accident, but he could see others thinking otherwise. If word got out, Hector's life would be as good as over. I got rid of the Boarlord's body myself, Sosha forgive me. What a fool I was."

Manfred patted Figgis on the shoulder. "Your loyalty to Vega, even in death, is commendable, but you've done the right thing by telling us."

The Staglord fixed each of them with a steady gaze. "It's more important than ever before that we remain tight-lipped over what we've discussed here tonight. This is a dangerous game we play with the Boarlord. Hector appears deadlier than I could've ever imagined. He can never know our plans."

"But what *are* our plans?" said Amelie.

"I need to inspect the count's sea charts," said Manfred. "Vega may yet be able to help us, from beyond the grave."

2

IN THE JAWS OF THE JACKAL

"YOU'RE A LONG way from home, Wolf."

The two captives stood alongside one another, surrounded by the royal court and twenty of Azra's finest warriors. While Djogo's gaze was fixed on his feet, Drew's eyes lingered on the frescoed domed ceiling above, the centuries-old art predating anything he'd seen in the galleries of Highcliff. He looked around. Majestic marble pillars and busts of ancient kings, fluttering curtains laced with gold and priceless artifacts from Lyssia and beyond—the show of opulence wasn't missed by Drew. He'd grown up under the mistaken belief that the Omiri were savages. A quick glance around the palace revealed that nothing could have been further from the truth. Here was an ancient, rich culture to rival anything in the Seven Realms.

Drew let his gaze return to the figure on the throne who had spoken: King Faisal, the Jackal of Omir.

"Not by choice. I'm sorry if my arrival has caused you any concern," Drew said, raising his bound arms toward the seated figure. His forearms had been lashed together, knotted behind his elbows. "If you could remove these ropes, I'll be on my way."

The crowd laughed, all except the king, who rose from his throne. The audience quieted instantly as he strode gracefully down the dais steps toward Drew and his companion. By Drew's reckoning, Faisal had to be as old as Bergan if he'd fought Wergar during the Werewar. If so, he wore his years well, the Werejackal's tanned skin smooth without scars and wrinkles, his features fine and unspoiled. He wore a simple white toga and a crown of twined golden rope. His feet were bare and paced silently across the polished marble floor. Beautiful wasn't a word Drew would ordinarily use to describe a man, but in Faisal's case no other would fit. The king came to a halt before Drew, his almond eyes inspecting the Wolf intently.

"You have your father's arrogance." His voice was rich and honey-toned, matching his appearance. Although Western wasn't his first language, he was as fluent as any lord of Lyssia in the tongue.

"If I do, it's dumb luck," said Drew. "I never met Wergar."

"Then your arrogance is your own, Wolf. Your dead, arrogant father would be proud."

Drew prickled. He'd never known Wergar and stories of his exploits were mixed, his role ranging from hero to barbarian. Regardless, Faisal's words cut deep.

"I understand Wergar waged war with Omir, Your Majesty," said Drew. "But that was his war. Not mine."

"Your father was the only Werelord ever to break the defenses of Azra, and without the forces of Brackenholme and Stormdale to assist him. It cost him the lives of many. For months he campaigned in my burning deserts, his men dying of thirst and starvation. If he hadn't had the help of the Hawklords, his bones would have joined those of his Wolfguard in the sand."

There was mention of the Hawks of the Barebones again, loyal to Wergar.

"The Hawklords helped him win that war?"

"The Hawklords would side with anyone who might help feather their nest!" shouted a pale-skinned, stocky man in a long black cloak. He looked out of place in the Omiri palace.

"I don't believe that," said Drew. "Griffyn's a good man, a noble therian, one of the last of his kind."

"You claim to know the old Hawk?" scoffed the man in black. "He's probably dead now, a relic of the past. There are few of them left, and the only good one sits in Windfell: Baron Skeer!"

Faisal smiled. "You'll have to forgive my guest, Lord Rook. The Crowlords have never seen eye to eye with the Hawklords. I'd have to say I agree with him. Then again, the Crows never attacked my city, did they?

"I swore fealty to the Wolf to end the siege of Azra, but that agreement didn't last long. By the time he limped home to Westland, bloodied and battered from the fight in Omir, his therian brothers had turned on him, handing his head to the Lion on a platter. They tell me you consider those who betrayed your father your friends and allies: the Bearlord and Staglords?"

"Bergan explained what happened long ago. He kept no secrets from me. If you're hoping to make me doubt my friends, you're barking up the wrong tree, King Faisal."

The king sneered, disappointed. "No doubt you now know that your precious Wolf's Council is broken? The Bearlord's dead, I hear, and the surviving Staglord lost. You'd be the last flame the Catlords need to snuff out, and then Lyssia will finally be rid of the Wolf."

Drew hung his head, the blow hitting home. Faisal nodded, content to see the youth's heartache.

"How have I wronged you, Your Majesty?"

Faisal's laughter was musical, joined by the guffaws of his courtiers. The king shook his head and sighed.

"It's bad enough you come to my city, the son of the only therian ever to defeat me in battle. Yet look who *accompanies* you."

The king turned to face Djogo, his hand reaching out and gently taking the tall warrior's jaw in his slender fingers. He lifted the brute's head, almond eyes widening as he stared into Djogo's one good eye.

"Djogo," he whispered. "Kesslar's hound, returning to the scene of the crime."

"What crime?" asked Drew.

"Your companions didn't explain what business they'd had in Azra previously, then? Splendid. Let me elaborate."

Djogo glanced at Drew briefly, the look apologetic. *What in Brenn's name did you do, Djogo?*

"The Goatlord, Kesslar, lodged here for a time," continued the king, pacing around the bound men. "Initially, he was a generous, thoughtful guest, and we were most gracious hosts."

"He was a slaver!" interrupted Drew.

"Look around you, Wolf. Azra is built on slaves. They're a currency like any other in Omir.

"It didn't take him long to betray our trust. He invited three of my cousins aboard his ship to dine. They took gifts, as is our tradition: gold, jewels, and spices. My cousins and their entourages stayed with him aboard his vessel as guests that night.

"When the morning came, they were gone. The bodies of several guards were found in the Silver River, throats slit. Your work, Djogo?"

The ex-slaver said nothing, his eyes returning to the floor.

"Where are they now, fiend? My people, my cousins? Do they live, or did they die in some distant arena, for the amusement of Kesslar and his friends?"

Djogo spoke at last. "All were sold into slavery, but only the strongest went to the arena. Two Jackals died in the Furnace in Scoria. The third, the youngest, was sold to a Bastian Catlord."

"Brenn, no," muttered Drew miserably. "Why, Djogo?"

The tall warrior looked at Drew, his face emotionless. "I worked for Kesslar. I was a slaver. It was the only world I knew. There was no right or wrong; it was my job."

Drew thought Faisal might strike Djogo at any moment, the king's face shimmering with fury. He bared his teeth as he looked at each of them, speaking clearly and with deadly purpose.

"I see you each bear the mark of gladiator upon your shoulders. That pleases me greatly."

As he spoke, the crowd backed away, while the golden-helmed palace guard stepped forward, long spears and scimitars raised.

"You've got us wrong, Faisal," said Drew. "We're not friends of Kesslar's—we're his enemies, as are you!"

"Finding your voice now, Wolf? Do you plead for forgiveness?"

Drew growled as he answered. "I've done you no wrong. We brought a child to your gate, a girl who'd been attacked upon the river."

"You brought the body of Prince Fier to our gates, Wolf!" shouted the king. "The child who accompanied him was nowhere to be seen!"

"That's not true! We had no idea who that corpse was,

only that he was heading to Azra when he was attacked! Why *else* would we bring his body to you? The girl was the only survivor—"

"They killed Prince Fier," interrupted Rook. "You can't trust the Wolf—no wonder half of Lyssia hunts him. No doubt he and Kesslar's people are agents of the Doglords, sent here to cause your family further harm. Kill him now, Your Majesty. Do every realm a favor."

"The child!" cried Drew. "Someone must have *seen* her! We brought her here along with your slain lord!"

"There was no child," said Faisal. "What? You thought you could show us the body of my uncle and demand a ransom for my daughter?"

"Your daughter? We brought her back to you! Search for her; you'll find her!"

"Just words!" cried Faisal as he paced back up the marble steps to his throne. "Even now my warriors make their way to Kaza to seize your ship. I'll find my daughter, wherever you've hidden her, so beg away, Wolf. You'll say anything now to spare your life!" He turned to his guards adding, "And throw the cyclops a weapon; he'll need it."

Two guards hastily untied the captives. As they stepped back, one threw a scimitar on to the floor, the blade ringing as it struck the marble. Djogo glanced at it and then back to Drew.

"We won't fight," said the ex-slaver, standing shoulder to shoulder with the man he'd sworn his allegiance to.

Drew spoke. "The Djogo you knew may have been a killer, Faisal, but he's a changed man now."

"Nobody ever truly changes. Bring the woman."

Drew and Djogo watched in alarm as the struggling figure of Lady Shah was dragged into the throne room. She kicked and fought as she was hauled before the king, her hands bound and her face bearing bruises. A white gag was looped around her face, muffling her screams.

"I never forget a face. Lady Shah, isn't it? A friend of yours and Kesslar's?" said Faisal. He aimed the question at Djogo.

Lord Rook walked over to Shah and gripped her tightly by the arms. The Crow held his cheek close to hers, as a lover might in an embrace.

"Lady Shah," he whispered. "Daughter of Baron Griffyn. How the Hawks fall . . ."

Rook raised a stubby silver dagger to Shah's throat, placing the point into the hollow beneath her chin. Her eyes widened, pleading for him to stop.

"You *will* fight," said Faisal. "Or the woman dies."

"Don't do this, Faisal!" yelled Drew.

His words were wasted though and should have been directed at Djogo. The tall warrior bent down to the ground, snatching up the scimitar. His good eye blinked, as he shook his head.

"I'm so sorry, Drew," said the ex-slaver.

The scimitar scythed through the air.

3
DUEL

DREW AND DJOGO paced around one another across the patterned throne room floor, a black marble mosaic flecked with the bright white stars of the heavens.

"We don't have to do this," said Drew, his feet moving, keeping the distance between them constant. The guards formed a circular wall of spears and swords around them, weapons lashing out when the combatants got too close. A transformed Drew might have bounded over them, but he didn't fancy his odds of clearing the long spears from a standing jump.

"We do," said Djogo, shifting the scimitar in his grip.

"If either of us dies, it's for what?"

"If you die, it's so that Shah lives," said the warrior. "If I die, it's Brenn's wish that you go on from here."

"And if neither of us dies?"

"If neither of us dies . . . they kill Shah." Djogo glanced to where Rook held the Hawklady, the knife jutting into her neck. "You heard what he said."

Faisal watched from his throne as the other nobles gathered around him, fellow Jackals who shared his hatred for the Wolf and the Goat.

Rook suddenly shouted, jabbing Shah in the jaw, the blade breaking the surface of her flesh.

"Fight!"

Shah kicked her heels, boots squeaking as they scraped the marble, unable to writhe away from the Crow's grip.

That was enough for Djogo.

The warrior lunged at Drew, the scimitar cutting an X through the air. Though still weary from their encounter at the River Gate, both men were recovered enough to fight for their lives.

Drew rolled clear as a sword blow hit the marble floor, sending sparks flying. A chunk of the ancient mosaic broke away, skittering across the court. Drew had to keep moving, evading, while he thought of a plan. *I can't kill Djogo. He's shown faith in me. What kind of man would I be if I betrayed that trust now? He might be blinded by his love for Shah, but there has to be another way!*

Of all the human foes Drew had faced in battle, Djogo was the one he feared the most. He'd been relieved when the tall warrior pledged his allegiance on Scoria, removing the threat that he'd ever fight him again. Drew had given his all, but this was different; he didn't want to see the man dead. He wanted him to live. He wanted the *three* of them to live.

Djogo brought the scimitar down lightning fast toward Drew's chest. The young Wolflord leaped back, narrowly missing having his stomach opened, only to feel the cold bite of a spearhead in his back. The guard propelled him forward toward Djogo's return swing, leaving Drew with no option but to dive at him, tackling him around the chest and wrestling him to the floor.

The two rolled, Drew's one hand his only means of holding the scimitar back.

"Please, Djogo!"

"There's no other way!" grunted the ex-slaver.

Djogo butted Drew in the face, sending him reeling away, blinded. Instincts kicked in as the Wolflord scrambled, eyes streaming as blood poured from his nose. The scimitar clanged against the floor inches from where he'd landed. The therian shook his head and prayed his vision would return. He heard the scrape of the scimitar as Djogo got to his feet, the blade dragging along the floor. Drew scrambled away from the telltale noise, foolishly forgetting the other perils that faced him in the arena. A guard's scimitar ripped across his back, felling him with a scream of pain just as his vision cleared.

Surrounded by a wall of armed warriors, he faced an

opponent focused on slaying him. That's all the Omiri nobles wanted—two hated enemies fighting to the death, slaver versus Werewolf. Drew spat blood on to the marble floor, letting loose a monstrous growl that caused the guards to shift warily.

Time to give the people what they want.

The guard with the scimitar took another potshot at Drew, but his timing couldn't have been worse. Drew had embraced the change, and all he now saw was a room full of enemies. His clawed foot shot up from the floor, kicking the warrior hard in his chest, sending him flying back through the air. He hit a marble pillar, landing in a crumpled heap, his polished breastplate battered out of shape. By the time his scimitar fell from his unconscious grasp, Drew had fully transformed, the Werewolf crouching on the floor, ready for battle.

Djogo swung at a surprised guard, disarming him with a deft flick of his scimitar. The guard's weapon flipped through the air and into Djogo's other hand, the Werewolf now facing an even deadlier foe. The ex-slaver spun the scimitars at his sides as he closed on the therian.

Drew watched Djogo's swirling blades, searching for a way past them. They weren't silver, but Djogo was adept enough with any weapon to open him up in moments. No therian healing would help him against such serious wounds. The warriors who ringed them were ready now, should either combatant turn on them again. Spears and scimitars hovered, ready to strike out at therian or human should they stagger too close.

"You can't win this fight!" growled Drew, moving quickly around the arena.

"One of us has to," said Djogo, his voice laden with anger and regret.

Djogo ran at Drew, preparing to leap into the air to cut down at the Wolf. At the last moment, Drew realized it was a bluff, the warrior hitting the marble floor in a diving slide aimed at taking out the Werewolf's legs. Drew hurdled the swordsman, narrowly missing his booted feet, but the scimitars left a trail of red mist in their wake as they scored the Wolf and he hit the floor with a snarl.

The Jackals cheered at the sight of the Wolf's blood. Drew looked down at his torso, his dark, clawed hand dabbing at the wounds the scimitars had left behind. *They won't be content until either Djogo or I lies dead.*

Djogo leaped back again, blades cutting downward in deadly swipes. When Drew ducked one way the warrior followed, closing off his escape route. He'd switch to the other, only to find him waiting. Years of fighting in the Furnace and across Lyssia had honed Djogo into a formidable fighter, predicting Drew's every move.

With an imperceptible glance, Drew marked two spearmen next to one another in the wall, their long weapons poised. Quickly he maneuvered toward them, avoiding Djogo's blows while ensuring the two were eventually at his back.

The Werewolf allowed his huge, clawed feet to strike the ground loudly, black claws scraping the marble and drawing attention. He retreated, one step after another, his head dipped at such an angle that he could still see the guards behind through the corner of his eye. One was unable to resist any longer, bringing his long spear back and stabbing at the Wolf.

The lycanthrope twisted, turning on his haunches and snatching hold of the spear. With a hard tug on the shaft Drew brought the man flying forward, the guard releasing his grip on the spear and flailing toward Djogo. The one-eyed warrior deflected the hapless spearman with his forearms as the guard struck him, the two hitting the marble together.

Drew was moving before they'd landed, whipping the long spear around and sprinting. He lowered the spear haft, praying it would find purchase. The hard, wooden end of the weapon clunked into a hole in the broken mosaic, halting his run instantly and sending the Werewolf into the air. To his relief, the spear buckled but didn't break, launching Drew skyward, vaulting him high over the guards. Their long spears jabbed up but in vain; the monstrous, gray Wolflord sailed above and beyond them.

And landed on the throne.

The nobles roared at the sight of the Wolf straddling King Faisal, pinning him to his seat. Canine features appeared in a wave, the Jackal-lords changing and howling for the Wolf's blood. Faisal bellowed with shock as Drew snatched him around the throat, his clawed feet digging into the king's thighs, drawing blood through the once-pristine white robes. Though the king's head expanded, transforming into the Jackal as his features distorted, his throat remained the size of a mortal man's in Drew's lupine grip. Faisal choked, his airway cut off. The Jackal's eyes bulged as Drew bared his teeth, holding his grip as the king floundered in a blind panic.

While many warriors rushed to their king's aid, others overpowered Djogo, tearing the scimitars from his grip before he was inspired to do anything foolish. He looked on with awe as the Wolf held Omir to ransom.

"Kill the Wolf!" screamed Rook from nearby, baring Shah's throat once more, a jagged red cut now visible where he'd sliced her with the blade.

"Call off your dogs!" said Drew, his lips peeled back as he growled into the Werejackal's ear.

Faisal glanced frantically from side to side, his hands out to his family, warning them to retreat. Drew allowed his grip to relax, enough to allow the Jackal to breathe. He gasped at the air, struggling to get oxygen past the Werewolf's claws.

"Tell the Crow to release Shah," said Drew. *"Now!"*

"Let . . . her . . . go!" whispered the king through his clenched throat.

Rook watched with disbelief, shaking Shah like a rag doll.

"But, Your Majesty . . ."

"Release her!" said Faisal.

Reluctantly the Crowlord let Shah go, the Hawklady stumbling to Djogo, who pulled himself free of the guards and tore her gag away. The two held each other as if their lives depended upon it.

"You won't get out of this palace alive, Wolf!" spat Faisal, strangled in Drew's grip.

The Werewolf tightened his hold again. "I'll get all the way to Westland with my hand around your throat if I have to, Faisal!" snarled Drew. "It didn't have to be like this," he went on, the fury momentarily gone from his voice. "I told you the truth, Faisal, and you chose to ignore me. We came here in peace, but you ensure we leave as enemies. . . ."

"She's returned!"

The woman's cry echoed through the throne room as her footsteps raced through the hall toward the throne. Whoever she was, she was oblivious to the drama that played out in front of her. Her voice was cheery as she approached, more guards accompanying her into the chamber.

"See, my love! She's returned to us!"

The woman looked up at last. Jackals' heads looked down upon her as her shocked eyes landed upon the king, helpless in the Werewolf's grip. She held the girl from the skiff in her arms, the child's big almond eyes wide as she clutched the woman's chest.

"My daughter . . ." Faisal choked out, the fight instantly gone from his body.

Drew looked from the king down to the child, who raised a trembling finger toward the Werewolf.

"It's him, mother," she said, sniffing back the tears. The girl's featured softened suddenly, from fear to admiration.

"He's the one who saved me."

4

THE PORT AT THE END
OF THE WORLD

THERE WERE FEW places in Lyssia as remote and in-hospitable as Friggia. Situated on the northernmost point of Beggars' Bay, it was the one port in Sturmland that the Sturmish people avoided. The Walrus had claimed the town linked by road to the Rat city of Vermire and Lady Slotha's city of Tuskun, for herself. While the majority of the Tuskun fleet was harbored in Blackbank on the southern coast of the Sturm Peninsula, a few of her warships considered Friggia, on the northern coast, their home, launching raids against those brave souls who dared sail the Sturmish Sea. Like their neighbors in Vermire, the Tuskuns were pirates to the core.

With a snowstorm having descended, any other harbor

in Lyssia would have been deserted, but not Friggia. The hour was late and the weather grim, but the Tuskun port was in no mood to sleep, with both streets and ships busy with activity. However, while the largest piers and docks that housed the bigger ships were bustling, the smaller jetties were quieter, all but deserted, with fishing boats moored for the night. Three figures stood on the end of one such jetty, shrouded in swirling snow. Behind them, a rowing boat was being tied up, and a handful of men clambered up from it on to the wooden walkway.

"By Brenn's whiskers," said Manfred. "I thought it was cold in the Barebones but this is something else!"

"You're in the north now, Your Grace," said Hector. "They don't do anything by half measures up here."

The reluctant new captain of the *Maelstrom*, Figgis, had nothing to say, watching the six other men finish securing the rowboat before they came over to join them.

"Are we clear as to our tasks?" asked Manfred, looking to each of them. "Captain Figgis is to remain here with the boat while we split into two groups."

Manfred pointed to the ship's cook, Holman, and the gray-looking fellow nodded back. "Master Holman, I'll accompany you while you see about getting some fresh produce for the stores—meat, vegetables, whatever passes for food up here in the rear end of nowhere. Hector"—Manfred nodded at the young Boarloard—"you'll procure drinking water for the ship, in addition to something a bit stronger as a reward for the boys. Let's keep it quiet, eh? Last thing we want to do is attract unwanted attention to our visit."

Hector's face was stoic and humorless. "You can count on me, Your Grace."

Ringlin and Ibal waited for their master a short distance away along the jetty. Both were well wrapped up against the elements, while Hector wore his cloak hood down, careless of the bitter snowstorm. The magister was about to follow his men when he stopped, turning to Manfred and placing his gloved left hand on the duke's arm.

"Is everything all right, Manfred?" asked Hector quietly and earnestly, dropping the formalities he'd used before the men.

"Whatever do you mean, Hector?" blustered the Staglord, glancing at the magister's hand on his wrist.

"You haven't seemed yourself lately, especially since that awful business with Vega and that poor boy going missing."

Manfred sighed, wearily staring at the young Boarlord from beneath his bushy gray brow.

"Which of us *has* been ourselves since the disappearance of the count, Hector? It's a terrible thing to come to terms with. It's . . . unbelievable . . . that something so tragic could befall our friend on his own ship, no?"

"Unbelievable," said Hector, nodding. "Just so you know,

I'm always here to talk to, should you wish to unburden your-self of anything. We friends must stick together."

"Friends," agreed Manfred, smiling sadly. "Together."

The duke shook the baron's hand before turning back to his complement of men from the *Maelstrom*. With no further word, the group split up, setting off into Friggia with their own very different agendas.

"That wasn't the agreed upon price," said Hector, wagging a finger at the innkeeper.

The two men stood on the frozen cobbles of the alleyway that ran the length of the Black Gate Tavern, cellar doors open at their feet. Lantern light from below was cast skyward, il-luminating the haggling pair, their men working together be-neath the inn.

"That's the price now," said the innkeeper, jutting his jowls out confidently.

"Is that how you do things up here? Renege on business deals at your whim?"

"That's how we're doing things tonight. I don't give a tin-ker's cuss how you do things in . . . Highcliff . . ."

The innkeeper let his sentence trail away, grinning.

So, whispered the Vincent-vile. *He knows where we're from, eh? Sounds like a threat, brother. He's a cocky one, isn't he?*

A solitary dray horse stood nearby harnessed to a cart, its head bowed, eyes fixed on the men in dispute. Ringlin and Ibal were working with the innkeeper's hulking barrel boy in the cellar, rolling three large barrels toward the hatch ramp. The barrel boy was a mute giant of a man who said nothing and did all his master commanded; a child trapped in a man's body was the expression that leaped to Hector's mind. The two rogues glanced up as Hector negotiated, paying close attention to where the conversation was heading.

"It sounds like you're getting greedy, sir," said Hector, his gaunt cheekbones lifting slightly as he managed a sickly smile.

"I'm a businessman, that's all. Way I see it you're not just paying me for the barrels of brandy, boy." He lowered his voice. "You're paying for my silence."

Hector shook his head from side to side. "I swear, why does it always have to end this way?" he said in a tired and irritated voice. He lifted his left hand and opened his palm.

Instantly the innkeeper was spluttering as he struggled with the invisible force tangled around his throat. Hector tightened his grip in the air, watching his brother's vile twist around the neck of the innkeeper like a deadly black noose.

"You had every chance of doing a nice bit of business with me tonight and walking away with your life. Three barrels of brandy, that's all I asked for. We had a deal; we shook on it. I distinctly recall shaking on it, don't you?"

The man collapsed to his knees, eyes bulging as his fingernails clawed at his fat throat, tearing the skin away in strips.

"Greed, sir; a terrible, ugly thing, I'm sure you'll agree. I'd love to say it was pleasant doing business with you, but . . ."

Hector clenched his fist tight, mind focused solely on the vile as he saw the phantom's attack through to its grisly end. Whereas previously, back in Highcliff, his control over the vile had been sporadic, inspired by surging emotions, since his encounter with the host on the White Isle he had a deeper understanding of his abilities. He yanked his hand back through the air, as if tugging a rope. The innkeeper's throat made a wet snapping sound before he fell to the floor, neck broken.

Hector looked into the cellar where Ringlin, Ibal, and the barrel boy stared back. The man-child looked worried now, the realization of what had just happened suddenly dawning on him. He stared at the Boarguard, who let the final barrel roll to a halt at the base of the ramp. Ibal pulled his sickle from his belt, while Ringlin gently unsheathed his long knife, twirling the blade as they advanced on the barrel boy. From his vantage point above, Hector lost sight of the trio as the giant mute retreated fearfully into the recesses of the cellar.

Done, brother.

Hector was surprised at Vincent. There was a new understanding between magister and vile, as if the spirit realized its master had unlocked a great many secrets. The Vincent-vile was showing a newfound respect for Hector, fear playing a large part in that. The host had hinted many things to Hector as it fed from his throat. It had shown him how to inflict pain, not just on the living, but the dead.

Even with a world of dark magick at his fingertips waiting to be explored, Hector found himself wavering. He'd done what had to be done to get rid of Vega. He knew the Sharklord would have betrayed him in time; he'd already humiliated him in front of Bethwyn at every opportunity. Hector only regretted the fact that he'd allowed the sea marshal to get so close to him. He wouldn't make the same mistake again. For the first time ever, Hector felt in control of his magistry.

The innkeeper had brought it on himself. He'd been an enemy of the Wolf's Council, and Hector had to eliminate him. Who could have imagined that his knowledge of dark magicks could actually be used for *good*? Despite the freezing cold that bit at his face, Hector felt a warmth in his heart that had been missing for too long. He was helping Drew once again, helping what was left of the Wolf's Council, with his Brenn-given gift.

Stepping over the dead body, Hector made his way toward the street, where the singing of folk inside the Black Gate Tavern spilled out of the door. It was only a matter of time before the innkeeper's clientele realized he was missing. Hector looked back over his shoulder as the first barrel emerged from the cellar, the Boarguard working it into the alley. It was time to return to the *Maelstrom*. Hurriedly, the two rogues loaded up the wagon before setting off back to the harbor.

Ibal cracked his whip over the nag's head and the dray

horse picked up its pace along the slippery dock road. With their task completed quicker than expected, Hector was hopeful they'd be back at the rowboat first. It'd be good to show Manfred how capable he was, after everything that had gone on in the recent weeks. The duke's people had looked after Hector in Highcliff when he'd been taken ill, allowing him to convalesce in Buck House. After the chaos in Moga and the White Isle, and with Vega finally out of the way, Hector felt it was time to repay the Staglord for the many kindnesses he'd shown him. Arriving back at the boat, mission accomplished, was the first step toward Hector proving his trustworthiness to Manfred once more.

Three barrels of brandy and four casks of fresh water sat in the back of the cart with Hector, his men riding up front. As they pulled away, the magister couldn't help but stare back in the direction of the Black Gate Tavern. Customers were already exiting the inn as they'd left, in search of the fat oaf who had run the place after he'd failed to return to the bar. Judging by the shouting that had begun to chase them down the lane, they'd found his body, and that of the slain simpleton in the cellar. Hector glanced back nervously at the thick grooves the wagon wheels had cut into the snow-covered floor of the lane. A trail to follow: the sooner they were back aboard the *Maelstrom*, the better. The last thing Hector needed was a hue and cry on his back with the miserable servants of Slotha hunting him.

Pulling up at the jetty where Figgis had moored the boat,

the Boarguard jumped into the back of the dray, clambering past Hector to unload the barrels. The distant cries of angry men told the Boarlord all he needed to know. *Here's hoping old Manfred's right behind us, then*, thought Hector as he jumped down on to the frozen cobbles.

He walked up the jetty, boots slapping the frosty timber planks as he strode through the stiff gale. He slowed as he neared the remaining length of the wooden pier, coming to a staggering halt.

The rowboat was gone.

Initially Hector thought he'd come to the wrong jetty, but that was impossible; there were only a couple at this end of the harbor, and this was certainly the one. He then noticed the other vessels that had been moored along the jetty had been cut free—coracles, fishing boats, and the like. A couple drifted some distance away in the choppy, black water.

Cut free.

He looked across to the next pier; again, the rowboats had been released, their only means of returning to the *Maelstrom* snatched away. He ran back to the dock road, finding his two companions rolling the first barrel along the planking toward him.

"Stop what you're doing," he said. "The boat's gone. We need to find Manfred, let him know Figgis has abandoned us."

But even as he said it, he knew what had happened.

310

"What's that, my lord?" asked Ringlin, his face white with worry. Ibal gave a sickly, nervous giggle, looking back up the docks toward where torches and lanterns had begun to appear. Ringlin was shocked to see his master smile.

"So that was your game then, Manfred?" Hector said, to himself as much as anyone else.

If his men understood, they didn't respond, instead drawing their weapons.

The Stag shows his true colors, brother; the last of the Wolf's Council stabs you in the back. You can trust nobody.

"You're right for once, Vincent," Hector said, walking past Ringlin and Ibal to stand in front of the horse and cart.

"What are you doing, my lord?" said Ringlin, his voice etched with panic as the approaching mob materialized through the swirling snowstorm, following the telltale passage of the dray through the white streets.

Hector stood calmly as the men appeared. Within moments they had surrounded the Boarlord and his henchmen. Ringlin and Ibal held their weapons at the ready; if they were to die, they'd take some of the Walrus's men with them. The locals were already shouting, calling to see the color of the Westlanders' innards.

Hector raised his hands, palms out to the mob. "Silence," he said simply.

A cold unlike anything the men of Friggia had experienced

before suddenly descended over the mob. To each man it felt as if Death's skeletal hand had traced a bony finger across their hearts, silencing them instantly. Hector smiled.

"Take me to Lady Slotha."

"It is done," said Manfred as he clambered back aboard the *Maelstrom*, the crew helping the elderly duke find his footing on the icy deck. Amelie and Bethwyn stood waiting for them, arms around one another as the frosty wind whipped around them.

"He cannot follow?" asked Amelie.

"Not unless he fancies a bracing swim," replied Figgis, the last man to climb up from the rowboat.

"I hope to Brenn we've done the right thing," said the queen, squeezing her lady-in-waiting in a fearful embrace.

"Don't you be worryin' about nothin,'" said Figgis, before turning to the Staglord. "Where to, Your Grace?"

"Onward to Roof, dear Captain," said Manfred. "And from there to Icegarden, and the protection of Duke Henrik. I pray he's in a generous mood."

5

A Captive Audience

FROM THE LOFTY balcony, Drew's view of Omir was as great as any in the Desert Realm. To the east the Saber Sea bled across the horizon, separating sand from sky. To the west the Barebone Mountains stood tantalizingly close, their snow-capped peaks glistening like diamonds. Drew glanced down. The city sprawled below the palace, while the gleaming outer wall of Azra kept it safe. A road ran atop the wall's entire circumference, with soldiers, wagons, and teams of horses moving along it, above the city. Only two gatehouses allowed entrance to the city: Copper Gate to the north and Silver Gate to the south. These structures were as big as many castles in the west, housing garrisons of warriors who manned the defenses; so long as the walls stood, Azra remained Faisal's.

The *Banshee* was still in Kaza under armed guard. Regardless of the fact that Drew's company had brought the king's daughter safely home, the Omiri took no chances. Drew wanted to be away as soon as possible but realized that he wouldn't be able to leave now. Not while an army gathered in the north.

Tents of all sizes dotted the desert several miles from Azra, the amassed force as huge as any Drew had seen. Siege engines intermittently towered into the sky, their definition wavering in the intense heat haze. He counted at least thirty of the machines, the sole purpose of each to break down Azra's fabled walls. Drew looked down at the city's defenses once more. Faisal's force was overwhelmingly outnumbered, the wall just about evening up the contest. *One wall to stop this mighty army.*

"Impressive, no?" said King Faisal as he joined Drew at the balcony.

"The walls? Or the army on your doorstep?"

"Both."

"How long have they been there?"

"They began to gather a week ago. More arrive each day, so our scouts report. Who knows how many more shall arrive or when they intend to attack?"

"Who are they?"

"It's Lord Canan and the Doglords. For ten years he's waged war in Omir, each year taking more of the desert from me. While fighting has intensified recently, he's never dared an assault upon Azra before. I wonder what now makes him so brazen. . . ."

Faisal turned and walked back through his throne room. Drew followed, the yellow-cloaked warriors of the palace guard shadowing him all the while. He wore no manacles, but he was their prisoner nonetheless. *Does Faisal know about the Dogs' alliance with the Cats? Has he heard the rumor of Hayfa joining forces with Canan?* Drew had a terrible feeling in the pit of his stomach. *Three armies against Azra? This city will fall. . . .*

After yesterday's drama, the king was a changed man. Drew and his companions might have been captives, but that didn't stop Faisal from extending every courtesy to them. The three had been taken to separate quarters under armed guard, where they could bathe, dine, and sleep. Drew's body cried out for rest and the time to allow his injuries to heal properly, but they needed to be moving again, and swiftly. It was mid-morning when they finally returned to Faisal's throne room. Shah now stood with Djogo, the two talking quietly while courtiers eyed them suspiciously.

"How's your daughter this morning?" asked Drew, as Faisal went to sit on his throne. A slave knelt at his feet with a tray of olives and grapes at the ready, raising them up instinctively whenever the king's hand reached out.

"Kara is better. Thank you again for bringing her safely home. My wife is herself once more."

"I wasn't alone," said Drew, casting his hand toward his companions. "It's Shah you must thank. It was her superior vision that allowed us to stop the Doglord's attack when we did. Without her, the outcome might not have been so joyous."

Faisal nodded to the Werehawk, his smile forced.

"You must understand, Lady Shah, I find it . . . difficult, to express my thanks to a Hawklord, after the part your kind played in breaking Azra's walls so many years ago."

"Understandable," said Shah, stepping beside Drew. "But it's alarming that your enemies might attack your own so close to home. What was your daughter *doing* on that boat in the first place?"

"Being brought home." Faisal's face was serious as he considered how close he'd come to losing his daughter. "The body you returned was that of my uncle, Prince Fier. He'd been schooling Kara in Denghi, where he served as my envoy. Word had reached us that Canan's forces were marching on Azra. We had no choice but to have them return."

"How was it they came under attack?" asked Drew.

Faisal frowned. Before he could answer Lord Rook stepped forward and spoke for him. "The king's enemies have a long and deadly reach, Wolf."

"But it was Doglords who attacked the skiff," said Drew. He watched the black-robed man carefully, the Crow having taken far too much delight in tormenting Shah the previous day.

"We have only *your* word that it was the Dogs who attacked them," said Rook. "It was probably just river pirates. Either way, she's safe now."

"It was a Doglord, all right, your daughter will vouch for that, Your Majesty," said Drew. "I left one at the bottom of the Silver River."

"I would imagine poor Kara can remember little from the traumatic event. The child is still in shock. How very convenient that you left the villain's corpse on the riverbed," said the Crowlord.

"Let's talk about convenient," said Drew, facing Rook. "How did the Dogs know that the king's daughter was traveling to Azra? I know maps and I understand distance: how did word reach the Doglords in the north, alerting them that the child was on her way? To get a message to the Dogs so swiftly? That sounds like something that would require *wings*, don't you agree, Lord Rook?"

"Mind what you insinuate, pup," said Rook. "They were simply pirates; bandits, Your Majesty."

Drew turned to the king, fed up with the Crow's interruptions.

"Armed with silver weapons? They're wealthy bandits Rook speaks of," said Drew. "This sounds like a coordinated attack. Your enemies are mobilizing against you, Your Majesty, and I fear their number is far greater than you imagine, and that some are closer than you know."

Rook took hold of Drew, turning him about so they were face-to-face.

"You think the king isn't *worried* about yesterday's events? You assume an awful lot, son of Wergar. Your greatest concern should be your own immediate future."

"As I understood, this is the court of King Faisal, not the Crows of Riven," Drew snapped. "While your interest in my welfare is appreciated, Rook, it's the king I sought audience with. Not some visiting dignitary from a small town in the Barebones."

"Mind your tongue, Wolf!" said Rook. "You and your *friends* are enemies of Omir. The good people of the Desert Realm have long memories. They remember Wergar's war all too well."

Drew ignored the man, speaking directly to Faisal.

"You have Kara back, Your Majesty, thanks to our actions. One of my companions, Drake, died saving her. A brave man and a Werelord of the first rank, he gave his life for a complete stranger, many miles from his homeland. Surely you can let us go?"

Faisal stroked his jaw as Drew spoke, pondering the young Wolflord's words.

"You're the reason there's a war in the west, boy," said the king finally. "The Seven Realms fight over Highcliff's throne. Some say it should be yours. I've yet to hear your thoughts on the matter."

Drew grimaced. The Jackal understood all too well the young Werewolf's value.

"Up until recently I'd no interest in the throne of Westland. But that was before I saw the cruelty that takes place across Lyssia in the names of monsters like Leopold, Lucas, and Kesslar."

Djogo and Shah looked down, ashamed, when Drew mentioned the Goatlord.

"The people of Lyssia have made a stand; they've rallied behind the Wolf's banner, risen in my name. I'd betray them all if I didn't fight now to free them from tyranny. Brackenholme, Westland, the Longridings, and the Barebones—"

"Don't mention my homeland as your ally, Wolf," said Rook. "The Staglords might have made a stand at your side, but what good did it do their home?"

Drew cocked his head at mention of the Stags. "Why? What's happened?"

The Crowlord jutted out his jaw as he relayed the news from the Barebones. "Highwater is surrounded by Onyx's forces, and sure to fall. As for your Staglords, no doubt you're aware that one brother's dead and the other's disappeared. So please, Wolf, don't tell me you've friends in the Mountain Realm. You'll find none there."

Shah stepped toward the Rook. "Highwater laid siege to? Tell me, Crow, where do the black birds of Riven fit into this picture. Highwater is on your doorstep, is it not?"

Rook prickled at the Hawklady's words.

"We Crowlords remain removed from conflict. We seek nothing but peace and neutrality."

Shah laughed out loud, but when she looked back at Rook her face was stony.

"How can you stand there and say the Crows of Riven want nothing but peace? Your father, Count Croke, has perched on that pile of slate for almost a century. In all those years he's bullied and bickered with his neighbors, trying to wrestle control of the Barebones away from the Stags of Stormdale. You expect me to believe he sits neutral while his lifelong nemeses are beaten black and blue by the Catlords? Tell me: how soon before a Crow resides in Stormdale, Rook?"

Rook lurched toward Shah, lashing out with a fist, only the swift action of the palace guards restraining him in time.

"You witch!" spat the Crowlord. "You dare lecture me on what's best for the Barebones? Your kind don't belong in my mountains any more than a fish belongs in a tree! You're relics, Shah—you and whatever Hawklord scum remain! Skeer's the best of your bad bunch, and he did right striking a deal with Leopold back in the day. He rules Windfell now, the last of the Hawks. Soon enough we'll see how Windfell looks with black feathers on the throne!"

Ignoring the Crow, Drew turned to Faisal. "A Doglord army approaches, Your Majesty, possibly the same one that was allied to the Catlords that attacked Westland. Now they gather north of Azra, the Cats returning the favor to the

Dogs. I wager you'll find Bastians fighting alongside Omiri."

"Let them come!" cried one of Faisal's cousins. "Their bodies will litter the base of Azra's walls!"

"We can defeat this army from the north!" shouted another.

"And the one from the south?" asked Drew, turning to the crowd. "Talk spreads like wildfire in Denghi. Lady Hayfa has struck a bargain with Lord Canan. Her army will come to the aid of the Doglords as well. Send scouts south—I guarantee you'll find her. That's three armies, my lords, surrounding your city. They're going to carve Azra up between them!"

"Preposterous!" scoffed Rook. "Don't listen to him, Your Majesty. He spreads mistrust and fear. You should have killed this monster and his companions when they landed here."

"Let us continue our quest," Drew went on. "We head into the Barebones with Baron Griffyn's blessing. He will lead us to the ancient tomb of his forefathers, the Screaming Peak. From there, the baron shall summon the Hawklords from every corner of Lyssia."

Drew held the king's gaze as he spoke, the room quiet but for the spluttering of Lord Rook.

"Your aid won't be forgotten, King Faisal. We'll return, in number, and help you defeat the army that approaches Azra, be they Dogs, Cats, or any other kind of beast. You shall have the Hawklords as allies this time!"

Rook moved past Drew, bringing his lips closer to Faisal's ear. But Drew still heard his whispers to the king.

"The Wolf will promise you anything to save his hide, Your Majesty. Kill him now and let all Lyssia know—you'll be a hero throughout the Seven Realms! With one thrust of your blade you can end this war!"

Slowly, the king turned to the Crowlord. "My dear Lord Rook," he said, smiling as he spoke. "I think you may have just outstayed your welcome."

"You're not serious," said Rook, his face frozen in a shocked smile.

"I'm very serious. I shall be closing the gates of Azra tonight for the last time to all but my allies. Anyone else should leave. That would include you."

"But I'm here on my father's behalf. We *are* your allies."

"These are turbulent times, Lord Rook. Your father would no doubt appreciate your presence in Riven, with war threatening us all. I want only those loyal to Azra within these walls."

Rook was furious, spittle frothing at his lips as he looked around the room snarling, his eyes settling on Drew and his companions.

"You side with your prisoners, Faisal? Is this how little you think of my kind? You take a Wolf's word over mine?"

Faisal rose and walked toward the enraged Lord of Riven.

"This has nothing to do with the Wolf and everything to do with the Crow. Many questions remain unanswered regarding the enemy at my gates and allegiances in the Barebones. You offer little to put my mind at ease."

"Don't be fooled by the Wolf's gossip," said Rook, but he choked on his words, struggling for conviction.

"I gave you every chance to walk away from Azra with your reputation intact. I tolerated your actions yesterday, taking such delight in holding the Hawklady hostage. I thought the Wolf and Hawk were my enemies—"

"They *are* your enemies!" said Rook. "You should kill them!"

"And now you attack a guest in my palace, a lady no less."

"She's no lady!" squawked Rook. The Crowlord was now surrounded by palace guards, the other nobles having moved clear of the volatile therian.

"What good does your presence here do me and my people, Rook? Why do you wish the Wolf dead so dearly? Whom do you truly serve?"

"If you don't kill them . . ."

"If I don't kill them, what exactly?" exclaimed the king, releasing the Jackal at last.

He arched his back, letting the white robes that draped across his shoulders tumble away as his tanned torso tripled in size. His arms popped with muscles, fingers shifting into claws that pointed menacingly toward Rook. His neck and head broadened, the smooth fur of the Jackal racing through his flesh as sharp ears rose and a long, canine snout worked its way through his face.

"Hold your tongue, Crowlord, before you say something you regret," growled the Werejackal.

Drew heard the snarls of the other therians in the court. A cloud passed in front of the sun, darkening the throne room. His cousins and fellow Jackal-lords growled in unison, the beasts all too visible in their angry faces.

"You have one hour, Crow," said Faisal. "The death of my dear uncle Lord Fier is shrouded by the stench of treachery, and the young Wolflord's words have allowed me to see clearly. Gather your belongings and leave my city. If you're still here after that, I shan't be responsible for my fellow Jackals' actions. A threat against their king is a threat to all."

Rook looked quickly around the room, noticing the assembled Jackal-lords' state of agitation. He backed up warily, eyes flitting between the warriors and therians.

"You've made a grave mistake siding with these beasts, Faisal," warned the Werecrow as he retreated through the throne room, armed guards escorting him closely. Turning on his heel, the Lord of Riven stormed from the chamber, long robe billowing as he left a shower of black feathers in his wake.

Drew kept his distance as the transformed Werejackal watched the Crow disappear. Faisal's broad shoulders heaved up and down. Gradually he returned to human form, the Jackal and his temper subsiding.

Finally the king looked back at Drew. "The black bird says I'm mistaken to trust you," said Faisal, his narrow eyes studying the young therian carefully. The look he gave the Wolf seemed as if he were laying down a challenge as he continued: "Prove him wrong."

6

NOWHERE TO RUN

THE CALLS OF the chasing pack seemed distant, their cries carried away on the chill wind that raced across the Longridings. Their torches were visible, flaming brands held aloft by the riders as they scoured the grasslands for fugitives. Trent spurred Storm on through the long grass, keen to put distance between himself and his comrades. With their constant shouting they were making enough noise to wake the dead, and if their enemies were to be caught, stealth had to play a large part.

The tall fronds whipped at horse and youth as they sped along, Trent's eyes picking out the broken grass ahead that marked the route his quarry had taken. Once again, his mind raced back to the Cold Coast where he and his father—and brother—had hunted by night, often on foot, occasionally on horseback, but always by the light of the moon. The pale light of the heavenly body illuminated the path ahead—the saw grass clumsily broken in his foe's desperate desire to escape. The man was injured, of that much he was sure, judging by the blood he caught sight of on the pale yellow blades of grass.

The trail came to a halt as the grass fell away suddenly before him. Trent reined Storm in, the horse snorting as she skidded to an abrupt stop, her hooves kicking at the frozen earth and sending a shower of pebbles skittering off the lip of the ravine. Trent lurched forward in his saddle, patting Storm's neck as clouds of steam snorted from her nostrils. Directly below them a small gorge cut through the grasslands, rocky inclines rising steeply from either side of a rushing, bubbling brook. Storm stepped nervously as Trent surveyed the terrain, looking north and south up the length of the rocky valley.

"He went down here," he said, as much to the horse as himself. "And so do we."

He gently prodded his heels into Storm's flanks, urging her over the edge of the ravine. Reluctantly, the horse proceeded, hooves gingerly picking a path down the steep, rocky slope. Occasionally they passed a bloodied rock, a red handprint smeared against a slab of stone where the fugitive had scrambled down to the gorge's bottom. Arriving at the base of the slope, Trent hopped down out of the saddle for a moment, leading Storm to the stream, his eyes wide and alert, searching the shadowy valley for a sighting of the enemy. He let Storm drink from the noisy stream momentarily, jumping across to the other side and searching the other bank. There was no bloody trail, no telltale marks left behind on the rocks. He glanced south down the ravine where the brook disappeared into the distance, back in the direction of the rest of his force.

"He won't have gone back that way, not after he witnessed what was done to his companions."

He jumped back up into his saddle, his horse refreshed by the cold water. "North it is. We follow the stream."

Lord Frost's force had encountered a large band of travelers earlier that day, around dusk, making their way west through the Longridings. The group had numbered nearly two hundred, mainly civilians—farmers, traders, and a smattering of Romari. There were also a number of Horselords within their ranks, the Werelords immediately rushing to the defense of their companions when the Lionguard launched an unprovoked attack against the caravan. The initial offensive had left a sour taste in Trent's mouth. The fact that Romari were present had been enough for the Redcloaks to decide that the group was the enemy, the travelers' loyalty to the Wolf and their antics in Cape Gala still fresh in their minds. As it transpired, their hunch had been correct, but Trent had put that down to blind luck rather than reasoned deduction.

The initial battle had been fierce, the Romari and Horselords engaging Redcloaks and Bastians while the remaining refugees fled across the grasslands. Once the enemy had been defeated, at some cost to Frost's small army, the Catlord had questioned the surviving prisoners. With the aid of Sorin, he had prised a great deal of information from the group, including the knowledge that more Werelords had been traveling with the group, escaping with the other civilians when the battle had commenced. Putting the prisoners to the sword, the Lionguard and Bastians had given chase, gradually picking up those who had fled. The soldiers had cheered as one after another of the refugees had been rounded up and clapped in irons. Only a handful remained at large, and Trent was determined to return to the camp with a trophy of his own.

Trent pushed on along the banks of the brook, Storm picking up pace as the outrider grew in confidence. *This is the only way he could have gone. Nowhere left to run. I have you now.* The foe must have thought the stream would mask his passage, which it would have done ordinarily. However, the noise of the water rushing over the rocks would also conceal Trent's approach, the constant gurgling covering the approach of Storm's hooves. He unsheathed the Wolfshead blade as he rode, controlling his horse by his thighs and heels alone, letting the longsword trail through the air to his right. He sat up in his saddle straight, eyes searching the ravine ahead.

"There you are."

The figure had collapsed ahead, leaning hard against a boulder that sat in the middle of the stream. The fugitive looked up as he caught sight of the approaching rider. The bearded man grunted, clutching his chest as if in pain. Then he was off, running along the shallow streambed. Trent kicked Storm's flanks, forcing the horse into a canter.

The fleeing man tripped and stumbled, feet splashing through the icy water. He glanced over his shoulder as Storm thundered closer, gaining on him swiftly. Trent allowed the horse to charge past, her hooves narrowly missing the man but frightening him enough to send him spread-eagled into the stream. He landed face first in the cold water, momentarily blinded as he surfaced, gasping for air. Trent turned Storm around, squeezing his thighs against her back and urging her to rear up, her hooves threatening to strike the enemy.

The fugitive began to change, heavy horns emerged from the old man's skull, twisting and curling about his head. His short gray beard began to lengthen as his ribcage cracked within his chest, a sound like hammer hitting steel. Trent showed no fear. Here was the trophy he had sought: an enemy therian, a traitorous Werelord. He expertly prompted Storm to lash out, the horse's hooves connecting with the shifting Werelord's horned head with a hollow *crack.*

The man went down on his side, his head bouncing off the rocks on the streambed, his face half submerged in the water. Trent could see the cold liquid rushing through his enemy's slack mouth, racing into his airways and threatening to fill his lungs. He quickly dismounted, landing beside the Werelord in the water, hooking his arms beneath the fellow's partially transformed torso. He heaved the therian on to the bank, throwing him on to his stomach and binding him swiftly with ropes.

More riders arrived, the snorting of horses mingling with the cheers and jeers of the soldiers as they looked down at the hog-tied Werelord. The horns around his head reminded Trent of the old ram they had kept on the farm, the tuft of a gray beard beneath his chin further enhancing the resemblance. A Ramlord? There had been one in Cape Gala, at the court of High Stable. Was this the one of the Werelords they'd been searching for? Trent looked back at his companions, smiling proudly. The old therian snorted, rolling on to his side to view his captors.

"Well done, boys," the aged Ramlord spluttered. "You chased down an old man."

"Chased down a traitor," replied Frost, his voice rich and smooth. The Catlord jumped from his horse and landed in the stream, hardly making a splash. His pink eyes widened as he waded toward the bank where the Ram lay, coming to stand beside Trent. He patted the young outrider's back.

"Good work, Sergeant Ferran."

"Ferran?" said the Ram incredulously, but the only reply he received was the albino's boot to the temple. Trent stared down at the bound captive as two of the Bastian warriors hauled him onto the back of one of their horses, puzzling over the prisoner's reaction to his name.

He knows my name, Trent mused as he clambered back on Storm's back. *He knows Drew.*

7

THE STARS OVER AZRA

ALONE IN THE heavens, with only the stars for company, the young Wolflord was transported through time and space. He was a child, back at the farmhouse on the Cold Coast, Tilly Ferran rocking him in her chair while the two of them gazed into the night sky. His mother had the gift, so old Mack always told him: she could read the stars, divine a person's fortune on a clear, cloudless night. He tried to recall the things she'd promised him, the events she predicted would come to pass, but all he could remember was the smell of her hair and the feel of her hand over his. For the first time in months, Drew felt a tear roll down his cheek.

"I'm not interrupting you, am I?"

Drew glanced up from the star chart mosaic, wiping the

332

tear from his face with the flat of his hand, as King Faisal paced through the darkness toward him. The rest of the king's guests were still gathered at the far end of the throne room, feasting one last time on the eve of war. Djogo and Shah were with them, the frosty relations between the two factions thawing, speeded along by fine food and drink. The Hawklady occasionally looked across the room, concerned by the Wolf's dark mood. Drew had no appetite for feasting, and even less for company.

"I'm sorry, Your Majesty. I was a world away."

Faisal walked around the mosaic, circling Drew as he remained rooted in the middle.

"They say Azra is the home of all Lyssia's knowledge. The art of magistry began here. The libraries beneath the palace would rival any in the Seven Realms, Drew. This city was the seat of learning for Brenn's wisest children at one time. Terrifying to think that this could all be lost if the Dogs and the Cats overrun our walls."

"I recognize the stars," said Drew, gesturing to the marble constellations. "There's the Stag, the Serpent. Over there are the Twin Boars."

"And you're standing on the Wolf," said Faisal, smiling.

Drew took a step back.

"So I am."

"Not in the mood for a feast? You surprise me. The morning brings danger to all of us; you, with your journey, and us, with impending war. We Jackals always dine as if it's our last meal on the eve of battle."

"I can't stomach it." Drew sighed. "Have you heard back from your scouts?"

"You were right, Wolf. The Hyena's forces amass to the south of the Silver River. You'll have to leave swiftly at first light if you're to sail out of Kaza before they take the port town."

"Are you prepared for them?"

"Azra is always ready for war. This is the Jewel of Omir. It's been fought over for centuries. This is just one more chapter in this city's rich history."

"You sound as if you're looking forward to war."

"I look forward to action. It's the waiting I can't abide. My warriors are ready. Azra's ready."

"But still . . ." said Drew, scratching the back of his head as he stared out of the archway that led to the balcony. Hundreds of fires dotted the horizon to the north, twinkling like fireflies over a pitch-black meadow.

"Don't hold your tongue now, Drew. If you truly are the king of Westland, then speak freely. It's been long years since another king has been my guest."

Drew looked wearily at the handsome Jackal. "There are so many of them. You're badly outnumbered."

"You underestimate our defenses. Besides, the people will man the walls should the warriors fall."

"I fear for your people."

"This is their home. They take pride in their land."

"Even the slaves?"

Faisal grimaced, shaking his head at the Wolflord. "I wouldn't bring such a matter up if I were you, Drew. We're just getting to know one another. Politics have killed the greatest friendships as sure as swords before now."

Drew bit his lip, shaking his head. His mind went back to the belly of the *Banshee*, to the Furnace and the cruel antics of Kesslar and the Lizardlords. "I can't stand here silent. It goes against all I believe in. I've *been* a slave, Faisal. Walk even one step with a collar around your throat and you may change your tune. No man should be owned by another."

"We shall have to agree to disagree, Wolf Cub."

"Don't mock me, Faisal," said Drew, angry now. "I haven't fought my way back to Lyssia just to sit quietly while a fool spouts barbaric beliefs at me, be he a beggar or a king."

The Jackal snarled. If any of the palace guard had been present, they might have seized Drew for offending the king so. But the two were alone, facing one another across the ancient mosaic.

"This is my land, Wolf—my city. Your place is in the West. Keep your so-called enlightened thinking on the other side of the Barebones."

Drew stepped forward, eyeballing the king. "How many slaves are there in this city?"

"I've no idea, they are too many to count."

"Estimate for me, Your Majesty."

"Tens of thousands, I should imagine."

"Tomorrow, your city will be overrun, even if we can call the Hawklords to our side. You haven't enough warriors to man the walls against three armies."

"And what would you propose?"

"Free them."

Faisal recoiled as if he'd been slapped in the face.

"Release the slaves. Grant them citizenship of Azra as free men. Free the slaves and you'll save your city."

Faisal stared at Drew, weighing the youth up. He clearly hadn't expected Drew to speak so frankly to him. Perhaps Drew might have kept silent if he hadn't been so weary. The thought of journeying to Tor Raptor made his legs feel heavy suddenly. He stifled a yawn.

"It's been a long day, Your Majesty, and I must be away before dawn's first light. I thank you for your hospitality, and your understanding. Until I return, with the Hawklords . . ."

Drew bowed, turning to walk away, as King Faisal called after him.

"I don't understand how turning slaves into free men will save Azra."

The Wolflord continued to walk away, calling back as he went. "Put a roof over a man's head and you give him a home. Put a sword in his hand and pride in his heart—you give him something to fight for. You give him hope."

The fire had burned low by the time Drew returned to his bedchamber, just a handful of coals still kicking out heat as the cold air of the desert spread through the room. The guest quarters could have housed the entire Ferran family and their neighbors, the opulence on a scale Drew had never seen before, not even in Scoria. An enormous round bed dominated the room, circular steps leading up to it like a sacrificial altar. The carvings around the marble fireplace were as intricate as anything he'd seen in the Temple of Brenn in Highcliff. Bejeweled curtains billowed around the door on to the balcony, gems flashing like the stars in the night sky beyond. The Azrans did nothing by half-measures.

Even with the thick doors closed at Drew's back, the noise from the throne room below still echoed through the walls of the palace. Faisal wasn't lying when he said the Jackals liked to feast the night before a battle. He looked around the room, a nagging sensation descending over him. *Something isn't right.* He paused, trying to figure out what irked him, but couldn't put his finger on it.

Drew shivered, striding toward the balcony, the freezing air raising goose bumps on his flesh. The room felt like a mausoleum, the cold marble only enhancing the sensation. He stared at the fires of the enemy encampments beyond the walls, spreading east to west as far as the eye could see. *Does Faisal truly understand the magnitude of what he's facing? Will he take the advice of a boy like me?*

Drew grabbed the handle and pulled the balcony door closed, stopping before he dropped the latch. He suddenly realized what was nagging him: the doors had been closed when he'd left the bedchamber. Drew turned quickly, eyes searching the room. He channeled the Wolf's senses, his vision heightening instantly as he sniffed at the air. Stepping carefully across the chamber, he reached over to the chest at the foot of the bed. A sheathed longsword rested atop it, a gift from the king and a small token of apology for the treatment Drew and his friends had endured. Drew snatched the handle, shaking the scabbard from the blade where it fell quietly on to the rug.

He snorted at the air once more, picking up the scent of the intruder. With his lupine eyes now adjusted to the dim light, he could see through the gloom as if it were day. He pulled at the jewel-encrusted curtains, tearing them clear of the windows to reveal what they hid, but found nothing. He leaped across the room toward the tall closet, flicking the door open only to find it empty. Lastly he dashed back toward the bed, dancing up the steps and pulling back the sheets from where they hung to the marble floor. Ducking down, Drew looked beneath the bed. There was nobody there. The prowler was gone.

He collapsed onto the enormous bed, his heart beating fast, relieved to not be caught in a fight once more but disappointed to have not captured his intruder. He turned his head, the moonlight that streamed through the glass doors illuminating the clean white sheets that spread out before him. Drew's eyes widened. *There you are.*

A single long feather lay on his pillow, black as night itself. Drew shivered as he reached across and picked it up, the waxy texture sliding against his skin. He turned it between his fingertips, considering the gift's meaning. Rook was watching him. There would be no hiding from the Crowlord.

8

A Welcome in Tuskun

THE DOGS' PAWS pounded through the deep snow, hauling the sleds through the blizzard, whipcracks urging them on their way. Hector lay on his side, lashed to the sledge as a hunter might bind his kill. Goyt, an old Sturmish pelt trader caught trapping in the queen's woods, lay strapped down before him, head tucked to his chest, the cold and exhaustion having taken their toll on him. Hector felt Ibal's fat belly at his back; the magister was grateful for the warmth of his portly Boarguard. The rogue's giggles had ceased two days ago back in Friggia, the mob having worked some of their anger out on the three southerners before throwing them in the jail for the remainder of the night. They'd departed the Sturmish port at first light, heading inland on a handful of dogsleds, toward the City of the Walrus.

Ringlin was on one of the other sledges, bound to some other criminals who were being transported to Tuskun. The cold was unbearable, the temperature having remained well below freezing during their entire journey. Hector's teeth chattered incessantly, his entire body struggling with the extreme conditions. Who could have imagined the warmth of Ibal's fat belly might keep him alive? His show of strength in Friggia had struck awe into his captors' hearts, the chill touch of his Dark Magistry unnerving the angry mob. But Hector was no fool, and neither were the Tuskuns; they had numbers on their side. Had the Boarlord tried to fight his way out of his predicament, he might have brought two or three of the enemy to their knees before he and his men were overpowered, probably killed. No; surrendering was the only way he could gain audience with Slotha. There were six of them in all being taken to her, each responsible for very different crimes. The queen of Tuskun was a notoriously ill-tempered, violent woman: he hoped the Walrus would allow him the chance to speak in his defense.

The driver let out a cheer, the noise echoing over on the chasing sleds. Hector craned his neck, looking up ahead to where they headed. The blizzard lifted briefly, allowing the magister a clear view of Tuskun's jagged black walls as they loomed into view. To describe the outer defense as a wall was an exaggeration; giant slabs of gray slate had been driven into the ground around the entire city, dozens of tall wooden watchtowers dotted around its circumference. The sharp, splintered defenses reminded Hector of Vega's teeth when the Sharklord was transformed: fearsome and deadly.

Not so deadly in the end, eh, brother? whispered the Vincentvile slyly.

Timber gates groaned open, a portcullis grinding clear out of the sleds' path as they raced past beneath it. The city within bore little resemblance to any civilized settlement Hector had ever visited. It was little more than a shantytown, a crowded slum, the locals standing aside as the dogsleds raced up the slippery, stinking streets, a river of feculence steadily streaming beside the road. Hector gagged at the stench as the whip cracked overhead and the driver yelled at his hounds.

The buildings in the city were wooden for the most part, though the Boarlord spotted the occasional stone structure as they raced by. Bones of all shapes and sizes featured everywhere, the skulls of wild beasts adorning doors, giant animal ribs and femurs woven into the rooftops, walls, and windows of the houses. Clearly, this was a city of hunters. These people lived to kill.

The sledge jostled up the rutted avenue, slush and filth splashing off the road surface into the faces of the prisoners. Hector thought he might vomit, smearing the sewage from his face against Goyt's shoulder at his side. The driver pulled hard at the reins, the dogs yelping and barking as they slowed, the sled grinding to a halt in the blackened slush before a great black building. Enormous whale jawbones formed an arch above the open doors of Slotha's Longhouse. Two heavy-set guards stood at either side of the entrance, each carrying a long barbed harpoon. The pair didn't move as the driver jumped off the sled, waiting for the others to join him.

"Goyt. Ibal. We're here," Hector whispered. The fat Boarguard grunted a brief acknowledgment.

Hector gave Goyt a shove with his knee. The impact was enough to jar Goyt's head, which lolled back from his chest with a *crack*. The old trapper's face was blue, his eyes wide and frozen over.

Welcome to Tuskun, brother.

The Longhouse resembled the hull of an upturned ship, the interior an arched tunnel that disappeared into darkness. An enormous firepit dominated the hall, belching clouds of black smoke to the ceiling where it struggled to escape through a single round hole. Guards like those at the entrance occupied the chamber, each carrying harpoons and axes, and clad in sealskins and furs. Their faces were leathery, with long drooping black mustaches and beards obscuring their mouths. Each of them stared intently at the five prisoners as they were marched toward the roaring fire, manacles jangling, and forced to their knees.

Hector looked back over his shoulder. Outside, beyond the open doors, he could hear the snarling of sled dogs as they tore into Goyt's corpse, an unexpected reward for their hard run to Tuskun. Hector shivered, despite the heat, and turned back. Beyond the fire he saw a great mass advancing through the shadows. As she got closer her form was illuminated by the dancing flames. Her flesh was on show to all, between tattered leather strips pulled tight across her broad frame, the skin bulging between the straps. A bearskin robe was draped from her shoulder.

"So," grunted Slotha, the Werewalrus, as she strode around the firepit and made her way behind her captives. "These are the prisoners the good people of Friggia have delivered to me? This is the *fresh meat.* . . ."

I don't like the sound of this, dear brother. . . .

The sled drivers standing to one side bowed, their hands clasped together as if in prayer.

"Go get yourselves fed."

The three departed, apparently happy to be away from their queen, while a man who looked like a councilor unrolled a scroll. The vicious-looking Ugri warriors stepped forward, one standing in front of each prisoner as Slotha maneuvered behind them.

"What crimes?" asked the therian lady as she settled behind the first man to Hector's right. The man's eyes were fearful, darting from the guard to the councilor and then back to the magister.

"Defamation of Your Majesty's character in a tavern," said the councilor, sneering as he read the charge.

"What did you say, man?" whispered Slotha, momentarily lowering her head between the terrified man and Hector, her lips wobbling as she muttered into his ear. Hector got a whiff of the woman's breath, as foul as a bucket of rotting fish.

"I . . . I . . . but I . . ." The man couldn't speak, his whole body trembling as he began to shuffle forward away from her. The warrior standing in front of him reached over, clasping the man's hair in his fist and holding him firmly in his place. Hector could hear Slotha grunting behind him now, her bones cracking as her body shifted. He recognized the noise of a therianthrope on the change instantly. The councilor finished the stuttering man's sentence for him.

"He called you a 'fat cow,' Your Majesty."

The man's eyes widened further as the wet sound of blades tearing through flesh cut through the air beside Hector. The Boarlord took a brief glance at the man as he spluttered blood from his trembling lips before the guard released his head, allowing the body to topple forward to the floor. Two great gashes were visible in the man's back, his spine exposed where a pair of blades had sunk through his body, butchering him on the spot. With a grunt, Slotha moved behind Hector.

"Next," she snarled, her voice deep and wet, her teeth grating.

"Murder," said the councilor. "He and his companions killed an innkeeper and his man."

Hector heard the queen shift her bulk behind him, as a warrior reached forward and took hold of his scalp in a dirty hand.

"A moment, I beg of you!" said Hector quickly.

The councilor arched his eyebrows as Hector struggled in the warrior's grasp.

"The charge is quite straightforward; you apparently admitted to your crime in Friggia."

"I believe Her Majesty would benefit from the full story!"

"Spit it out, then!" she said, smacking her lips.

"I'm Baron Hector, the Boarlord of Redmire. I'm one of the Wolf's Council."

The councilor looked astonished as Slotha grabbed Hector by the shoulder and spun him about, his hair tearing from his scalp as he turned to face the queen of Tuskun.

"Oh, but what good fortune!" she roared, clapping her hands together. "Sosha smiles up at me!"

Nothing had prepared Hector for the sight of the monstrous Werewalrus. The scraps of clothing that had clung to her had been ripped away; her pasty, pale skin was now mottled dark brown and covered in calluses, her stocky legs having transformed into huge, flat flippers. Her clawed fingers were long and webbed, her hands wide and wobbling as she clapped them together. Her long, greasy hair hung down her back, neck and lips bristling with oily whiskers. A pair of yard-long tusks protruded down from her top lip, ivory blades that dripped crimson with the dead man's blood.

"You have the look of your father," she grunted, clawing at his face with a flippered hand. "He was an ugly pig, too!"

You have my permission to roar at the irony, chuckled the Vincent-vile to Hector.

"Hold him still," she gushed excitedly as her warrior grabbed his head once again. "I want to look into this one's eyes while I run him through. Imagine Prince Lucas's joy when I deliver a spitted Boarlord to him!"

"Wait!" shouted Hector, as Slotha raised her tusks, ready to strike his chest. She paused, waiting for him to speak.

"I know there's a price on my head, but grant my sorry life a few more days, I beg of you, Your Majesty. Killing me would be too easy—the prince would prefer it if you delivered me alive, I can promise you. I know him, I served him for years. Let him do what he will with me. I guarantee he'll be doubly grateful. . . ."

Slotha looked from Hector to her councilor. The man shrugged, leaving the decision entirely to her whim.

"You say I should let you live and go to Highcliff?"

"Hand me over as a gift alive rather than dead. I have information that will aid the Catlords in their war."

"Tell *me* your information then, Piglord."

Hector managed a thin smile.

Roll the bones, brother!

"My information is for Prince Lucas and him alone. Deliver me to him and your reward shall be greater than you could possibly imagine, Lady Slotha."

"That's *Queen* Slotha," she snorted.

"I know," said Hector as the warrior's grip on his hair tightened. "The queen of the North and the king of Westland; can you *imagine* what you might discuss together?"

Slotha smacked her lips as if savoring a previously un-known taste. Hector kept his eyes fixed on her.

She's taken the bait, Hector! Well done!

"I deliver you alive to Highcliff?"

"Myself and my two men." Hector gestured to Ringlin and Ibal at his side with a quick glance.

"Very well," said the Werewalrus, shuffling past the two rogues who breathed audible sighs of relief at their temporary pardon. She settled behind the last prisoner, who was afforded no such kindness.

"That one's a thief, Your Majesty," said the councilor, an-swering her unvoiced question.

"But remember, Piglord . . ." she said, rearing up behind the bound man as he knelt before her. The Ugri warrior held the prisoner's head as he kicked out, trying to roll clear. She lunged down fast, the tusks puncturing the man's back and disappearing up to her gums. The blood erupted as she tore them free.

"No tricks."

Hector bowed on his knees, his heart near exploding.

"Ready the *Myrmidon*," said the Walrus of Tuskun. "We sail to Highcliff to meet the prince."

PART VI

TALONS AND TURNCOATS

I

TWO RIVERS

ANY OBSERVER WITNESSING the *Banshee* disembarking into the border town of Two Rivers would have been hard-pressed to imagine a more unusual party of people. Drew led the way, the mountainous figure of the Behemoth, over seven feet of towering muscle, following behind him. The Weremammoth carried an enormous stone mallet across one shoulder, a weapon the strongest man would struggle to lift with both hands. Following him came the crooked figure of Baron Griffyn alongside the Catlady, Taboo.

Krieg awaited them at the head of the docks, his spiked mace swinging from his hip, grimacing as they approached. A chill wind blew through the ramshackle harbor, sending sand through the air like a shower of broken glass.

"Good to be off that wretched boat, isn't it?"

"It's good to be on our way again," said Drew, the passing townsfolk eyeing them suspiciously. "I just hope our friends are safe in Azra. Did you find horses?"

The Rhino nodded and set off up the street, Drew at his shoulder and the others behind.

"How's the old man?" asked Krieg, without looking back.

"He misses her, which is understandable, but she has Djogo. She'll be fine."

Faisal had insisted the Hawklady and Djogo remain behind in Azra as his guests. Effectively, the Jackal was holding her ransom, a guarantee that the Hawklords would return and fight for him, honoring the promise Drew made on their behalf. There had never been any doubt in Drew's mind that the Hawklords, *if* they could summon them, would aid them, but that clearly hadn't been the case for Faisal. Considering the previous visit of Wolf and Hawk to Azra years ago, the king had fair reason to feel that way.

Faisal had passed a decree that very night, granting every single slave in the city of Azra his or her permanent freedom. While the therian lords of the city had accepted this without challenge, the merchant classes had been horrified; it would take all of Faisal's political know-how to put their minds at ease in the following days. Delighted, Drew was in no doubt that the Jackal would bring his people in line; overnight their militia had swelled by tens of thousands as former slaves volunteered to help protect their city. Suddenly, the odds for the people of Azra against the three advancing armies didn't seem so grim.

Furthermore, the hundred gladiators who had journeyed from Scoria had joined Djogo and Shah in the desert city. The men were an elite fighting force who could be put to good use by Faisal, under Djogo's command. There was no need for Drew to drag his small army up into the Barebones. It seemed a far sounder plan to leave them in Azra to aid the Jackal in any way they could. As shows of goodwill went, it was much appreciated by Faisal, who immediately set them to work alongside his own soldiers, training and drilling the civilians and former slaves in preparation for battle. A skeleton crew had remained on the *Banshee*, transporting the remaining therians to Two Rivers.

A prospecting town, Two Rivers was the last place a ship the size of the *Banshee* could navigate up to on the Silver River. Being on the border of the Desert and Mountain Realms, it was a wild old town with little law or order, home to gem diggers, bounty hunters, the crazed, and the criminal. Drew hoped they could pass through the town quickly. A ramshackle avenue ran through its center, low buildings lining the pitted road on either side. Trading posts and taverns made up the majority of businesses, jostling for the attention of passersby. The group kept their heads down as they followed Krieg, aware they were being watched, the townsfolk making no attempt to hide their interest in the travelers. Krieg led them to the end of the street, marching up to a squat stable block with paddocks attached.

The wind stirred up dust devils, sand whipping through the air as they hurried toward the horse trader's establishment.

As they approached, Drew pulled up short, placing his hand on Krieg's shoulder.

"You're sure he can be trusted?"

"As trusted as anyone can be in a fleapit like Two Rivers. Why?"

Drew shivered as he tried to shake off the uneasy feeling. "No matter, Krieg. Lead on," he said as the Rhino entered the building.

The stable was split down the middle by a filthy path, with camels on one side and horses on the other. A bearded man in brown robes emerged down the passage, dragging a sack of grain behind him. He looked up, recognizing Krieg immediately.

"These your friends, then?" he said in a thick Omiri accent.

The man straightened, looking past Krieg toward his companions. His eyes seemed a little too large for his features, as if his face had frozen mid-choke and refused to return to normal.

"The horses," said Krieg, wasting no time on banter. The Rhino unstrung a pouch from his hip, jingling it in his hand. "I have the money, as agreed."

"Is that everything?" said the big-eyed man, watching Krieg weigh the bag of coins. Krieg tossed it, the trader catching it midair.

"Count them, if you distrust me," said the Rhino, his voice serious.

Drew took a moment to look around the interior of the building while the horse trader rooted through the money pouch. It was the largest structure they'd seen in Two Rivers, with a hayloft above that ran around the entire stable. Bright though it was outdoors, it was dark in here, a couple of lanterns keeping the filthy walkway illuminated, but all else shrouded in darkness. Taboo and Griffyn held a quiet conversation at Drew's back while the Behemoth stood to the rear, staring back at the doors.

Drew still felt on edge. Although the atmosphere in the stable was heavy with the smell of captive animals, a gut feeling told him that something wasn't right. Not wanting to alarm the horse trader, Drew let a little of the Wolf in. His heightened sense of smell revealed something else beyond the stench of animal feces. He smelled alcohol, sweat, and steel. His ears pricked as he concentrated, listening beyond the snorting horses and spitting camels. Floorboards creaked in the loft above.

"Do you work here alone?" asked Drew.

The man looked up, lips smacking nervously as Drew's eyes remained fixed upon the shadowy first floor overhead.

"Indeed. Why do you ask?"

"It sounds like you've rats in your hayloft, in that case. Big ones, judging by the noise they're making up there."

Instantly Krieg had his spiked mace out, while Taboo raised her spear. Drew kept his eyes focused upon the hayloft, catching sight of movements now as would-be assassins darted through the darkness.

"What treachery is this?" spat Krieg. "I make a deal with you in good faith."

The trader's eyes widened further as Krieg stepped toward him, twirling the mace in his grasp, the spikes spinning menacingly.

"They . . . they saw you come!" stammered the man, his eyes looking up. "This isn't my . . ."

The trader collapsed to the floor, unable to complete his sentence, the feathered flight of an arrow sticking out of his throat as the coins showered down on top of him. An arrow hit Griffyn's back, while Krieg crashed through the partition fence, an arrow protruding from his chest. Instantly the therians dived into the pens, camels and horses panicking at the intruders in their enclosures. Taboo had found a ladder on the rear wall, and leaped halfway up in one bound. She thrust her spear up through the hatch, a foe screaming as it struck home.

Feet hammered along the walkway above, the ambushers scrambling to find better positions from which to strike. Drew stayed close to Griffyn, supporting the winded Hawklord as they dashed for cover. A horse whinnied beside him as an arrow punched into its flank with a wet snap. It kicked out, striking another animal at its side, the pen transformed into a deadly arena.

"They could have avoided this," said Drew, the Hawklord grimacing as they ducked behind a post.

"It appears they'd rather fight," said Griffyn. "There must be quite a reward on your head!"

Drew pulled the arrow from the Hawklord's back, the tip embedded in the leather strapping of his breastplate. Griffyn grunted as the pair stared in shock at the shining silver arrowhead.

"These are no regular bandits, young Wolf."

"Stay here!"

A mountain of crates lined the rear of the horse enclosure, providing Drew with a means to reach the first floor. He changed as he bounded, feet elongating into gray, clawed paws as he raced up the stacked boxes toward the hayloft. He burst onto the dark landing, and his longsword arced through the air, striking a drawn bow from an assassin's hands. The man in black reached for a scimitar on his hip but was already flying through the air, the Werewolf catching him in the chest with a kick. The attacker disappeared over the hayloft rail, vanishing into the enclosure below.

Another black-kashed warrior lunged at Drew, his silver scimitar tearing a cut down the Werewolf's back. Drew roared, bringing his trident dagger around to disarm the man on his following blow. The scimitar flew from the man's grasp as Drew's longsword struck home.

On the opposite hayloft Drew caught a glimpse of Taboo,

the Weretiger cornered, jabbing with her spear and slashing with her claws. She was outnumbered three to one, and if her enemies had silver weapons, she was in terrible danger.

Glancing below Drew spied the Behemoth, dragging the wounded Krieg to safety through a crowd of alarmed camels. By Brenn's grace the silver arrow embedded in the Rhino's chest hadn't proved fatal. The Weremammoth looked up, noticing Drew as he pointed across to the other hayloft with his sword.

"Take its legs!" shouted Drew, and the giant instantly understood.

Leaning Krieg against the wall, the Weremammoth swung his enormous stone mallet around his head. The therianthrope transformed with each rotation, the weapon's speed increasing with the Mammoth's burgeoning muscles. Finally he brought it around into one of the supporting posts that held the hayloft up. The mallet's stone head shattered the pillar in two, sending the ceiling crashing down around him. Fearless, the Behemoth remained where he was, raising a huge arm over his head as beams and floorboards crashed down on top of him, along with the trio of assassins.

As the dust settled, Drew looked across the stable, searching the debris below for Taboo. There was no sign of her, only the broken-limbed corpses of the black-kashed warriors.

"Up here, Wolf!"

To his relief, Drew saw the Weretiger suspended from a

rafter across the way. She hauled herself over the beam, holding a hand to her bloodied side. Drew leaned on the balcony, chest heaving as he returned to human form. Below, Griffyn staggered over to Krieg, the two Werelords comparing their near-fatal wounds. The Behemoth, cloaked in sawdust and splintered wood, waved a mighty hand up toward Drew, his voice rumbling through the devastation.

"We need to go."

By the time the people of Two Rivers had investigated why camels were roaming their miserable, dust-ridden streets, the five therians had departed. Taking the sturdiest mounts they could find, the riders took a trail through the foothills that followed the southern branch of the river, leaving the barter town behind them.

The terrain was barren and rocky, vegetation sparse, the environment utterly inhospitable. Here and there the odd gnarled tree had managed to survive against the odds, its roots gripping the rocky slopes for dear life as the cold winds battered it.

The Behemoth brought up the rear of the group, riding the stockiest workhorse any of the therians had ever seen. Taller and uglier than the mountain ponies the others were riding, it had a broad back, thick legs, and a desire to carry heavy burdens. None came heavier than the Behemoth, or less ex-

perienced at riding for that matter. After suffering the horse's attempts to buck him off, the Weremammoth had struck an uneasy alliance with his mount, riding in stalemated silence. His companions bit their lips, resisting the temptation to tease him over his newfound friend.

Griffyn led the way, with Drew at his back. Taboo followed the Wolf, with Krieg close behind. Taboo had declined her companions' attention, insisting the cut along her side was a mere graze. *I've never encountered a tougher woman*, thought Drew, ever amazed by both her strength and her stubbornness. The Rhino had taken care of his chest wound while the others readied their horses, Griffyn staunching the bleeding with dressings from his pack. In obvious discomfort, Krieg had stifled his complaints on the uncomfortable ride.

"So who were they?" said Drew, his pony shadowing Griffyn's in front.

"I doubt we'll ever know," replied the Hawklord. "They carried no clues as to who was behind the ambush."

"They could have been anyone's agents: Dog, Cat, Hyena ... Crow!"

"Their choice of weapons is most alarming: silver. The Scorians used it to keep therian gladiators in check, but in Lyssia? It was outlawed across the entire continent, yet these assassins used it by blade and bow. Such a deadly metal doesn't come cheap; our enemies have wealthy benefactors."

Drew thought back to the scars on his back from his time

as a prisoner in Highcliff, whipped by the silver-studded whip of Captain Brutus.

"The Catlords reintroduced silver to Lyssia."

"Another connection then, tying your enemies together, Wolf," said Griffyn, kicking his pony's flanks to encourage her on.

The night was beginning to close in as Drew looked back. The lights of Two Rivers shone below; would anybody follow them, seeking retribution for the death of the men in the stable? Farther back, across the desert, the horizon glowed: Azra. *Are those the fires of the enemy camps? Or does the city burn?* Drew looked ahead once more at the trail disappearing into the distance, following the stream that tumbled down the rocky slope toward them. He stared up at the mountains, their snow-capped summits glowing dully in the twilight.

"I just hope we stay well ahead of our enemies," said Drew, urging his mount after Griffyn's.

"We must remain alert, Drew," said Griffyn, his eyes scanning the mountains in front of them. *His mountains.* "I fear we've been watched since we first set foot on to Omir's sands, young Wolf. The enemy follows our every move."

2

THE WRONG ANSWERS

THE SOLDIERS OF the Lionguard were in a relaxed mood, gathered around their fires, playing cards and tossing bones. Sorin led the festivities, winning more than his fair share of coin from his men. The Bastian contingent of Lord Frost's force remained removed from their comrades, polishing armor and sharpening weapons. The albino Catlord had retired to his tent, dining on the best food that his warriors had confiscated from the people of the Longridings. With the camp preoccupied, it was relatively easy for Trent to enter the prisoner's tent unnoticed. Letting the door flap swing shut behind him, he looked down upon the captive Werelord.

"Tell me," Trent said, standing over the bound prisoner. "What was he like?"

Baron Ewan looked up slowly. The Ramlord's face was a rich palette of bruises, a mask of purple, black, and blue. Sorin had used the flat of his silver-blessed longsword on the Lord of Haggard, beating the old man about head and body, dealing him injuries that could only heal over a mortal span of time. Nobody had tended the old man's wounds.

"Who?" asked Ewan, through broken lips. His left eye was closed shut, while his bloodshot right was fixed squarely on Trent.

"The Wolf—Drew," replied Trent, trying to sound cold and impassive.

The old Werelord studied him. "Why so interested?"

"What kind of man is he? We hear so many things. How did you find him?"

Ewan smiled, his swollen lips tearing anew through the bruising. He winced, arching his back, catching his breath.

"What's the matter?" asked Trent, concern creeping into his voice.

"Chest," said the Ram.

Lord Frost had ensured that his interrogators had worked Ewan over thoroughly. The Catlord had even participated himself, the Ram's greatest screams caused by the albino. Trent hadn't the stomach to witness the torturing of prisoners. He could kill a man, at the command of his superior officers, but torture wasn't why he'd signed up to the Lionguard.

Trent could see the rolls of tightly bound ropes that wound

around the beaten old man, securing him to the stake in the ground. Therianthrope or not, the bonds were excessive. Sorin and his cronies had battered the baron to within an inch of his life, his hands broken by the cruel captain's zealous work. Trent crouched and loosened the ropes, letting a clutch of them fall to the ground.

Ewan relaxed a little, leaning back and straightening his bent legs, bringing his bound hands up before him to massage his chest. Trent filled a mug of water for the Werelord, holding it to his lips as Ewan drank thirstily.

"My boy," he whispered. "Thank you."

"Why?"

"That was the greatest drink I've ever savored in my long and glorious life. A barrel of the Redwine's finest couldn't compete with it."

Trent smiled, taking the cup away. "The Wolf," he said again. "What of him?"

"He came to me in Haggard, a prisoner of the Goatlord, Kesslar. He was thrown into the cells beneath my keep alongside my people and me. We got to know one another. He had no reason to lie when he recounted all he'd been through. The death of his parents at the hands of the Lion and the Rats—"

"*He* killed his mother!" interrupted Trent.

Ewan sighed. "Did you want to hear my story?"

Trent grimaced, before nodding.

The Ramlord continued. "Drew was instrumental in freeing my people, helping us rise against our enemies. He then rode south, and I accompanied him as he sought to save Lady Gretchen from the claws of Prince Lucas."

Ewan paused, expecting the young Redcloak to cut in once more. When he didn't, he carried on.

"Lucas and Vanmorten took Cape Gala from the Horselords, stole the sovereign state from the people of the Longridings— *my people*—with the help of the Bastian invaders. While the majority sailed north to attack Highcliff, a small force was left behind in Cape Gala. Once again, Drew came to the aid of his friends, trying to rescue them from Vankaskan."

Ewan hung his head.

"I betrayed him. I handed him over to the monster Vankaskan. I recognize that villain, Sorin, as one of his. My boy, they turned High Stable into a monstrous circus, slaying Werelords and humans alike. Only their torment didn't end there. The Rat did such vile things . . ."

"What more of the Wolf?"

"He was gone," whispered Ewan. "Disappeared. At one moment, he was on the balcony; the next, gone. Vanished on the wind. I don't know what happened to him."

Trent couldn't look at the baron. He didn't want to believe him, but much of what the old therian said made sense. Still, he'd seen what had happened back on the family farm. *Drew had turned on Ma.*

"But Drew," said Trent, "he's a monster! He's a Werewolf, for Brenn's sake!"

"There are monsters across Lyssia—human and therian alike. Your brother's a good man."

"He killed our moth—" Trent stopped, biting his lip. "How did you know he was my brother?"

"You didn't say as much, but I'd heard mention of a Sergeant Ferran." Ewan sighed. "They might have beaten me, but not entirely senseless. My hearing works well enough. You and Drew are brothers?"

"*Were* brothers," corrected Trent. "Until he killed my ma."

Ewan shook his head sadly. "You believe everything you're told, lad?"

"I saw her corpse with my own *eyes*, old man! Don't think to lecture me on the Wolf's true nature. Nobody knows Drew better than I!"

"I fear you believe what you want to, Master Ferran. Could it be you're mistaken?"

"You know nothing. He's pulled the wool over your eyes, Sheeplord, clearly. My brother could charm his way into any fool's heart."

"There you go," said the old man. "*My brother*—the bond is strong between you. Search your heart, boy. You know I'm telling you the truth . . ."

Ewan was cut short as Trent stepped forward, his fist

raised above his head, ready to strike. The Ramlord's bruised eyes went as wide as the swelling would allow, the aged therian shrinking back in anticipation of the blow. Trent wavered, snarling. He stepped behind him swiftly, binding Ewan's ropes once again. Trent knew rope mastery as well as anyone, having learned under his father back on the Ferran farm. He gave them a sharp tug, the Ramlord's battered arms creaking as he was secured once more.

Trent got up. "Keep your poisonous words to yourself in future, you old fool," he said.

"It was you who came to me, seeking answers," said Ewan as Trent strode out of the tent—straight into Lord Frost, chewing on a haunch of bloody meat. Trent jumped with shock.

"It's lamb," said the Catlord, offering it to Trent. The youth looked at the meat: any rarer and it would still be bleating.

"No thank you, my lord," replied Trent, regaining his composure. "My appetite is lacking."

"Speaking with the prisoner, eh? Did he offer us anything new?"

"No, my lord."

"It's Frost, remember. You and I are friends now, Trent, just remember that." The Catlord took another bite of the lamb and looked at the tent door. "You've just reminded me. Our prisoner should never be left unguarded. I'll speak with Sorin; arrange for a guard to be posted on the Ram at all times. Good man, Trent. Go get yourself some rest."

Trent bowed nervously, his cheeks flushed with color at having been discovered speaking with the prisoner. He strode away in the direction of the corral; his horse, Storm, needed bedding down for the night. He glanced back as he walked away. Frost watched him go, tearing another mouthful of meat from the joint of lamb. Trent turned his gaze to the ground, feeling the Catlord's eyes burning holes in his back.

Fool, Trent, he berated himself. *Giving Frost cause to distrust me. That's the last time I seek answers.*

3

TOR RAPTOR'S MERCY

IF THE FOOTHILLS of Omir appeared treacherous, nothing had prepared the travelers for the perilous trail through the Barebones. Another old mountain road had led to Windfell, but the group had passed it by. The city of the Hawklords wasn't their destination; it was their tomb they sought, high up in the sky. Only Griffyn seemed at ease, the old Hawk returning home for the first time in fifteen years, while his fellow therians gripped the reins of their mounts with white knuckles. At the rear, the Behemoth was slumped in the saddle of his stocky horse. Krieg and Taboo were in front of him, the ravine drop to their right bringing on terrible bouts of vertigo. Farther ahead, Drew followed Griffyn closely, his reins wrapped around his trident dagger.

Occasionally Drew glanced into the chasm, a morbid fascination with the deadly drop luring him like a moth to candlelight. With each of his horse's steps, the hooves dislodged stones that skittered away from the path, bouncing off the sloping rock and disappearing into space. Drew brought his eyes back to Griffyn ahead, smacking his lips as he breathed the cold, thin air. The wind changed direction with alarming frequency, sudden updrafts replaced by blustering downdrafts that threatened to knock the riders from their saddles. As they climbed Tor Raptor the Mighty, giant of the Barebones, wispy clouds drifted all about her and the surrounding peaks.

Griffyn twisted around, smiling at the pale-faced Wolflord. "Breathtaking?"

"Literally," replied Drew as another gust of wind hit him. "I'm struggling to breathe, here. How much farther?"

"Some way yet, cub. See that?"

Griffyn pointed ahead to where the cliffs of Tor Raptor appeared to collide with those of the neighboring mountain, as if the two giant landmasses had collapsed against each other. The path was all but invisible, with a thin sliver of vertical light the only indication that the trail emerged on the other side. The drop between the two vanished into gloomy blackness, swallowed up by the enormous ravine's dark depths.

"I see it," shouted Drew over the wind. "But I don't like it!"

"The Falling Road: it's not to be liked, it's to be endured!

We travel to the tomb of my fathers. Look about you, Wolf— see the burial sites and barrows of my kinsmen."

Drew looked up, scouring the cliffs for sign of human or therian touch. There they were, dotting the mountain hundreds of feet above. At first glance they appeared to be rock formations, but closer inspection revealed them to be cairns, tall spires of rocks that the Hawklords had placed to mark out the chambers of the dead.

"The tombs of the Hawklords, Baron Griffyn? Left unguarded on a mountainside?"

"You think we fear graverobbers in the Barebones? If the mountain doesn't kill you, there are other things on Tor Raptor that protect our tombs. My forefathers do not readily relinquish their worldly goods, even in death . . ."

Griffyn let this last statement hang in the air, the sinister implication not lost on Drew. *Even in death?*

The Hawklord swung in his saddle, leaning precariously out to see around Drew. The Wolflord blanched when he imagined the old man tumbling from his seat.

"Our friends look unwell," chortled Griffyn. "It appears the Barebones aren't for the fainthearted!"

"You might feel like them if you weren't a Hawklord!" said Drew in their defense.

"You forget, young Wolf," said Griffyn, gesturing at his shoulders with a hooked thumb. "My wings were taken from me many years ago. If I fall here, I'd be as dead as anyone else.

Lean forward in your saddle, respect the path, and pray the mountain remains merciful."

The Hawklord cast his hand heavenward, the snowcapped giant of the Barebones towering above them.

"You are in Tor Raptor's talons now!"

As fierce as the winds had been on the cliff path an hour before, nothing had prepared the therians for the gale that greeted them on the Falling Road. Dismounting when they approached the monstrous chasm, Drew had marveled at the sheer cliffs on either side as they reached across to one another. He whispered a brief, heartfelt prayer to Brenn as he followed Griffyn into the darkness, leading his pony along behind.

The Hawklord had warned them to keep their voices low when traversing the Falling Road. Avalanches were commonplace, where massive boulders had caught between the cliffs, weighed down with packed ice, waiting for the chance to break free and plummet toward the road. As if the threat from above and raging winds weren't enough, the path was nothing more than scree. The therians' feet and ponies' hooves scrambled for purchase as they passed over the ice and gravel. Frequently, Drew found himself casting his trident dagger out, grateful for the barbed weapon as he snatched hold of the cliff wall to stop himself from falling.

While Griffyn had little trouble on the path, the same could not be said for Taboo, Krieg, and the Behemoth. The Weremammoth had taken some persuading to traverse the treacherous road, and his companions shared his concerns. These people were from jungles and savannas, not freezing mountains. This world was alien to them. With words of encouragement from Drew and Griffyn they'd continued on, none wishing to break their oath to the young Wolflord. Their loyalty and courage filled Drew's heart with hope.

Ahead, Griffyn waited, cloak wrapped around his body as defense against the freezing wind. His pony hunkered against the cliff face, sheltering as best it could, as Drew slowly and carefully approached. His voice was controlled when he spoke over the howling gale.

"We need to pick up our pace, Drew. The night closes in. If we can get beyond the Falling Road, we may find somewhere to pitch camp before tackling the summit tomorrow."

Drew looked back, spying Taboo appearing around the cliff path a hundred yards or so behind. The others were behind the Weretiger, somewhere—hopefully making steady and safe progress.

He turned back to Griffyn, squinting as sleet peppered his face.

"How far to the end?"

"We're halfway through," replied the Hawklord.

Only halfway, thought Drew. *And we've been on this murderous road for over an hour.*

His nerves were shot, his body on the brink of exhaustion, adrenaline the only thing keeping him moving. Drew noticed that Griffyn was looking up. He followed the Hawk's gaze. The black wall of rock rose at a skewed angle overhead, meeting the opposing cliff high above, boulders the size of houses buttressed and braced against one another. It looked like a monstrous cathedral ceiling, hewn crudely from the mountains. With such an awe-inspiring, religious feel to the place, it was no wonder the Hawklords had chosen Tor Raptor as the site of their oldest tombs.

As he watched, a few blocks of ice came away from the natural ceiling, falling from where they'd been packed in place. They were closely followed by a large slab. Drew leaned back against the cliff wall as the frozen debris rushed by. The sound of them crashing on to the ravine bottom bounced back up toward them from hundreds of feet below. Drew held his breath as the reverberations disturbed the ice overhead, cracking noises from the strained ceiling audible over the wind, but was relieved to see nothing else break free.

The Hawklord beckoned him frantically now, urging him to follow swiftly. Drew's booted feet scrambled along the smooth path, the rock pitched at an angle ensuring that one false step would send the Wolflord slipping to his doom.

Then a sudden, terrible shriek echoed overhead, as if the mountain itself cried out in agony. After a couple of awful, ponderous heartbeats, the scream was joined by the sound of the monstrous ceiling cracking. The noise shook Drew's body as he pressed himself once more against the cliff, the rock at his back trembling and shuddering as stone, ice, and snow high above them buckled and began to fall. He looked up in horror as the crashing cascade of black and white death hurtled toward him. Drew glanced back along the ledge as Taboo was suddenly engulfed by the icy downpour, disappearing from view in the blink of an eye. Rocks and snow rained down around him. A fist-sized block of ice hit his shoulder, narrowly missing his skull but still sending him staggering to his knees, while a great lance of granite fell like a guillotine, shearing his pony in two and dragging it over the edge. Boulders hit the path, smashing and tearing the narrow trail away all around him. Drew's scream was cut short as the deafening roar of the avalanche choked the breath from his battered body.

4

THE SCENE OF THE CRIME

AS THE *MYRMIDON* eased into Highcliff, six of Tuskun's finest Ugri warriors stood to attention on the icy foredeck. Before them, Hector took in the city, the night casting a brooding menace over the all-too-quiet port. This city had been his home for a time, a metropolis that brimmed with life from all over Lyssia. Before the curfew of the Wolf's Council, Highcliff had been a city that rarely slept. Now, with the Lord Protector and his friends gone, as well as the majority of the city's inhabitants, Highcliff was a ghost town. Hector placed his black-gloved hands on the frosted rail, manacles jangling between them, as he surveyed the results of the Lion's vengeance.

The pier that the *Myrmidon* pulled alongside had once sported tall lanterns that lit the way for sailors and fishermen alike. Now it was dotted with gibbets that contained the dead and dying. Hector stared at the rusting cages, crows and gulls squawking as they bickered over the morsels within. The unmistakable Graycloaks of the Wolfguard hung around the throats of corpses and captives alike. The moans of the unfortunate souls could be heard by the crew of the warship, but the Tuskuns ignored them. The Ugri were the toughest, most fearsome men the frozen north had spawned, each over six feet tall and seemingly as broad. During the journey, Hector couldn't so much as scratch his nose without one of them glowering or growling. They stood to one side as the heavy barefoot steps of their queen approached.

"Is it as you remember, Piglord?" Slotha, the Walrus of Tuskun, laughed. While many of Lyssia's Werelords chose to keep their human appearance on most occasions, saving their shape-shifting for when the time arose, Slotha held no such discipline. Her hold over the Ugri warriors was to the result of her many victories in battle combined with her intimidating presence. Easily the tallest woman Hector had ever met, and as broad as any barbarian who worked in her service, she revelled in her frightening therian image. While not completely transformed, there were enough elements of the Werewalrus on show to strike fear into the hearts of most men. Her large hands were still webbed, her fingernails sharp claws, and her wide feet slapped the deck with each step. Her muscular arms held the dark, mottled texture of the beast, while her head kept the key features of the walrus, dark whiskers sprouted from around her lips while a suggestion of her tusks remained in evidence, protruding from her upper jaw.

"It's quite . . . changed," managed Hector, trying not to look at the monstrous woman. He'd endured days at sea in her company, and every additional moment in her presence made him fearful she'd back down on their agreement. He'd seen first-hand how vicious she could be with her prisoners. Here was a therian who enjoyed the kill.

"Changed how?"

Hector looked back at the swinging bodies in their cages. "They've done away with the sea lanterns, I notice," he said calmly.

Slotha snorted at Hector's dark humor.

The *Myrmidon* secured, the crew extended their gangway across to the stone pier. Two dozen torch-carrying Lionguard awaited them, alongside half as many Bastian warriors. More cavalry gathered on the docks, along with an empty carriage awaiting the visitors. The Ugri grunted, unimpressed by the southerners' show of strength.

"Take him ashore," grunted Slotha, shifting her great mass to one side. "We've an audience with Prince Lucas."

As the procession climbed through the steep city toward Highcliff Keep, Hector's mind cast back to the frantic escape he'd endured, chased through the streets by Omiri warriors. That seemed like another life now, the youth who'd fled bearing little resemblance to the man who returned.

Looking out of the carriage he noticed the city was far from deserted. Lights were on in many homes and taverns, showing that Highcliff was still inhabited, but the streets were devoid of life, the curfew he'd helped set in place still standing. A veil of fear had settled over the city.

An Ugri warrior sat on either side of him, while opposite the huge frame of Slotha filled the entire padded bench.

"What's the matter, Piglord? Upset with what they've done to your city?" asked the Walrus.

"This isn't my city, Your Majesty. My home is far to the east of here—Redmire, capital of the Dalelands. But I'd be lying if I said Highcliff meant nothing to me. This is the city where I learned who my friends were."

His voice was clipped, the words catching in his throat.

Slotha smiled. "You've got a world full of regrets, boy."

"Only one," answered Hector, looking at his manacled hands. "I never truly said good-bye to him."

Since Friggia, Hector had tried not to think about Drew, but it was impossible. The Stags, Shark, and Bear might have betrayed him, but Drew had been long gone by then. He'd heard the rumors about Drew falling to his death in Cape Gala. The Wolf had been the only true friend he'd ever known. But his hatred for the things done in the Wolf's name, in his absence, remained undiminished. Each of the other Werelords had betrayed him over time and each had paid the price. First the selfish Earl Mikkel had fallen, the Doglords of Omir having slain the Staglord as he'd fled to his home in the Barebones. Then Duke Bergan, the Lord Protector who had humiliated him, stripping him of power within the Wolf's Council, had been slain in Highcliff. Count Vega had held Hector to ransom, dangling the grisly truth of Vincent's death over his head like a guillotine. The Sharklord's reputation had been built upon dishonesty— Hector had done the right thing, getting rid of the count before the Shark could bite.

The last of the quartet had disappointed him most of all, Duke Manfred having left him for dead in Friggia. With dear Drew no doubt dead and those he'd once considered friends having turned on him, what choice did Hector have but to switch his allegiance to the Catlords? They wouldn't punish him for the power he commanded. They would embrace his magistry. And Manfred? He would pay for his betrayal.

That's it, dear brother, whispered the Vincent-vile. *A reckoning comes . . .*

"Sounds like the Piglord was in love," teased the Walrus.

Hector directed the conversation back at her. "I know very little about love, Your Majesty," he said. "A lifetime with my head buried in books has allowed me few opportunities to enjoy the company of the fairer sex."

"A bookworm, like your father was, then?"

"You knew him?"

"Lord Huth visited Tuskun when I was in my youth. For a while my father petitioned his to arrange marriage."

Hector coughed suddenly, shocked at the news that his father might have been wed to such a fearsome warrior queen as Slotha. Never could a match be more misplaced. The Werewalrus glowered at her captive Boarlord.

"And what stopped the marriage from taking place?"

"Your father's constitution, apparently," she said, strangely wistful for the briefest moment at what might have been. "The cold northern air played havoc with his breathing."

"That sounds about right," said Hector, slowly regaining his composure.

Slotha sneered at him. "Weakling Boars: it was the best thing that could have happened. Any child of that union would have polluted the bloodlines of the Walruses. My father did right by me. He spared me the embarrassment of a marriage with your kind, and saved me for something greater."

"You mean to impress Prince Lucas?"

"He's a Prince," she said stiffly. "I'm the queen in the North.

Who knows what ... *alliance* we can agree upon. This is my first visit to Highcliff. I intend to make it memorable."

"I'm sure it will be," said Hector, dabbing at his lips as he reclined in his seat. "The Court of Highcliff won't forget you in a hurry."

5

THE SCREAMING PEAK

THE TRIDENT DAGGER remained buried within the ice, the battered old blade the only thing stopping Drew from sliding off the slope into thin air. The muscles in his left arm strained, his elbow locked as he struggled to remain motionless. The toes of his torn boots were braced against the ice as if they might somehow stop his body from falling should the trident dagger snap. The blade was bowing, the metal bending back on itself as it threatened to break. Drew looked up, grimacing, as the old Hawklord skidded down the incline toward him, somehow keeping his balance.

The avalanche on the Falling Road had been no accident. A loud shriek had set the rock- and icefall in motion, timed to perfection. While Drew and Griffyn had avoided the deadly deluge, what fate had befallen their companions wasn't known. The path behind them had been cut off, choked in a cloud of dusty ice and broken stone. Drew's stomach lurched when he thought about Krieg, Taboo, and the Behemoth. The trio had followed him to Lyssia to fight by his side: that the mountain might have killed them broke his heart. The two survivors had continued on alone, minus their ponies and provisions, which had been carried away by the barrage of boulders. Drew and Griffyn were left to pray that their friends had survived and could find their way back to the lower path to Windfell.

"Your hand!" called Griffyn, reaching his out, palm open.

Drew threw his body forward, the hands of the two Werelords clamping over one another's wrists. The baron deftly hauled Drew back up the slope and onto the sliver of a path they'd been following. The young Wolflord collapsed against the cliff, body trembling as he struggled to regain his composure, while the Hawklord seemed perversely relaxed.

"I can't go on!" Drew cried, gasping for breath, the air so thin his lungs ached.

Griffyn looked down, fine hair whipping across his face as he smiled. "It appears youth counts for nothing: experience everything. Remember, these are *my* mountains, Drew. Come, we mustn't delay. We approach the summit, my friend. We must try and reach the Screaming Peak before nightfall and find shelter by the tomb. The last place one wants to be stranded at night is on Tor Raptor's back!"

Drew rubbed the strained muscles of his arms. "Any sign of our enemy?"

"None," said Griffyn.

"Perhaps we've lost them. You did say this path's location was guarded by the Hawklords, didn't you?"

"Yes, but that's not to say our enemy hasn't found another route to the summit."

"Are you sure the Hawklords will hear your call?"

Griffyn stroked his grizzled jaw, glancing at the sky around them. Below, the clouds rolled like a smoky sea, the jagged peaks of Tor Raptor's sisters visible like islands through the fading light.

"They'll hear it, Drew, no matter where they are. How many still live, however, is another question entirely."

Griffyn helped Drew to his feet, the young Wolf craning his neck to look toward the summit. Drew shook his head, trying not to linger on the dizzying sight.

"If I don't die of a broken neck, the vertigo might give me a heart attack," he murmured. "How in Brenn's name did you get your dead to the summit?"

"How do you think?" The Hawklord smiled grimly. "We flew them."

The dark settled over the Barebones as the two therians struggled on, their hopes of beating the sunset long gone. Drew caught sight of Griffyn disappearing over a ledge above. There were hand and footholds aplenty here, but they were hidden by the ice and the night. Drew waited a moment for the old man to reappear, to offer a hand to help him climb up, but Griffyn didn't appear.

Cursing, Drew hacked at the ice, forcing the trident dagger in once again, crying in pain as the cold metal rubbed against the stump of his wrist. He thought he'd got used to the feel of the basket handle against the sheared bones, but the freezing weather that crowned Tor Raptor caused a new, unknown discomfort. He reached up with his right hand, black and blue fingertips desperately trying to catch the ledge.

He could feel his will slipping, along with his grip on the mountainside. His eyes drifted down into the empty sky. Death would be swift if he fell. There were worse ways to die.

I can't stop now, I have to fight on. For my friends and my people! For Taboo and Krieg and the Behemoth!

Drew brought his head up and stared at the moon.

Her light might have been cold, but the warmth he felt inside was unmistakable, and he let it flood through him. Not for the first time on the mountain, Drew let the Wolf in, just enough to feel his fingers tearing into claws, a lupine hand taking a firm grip on the overhang. With a growl he hauled himself high, ripping the dagger free as he kicked back against the rocks below.

His torso landed on the ledge, the rock digging deep into

the fur that covered his stomach. Drew grunted as he scrambled and snatched at the darkness ahead, legs kicking out into space, threatening to send him toppling back into nothingness. The bent and battered trident dagger bounced off the ledge ahead, causing the sheet ice to shatter in great shards. Gradually, he inched forward, his right leg finally finding its way above the overhang, his knee finding purchase as he rolled his exhausted body on to the ledge.

"You took your time, Wolf."

Drew turned his head, looking toward the voice as the wind tugged at his legs where they dangled across the overhang. The ledge opened onto a rocky platform perhaps twenty feet across, receding toward a sheer wall of rock that rose the remaining fifty feet to Tor Raptor's peak. A jagged, triangular crack was visible at the wall's base, rising ten feet up to a point, a dark doorway that disappeared into the mountain. A figure stepped out of the shadows into the moonlight, Baron Griffyn held before him, with his head pulled back and a familiar short, silver knife pressed to his throat.

"We've been here before, Rook," said Drew to the Crowlord, rolling over on to his stomach, inching away from the overhang. "Only last time it was a woman you threatened as opposed to an old man. Let the Hawk go. Face me like a therian."

"Hawk? This cripple? If he was a Hawk, he'd have wings! Let's see how he flies, eh?" To emphasize the point, Rook skirted Drew and marched toward the edge, instantly causing the young Wolflord to raise his hand.

"No, wait!"

"What do you want?" gasped Griffyn, his feet struggling in vain to halt the Werecrow's progress toward the drop.

Drew looked about frantically, his hand catching hold of a long dagger of broken ice.

"Riven, Stormdale, Windfell: everything! I want the Barebones, Griffyn!" shouted Rook, propelling the old man forward.

The dagger of ice hit Rook square in the face; Drew's aim was faultless. The Crow cawed furiously, instantly releasing Griffyn, who hit the ice and slid toward the edge. Rook collapsed, screaming obscenities as his hands went to his shattered face. Drew dived for the Hawklord's arms, catching Griffyn's hand as he disappeared from the ledge. The old man hung there for a moment, the weight of his body drawing the young Wolflord ever closer to the edge. Behind, Drew heard the screams of the Crowlord as Rook began to change.

"Release me, Drew, before we both fall!" shouted Griffyn, eyes wide with fearful sincerity.

"I won't let you go," gasped Drew, tears streaming as he struggled to keep hold of the Hawklord, his body still sliding closer to oblivion.

"Beware the dead, Drew. Open the windows; call my people

to you and take what's yours by rights. I brought it here," whispered Griffyn. "I kept it safe."

Drew growled, calling upon whatever lycanthropic strength remained inside, but it was no use. The Werewolf's clawed hand was gripping at the Hawklord's tearing sleeve. Griffyn glanced past Drew's shoulder, his face a mask of alarm as his eyes settled on the enemy at Drew's back.

"Brenn protect you, Drew!" he cried as he tore his arm loose and fell into the night, swallowed by the darkness below.

Drew rolled quickly, almost following Griffyn over the edge as the ice shattered beside him, a longsword crashing into the ledge. He looked up to see clouds pass over the moon above.

With a blood-curdling screech the Werecrow threw his arms out, wings erupting from his back in an explosion of feathers. The lord of Riven had fully changed—Rook's features had utterly gone, replaced by the monstrous head, sharp black beak open and tongue rattling within. His arm came back down, the sword smashing into the ground where Drew had lain moments earlier. The Wolflord scrambled across the ice, making toward the rock face as the Werecrow followed. Rook was in no danger of slipping, his feet having shifted into long, dark talons that gripped the ice securely.

"Where do you run to?" squawked Rook, his huge chest rippling, muscles and feathers ruffling as he stalked closer. "Wolves don't belong in the sky!"

Drew reached the rock wall. Every muscle burned, every

ounce of energy had been spent climbing Tor Raptor. He tried to call on the Wolf, but there was little left. Tugging his longsword from its battered scabbard, he glanced at the dark doorway. A series of runes were carved around the triangular entrance.

Beware the dead, Drew . . .

The Werecrow leaped suddenly, closing on the Wolf with a beat of his enormous wings. Rook's sword came down, Drew raising his own in defense, the metal ringing in his grasp with the full weight of the Crowlord behind it. With the steel shattering, the weapon flew from his grip, the blade broken in two. Drew didn't wait, crawling quickly through the dark arch. As he passed over the threshold, the runes began to glow with a pale silver light, their ghostly illumination bouncing off the rock walls within.

Behind, Drew heard the Werecrow laugh, a wheezing screech of glee, as it followed him into the tomb. He scrambled on, staggering briefly to his feet before tumbling down a flight of stone steps. Drew rolled to a halt in the center of a great round chamber, the walls of which were inscribed with silver sigils like those that glowed outside. A large window was cut through the rock overhead, open to the night sky beyond. The runes seemed to beat with a rising rhythm, the thrum of which reverberated through Drew's ears, causing his teeth to chatter and his bones to ache. It was like a slow, drawn-out heartbeat, as if Tor Raptor's summit were alive, awakening with his arrival. The noise gripped his chest. Drew wearily climbed to his feet, squinting through the otherworldly light.

At first glance it looked as if a series of caves were carved within the domed walls, but then he saw the wrapped bodies set within each of the alcoves: the mummified remains of the Hawklords of old. He counted twelve such catacombs pockmarking the chamber, with chests laid at the feet and head of each mummy. He might have stared at them in wonder longer if it had not been for the dark, feathered monster that descended the steps into the room.

Rook let his wings flap once more, sending clouds of dust swirling through the air. His feet scraped against the cold stone floor, talons grating and sending shivers racing up Drew's spine. The young Wolflord retreated, soon finding the wall at his back.

"Done running, Wolf?" sneered the Werecrow. "Griffyn will have to make do with the mountainside. You can have his bed in this dead birds' nest."

Rook took another step into the chamber just as moonlight began to stream in through the window above. The disturbed dust glittered in the air like tiny silver stars as the light settled on the catacomb behind Drew. The alcove glowed suddenly as the moon's rays landed upon it, and a shaft of pale blue light glowed dimly on the mummy's chest; it held a sword in its grasp.

"What dark magistry is this?" squawked Rook, taking another step closer to Drew, but less steadily now, looking over his mighty winged shoulders around the room.

Drew's instincts told him what to do. He reached behind, his fingers settling around the sword's handle. The mummy instantly released its grip. With his hand closing around the sword, the blade glowed brighter, its pale blue light flashing bright white in Drew's grasp.

"There's nothing dark about it," said Drew breathlessly, his eyes fixed on the shining blade in astonishment. The young Wolflord was so entranced by the weapon that he didn't notice Rook raise his own blade.

Before the Crow could strike, a sudden, violent wind whipped through the tomb, throwing the young Wolf to the ground. He looked up, his left arm sheltering his eyes from the blinding gale. Lord Rook teetered forward and backward as the wind hurtled around him, buffeting him from side to side and lifting him into the air.

Drew could make out a series of dark shadows racing from each of the alcoves and joining the cyclone. The Werecrow let out a scream as the speeding winds smashed into his wings, cartilage snapping and feathers flying in a ghastly black shower. His cry increased in pitch as cuts began to appear across his body, first his arms and legs, flesh tearing and bones breaking. Next the wounds appeared across his chest and back, as shadowy talons slashed into his torso. As the feathers and blood flew, the Crowlord of Riven's screams reached a deafening roar, forcing Drew to look away.

The wind dropped suddenly, as did the body of the Crowlord. Spluttering and coughing, Drew looked back into the center of the tomb, his eyes settling on the corpse of Rook, his head back-to-front and his body sliced to ribbons. Feathers floated through the blood-misted air as the moon continued to shine into the chamber. Drew felt his heart constricting once more as the shadows that had joined the deadly whirlwind began to take a more solid form.

Twelve dark figures appeared, their form shifting all the time as they closed in around him. Drew's mouth was dry, and when he tried to breathe he felt the pressure growing in his chest. Skeletal black hands emerged from the wraiths, reaching out toward him, their taloned fingers grasping. He brought the white sword around, holding it in his trembling grasp, a hopeless attempt at warding the demons away.

As one, the phantoms retreated, and the air returned to Drew's lungs in a surging, life-giving wave. His chest heaved as he watched the dozen shapes suddenly switch from grim black wraiths into ethereal white angels. Dazzled by the stunning light, Drew looked on as the dozen figures seemed to shrink in height. The Wolf righted himself, standing gingerly as he looked over the glowing shapes. *Are they kneeling? Bowing?*

Beyond the sentinels, Drew could see twelve runes carved

into the tomb wall shining as bright as the sword in his hand, forming a perfect circle. He limped over, between the ghosts, taking care to avoid touching them. The runes encircled a round stone set in the rock, similar to a small millstone, with a dimple carved into the middle. Hooking the sword beneath his left arm, he tried to prize the stone's edge, but there was nothing to take hold of. Returning the sword to his hand, he smashed the twisted end off the trident dagger, sending it to the floor with a clatter. He then placed the metal-capped stump into the hollow and pushed. The stone grated, sliding back against the rock around it. With a sudden *clang* the stone fell away, revealing a tunnel that began to rip the air from the room.

Drew dropped to the floor, his tattered cloak flapping and shearing free from his shoulders, sucked away through the hole and out into the dark space beyond the mountain. One after another the white ghosts were drawn through the hole, screeching and screaming as they went, the sound deafening, their light blinding, as Drew gripped the cold stone wall for fear of being torn through the tunnel after them.

6

A GIFT FROM THE NORTH

HECTOR COULDN'T BELIEVE the change that had taken place in the prince. Having spent a torturous time in Lucas's service under the tutelage of the wicked Vankaskan, he'd seen the young Lionlord change from a boy to a man well before his years. An expert warrior with blade in hand, with total mastery of his felinthropy, he was the image of his dead father, King Leopold, a worthy successor to the Lion King's crown. But the figure that sat on the throne before him was a shadow of that bold, impetuous youth, a ghost of the Werelord he'd once known and feared. Where was the old Lucas?

He's in there, brother. Just you wait and see. . . .

Prince Lucas had remained silent when the Tuskun party arrived. He'd stayed silent while Queen Slotha had announced, with much bluster, that she'd brought a gift from the north to the Lion of Westland. The Lord Chancellor, Vanmorten, had gone through the formalities with the Werewalrus, willing her to hurry to the end of her grand speech, his eyes fixed on the young Boarlord who stood manacled between her guards. The Ugri warriors propelled the magister forward, sending Hector to his knees.

"Kill him."

Lucas's voice was clear and calm. This was new to Hector— the prince he'd served had been prone to great emotional rants and tantrums. Vanmorten turned slowly and stared at the throne. His face was hidden within his cowl, the scars from his battles with Drew having left him hideously disfigured twice over.

Lucas was sitting upright in the stone chair, spine stiff against its back. The rear of the hall was shrouded in darkness, the torches unlit in their sconces around the throne. Lucas's hands rested on the carved snakes on the chair's arms as he stared at Hector. Leopold's iron crown sat firmly upon his head, his son's blond hair lank and lifeless beneath it.

"I don't think so," replied a voice from behind the throne. "Let's hear what the Boarlord says before rushing to any judgment, Lucas."

The woman who stepped into the light was the polar opposite to the queen of Tuskun. Whereas Slotha was a towering figure who cast a huge, intimidating shadow, the other was slight and slender. Hector had seen nobody like her in all of Lyssia, her skin so black it seemed to glow with a dull purple light, while her eyes shone yellow like the sun. She came to a halt before him, looking down at the kneeling magister. Her head was shaved smooth, every bump of her skull visible in the torchlight. While others in the chamber avoided eye contact with her, Hector was unable to draw his eyes away. He'd heard the tales about her, and she was even more fascinating in the flesh: Opal, the Catlady of Bast. She arched her eyebrow in surprise as the Boarlord fixed his gaze upon her.

"I would have his head on a spike, to go with those of other traitors," spat the young Lion, his lips peeling back to show a full set of sharp, white teeth. "What can he possibly say that will spare him my wrath?"

"It might be wise to listen to his final words, Your Highness," said Vanmorten, trying to reason with the impatient prince. "Think of it as an amusement!"

"If the prince wants him dead, so be it," declared Slotha, clapping her huge hands. An Ugri stepped forward, unhitching an ax from his belt. The audience gasped as he raised it over Hector's head.

"Put that away!" shouted Vanmorten.

"He's *my* prisoner," growled Slotha, bearing her tusks in a jutting snarl.

"He *was* your prisoner," corrected Vanmorten. "Until you presented him as a gift to Prince Lucas."

The Ugri warrior glanced at his queen who, with a nod of the head, commanded he step down. She glared at the Wererat as the Lord Chancellor turned back to the prince. Opal watched, smiling, enjoying the tension in the great hall.

"Hear what he says, Your Highness, then do what you will," said the Ratlord.

Lucas nodded. He looked tired to Hector, his former vigor and energy having all but disappeared, to be replaced by pale flesh and red-ringed eyes. Something wasn't right.

"Go ahead, Piggy. Speak your mind for the last time."

Hector struggled to his feet, the manacled hands making the task awkward. He pulled his eyes from Opal, focusing on the prince.

"Your Highness," he said, which caused Lucas to chuckle.

"You dare call me that after your betrayal . . ."

Vanmorten and Opal looked at the prince, their glares encouraging him to quieten. Miraculously, this seemed to work.

The prince pays heed to his advisers' words, brother, whispered Vincent. *Let's hope his advisers in turn are open to suggestion. . . .*

Hector cleared his throat, the interruption having thrown him. His guts were knotted, twisted around themselves with anxiety. He'd placed his throat in the Lion's jaws on an all-or-nothing roll of the bones.

"As Baron of Redmire and Lord of the Dalelands, I offer the Emerald Realm to you, Prince Lucas, as well as my services as magister and councilor."

The room was quiet as the members of Lucas's court looked at one another in astonishment.

Finally, Vanmorten spoke. "Is this some kind of trick, Boarlord?"

"It's no trick. I'm giving you the Dalelands, Prince Lucas: hilt, blade, and scabbard. You have our allegiance and my support as you secure lordship over Lyssia. What does that give you: Westland, the Cluster Isles, the Longridings, and now the Dalelands? That's four of the Seven Realms: the throne is yours, Your Highness."

"I've already taken the Dalelands, Piggy," said Lucas, glaring at Hector with utter contempt. "It's no longer yours to give."

"But it is, Your Highness," said Hector. "You can attack the Dales, but Brenn's law stands above all others: the Boars of Redmire rule the Dalelands, and as Baron of Redmire I speak on behalf of all my people. The support of the Emerald Realm is mine to give, and mine alone. You have our fealty."

"Do I hear you correctly?" said the Ratlord. "This is the same young Boar who was a founding member of the Wolf's Council, a traitor who turned against the House of Lions and all that was lawful? Why the change of heart, boy? Why the sudden allegiance to your rightful monarch? It doesn't have anything to do with your capture in the north and your friends being defeated, does it?"

The manacles jangled as Hector lifted his arms, right hand raised as he begged permission to speak.

"I wasn't *captured* in the north. Had I chosen to, I could have left Friggia at any point in time. I asked to be escorted to Slotha in . . ."

"That's *Queen* Slotha!" shouted the Walrus, backhanding him.

Hector looked up at the massive Werelady as she hulked over him. He winced, his split lip torn and streaming as he spoke through gritted, bloodied teeth.

"I asked to be escorted to *Queen* Slotha, so I could be brought here to parlay with you. I was never caught by the Tuskuns. I come here willingly. I'm worth more to you alive than dead."

"What possible value do you have?" asked Vanmorten. "I could have you sign a declaration right now, declaring your allegiance, before removing your head from your shoulders. You're a bumpkin, Hector—a child of the country who has wandered into a man's city. You offer nothing. You're out of your depth."

Vanmorten stepped up to the magister, his face inches from Hector's. The young therian could smell the awful cocktail of flowers and rotten flesh, the rose water applied to mask the Ratlord's ghoulish stench. He could see inside the cowl now, one half of the Lord Chancellor's face bare skull, the other blackened flesh. The Rat spoke again through his lipless mouth.

"You're drowning."

They don't fear you, brother. They don't respect you. They mock you. I fear you may join me, Hector, all too soon. . . .

Hector could sense the mood shifting in the chamber. They'd heard enough. They'd take his signature and then his life. *Last chance to shine.* He raised his voice so all could hear.

"I'm your ally, Prince Lucas, whether you like it or not. My foes are your foes, and I've already slain one of them."

Lucas leaned forward and guffawed, his weariness lifting for a moment before he collapsed into the stone chair once again. Vanmorten and Slotha also laughed, joined by a chorus of jeers from the Lionguard. Only Opal remained straight-faced.

"Who've you killed?" she asked.

"Vega. I killed him aboard the *Maelstrom*. The count is dead."

"Lies!" shouted Vanmorten.

"Kill him!" Slotha laughed. "I'll do it myself," she added, snatching the ax from her Ugri bodyguard.

"Stay your hand, woman," growled the Werepanther.

The Ugri and their queen stared at the woman in shock, but her command was followed. Slotha reluctantly released her hand from the ax haft, glowering at the Catlady.

"How in Brenn's name do you expect us to believe you killed Vega?" asked the prince.

"As much as I hate to admit it, Vega's the most cunning captain on the White Sea," said Slotha. "There's no way this wetling fool could've killed him, my dear prince."

Oh she is *keen, isn't she?* hissed Vincent. *Perhaps there'll be a royal marriage after all, although Slotha's quite a step down from Gretchen.*

"Unlikely," said Hector, accidentally aloud.

"What's unlikely?" said Vanmorten.

"My killing Vega," replied Hector, covering his tracks. "Unlikely, but not impossible: I buried a silver arrow within him, and then I had my men toss him overboard. That arrow is still in my possession, stained dark with the Sharklord's blood. That is, if Slotha hasn't taken it from my belongings. The Wolf's Council is dead to me. My future lies in your service, Your Highness."

"You've worked for the prince before, young magister, and it didn't end . . . well," said the Lord Chancellor. "Even if his Highness were to allow you to live, a notion that I struggle with, what guarantee do we have that you wouldn't bite your master's hand again?"

Lucas nodded. "I've heard enough," he said, turning to the Wererat. "Get him to sign over the Dalelands, and a confession while he's at it. Cut him up into tiny pieces if he resists, Vanmorten."

The Ratlord bowed low as Hector felt the hands of the Ugri warriors on his shoulders.

"You're making a mistake!" cried Hector, struggling against the men as Slotha stepped in front of him.

"You're the same dreadful wretch who sniveled around in my shadow, Piggy!" shouted Lucas, waving his hand dismissively. "You haven't changed one bit!"

"I enjoyed our time together, Boarlord," said Slotha, smiling, unable to resist one last slap. Her clawed fingernails raked across Hector's face, leaving bright red ribbons of torn flesh in their wake. The magister broke free of the Ugri's grasp, raising both his hands, gloved fingers splayed wide, the manacles taut. The prince jumped back in his throne suddenly, the old Lucas coming to the fore as he growled defensively. But if he feared Hector might attack him, he was mistaken. The Boarlord had another target.

The Vincent-vile flew from his grasp, fast as an arrow, whipping around the enormous throat of Lady Slotha. Her huge jaw hung open as the spirit coiled around her thick neck, slipping between the folds of her chin like an invisible garrotte. She stumbled toward the throne, staggering up the dais steps, hands grasping at Lucas. The prince leaped up to stand on the stone chair and lashed out, striking her hands away. He roared to try and warn her off, but she was wild beyond reasoning.

The Ugri warriors realized what was happening, the magister's hands moving as they manipulated the space before him, black leather fingers throttling thin air. They leaped, but not quickly enough; Opal was before them in a flash, her face shifting into that of the Werepanther, clawed hands ready to rip into them if they moved an inch closer. The Ugri stepped back, neutered and helpless as their mistress fell to her knees.

Her tongue lolled from her mouth now, purple and snake-like, as her bulging eyes rolled in her head. The tusks of the Walrus jutted down, ivory sabers that sawed vainly at the air.

Hector yanked his hands back, as if pulling a rug from beneath a giant's feet, hauling the vile back with all his might. The neck of the Werewalrus made an awful, wet cracking sound as her huge head collapsed into her shoulders. With a wheezing death rattle, the queen of Tuskun fell to the flagged floor with a loud thud.

Brilliant, dear brother, panted Vincent, fresh from the kill.

Hector's heart shook like a rattle within his chest, his skin covered in sweat as he looked at the Lion, the Rat, and the Panther.

"You're wrong, Lucas," he said, sounding calmer than he felt. "I've changed more than you could ever know."

"Whatever . . . whatever he just did," stammered Lucas. "He could do that again. Kill him. Kill him now, before he uses his dark magick upon me!"

Opal raised her hand to the prince, demanding silence.

She's the one you need to talk to, brother. She's the one who makes the decisions around here.

"I've seen dark magistry before," said Opal. "In Cape Gala. Your old mentor, Vankaskan, he knew a thing or two. But that trick you just played. That wasn't one of his, was it?"

"I heard he died," said Hector, avoiding answering the question.

"He was slain by your friend the Wolf," snarled Vanmorten, stepping forward and towering over the Boarlord. If he feared Hector's power, he didn't show it.

"I would pay my respects to him," said Hector. "He set me on my path."

"Then let me escort you up Grimm's Lane to Vermire, Pig. Visit his skull in my father's tomb and see how my brothers greet you!"

"Quiet, Vanmorten," said Opal calmly. She looked at Hector, her big yellow eyes unblinking. And she smiled.

"You risk much allowing yourself to be brought to Highcliff by the Walrus, offering yourself to us. What you bring—this great power of magistry—would make our enemies quake. What do you want in return, Hector?"

All eyes were on the Boarlord.

Take the leap, brother. Leave the Wolf. Embrace your own destiny.

"I want a pardon," said Hector, "a guarantee that no harm will befall me at the hands of your forces. I need unhindered access throughout the realms, no restrictions on my movements. There's much I need to research if my magistry is to be a true weapon at your disposal. The Wolf's Council saw it as an aberration. They were feeble-minded fools."

Good, Hector, keep going.

"And I'll need a position within the royal court; Lord Magister to the king would be nice."

"Never," spat Lucas, while Opal raised her hand to silence him again.

"Go on," she said.

"Duke Manfred's the only remaining member of the Wolf's

Council, discounting myself. He wronged me, and I'd have his life, too. He's taken your mother to Icegarden, Your Highness. I want to be there when we capture him, to play my part in bringing the Stag down. Then, finally, your enemies will all have been defeated."

"Not all of them," said the prince. "The Wolf. What of him?"

Hector's bloody lips felt suddenly dry as he cleared his throat. "They say he fell to his death. But if he yet lives, I'll help you bring him down."

You really mean that, brother? If it came to it, you'd kill Drew?

Opal looked to Vanmorten and the prince. While Lucas sneered, Vanmorten allowed the briefest of nods. Opal turned back to Hector.

"We appear to have an agreement, Boarlord," she said, her yellow eyes finally narrowing as she grinned. The Catlady leaped over the corpse of the Walrus and extended her hand to Hector. He reached a gloved palm out and shook it.

Vanmorten watched, his face hidden within his cowl. Hector couldn't tell whether the look he gave them was one of approval or disgust.

"So, Icegarden," said Lucas. "That's where they've taken my mother. We'll wipe those Sturmish scum off the map for harboring traitors."

Lucas stood, uneasy on his feet as if drunk. Hector watched the young Lion warily; he'd never seen him like this. He could see him by torchlight, unkempt and disheveled. The old Lucas would never have allowed himself to be seen in such a state. The look in his eyes was wild.

"I wouldn't have just four of these realms bowing down before me. We must assemble our armies, Opal: the Lions, the Cats, the Rats, and the Dogs. I'll have all of the Seven Realms kneeling before me, with my foot on their backs and my sword at their throats if that's what it takes!"

"And we'll have the Boars to assist us, too," Vanmorten sneered.

"You shall," said Hector, turning to the Ratlord and smiling. "But first, I'll take you up on your offer, Lord Chancellor. Please, take me to Vermire."

7

RETURN TO THE PACK

THE BAREBONES LOOMED large over the eastern horizon, their snow-capped peaks faintly visible by the starlight. Trent Ferran found himself staring at the distant mountain range as the wind raced through the Longridings around him. His red cloak flapped, clapping at the air, as he gripped it tightly about his throat. He shivered as he glanced at the peaks one last time, the hairs prickling on his arms, before turning and pacing through the camp toward the prison tent.

One guard stood to attention in front of the weighted door flaps. Trent quickened his pace into a brisk, officious stride as he approached. He made to walk past the guard.

"Sergeant," said the man, older than the young outrider

and clearly resenting having to call him his superior. He remained barring Trent's path.

"Stand aside, Eaves," said Trent, staring the man down.

"Can't do that, Sergeant," said the man, revealing a hint of a smug smile. Very few of Captain Sorin's friends in the camp respected the young sergeant, Trent having received the promotion at Lord Frost's insistence. The albino Catlord had his favorites, none more blessed than the youth from the Cold Coast.

"Why's that, Eaves?"

"Captain's orders."

"Forget Sorin. I'm here on the command of Lord Frost, to question the prisoner. You want to take that up with his lordship?"

Trent eyeballed the man. He might have been twenty years his junior, but he was the same height, and equally as broad; the apple hadn't fallen far from the tree with Mack Ferran's son. Reluctantly, Eaves stood aside. Trent stepped past, glowering as he went, allowing the tent flap to swing shut behind him. The young soldier paused for a moment to tie the door cords, fastening it tight so it couldn't be opened in a hurry. Satisfied it was secured, he walked quietly into the heart of the dark tent, to the beaten figure kneeling in a slumped heap.

"One more thing," said Trent as he stood over Baron Ewan.

The Ramlord looked up. "You came back?" he whispered through broken lips.

"You don't believe Drew killed my mother. Then who did?"

"The Wererat Vanmorten killed your mother, lad."

Ewan's voice was serious and hard.

"How can you *know* that, though?"

"Drew's word would have been enough for me. I wouldn't doubt anything that lad told me. But you forget: I spent time in Cape Gala, while the Wererat Vankaskan lorded it around High Stable. That one couldn't hold a secret if his life depended upon it; his brother's murder of your mother was something they were proud of. I heard him gloat as much with my own ears."

Trent's skin felt suddenly cold all over, a clamminess that spread from his extremities up toward his chest and throat. He felt a chill seize his heart, fearing the broken Ramlord spoke the truth.

He has *to be lying!*

"You'll say anything if it spares you Sorin's beatings," said Trent, struggling to hold back the tears. But his voice was trembling, the young outrider assailed by doubt.

"What more can possibly be done to me?" The Ramlord laughed quietly. "My body and heart are weak after your captain's work. I am already at Death's dark door. The long sleep would be a blessed relief after what your *friends* have done to me."

"This can't be true," sobbed Trent, unable to hold back his emotions any longer.

"Not a day has passed since your mother was murdered when Drew hasn't thought about the horror done to his family.

And that his own father—*and brother*—should think he'd killed her? Can you imagine the torment?"

Tears rolled down Trent's cheeks, a steady stream that couldn't be stopped. He hunched double, retching, a dry heave causing his back to shudder. He dropped to his knees, choking, wanting to shout, but instead silently screaming. *What have I done?*

"I've hunted him," he whispered. "Hunted him for . . . for those who killed my family! What have I done? I'm damned . . ."

"All is not in vain," urged Ewan. "You can still help him. Lady Gretchen and Lady Whitley: your masters believe they've fled to the south, to Calico or Port Stallion."

"They haven't?"

"No! They've gone north, to Brackenholme! Go after them, help them, boy: they're in grave danger!"

A slow handclap caused both of them to look up. The lithe figure of Lord Frost prowled into the room, the severed cords that had bound the door shut fluttering behind him. Trent looked back at Ewan, the look on his face as surprised as the Ramlord's. Ewan smiled sadly at the young man, Trent's eyes wide with horror as the full ramifications of Frost's presence dawned on him. He'd heard *everything*. The Catlord wore a pair of leather breeches and nothing else, his pale feet padding silently across the earth floor. Sorin followed at his shoulder, the broken-nosed captain grinning broadly.

"Excellent work, Trent," said the albino. "Excellent!"

He placed his white hand on Trent's shoulder and gave him a squeeze. Trent felt the Catlord's claws through the material of his cloak, digging into his flesh.

"You've outdone yourself, my friend. I didn't hear it all, but you unearthed the gem at the end: Brackenholme."

Trent wearily rose to his feet, red-ringed eyes still wet with tears. Ewan looked up, his broken face trembling but forgiving. Sorin paced across and launched a vicious kick at the old therian, his booted heel hitting him square in the breast. Ewan collapsed, slumped against his ropes.

"Kill him," said Frost, clapping Trent's back.

The young man's hand hovered over the pommel of the Wolfshead in his scabbard. *All this time, helping my enemy, hunting my brother, betraying my family* . . .

The Wolfshead blade slid out of its sheath, rising up in the air over the Ramlord in a smooth motion. It hovered there, the executioner's steel poised to fall. Every ounce of Trent's rage was unleashed as he let the sword fly in a furious swing, not down toward the Ramlord, but around him in a fluid arc.

Frost stood motionless, his pink eyes widening in wonder as he stared at the young outrider, poised to strike again. The Catlord's eyes settled on the Redcloak's sword, the edge of the blade dark with blood. He glanced down to his stomach, disbelief spreading across his face as a widening red line appeared across the toned flesh. The albino changed quickly, calling upon his felinthrope healing to try and halt the wound's

413

progress, but it was hopeless; the Wolfshead blade was blessed with silver, at the Catlord's own command.

As Frost fell to his knees, mid-change, Sorin leaped past him, his own sword meeting Trent's as the young sergeant defended himself.

"You traitorous scum!" shouted Sorin, raining blows down on Trent as the younger man parried. "You're as bad as the other Ferrans! A Wolf, just like your brother and father!"

Trent had heard enough insults. He could take the barrage of sword blows, but he wouldn't listen to Sorin besmirch the Ferran name. The next time Sorin's sword struck Trent's, the young man dived forward, catching him in the ribs with his shoulder. The air exploded from Sorin's lungs as the two crashed down to earth, both swords flying, Trent on top of the captain.

Sorin threw a wild punch upward, but with little power, and the young man batted it away and landed a flurry of blows on Sorin's face. The captain stopped moving, his features battered, as Trent rolled away, panting and panicked.

The tent flaps swung open as the guard entered, stumbling blindly into the scene. Trent wasted no time on Sorin's man, snatching up the Wolfshead blade and leaping up from the floor in a savage lunge. The sword disappeared through Eaves's stomach, rising up out of his back. The guard fell to the floor, dead in an instant.

Trent scrambled across to Ewan, cutting the Ramlord's bonds as he tumbled into his arms.

"Come, my lord," said Trent. "We need to go."

Before Ewan could answer, another voice cut in.

"They'll find you and your kin. They'll kill you all. My brothers and sisters won't stop."

Trent looked up and saw Lord Frost yet lived, the albino Catlord kneeling, his clawed fingers failing to hold his open stomach in place. He'd partly changed, the White Panther visible throughout, but he looked paler than ever, like a ghost, the enormous puddle of blood that he knelt in steadily growing. His pink eyes fluttered as he stared at Trent, head lolling, a sickly smile across his jagged feline mouth.

Trent rose and walked over to him, dragging the Wolfshead blade behind him.

"You strike a blow against a Catlord, you strike a blow against all my kind."

Trent lifted the sword high before answering. "You strike a blow against a Ferran, you strike a blow against our whole family."

The sword sliced down, the severed head of Lord Frost rolling to a halt beside the body of Eaves. Trent looked back to Ewan in time to see Sorin at his back, risen from the floor, his face a red mask, his sword raised to strike. The captain's face was twisted, bloody skin broken by white snarling teeth and even brighter eyes. Trent began the turn, bringing the Wolfshead blade up to parry the below, but he was too slow, his poise all wrong. Sorin's sword was descending.

The killing blow never struck, the sword clattering from the captain's dying grasp. A horn burst from Sorin's chest, his ribcage splintering, as the changed Ramlord launched himself from the floor into his back. Shock, agony, and horror flashed in Sorin's eyes as he and Baron Ewan collapsed. The Lionguard captain was dead before he hit the dirt. Trent skidded along the ground to catch Ewan as he rolled away from Sorin's corpse, wheezing with the strain of the transformation. The Ramlord was heavy, his head lolling against the youth's chest as his strength faded fast.

"We need to go," cried Trent.

"No, boy," he said. "Go on your own."

"I can take you with me, if we leave now!"

"Slow you down," spluttered the wheezing old Ram.

Trent shook his head, dragging the Werelord toward the wall of the tent, but Ewan was right. Fully transformed, he was a deadweight in Trent's arms, his limbs useless.

"My time's up," said Ewan. "The long sleep awaits me. Go. Help your brother. His friends."

Trent choked back the tears, nodding. Outside he could hear shouting, the commotion in the tent not having been missed by the rest of the camp.

"The girls," whispered Ewan, his voice trailing away.

"What?" asked Trent, bending his ear closer to the Wereram's battered face.

"In danger. Gretchen, Whitley . . . Brackenholme."

A rattling wheeze escaped Ewan's chest as his voice trailed away. His eyes stared at the tent ceiling, the light fading from them.

"They travel . . . with . . . Baba Korga . . ."

Then he was gone, his broken chest no longer moving, the fight over.

Trent didn't wait. More shouting from the camp told him he'd overstayed his welcome. He rushed over to the wall of the tent, slashing through it with a swing of the Wolfshead blade. Trent slipped out of the tent, pacing swiftly through the camp, striding between his fellow soldiers as he headed to where the horses were tethered. Bastian and Lionguard alike hurried past him in the opposite direction as the cry went up from the prison tent. He was sure they were looking at him, could feel their questioning gaze as he strode by, but none stopped him.

When Trent found his horse, Storm, the rest of the camp had descended upon the prison tent. By the time the Bastians and Lionguard began looking for the culprit, the outrider was already on his way, galloping across the Longridings, toward the Dyrewood.

Toward Brackenholme.

8

THE HEIRS AND
THE HONEST

TALONED FINGERS SQUEEZED Drew's windpipe, rousing him from his fevered slumber, threatening to tear his throat out in a flash. His eyes were instantly open, feet scrambling against the freezing stone floor of the Hawklords' tomb as he struggled in vain to slip free of the deadly hold. He brought his hand up to prize his attacker's fingers loose, but the other's free hand shoved him away, the grip tightening suddenly and shutting off Drew's airway. Drew went limp in surrender, eyes fixed firmly on his foe.

The therian was unmistakably a Hawklord, although dramatically different in appearance from Shah. When Griffyn's daughter had transformed she had looked elegant, majestic, a true mistress of the sky. The falconthrope who held Drew's life in his talons was a rougher-looking character. Rusty brown wings folded behind his back. The red feathers were tattered and threadbare in places, old wounds visible beneath missing plumage. A shortbow swung from his hip as he towered over Drew, his head craning in close to better inspect the young Wolflord. One long scar ran down the left side of the Hawklord's face, from the top of his crown, over his eye, disappearing beneath his jaw. His razor-sharp yellow beak snapped at Drew's face, and his big, black killer's eyes blinked suspiciously.

"You're well off the beaten track, boy," croaked the Hawk. "Thought you'd try and take from our kin, did ya?"

Drew's mouth gasped at the air like a fish out of water, no words escaping. Changing into the Wolf wasn't an option—the clawed fingers of the Hawk would puncture his neck like a knife through soft fruit. He could sense unconsciousness—and ultimately death—fast approaching. The Hawk looked across at Rook's corpse where it lay on the floor, illuminated by a shaft of morning sunlight from the window above.

"Thieves!" snapped the Werehawk, shaking Drew like a rag doll. "The Crow promised you a fortune if you helped 'im rob our tomb, did he? Well the Crow's dead, boy, and you're about to join 'im . . ."

"Red Rufus!"

The Hawk bobbed his head, opening his beak to hiss in

the direction of the staircase that led into the Screaming Peak. Another figure descended the steps, striding over toward the rust-feathered falconthrope and his prisoner.

"Let him breathe," commanded the newcomer, a blur before Drew's cloudy vision as he was about to pass out.

Reluctantly, Red Rufus released his grip, letting Drew collapse on to the floor, snatching great lungfuls of air.

"Let me kill 'im, Carsten," said Red Rufus, flexing his talons, ready to lash out. "Let's see 'is gizzard, eh?"

The one called Carsten raised his hand, silencing Red Rufus. "Let the lad speak first, Red Rufus, hear what he's got to say. Then you can open him up."

As Drew's vision recovered, Carsten shifted into focus. In his fifth decade, he was stocky and broad-shouldered, with a mop of thick black hair. His eyes were bright blue, trained keenly on Drew, while his hands remained folded over the pommel of an upright broadsword, the blade turned down to the floor. Drew rubbed his throat, massaging life back into his vocal chords.

"Seems like the tombwraiths took care of your master, thief," said Carsten, stepping over Rook's body.

"I'm not . . . a thief!" gasped Drew.

"Lost your way did you, lad?" said Carsten. "Happens all the time up here. A boy's just wandering around through the vales and grasslands, takes a wrong turn, ends up on top of Tor Raptor. Easy mistake to make."

"I came here . . . with Baron Griffyn . . ."

Carsten gave Rook's body a kick, the corpse rolling over, black feathers fluttering around it.

"Rubbish!" sneered Red Rufus, clenching his taloned hands, ready to strike. "Griffyn died years ago. You're one of the Crow's men."

Red Rufus brought his hand back, fingers open, his big black eyes narrowing to slits.

"You're a dead man . . ."

"Wait!" shouted Carsten, causing Red Rufus to turn.

Another figure had descended the staircase. A tall, partly-changed Hawklord staggered down the steps. His wings were already retreating into his back, the beak grinding back into his jaw and skull, feathers disappearing beneath his skin. He was bald with a full black beard, a little taller than Carsten, but they had the look of family. In his arms he carried a body.

"Is that . . . ?" said Carsten, stepping closer.

"It's Griffyn," said the newcomer, his head bowed, beard bristling as he grimaced. "Dead: I found him below the cliffs."

Carsten and Red Rufus looked back to Drew where he lay on the floor, his eyes darting between them all.

"I told you I came with him!"

"And yet you live while my lord lies dead?" said Carsten.

"Let me do 'im, Your Grace," said Red Rufus, hopping from foot to foot now, keen to be on with the business of killing.

"Who is this?" asked the bald, bearded Hawklord.

"My name's Drew. Drew Ferran."

Red Rufus was about to strike when Carsten snatched him by the forearm, causing the red-feathered bird to squawk at his liege.

"*You're* Drew Ferran?" he said in disbelief, ignoring Red Rufus. "Half of Lyssia is searching for a boy by that name."

"This is Wergar's son?" asked the bearded falconthrope.

"Just words, Baum," replied Carsten. "I still think he's an agent of this dead Crow, sent here thieving. He'll say anything to live . . ."

"How *does* he live though, brother?" said Baum. "The Screaming Peak and the tombwraiths: '*None but the Heirs and the Honest may enter*'? This Crow lies dead, but the boy survives."

Carsten cocked his head to one side, aspects of the hawk never far away. He crouched on his haunches in front of Drew while Red Rufus paced anxiously behind him.

"Good question, Baum. Boy, how *do* you live while the Crow lies dead?"

Drew reached behind his back, his torn cloak falling to one side to reveal the sword he'd found in the tomb.

Carsten and Baum both gasped, while Red Rufus stuck his avian neck over his lord's shoulder, his eyes running along the length of the blade. Carsten moved from his crouch, dropping onto one knee, while his brother gently placed Griffyn's body onto the floor and did the same.

"What is it?" said Red Rufus, agitated by his falconthrope cousins' show of reverence.

"The sword," whispered Baum, recognizing the blade straightaway.

"He's Wergar's son, all right," said Carsten, taking hold of Red Rufus and drawing the old bird to the ground into a bow. "He's the rightful king of Westland."

Drew staggered to his feet, looking down on the three Hawklords who knelt before him. They reminded him of the tombwraiths he'd encountered that night, striking the same poses that the phantoms had when they'd seen the sword.

"I don't ... please, I don't understand. And for Brenn's sake, my lords, don't kneel before me!"

The three rose, Red Rufus a little quicker than the other two, stalking to the rear of the tomb.

"The runes beyond this crypt are a warning," Baum said. "None may enter the Screaming Peak but the Heirs and the Honest: this law the tombwraiths honor."

Only the just and rightful lord may enter: that's what Baron Griffyn had told Drew about the tomb.

"How did the tombwraiths know I wasn't a thief, come here to steal the sword? They tore Rook to pieces!"

"That sword," Carsten said, pointing to the gray metal blade, "was the weapon of Wergar the Wolf: Moonbrand, forged for his ancestors in Icegarden by Sturmland's greatest smiths centuries ago. The wraiths wouldn't have allowed you to pass if you weren't truly Wergar's heir. Did it glow when you touched it, lad?"

"It was already glowing, but when I picked it up it shone with a white light."

"The Sturmish enchanted the weapons of the Werelords," said Baum. "The steel glows like a torch under moonlight."

"And the rest," muttered Red Rufus cryptically.

"But what's it doing here?" Drew asked, trying to piece together the jigsaw.

"It would appear our dear, departed Griffyn brought it here for safekeeping after Leopold took the throne. Who could have known that one day Wergar's child would climb Tor Raptor and reclaim it as his own?"

Drew thought back to Griffyn's words once more: *I brought it here. I kept it safe.*

Drew had heard the sword's name before. Queen Amelie had mentioned it in Highcliff. *My father's sword.*

"My lords," said Drew, sliding Moonbrand into his battered weapon belt. It was his turn to kneel now, Baum and Carsten looking to one another in surprise while Red Rufus watched distrustfully. "I was here with Baron Griffyn's blessing. We came to the Screaming Peak because we needed to call you back. The war that has taken hold of Lyssia, we, the army that stands before the Catlords of Bast, are in dire need!"

"In need of what, son of Wergar?" asked Carsten, his blue eyes shining like ice.

"We need the Hawklords."

PART VII

DEATH FROM ABOVE

I

THE GUEST

THE FIRST RAYS of sunlight illuminated Windfell Keep as a trio of servants stood in the lord's chamber, watching their master frantically rifle through his desk. Each held a casket, lid open, half-filled with coins, gems, and artifacts. The Falconlord tugged loose a drawer, tipped its contents on to the table, and sifted through them with feverish fingers.

"It must be here somewhere," murmured Baron Skeer, clawing through bound scrolls and checking the seals of each.

The doors to his study were wide open, the booted sound of guards' feet echoing through the corridor beyond.

"What the devil's going on?"

The question came from the doorway, Skeer glancing up to find his guest, craning his head around the corner.

"I'm leaving," said Skeer briskly. "Ah, there you are!"

His eyes lit up as he snatched a scroll with a red wax seal: the Lionshead, King Leopold.

"Leaving? Are you insane, Skeer?"

"You'd leave, too, if you knew what was best."

The old Falcon checked the seal, making sure it remained unopened.

"What's the scroll?" said the visitor, striding into the room, looking back as another group of soldiers raced by in the corridor. They may have worn the brown, feather-trimmed cloaks of the Hawkguard, but each man there was now a soldier of the Lion. Windfell had been Leopold's foothold in the Barebones for fifteen years, in which time the soldiers had seen little by way of combat, growing careless and out of condition. Suddenly, conflict was approaching, and the Hawkguard's fear was palpable.

Skeer stashed the scroll in the belt of his robes.

"A decree made by the old king."

"That states what?" asked the Falcon's guest, trailing his hands over one of the open caskets that the servants held.

"That my position here as baron is lawful. Leopold asked me to rule here for the good of the Seven Realms."

His guest laughed, a rasping cackle that rattled in his chest.

"For the good of the Seven Realms? For the good of *you*, Skeer, and no one else!"

The guest slammed the casket lid shut, causing the

Falconlord to jump. The baron scooped up a further handful of trinkets and barged past his visitor, dumping them into another box.

"Why the concern over your position, old friend? Why the activity within the halls and corridors of Windfell? Why so fearful for your life all of a sudden, Skeer? Explain what's happening!"

Skeer stepped closer to his fellow Werelord, who was a good foot taller than the old bird. The baron stared up into the squinting off-center eyes of the crooked count.

"My cousins, Kesslar," said the Falcon. "The Hawklords return!"

"What do you *mean* they're returning?" shouted Kesslar as he marched after Skeer, the baron's servants getting under his feet as he tried to catch up. He shoved one out of the way, the young man crashing into the corridor wall and spilling half the contents of the casket on the floor.

"Pick those up!" squawked Skeer as his servant snatched up the jewels.

"How can the Hawklords return?" repeated Kesslar. "They're all dead, aren't they?"

"Not dead," corrected the Falcon. "Banished. Forbidden ever to return."

"Yet you say that's happening? How can you know?"

Skeer's eyes were frantic as he peered through one of the tall arches that looked out over the mountains beyond. He strode

to the stone sill, ducking his head from side to side, searching the sky fearfully. Beside the towering keep of Windfell,
the Steppen Falls crashed down through the Barebones, working their way to the Longridings far below. A line of bridges
spanned the falls, carrying a road from the city down to the
grasslands.

"Did you not *hear* it?"

"Hear what, Skeer? The waterfall? Of course I do. You
sound like a madman!"

"No! The Screaming Peak! It's calling them home. They're
returning to Windfell." He turned toward a set of double doors
guarded by soldiers.

"I thought only the Lord of Windfell could enter the crypt
of your ancestors?"

Skeer looked back at Kesslar briefly, as the Hawkguard
opened the great doors.

"Griffyn?" asked Kesslar. "That old buzzard's behind this?
I left him behind in Scoria—I'd be amazed if he got out of that
hellhole alive!"

"Well, he's out," grumbled Skeer. The soldiers followed
out of the doors and down a flight of steps into the huge circular courtyard within the keep. Curving granite walls rose
high around them, stone ledges lining them on every level, the
ancient seats of the Council of Hawklords. A carriage waited,
horses kicking their hooves impatiently, alongside a platoon of
Skeer's personal guard.

Kesslar was thinking fast as he stumbled down the steps behind the Falconlord.

"If Griffyn escaped Scoria . . ." he muttered. *Who else escaped the island of the Lizardlords? Surely few of them could have survived? If they find me here . . .*

Skeer spun, raising his voice.

"He *is* returning, and he brings the banished Hawklords with him!" he cried. "I don't give a flying spit about the where or why that helped him get here, but these are my *enemies*. They won't forget the part I played in this city's downfall. I was there when they chopped Griffyn's wings off, for Brenn's sake! If he's returning, do you think he'll be in forgiving mood?"

Kesslar watched the baron storm across the courtyard toward his waiting soldiers. He counted thirty of them, and they struck the Goatlord as an uninspiring bunch. Their armor and uniforms were pitted and shabby. A couple of the men glanced up at the skies nervously.

This is what happens when you're posted to a ghost town in the peaks of the Barebones.

"Why not stand and fight?" shouted Kesslar. "There may only be Griffyn returning."

"True," replied Skeer. "Then again, what if they all return?"

"Wave your precious scroll at them!"

"I'm not a fool, Kesslar: that scroll will provide me with protection throughout Lyssia, but in the eyes of the brethren whom I turned against? That's a risk I'm not prepared to take!"

432

"Where will you go?"

"You ask too many questions, old friend!" yelled Skeer as his men loaded his chests and personal belongings into the carriage. "If you hurry, there's a seat here for you! Make haste!"

Kesslar turned on his heel and ran, passing more soldiers who were hurriedly evacuating the keep. Following the curving corridors and sweeping staircases, the Goatlord crashed into the room he'd been occupying, dashing straight to the side of his bed. He reached under, gnarled hands catching hold of the five-foot trunk that was stowed beneath. With a heave it slid out. Kesslar took a key from his pocket and unlocked it.

The true fortune of Scoria lay inside: gems and jewels that had been captured from every continent. Rubies the size of fists; ingots of enchanted Sturmish steel; diamonds as big as apples; coins, crowns, and coronets; regal rings and magisters' rods. Kesslar allowed himself a momentary smile. That fool Ignus and his inbred brothers thought they'd get the better of him. Kesslar had already been plotting his heist, long before the Wolf boy and his allies decided to spoil the Lizards' party in the Furnace. If anything, their escape and the ensuing chaos helped Kesslar make his getaway.

He locked the trunk shut once more, heaved it across his back, and set off through the door. Kesslar shook his head as he ran, cursing his luck. With Haggard lost to him and his bridges with Scoria utterly burned, Windfell had been his last hope of a place to recuperate and re-form his plans. He and Skeer had always looked out for each other. Long ago the old Falcon had even sold Griffyn to him, along with his daughter, Shah. Their business relationship was about the longest standing friendship the Goat had ever known, Skeer being possibly the only therian he could ever truly trust.

His stay in Windfell should have been a quiet, relaxed affair. Let the rest of Lyssia crash and burn; he and Skeer would remain in the Barebones, looking down on the chaos below, ready to return once the victor was decided. Or, failing that, remain hidden away while all their foes slayed one another—it made little difference to Kesslar. Instead, the old wretch Griffyn had somehow sprouted a new pair of wings and flown back to Lyssia, even making it as far as the tomb on Tor Raptor. Kesslar couldn't hear the *Screaming*, as Skeer had described it, but he didn't doubt his friend for one moment. Something was coming.

The corridors were near deserted by the time Kesslar bounded down toward the double doors that led into the courtyard. He was too busy grunting, the box on his back heavy with treasure, to pay attention to what lay ahead. At the last moment he looked up, stumbling to a halt as his knees buckled beneath him.

In the brief time it had taken him to grab his trunk, the yard had been transformed into a scene of battle. The Hawkguard were trapped within the circular court, screaming and shouting as they defended themselves from aerial attack.

Their spears jabbed skyward, swords slashing at the air as they desperately sought shelter from their enemy. Many lay dead on the ground, and the unmistakable figure of Skeer could be seen with his back to the carriage while the chaos exploded around him, the horses bucking to break loose. He looked up, face stricken by terror.

A dozen therians rode the wind around the courtyard, great raptor wings keeping them aloft as they rained death down on the soldiers. Some wore breastplates, others were bare-chested; some carried axes and swords, others fired bows or threw javelins. While they favored different armor and weapons, they were inextricably linked as kinfolk; each was unmistakably a Hawklord, legendary warriors thought to be lost from Lyssia.

Their wings, with feathers of different shades of brown, red, and gray, rose majestically from their backs. Their muscular arms were still human in appearance, while their legs were those of birds of prey, wide splayed feet that ended in deadly talons. Most fearsome of all were their heads, hooked yellow beaks screeching with fury, dealing death in the blinking of a big black eye. They swooped through the Hawkguard, tearing them to shreds, ripping them apart, tossing their warm corpses into the air.

Skeer saw Kesslar and made a break toward his old friend. He darted through the screaming guards, deceptively agile, as dismembered bodies fell across the courtyard. The Hawklords were enjoying this moment, meting out long-awaited justice upon those who had pillaged Windfell. Even Kesslar, a man used to violence, blanched at the Werehawks' grisly work.

Skeer was close now, leaping up the steps toward the Goatlord. "Kesslar!" he wailed as he neared him, hands reaching out in desperation as a shadow passed overhead.

With a bone-shattering *crunch*, an Eaglelord landed on top of Skeer, knuckled yellow feet crushing the baron's body beneath him. He held a broadsword, but that wasn't the weapon he'd used on the turncoat Falcon. Dark talons clenched together, the hooked blades digging into the skin of Skeer's back, catching on his ribs and spine as they ground flesh and bone together on the stone steps. The Falcon cried out in horror, screaming Kesslar's name from his traitorous lips. The Eagle turned his head to stare at Kesslar, blinking briefly, before tearing Skeer apart with his feet.

Kesslar raced back inside, dropped the trunk, and slammed the doors shut, throwing the locking bars into place with a *clang*. His heart felt like it might explode, his hands shaking as he caught hold of the trunk handle again, dragging it away from the doors and the battle in the courtyard. He heaved the box over to the windows from where Skeer had, only moments earlier, stared out over the mountains. With few alternatives, Kesslar craned his neck out and looked down the keep's curved granite wall. There was a twenty-foot drop from the window to rough rock below. Windfell perched upon a sheer cliff face, protecting it from attack, the bridge road over the falls being the only way to reach it on foot. The cliffs were sharp and jagged, impassable to humankind, and to therians for that matter. *Most* therians.

He let the beast take over quickly, every moment's delay making his death more likely as the Hawklords hammered on the double doors. His chest expanded with three great cracks, ribs bursting to take on the Weregoat's mightier physique. He tore the robes from his back as wiry gray hair raced over his body. His legs transformed swiftly, huge, muscular thighs supported by powerful black hooves. His eyes shifted farther around his skull, long black pupils bisecting globs of molten gold. The horns emerged from his brow, thick as tree trunks, coiling around upon themselves—the devil incarnate.

Snatching up the trunk in one grotesque hand, the Weregoat clambered out of the window and jumped. Kesslar's hooves hit the rocks and somehow managed to take hold, his free hand grasping the wall for further support. To anyone other than the Goatlord such a feat would have proved deadly. Unperturbed, Kesslar shuffled and jumped his way around the keep's base, making his way around, past the outer walls that surrounded the city, toward the road ahead. Above, he heard the cries of Skeer's soldiers as they were chased through the palace, butchered where they were found.

Finally he approached the cliff road, a yawning chasm his only obstacle to freedom. The gap was fifteen feet, from a standing jump, but once more, Kesslar's faith in his therian ability and his own survival instinct provided all the impetus he needed. Shifting the trunk to his other arm, he crouched low and leaped, propelling himself forward as if his legs were spring-loaded. The Goat sailed through the air, landing safely on the road with some feet to spare.

Kesslar grinned triumphantly, glancing back at Windfell just the once.

"Good-bye, old friend," he said, before turning and sprinting toward the first bridge on his powerful therian legs.

The first bridge was the tallest and longest of all those that spanned the Steppen Falls, the white stone road riding the elegant arches that held it over the mighty torrent of water. Misty clouds from the waterfall shrouded the center of the bridge from view, the promise of freedom awaiting him beyond the veil. Kesslar kept his pace up, jogging away from the city, black hooves striking the white granite underfoot as he ran into the spray. He was unsure of where he was headed, but an opportunity would arise soon enough. Something would surprise him, sooner or later.

As it happened, he was surprised far sooner than he could have imagined. His hooves skittered to a halt on the wet road as the beating of wings caused the mists to part. A large shape loomed into view overhead, the spray swirling through the backdraft. With dread, Kesslar saw the Hawklord drop something from above, the dark mass landing on the bridge, barring his path. The figure rose to its full height, stepping forward, slowly materializing through the mist before Kesslar's bulging eyes.

"It cannot be!" the Goatlord gasped, staggering backward in disbelief.

Drew Ferran growled. The last of the Gray Wolves paced forward, Moonbrand raised and vengeance in his heart.

"Kesslar!" Drew shouted over the roar of the Steppen Falls.

2

THE STEPPEN FALLS

THE GOATLORD LOOKED back the way he'd come, the cries of battle echoing from Windfell. He tugged a long, black knife free from his belt, holding it up defensively.

"Stop running, Kesslar," growled Drew. "Surrender now and I'll spare your life."

"You believe my life is *yours* to spare?"

"Drop the knife," said the Werewolf, his teeth bared as he stepped closer to the Ram.

"You think you can intimidate me, child?" shouted the Goat, but there was a tremble to his voice. "Your father was the same! Bullied his way across Lyssia, and what good did it ultimately do him? His own friends turned against him!"

Kesslar laughed, backing nervously through the mists, losing all sense of direction. Drew kept his eyes locked on the Goat, ready to leap upon him at a moment's notice.

"They'll turn on you, too, Wolf! All those you hold dear! History repeats itself, boy: you're your father's son!"

"Drop the dagger," said Drew. "You've nowhere to run."

Kesslar's hooves backed up to the edge, sending chalky pebbles scuttling off the bridge.

"Your weapon, Kesslar."

The noise of the waterfall was all around them, a constant, tumbling cymbal clash. Kesslar looked behind at the deadly drop, and then squinted at the dagger in his hand. The Wolf towered before him.

"I've had a good life, haven't I?" Kesslar chuckled, his laughter false and grim. "Spent so long putting people in cages, maybe it's time I tried the view from the inside out? Perhaps the change will do me good?"

"The knife."

The Goatlord tossed it across the bridge, metal clanging against stone as it skittered to a halt. Kesslar put his long box down in front of him and dropped to one knee, his head sagging forward. Drew, trying to remain calm, felt dizzy with triumph, having forced the Weregoat to surrender without even drawing blood. *There's always another way*, he reasoned silently to himself.

"You've done the right thing, Kesslar. I'm no monster. I'm taking you back to Windfell, let the Hawklords judge you. See what they—"

The sentence was cut short as the large wooden trunk was propelled forward by the Goat, shoved along the floor in front of him. Drew had no option but to jump into the air to avoid being hit. By the time he was returning to earth, Kesslar had already leaped, springing forward from his crouched position, his powerful horned head catching the Wolf square in the chest.

The Werewolf sailed through the mist, landing on his back with a crunch. Stars flashed as the world spun. His vision blurred as he tried to right himself. The hammering of hooves on the road approached rapidly. Drew raised Moonbrand up, his hold on the sword flimsy. A powerful kick from the Goatlord's hoof almost broke Drew's arm, the precious sword flying from his grasp.

With a wheeze he rolled over, the fingers of his hand scrabbling over the white stone as he searched in vain. Another kick to his guts sent him rolling, over and over, before he shuddered to a halt by the bridge's edge. Grunting, he pulled himself on to all fours, wincing as his bruised ribs grated, nerves firing with pain. He caught the sound of hooves through the mist once more. He raised his left arm up, the stump deflecting the blow at the last second and slamming Kesslar onto the ground.

Drew dived for the Goatlord, but his movement was

clumsy, the youth still stunned from the injuries he'd been dealt. Kesslar snatched at the Wolf's throat, throttling Drew as the lycanthrope's jaws snapped toward his face. The Wolf's claws came up next, his right hand tearing at Kesslar's chest, arms, and wrists, trying to shake the Goat loose. The golden eyes bulged, the Weregoat snorting with exertion as he put all his strength into the chokehold.

Drew tried to bring his legs around, tried to grapple with the lower half of the Goatlord, but Kesslar's powerful legs kicked him clear. Drew felt his stamina faltering, his limbs growing weak as the fight began to slip away. He focused his energies into his throat, straining against the Goat's grip, concentrating solely on not letting the beast snap his neck. *A little longer*, he prayed. *Just a little longer . . .*

Kesslar rolled him over, first straddling him and then standing. Drew's hand and stump fell away as the Goatloard choked the life from him.

"This is how you die, Wolf," grunted Kesslar. "At my hands. Alone."

"Not . . ." spluttered Drew, the Werewolf's mouth wide now, tongue lolling. The veins and muscles bulged around his shoulders and throat, a last stand against suffocation. Kesslar shook him, coaxing the final words from the dying lycanthrope.

"Speak, Wolf!"

"Not . . ." croaked Drew. "Alone . . ."

He lifted his weak hand, a clawed finger pointing through

the mist. Kesslar looked up and saw three figures appear through the mist. Their features were unreadable through the spray, but their outlines were instantly recognizable. The giant figure in the middle carried an enormous mallet in his hand, a hammer that would take the strength of two regular humans to lift it over their heads. The prowling woman stalked forward, her spear raised, ready for attack. Last of all came the heavy-set warrior carrying the spiked mace, swinging his deadly club menacingly.

"No!" shouted Kesslar, as the Werewolf threw his arm out.

The clawed hand tore at Kesslar's hamstring, the mighty leg buckling instantly, loosening the Goatlord's grip. Drew collapsed as the Goat staggered back, bringing his hand to his throat as the Wolf vanished, his therian energies exhausted. He lay on the ground as the Goatlord screamed, clutching his bloodied leg. Kesslar tried to back away, but it was no good. His enemies surrounded him in the mist, shadows that would have their revenge.

With a furious roar the Weretiger dashed forward, lightning fast, her claws tearing across Kesslar's chest. Then he was flying in the other direction as Taboo caught him with another claw, this time across his throat. Then she was gone, returned to the mists.

"Turn on me, would you?" choked Kesslar, trying to staunch the wound at his neck. "They chanted your name in

Scoria, Taboo! I turned you into a goddess! This is how you repay me?"

The snorting sound from behind was the only warning the Were-rhino gave him. Krieg's huge horn punched into Kesslar's back, launching him into the air. Drew watched as the battered Weregoat sailed over him. He landed beside the trunk, his clawed hands fumbling over the wood as he struggled to rise, his back broken, leg snapped, and throat torn. The Goat still managed to pick up his precious box, holding his treasure close to his chest as the last therian gladiator advanced.

"Whatever he's paying you," spat Kesslar, his mouth frothing with bloody bubbles. "I'll triple it! I have here the treasure of Scoria. I'll share it with you. What do you say?"

The Behemoth brought his huge mallet back, his body shifting, doubling in size as his shadow filled the bridge. His broad head, tusks, and trunk rose through the air as he put all his weight behind the final blow. Drew looked away at the last, the Weremammoth's hammer flying, the stone block crashing through Kesslar's box, shattering the timber as if it wasn't there. The mallet shattered the Goatlord's ribcage as Kesslar's body took flight, disappearing off the bridge into the white spray, leaving a trail of blood, gems, and jewels raining through the air in its wake.

The Behemoth let the mallet fall to his side.

"Take it with you."

Krieg was at Drew's side, the horn slowly receding, the broad neck thinning once more as he cradled the young Wolflord in his arms.

"My throat . . ." whispered Drew, his voice hoarse.

"You'll live, Wolf," said the Rhino, as the Behemoth joined him.

"Thank you," Drew croaked.

"Thank your Hawklord friends," said Krieg as he helped the Wolflord to his feet.

Taboo slinked toward them, Moonbrand in her hand. For a moment, she examined the blade, checking its balance, giving it a few swipes through the air. Drew was momentarily transported back to Scoria and the wild, arrogant felinthrope he'd first met. That Taboo would have taken the sword for herself. She flipped the blade around, holding the round white metal handle out toward Drew.

"The king dropped his sword," she said, smiling, as the Steppen Falls thundered around them.

3

THE RATLORD'S SKULL

THE TORCHLIGHT SENT shadows racing down the spiral staircase ahead of them, flickering phantoms that danced out of sight. Each curving step down the narrow stairs took them deeper into the belly of the citadel of Vermire, closer to the tomb of the Ratlords. Vanmorten led the way, the Lord Chancellor's long black robes dragging over the wet stone steps, threatening to trip up the magister following. Hector stayed close behind the Ratlord, grateful for the illumination, fearful he might stumble and fall at any moment.

"Mind your step, Lord Magister. I wouldn't want you breaking your neck."

We can't have that happening, dear brother. Not when we're so near to our prize.

Hector's Boarguard, increased in number, had accompanied him on the two-day ride north. There were now eight, Ringlin and Ibal complemented by the six Ugri warriors who had been the bodyguard to Slotha. Hector had been unaware of the Tuskun tradition that dictated that a defeated lord's or lady's vassals would immediately swear allegiance to the victor. He now had six of the mightiest warriors from the frozen wastes at his disposal. The thought was comforting to Hector, especially considering their destination.

Vanmorten and a platoon of the Lionguard had traveled also, escorting the Lord Magister up Grimm's Lane. Word must have been sent ahead that Hector was on his way, for the Vermirian army awaited them in number at the top of Grimm's Lane. Armored pikemen, mounted bowmen, filthy foot soldiers, and black-cowled scouts; the escort grew as they neared the city of the Rat King, all wanting to catch sight of the magister who had once been Vankaskan's apprentice. Hector kept the Boarguard close at all times. He knew that Vanmorten despised him, the very act of escorting the young Boar to Vermire repulsing the Rat. His business was unfinished with the Lord Chancellor, just as it was with his dead brother.

Two other members of the Rat King, Vorhaas and Vex, remained upstairs in the Citadel, watching over the Boarguard, while the eldest sibling led Hector into the tomb. War Marshal Vorjavik was away campaigning, leading the Lyssian army through the Dalelands alongside Onyx's Bastian force. His twin brother, Inquisitor Vorhaas, had remained behind in Vermire, looking after the Rat King's homeland. He'd shown surprise at the decision to allow the magister into their family crypt, but had held his tongue after a glare from Vanmorten. The youngest brother, Vex, had looked on from a distance, apparently studying the Boarlord's every move. Hector no longer spooked very easily, but Vex set his nerves on edge.

You'll have to watch that one, brother, Vincent had hissed.

Arriving at the base of the staircase, Vanmorten strode across to an unlit torch that hung from a bracket. Lighting it, he walked onto a rusted iron gate, feet slapping through the puddles. The stench of damp and stagnant water was overwhelming, while the constant sound of dripping echoed around the catacomb. Vanmorten reached a scarred, skeletal hand into his robes and withdrew a key, unlocking the metal door. It swung open with an ominous creak. Hector followed him through.

Stone coffins lined every wall of the room, some recessed within the crudely carved ore-stained rock. The scurrying of rats replaced the dripping noise, as Vanmorten's distant, diminutive cousins fled from the torchlight. A black marble box, less than two feet square, stood on a pedestal in the center of the low-ceilinged chamber, yet to be moved into the walls like those of the Rat King's ancestors.

"Here he is," muttered Vanmorten unenthusiastically. Hector had known from his years in Vankaskan's service that the brothers disliked one another.

"This is it?" asked Hector, surprised to be faced with a small box and not a coffin.

"What part of 'only his skull remaining' did you not understand, boy?" snarled Vanmorten.

"If you could leave me alone," said Hector, smiling politely.

"That's not going to happen, little pig. You may have fooled Opal and the prince, but I won't be tricked so easily. You've had your fun. Say your piece to his box and let's be on our way. I won't dance to your tune a moment longer."

"With respect, Lord Chancellor, my business with your brother is a sacred and magisterial matter. The Guild of Magisters' secrets go back to the Great Feast. To have you present while I bless his remains would be blasphemous."

Vanmorten sneered under his hood. Hector got a whiff of the decayed, burned flesh within the cowl as the Ratlord grated his teeth in annoyance.

"You can find your own way back up, piglet," said the Wererat, tossing him the key. "Lock up when you're done. And leave *everything* as you find it. I shall know if you've disturbed anything. Understand?"

Hector nodded, smiling. Vanmorten stormed from the chamber, disappearing up the spiral staircase. Hector followed to check he was gone before closing the door as quietly as its rusted hinges would allow. He locked it, making sure it was firmly shut. Then he turned, walking back to the black box. Hector removed the lid and placed it gently on the floor before reaching into the box and lifting the grotesque bleached-white skull of Vankaskan.

Oh, dear brother, gasped the Vincent-vile. *He's beautiful!*

"Now, my old master," he whispered, marveling at the partially transformed skull. "To work."

The chanting was fast and breathless, ancient words of magick known to only the few. The black candle burned brightly in Hector's right hand, oily black smoke billowing from the flame and gathering under the ceiling above. He tipped the candle over his open left hand, the molten wax pooling in his blackened palm, pouring between his fingers, searing the flesh and racing down his arm. All the while the chanting continued as the Boarlord sat, cross-legged.

The box had been removed from its plinth, the skull of the dead Ratlord now gracing the stone pedestal alone. A circle of brimstone was carefully laid out around it on the ground. Hector's words rattled from his mouth rapid-fire, unintelligible to anyone other than a magister. He stopped chanting suddenly, clenched his fist and slammed it down on to the stone floor once, twice, three times. The skull shuddered on the plinth.

"Rise, creature, and answer your master's bidding!"

Hector felt the cold rush into the room. The candle flame sputtered, fighting the breeze, clinging to the wick and refusing to die. While the candle remained lit, the rest of the crypt darkened as the shadows crept in all around, the blackness all-consuming. The coffins and walls were swallowed by the darkness, and the gate that led to the stairs vanished. Even the torch at the foot of the stairwell spluttered out, leaving the candlelight as the only illumination in the chiling chamber.

A low chuckle bloomed slowly in the center of the circle of brimstone, the yellow powder shifting as if caught by a breeze. The laughter rose, rasping like a blade on a file, causing the skin on Hector's arms to bristle.

Well, this is a surprise, hissed the spirit of Vankaskan, tied to the dead Ratlord's skull in the form of a vile.

Hector listened for Vincent, but heard nothing, his brother silent in the presence of a spirit as powerful and steeped in magick as Vankaskan.

"I've surprised myself, my lord," said Hector. "I wasn't sure your spirit would still be here. I thought you might have moved on."

Alas no, sighed Vankaskan. *My time in the mortal world isn't over by a long chalk. One cannot be surrounded and immersed in magick one's whole life and not be affected by it in death. Once one crosses over, the bridge remains, and as easy as it is for one to pass along it . . . things . . . can always come the other way. But then, you'll know that already, won't you, Hector?*

The young magister shivered at the mention of communing; the dead Ratlord was clearly already aware of Hector's dab-bling in the dark arts.

"I'm in control, my lord," blustered Hector. "I know what I'm doing."

Do you? You've raised my spirit, awoken me from my slumber, bottled my soul in the form of a vile. You know what you're doing? Can you imagine how angry *you've just made me, calling me to you like some kind of plaything?*

Hector leaned back from the edge of the brimstone circle, as he felt the cold breath of Vankaskan's vile wash over him. He saw its shape now, a smoky black cloud of malevolence that paced the yellow line like a caged beast.

You think this sulfurous dust can stop me, Hector? You think I won't find a way out of this little prison you've constructed for me? Why did you summon me, Hector? Did you hope to get answers from me? An apology perhaps for the path I set you upon?

Vankaskan's words came thick and fast, loaded with hatred for the young Boarlord. Hector recoiled, turning his face as if the vile's spittle might spatter his cheek.

I will find you, Hector, hissed Vankaskan. *I'll come looking for you, once I'm free of this crypt. You've woken me now, Boarlord! I shall not sleep! I shall not return to the darkness!*

Hector turned toward the skull on the pedestal. Slowly, very deliberately, he reached out with his wax-covered, black-ened hand and placed it within the circle. The Vankaskan-vile gasped as Hector drew his hand back, clearing away the yellow powder. He lifted his hand, the brimstone mixing with the cooling wax that was setting over his fist and forearm.

"I'm right here," said Hector.

Are you mad? gasped the Vankaskan-vile. *Is this suicide?*

"No," answered the young magister, rising to his feet and stepping into the broken circle. He felt the dead magister's vile now enveloping him, its claws moving around his throat, trying to prize open his mouth and see his insides. Hector ignored the spirit, picking up the skull in his right hand. He opened his left hand and clicked his fingers, the wax cracking and tumbling to the flagged floor.

"I'm here for everything, Vankaskan."

The Vincent-vile was onto the Ratlord's vile in an instant, tearing it off his brother.

What is this? What's going on?

"You don't understand, Vankaskan. There are more powerful creatures of magick than you out there. I met one; it shared its secrets with me."

The Ratlord's vile screamed as the Vincent-vile tore into it, biting and clawing at the shadowy form.

Release your hound, Hector!

"Every ounce of knowledge your rotten skull has held on to, every scrap and cantrip of magick lore, I'm going to take from you, Vankaskan."

Hector ran his scarred hand over his throat where the

wound from his encounter on the White Isle still remained. Vankaskan's spirit continued to wail as the Vincent-vile devoured it, bite after bite, smoky black morsels of pure magick torn from the air. Hector's heart and head pulsed as the vile feasted on the dead Rat's secrets. He stared at the skull in his hands, Vankaskan's power rushing through his body, filling every corner of his dark and dangerous soul.

"You took your time, Lord Magister," said Vanmorten as Hector arrived at the top of the staircase.

Behind the Ratlord, Vorhaas and Vex huddled, deep in conversation, looking every inch like a pair of villains plotting treason. Ringlin and Ibal rose from where they sat with their Ugri companions. The soldiers of the Rats had formed a circle around the eight Browncloaks, watching the Boarguard all the while.

"Well, you will bury your dead beneath the pits of hell, Lord Chancellor," replied Hector, a note of derision in his voice.

Vanmorten covered the distance between them in a swift stride, his long robes swirling around him, dark as night. The Boarguard moved for their weapons, but the Vermirians' swords and halberds were already poised to strike.

"How dare you come here, thinking you can speak to *me* in such a way! What makes you think I won't—"

Vanmorten's speech was cut short as Hector raised his ungloved left hand to his face, placing his forefinger to his lips. "Hush."

The hand was unrecognizable, the flesh withered and clinging to the bones, seemingly drained of all fluid. Fingers, palm, and forearm were all black, as if burned by a raging fire, giving the limb a skeletal appearance. The necrotic flesh remained taut as the knuckles clicked against one another.

"Your hand . . ." said Vanmorten, shocked by the appearance of Hector's mummified limb. The Ratlord lifted his own disfigured fingers to his throat, running them over the scarred flesh of his neck.

Hector opened his palm and examined it, as if noticing the changed appearance for the first time. He turned it one way and then the other, as though it belonged to another person, alien to the rest of his body. The skin of his face was the opposite, drained of blood, white as a skull. A sickly sheen of sweat glistened across his features as he smiled at the stunned Ratlord.

Blackhand, whispered the Vincent-vile.

"My hand?" repeated Hector. "Oh, my hand is strong, Lord Chancellor. I have your brother to thank for that."

4

CROSSROADS

A CROWD HAD gathered in Windfell's great hall, returning Hawklords from the length and breadth of Lyssia and beyond.
Each stared at the rough stone wall behind the carved wooden
throne, their faces etched with sorrow. Drew stood among them,
watching with grim wonder. A pair of threadbare, tattered wings
hung staked to the brickwork, metal spikes having held them in
place for many miserable years. The skeletal frames now resembled
a moth-eaten spiderweb of thin white bones, the odd remaining
feather still clinging to the rotten remains.

"Take them down," said a choked Count Carsten.

One of the still-transformed Hawklords moved quickly,
flying toward Baron Griffyn's severed wings. Reverently, he
lifted the torn bones and feathers from the spikes, gently fold-

ing them close to his chest as he returned to the ground.

Thirty falconthropes filled the hall, each one ready for battle. More were sure to follow. Drew had expected them all to look similar to one another, but he couldn't have been more wrong. The Hawklords came in all shapes and sizes, as different as Krieg, Taboo, and the Behemoth were from each other: tall and rangy, short and wiry, heavyset, slight, young, old, fit, and out of shape. The tombwraiths had soared across the continent, seeking out the Hawklords wherever they hid, carrying Tor Raptor's screams to the four corners of Lyssia. Each had heard the call and answered.

As Griffyn's wings were taken away, the assembled Werelords looked to their most senior noblemen, Count Carsten and Baron Baum, the Eagles. Neither therian was as tall as Krieg or the Mammoth, but they were as imposing in their way, their muscular chests rippling beneath banded mail breastplates. The black-haired Carsten's broadsword remained sheathed in its scabbard, while the bald and bearded Baum leaned on his spear, the weapon fashioned from a deep red wood, filed and burned to a terrible point. Drew wondered if the spear was naturally that color or whether it remained stained from the recent battle.

"Take the throne!" called one of the Hawklords from the rear of the hall. A chorus of cheers broke out as the Werelords raised weapon and voice in support.

"The brothers!"

"Our new Lords of Windfell!"

Carsten raised his hands to quieten the crowd while his brother smiled and shook his head.

"Our enemies might have taken Griffyn from us before we could be reunited, but the baron's bloodline lives on," said Carsten.

"This throne is not ours to take," added Baum, his voice deep and rich. He lifted his spear and pointed it over his shoulder symbolically.

"Lady Shah is in the custody of King Faisal in Azra. *She* is the rightful Lady of Windfell and it's our duty to return her to her father's throne."

Nods and murmured agreements rumbled around the room, each Hawklord accepting the Eagles' words without question.

"How soon do we fly to her aid?" asked Red Rufus, his scrawny neck bobbing as he spoke. The scar that had been visible from the top of his head right down to his throat as a Werehawk was all the more livid in human form as it gouged through the left side of his face. He cut quite a different figure now from the fellow who'd wanted to kill Drew in the Tomb of the Hawklords.

Red Rufus continued. "How long has the Jackal held her prisoner? Wergar should have killed him when we had the chance. The only good Omiri's a dead one."

"It's not as simple as that, Red Rufus, as well you know,"

said Carsten, turning and holding his hand toward Drew.

The Wolflord looked surprised when Carsten beckoned him, painfully aware he was a stranger among these people—they didn't know him from the next man. The doubts had returned. What did Drew really know? What could he say that might convince them to aid him? Baum nodded, encouraging Drew to approach. Krieg's firm hand pushed him forward, through the crowd, the Hawklords parting as he walked toward the dais. He climbed the steps, standing between the two Eagles and turning to face the assembled room.

Humans had joined therians in the chamber, those hardy souls who still lived in the Barebones having returned after the sight of the Hawklords coming home to roost. Drew looked over to his companions. Krieg nodded encouragingly while the Behemoth looked on impassively. Taboo bared her teeth, somewhere between a snarl and a smile.

"Faisal isn't the enemy," Drew said at last turning to the assembled throng. "Azra's surrounded by the Jackal's foes: Doglords to the north and Hayfa to the south. Between them they'll overrun Azra."

"I fail to see why we should care about the demise of Faisal," said Red Rufus. It was clear to Drew that the old falconthrope still distrusted him.

"Aye," agreed another. "Leave the Hounds and Hyenas to tear one another apart. They're savages."

"The Azrans *aren't* savages. They're a proud people, not unlike yourselves."

Red Rufus scoffed, but Drew continued.

"Baron Griffyn's last wish was that his people should fly to Faisal's aid. That's why Shah remains there, already lending her wits and wisdom to the Jackal's cause. I understand the ill feeling you have for one another—the war you fought on Wergar's behalf has left wounds that have festered over the years. But a new enemy's at the gate. The world is changed."

"It's not so different," said Red Rufus. "I see we're still expected to follow a Wolf."

Drew winced. The old Hawklord's attitude was belligerent but well-founded. *Away from their homes for fifteen years and my first request is that they join me in battle? I'd feel the same.*

"This is *everyone's* fight. The threat won't go away. You can't stay out of a battle that rages around you—the Catlords will come knocking. We *need* you. I was told the Hawklords were the bravest warriors to fight by the Wolf's side, and loyal to the last."

"Loyal to old Wergar, young cub," said a voice from the rear of the group.

Another voice chimed in. "You expect us to swear fealty on account of the love we had for the dead Wolf?"

"We should fetch Shah!" cried a third Hawk. "Get her out of the desert. Leave the Omiri to butcher themselves."

Carsten and Baum watched and listened in silence, leaving the debating entirely to Drew.

It's my task to convince these men that they should join me, thought Drew. "It's not as simple as leaving them to fight it out," he said aloud. "The Catlords are behind the civil war in Omir. Canan's Doglords aided the Bastians' attack on Highcliff, and now Prince Lucas returns the favor. The young Lion sits on the throne, his counsel coming from the Rat King and the Werepanthers Onyx and Opal. So long as Lucas and his cronies rule, nobody is safe. They mean to take *everything*, to crush the uprising of the free people of the Seven Realms. The fighting in Westland and the Barebones, the battles in Omir—it's all one and the same. This is a war for Lyssia, and one that Bast is winning."

Drew felt his chest rising as he spoke, his words honest and true. His blood was up and his self-belief was solid. Although Red Rufus was the voice of doubt among the Hawklords, many of the old therian's brothers seemed unconcerned by him. They nodded as Drew spoke, jaws set, eyes glinting with steely resolve as they saw the fight that lay ahead. If Drew had doubted the cause previously, that reservation had been vanquished.

"Believe me, the Jackal's our ally. The Cats are the constant throughout. The Dogs, the Hyenas, the Crows, the Rats are just adding their muscle and might to these enemies of the free people of Lyssia. Lucas might reign in Highcliff, but he's a puppet, a mouthpiece. It's his friends from across the sea who seek control over the Seven Realms. Onyx and Opal are the power behind the throne. If we help defend Azra, break the back of this assault from Canan and Hayfa, then we have Faisal's army behind us. Each battle we win, we shall gain fresh allies. It starts with Azra. First we drive them out of Omir, then the Barebones and Westland. We chase them back across the Lyssian Straits, all the way back to Bast."

His voice had deepened now, his words coming out loud and heavy, bouncing off the walls of Windfell's great hall. Every man and therian watched intently, caught up in the Wolflord's passion.

"There are three other therians in this chamber who have joined me in the fight. None is Lyssian— each hails from a land far away. They fought me in the Scorian arena, and now they fight by my side: free therians, united against a common enemy. I trust each with my life."

He looked at his three friends from the Furnace. Each of them bowed back, as the assembled Hawklords stared reverently at them.

"These Werelords have traveled to a foreign land where they can expect little more than suspicious looks of fear and distrust. Their homelands have already been seized by the Catlords. They've seen firsthand what Onyx is capable of. I would return with them to Bast, once the fight here is won, lend my life to their cause in return for their sacrifice. They've put their faith in me, and Brenn be my witness, I won't let them down."

Drew glanced at the skin of his curled fist, the flesh now gray as the Wolf fought to emerge. His eyes had yellowed over, and he could see the Hawklords nodding as one. Falconthropes clapped one another on the shoulder, punched their chests, and raised their weapons.

"Join me," growled Drew. "Let's take the fight to the Beast of Bast."

The great hall of Windfell, silent for so many years, thundered with the sound of swords beating against shields and falconthropes cheering.

The Hawklords had returned.

Two hours had passed since Drew's passionate speech in the great hall, and that time hadn't been wasted. Windfell's circular courtyard was a hive of activity as the Werehawks prepared for battle. Drew, Taboo, Krieg, and the Behemoth had equipped themselves, replacing their battered gear and torn clothing with kit from the Hawklords' armory. Drew had found a studded black-leather breastplate, fashioned in the style of the Sturmish smiths, with buckles and clasps that allowed the armor to change shape as a therianthrope shifted. While there were steel breastplates and chain shirts that might provide stiffer defense against blade or bow, the leather felt right for Drew, more lightweight and less cumbersome. Besides which, the wide-eyed youth in Drew found himself grinning: it looked utterly fearsome. He even found a woodland cloak that wasn't a million miles from the tattered old Greencloak he'd been gifted by Bergan and, snatching it up, he was ready to depart.

The Hawklords looked resplendent, armed and armored, gathered and ready to take flight. News had spread quickly. The population of Windfell continued to swell with humans returning to the city. While the majority who'd left might never return, some had made new lives in nearby hamlets and settlements on the Barebones' slopes. With the sudden activity in the city above, they'd rushed home as if they'd heard Tor Raptor's screams themselves. Many now hurried around the halls of the mountain keep, helping their former lords make preparation for war.

In all, thirty-three Hawklords had returned, and thirty of them would fly to Omir. It wasn't the hundred Drew and the late Baron Griffyn had hoped for, but thirty falconthropes flying into battle was still a tremendous coup for the Wolf and his allies. Three would remain in the mountain city to prepare the people for what lay ahead, ensuring the last reminders of Skeer's reign were tossed from the parapets and Windfell was returned to its former glory.

The first "wing" of Hawklords had already taken flight, ten of them taking to the skies in the dim light of dusk. The second wing was now leaping skyward from the courtyard as they pursued their brethren into the clouds. Drew was the last of the therians from the Furnace to depart, Krieg, Taboo, and the Behemoth having been taken off in the first two wings. Two Hawklords had been needed to carry the Weremammoth, each holding an arm as they lifted the giant aloft.

Drew stood apart from the remaining Hawklords, lost in his own thoughts while they made the final adjustments to their armor ahead of the journey. He unsheathed Moonbrand and stared at the dark leather that spiraled about the handle, the wrappings centuries old yet unchanged by time. The white stone pommel was polished smooth, its likeness to the moon it was named after unmissable. In the warm light of day, the blade was steel gray, unremarkable.

"What tales you could tell," he whispered, imagining his ancestors' battles. An unending stream of questions ran through his head. *Will this sword help reunite me with my friends? With Hector, Whitley, and Gretchen? How many lives have been taken by this blade? How many wars won? Can one good soul really make a difference? Just a shepherd boy from the Cold Coast?*

"If ever a fight was just . . ." he murmured.

The flapping of the Hawklords indicated that the final wing was taking flight. He slid Moonbrand back into its scabbard before returning to the three remaining falconthropes. As he approached, two of them suddenly took to the heavens.

And then there was one, thought Drew, striding up to the Hawklord who would fly him into the heart of Omir.

"Hang loose like a bag o' bones, you hear me?" said Red Rufus, running his thumbs around the collar of his golden breastplate. "Limp as a dead man. That's what I need you to be."

The old therian was shifting as he spoke, rusty-colored feathers sprouting from his face as the yellow beak emerged. He straightened his bent frame as great red wings emerged through flaps of leather that ran down his armor's back. As old as Red Rufus was, he was in remarkable shape when in therian form, his legs transforming into those of a powerful, deadly raptor. The skin of his calves hardened, reminding Drew of the reptilian limbs of Ignus and Drake, while his feet split into four immense, long toes, ending in curling black talons. The big predator's eyes blinked as Rufus towered over the spellbound Wolflord.

"I'm carrying a precious cargo. I'd like to get you to the Jackal in one piece. Understand, boy?"

Drew nodded as Red Rufus shook his wings, ruffling the feathers. A shortbow hung from one hip and a quiver swung from the other.

"Ready, Wolf?"

Drew was about to answer when the clattering of a horse's hooves beyond the walls distracted him. It was swiftly followed by shouts from the men who remained in the keep. Drew made for the commotion as he saw a crowd gathering outside the gate.

"Where are you going? We need to be away—the last wing has already departed!" warned Red Rufus.

"A moment!" cried Drew, rushing off before the cantankerous old Hawklord could object further.

Directly outside the keep, the townsfolk had gathered around a horse, its rider slumped in the saddle. As Drew approached the man tumbled into the arms of the surrounding men and women. Some cried out when they noticed his cloak was dark with blood, broken arrow shafts protruding from his back.

Although he wore battered military clothes beneath the cloak, Drew reckoned he was much younger than himself. The youngster's face was ashen—a sheen of sweat glistening as his eyes fluttered. Drew counted four broken arrows in all, peppering his back and pinning his gray cloak to his torso. Recognizing the uniform instantly, Drew snatched his own waterskin from his hip. He bit the stopper off and held it to the boy's mouth. The boy drank greedily, spluttering on the liquid.

"Steady," said Drew.

"I'm a healer, my lord. I can tend to those wounds," said an old woman at Drew's shoulder, looking on with grave concern, but the Wolflord ignored her for the moment, pressing the injured Graycloak for answers.

"You're from Stormdale? A little young to be one of Manfred's men, aren't you?"

"His son," said the boy, a bout of coughing racking his chest.

"What news?" asked one of the men nearby.

"I have family in Stormdale," said another.

Drew raised his hand, calling for silence.

"Highwater's fallen. Stormdale's next. Villagers and farmers, women and children: surrounded," spluttered the boy, his
voice fading. "No mercy. Crows and Rats. Kill us all . . ."

The crowd at Drew's back parted as Rufus stepped forward,
flexing his wings and casting shadows over the townsfolk.

"Come, Wolf. You delay us. We need to go. We need to
leave now."

Drew looked at the young Stag, the boy's eyes closed, his
head lolling heavy to one side. Drew lifted him carefully, cradling him, feeling the fever-heat rolling off him. He turned to
the old woman.

"Lead the way," he said, holding the boy close.

Rufus grabbed Drew by the shoulder, holding him fast.
"You're not listening, Wolf!"

Drew tugged himself free from Rufus's grip, glaring at
him. "We're not going to Omir."

"Have you lost your mind, pup?"

"Not at all, old bird," said Drew, his patience worn thin by
the grumbling Hawklord. "You and I fly to Stormdale."

EPILOGUE
MAN AND BOY

NO SOONER HAD the lightning flashed than the thunder followed, tearing the sky apart above Moga. Ten ships blockaded the harbor, the Catlords' navy having chosen the Sturmish port as their base in the far north. Flags from Bast, Highcliff, and the Cluster Isles flapped in the fierce wind, the rain threatening to tear them from the masts. The fleet had arrived straight after the *Maelstrom*'s departure, on the hunt for the remainder of the Wolf's Council. While others had followed the pirate ship, the remaining force had taken Moga for their own.

Three men crept along the harbor road, hugging the walls and rushing between buildings. Passage was slow on account of the size of one of them, the man twice as big as his two companions. To be found on the streets after the ninth bell had tolled was punishable by death: fully two dozen Sturmish pirates swung from the gallows that had been set up in the crowded marketplace, two or three hanging from each of the scaffolds. Arriving at the ruined warehouse on the northern-most end of the docks, the two smaller men took up lookout positions in the shadows that shrouded the splintered building, while the enormous one squeezed through the broken door-way. The storm crashed overhead as the rain hammered down, the inside of the building exposed to the elements through the ramshackle roof. The big man shook the water from his heavy black cloak, the jewelry that adorned his hands and wrists jangling as he advanced into the heart of the warehouse. Another man emerged from the shadows, a weaselly looking fellow with a tatty black beard and a cutlass in his hand.

"My lord," he said, nodding humbly in the presence of the newcomer. The noble dismissed him with the wave of a fat, gem-laden hand.

"No time for pleasantries, Quigg. Where are they?"

The bearded pirate turned, leading the huge man deeper into the building. The floorboards groaned under the fat one's weight, threatening to splinter and carry them both into the harbor water below. The spluttering coughs of a young boy drew them through the shadows. The child sat on a barrel, a filthy old coat wrapped around him for warmth. He looked up as the two approached.

"Baron Bosa," said the boy, jumping down from the barrel to bow dramatically before the fat man. Bosa rolled his eyes at the lad's show of etiquette, considering the dire circumstances.

"You know me, child?"

"I've heard plenty about you, your lordship, from my shipmates and my captain."

"And where's your ship now?"

"Dunno, sir; she sailed off without us. They done him in, sir. Least they tried to."

"How is it you didn't drown, boy? The Sturmish Sea could kill any man, yet you live?"

The boy shrugged.

"And you claim to have saved your captain's life?"

The boy supplied no answer, simply staring at Bosa with big brown eyes. The Whale of Moga turned to Quigg.

"Where is he?"

The black-bearded pirate pointed beyond the boy toward the dark recesses of the warehouse. The fat Whalelord strode past them, searching the shadows for his brother therianthrope. He found the man lying within a grounded rowboat, a tarpaulin laid across him as a makeshift blanket. His face was white, eyes red-rimmed as he stared up at Bosa. The Whale reached down and pulled the tarpaulin to one side, revealing the injured man's torso; the usually pristine white shirt was stained dark.

"I see you have visitors in Moga," whispered the wounded sea captain, trying to smile through bloodied teeth. "How long have they been lodging with you?"

"My dear, sweet Vega." The Whale sighed, his voice thick with concern. "What have they done to you?"

ACKNOWLEDGMENTS

I need to say a few words of thanks to the elite team of guys and gals at Puffin HQ who have not only supported me while I wrote the Wereworld series, but also got the books into readers' hands. Clever birds, these Puffins.

Much gratitude to Francesca Dow, MD extraordinaire, and to publishing director Sarah Hughes—I should probably restrict thanks to 140 characters as she's fluent in Twitspeak! #cheekynorthernblighter

Huge thanks to Jayde Lynch, Julia Teece, and Vanessa Godden who've had to endure my company—and obsession with Full Englishes—while we've toured schools and festivals the length and breadth of Britain.

Cheers to Samantha Mackintosh, Julia Bruce, and Mary-Jane Wilkins in editing, for polishing my dirty lumps of coal into something that sparkled.

Thanks to Zosia Knopp and her amazing rights team, including Jessica Hargreaves, Camilla Borthwick, Joanna Lawrie, Susanne Evans, and Jessica Adams. Thank-yous to Winsey

Samuels in production, Brigid Nelson and the children's division sales team, and Carl Rolfe and the Penguin sales reps, and *merci* to Rebecca Cooney in international sales.

And they say you should never judge a book by its cover. While there's a great deal of truth to that adage, I have to say that a spiffy cover really does bring a book to life. Thanks to fab designer Patrick Knowles and ace artist Andrew Farley for helping to make Wereworld turn folks' heads. A special word of thanks has to go to Jacqui McDonough, Puffin's art director and the first person I ever reached out to many, many years ago when I was trying to get into publishing as an illustrator. When I say "reached out," a more accurate description would be "pestered for two years." Whodathunk we'd finally get to work together after all that time, missus?

Last two thanks go to my left and right hands: my editor, Shannon Park, for believing in Wereworld from the get-go, and my wife, Emma, for spotting my shoddy grammar and enlightening me in the process. Cheers, m'dears!

Thank you all.

Keep reading for an excerpt from the fourth
book in the thrilling Wereworld series,

NEST OF SERPENTS

I

TAKE NO CHANCES

"DID YOU HIT him, master?"

The Lionguard scout lowered his bow, ignoring his apprentice. He stared out across the Longridings, squinting through the twilight at the fleeing Greencloak. Gradually, the rider began to slouch in his saddle as his mount slowed, weaving up a rocky incline. The bowman grinned as he saw the distant figure keel to one side, sliding from his steed and hitting the frozen earth in a crumpled heap.

"Have you ever known me to miss?" the scout finally replied, stowing his bow alongside the quiver on his saddle before clambering back onto his own horse.

His companion, a youth yet to see eighteen summers, grinned with delight. For one so young, he'd seen more than

3

his fair share of bloodshed, having served his apprenticeship in the Lionguard scouts under his master's watchful eye. The boy wasn't shy about getting his blade wet: that would serve him well in the coming months as the Catlord armies mopped up the remnants of their enemies' ragtag force, scattered across the Seven Realms.

The scout had served in the army of Westland for three score years, his bow defending him against enemies of Wolf and Lion alike as they had fought for the throne. As a mortal man, he could never truly understand the noble therianthropes—their might, their majesty, and the old magicks—and it wasn't his place to question. His allegiances may have changed over time, but the role had remained the same: a life spent in servitude to the shape-shifting Werelords who ruled Lyssia.

"Let's see what we've bagged," said the scout as he spurred his horse on, his young protégé riding close behind as they raced across the barren slopes toward the fallen Greencloak.

Traveling apart from their comrades allowed the scout and his apprentice to move swiftly and stealthily across the Longridings, deep into hostile territory. Powerful as the Catlord army was in the south, the grasslands were still untamed, harboring the enemies of Prince Lucas the Lion throughout. Many of the Horselords had fled to Calico, hiding behind the coastal city's enormous seawalls, while others remained in the wilds. The Werestallions weren't the only danger to the Lion's forces in the Longridings: the traveling mortals known as the Romari had sworn fealty to the Werelord Drew Ferran, last of the Werewolves and the inspiration for this bloody civil war throughout the Seven Realms. The Romari were unpredictable and unconventional: they waged war through subterfuge and terrorism, striking the Catlord forces on their fringes, at their weakest points, before disappearing back into the grasslands. The scout and his charge had expected to run across the Romari; stumbling upon a Greencloak had been a surprise.

"What's a soldier of the Woodland Realm doing out in the Longridings, master?" called the youth from behind, his red cloak flapping in the stiff winter breeze.

"A straggler or deserter, perhaps," the man cried back. "Maybe he was left behind after the taking of Cape Gala."

"He could be a spy from Brackenholme!"

It was well known that the men of the Woodland Realm were aligned with the Wolf, which made this fool fair game in the eyes of the scout. They had encountered him by chance, the two Lionguard soldiers spying the lone rider as they had all crested hillocks in the grasslands; they were dangerously close and within hailing distance. While the Greencloak had spurred his horse away, the scout had leapt down with practiced ease, his bow quick to hand, and sent an arrow sailing on its way. He had taken only one shot: he rarely took more.

"Whoever he was, and wherever he was heading, his

message won't arrive." The man began to slow his mount as they neared the fallen woodlander, bringing their horses up the rock-strewn slope to where their enemy lay. "His war's over."

Twenty feet up the slope, the Greencloak lay motionless, facedown on the frozen earth, his horse nearby, its head bowed solemnly. A quarterstaff lay beside the body, hinting at the soldier's profession as a scout. The old tracker kept his eyes fixed on the fallen foe, although he could sense the movements of his companion beside him, keen to investigate. He heard the dry *shlick* of the young Redcloak's hunting knife sliding out of its leather sheath. The apprentice jumped down and began walking forward, shifting the dagger in his grasp as he approached the still woodlander. The thick green cloak covered the body like a death shroud, the hood obscuring the back of the man's head, only the scuffed brown leather of his boots visible, poking out from the hem of the long emerald cloth. A loud creak made the youth stop and turn. His master's bow was drawn and aimed at the body on the ground. With a sharp *twang* the arrow whistled into the body, joining the earlier one, buried deep in the Greencloak's back. The apprentice's eyes widened momentarily before he nodded.

"Best take no chances," said the scout as the young Redcloak covered the remaining distance to the body.

The apprentice kicked one of the fallen rider's legs, and the booted foot wobbled lifelessly. He looked back at his master and smiled. It was a brief moment of contentment, followed swiftly by a sensation of pure horror as the leg he'd just kicked lashed out, sweeping his own from under him and sending him crashing to the ground.

The scout's horse reared up, suddenly alarmed, as the felled Greencloak jumped into action. The old Lionguard let go of his weapon, the saddle quiver spilling its contents as bow and arrows clattered to the ground. The rider snatched at his reins in panic as the youth and the woodlander wrestled on the ground. The apprentice lashed out with his dagger, and his enemy raised a forearm to deflect the blade. In the split second before the weapon struck home, the Redcloak caught sight of his opponent's face. It wasn't a man at all, but a girl, her big brown eyes wide and fearful as she fought for her life. The hunting knife bit into her forearm, tearing flesh and scoring bone. The girl let loose a roar of pain.

The scout heard it, clear as a bell. The cry was deep, animalistic, primal. He'd heard it before, on the battlefield long ago, back in the time of the last Werewar. He'd switched sides, taking the Red at the first opportunity, and swearing fealty to King Leopold as the Lion seized Westland from Wergar the Wolf. The scout had been there when they'd brought Duke Bergan, the lord of Brackenholme, to his knees at the gates of Highcliff. That roar and this one were unmistakable. They were the roars of a Bearlord, and they chilled him to his core.

The saga begins with

Wereworld
RISE OF THE WOLF

"A fairy tale with fangs."　　*—Library Media Connections*
"[A] rousingly gory heroic fantasy."　　*—Booklist*